"NOW WHAT?" EMILY ASKED ANGRILY. "I SUPPOSE YOU INTEND TO RAPE ME!"

Drew swore under his breath. He shook her hard. Pins tumbled from her hair and her long golden tresses slipped down her back.

"I have no intention of raping you, Miss Parker. It's a bit too warm a day to be deflowering virgin schoolmarms who don't have the sense to stay out of brothels."

Emily gasped. How did this man know her name and that she was a schoolteacher? And this was a brothel! Good Lord, what had she walked into?

"Please forgive me if I was an imposition," Emily said indignantly. "You certainly have a high opinion of yourself! If you call your assault on me help, then I'd dearly love to see what you do when you set out to harm!"

He moved a step closer and took her in his arms. "Believe me, you wouldn't," he said, grinning audaciously.

SPELLBOUND

ALLISON HAYES

AVON BOOKS ◆ NEW YORK

AVON BOOKS
A division of
The Hearst Corporation
105 Madison Avenue
New York, New York 10016

Copyright © 1990 by Lynn Coddington
Published by arrangement with the author
Library of Congress Catalog Card Number: 90-93155
ISBN: 0-380-76214-5

First Avon Books Printing: October 1990

For my mother's people, past and present;
the pioneers, teachers, ranchers, and especially
the dreamers—
bound to the Mystery, the plains, the deep sky,
and the Black Hills.

With special thanks to Mom and Jan and Sarah.

Prologue

Somewhere near Bear Butte, Dakota Territory, 1861

The small flags of colored cloth snapped against their poles like wild ghosts in the night as the west wind lifted them. The wind brought the scent of new grass, damp earth, and promised rain, yet there were no clouds. A waning crescent moon dipped toward the horizon, and the boy sitting on a bed of sage, enclosed by the four poles, shivered as the breeze rippled over his bare, sunburned body. Goosebumps rose on his arms and stomach, but he didn't notice them. His eyes were fixed on a small, dark speck far away in the western sky, beyond the pale buffalo skull atop the cottonwood pole before him, beyond the dark humps of Mato Paha, or Bear Butte. Without blinking, the boy lifted the pipe that rested in front of him and raised it to the four winds, to the earth and the sky, and finally to the dark shape approaching him.

He stood motionless. Tiny sounds began to fill his ears, growing until they were almost deafening in the predawn stillness. He heard the grass stems bending and shifting in the wind, and the insects marching upon the moist spring earth. He heard the horses at the camp whinnying and snorting. And though the camp was far from him and beyond his sight, he heard the even breathing of the sleeping people, the small cries of babies, the snores of old men, and the creak of the lodge poles in the gusting wind as if he were present in each lodge.

The sounds spilled into the night. Then there were new

1

voices, and harsh, metallic noises coming from the east.
Noises he remembered from his childhood encroached on
the prairie night; crowds milling, engines churning with
cranking gears and hissing steam, wheels screaming
against steel tracks, and heavy wagons thundering over
uneven roads. The roar built in his ears until he could no
longer hear the earth and the people, but only the chaotic
din of machines and white men's shouting voices.

Suddenly, the rush of beating wings drowned out all
other sound, and the boy stared in wonder as the dark
shape above him descended, wide wings blocking out the
stars. Instinctively, he held his pipe aloft, and a sob escaped his lips. Tears streamed down his face, and he
thought he would faint from the excitement and fear that
coursed through him. Then the great bird dropped onto the
buffalo skull and looked curiously at the boy. It was an
eagle, strong and powerful, his dark feathers touched with
lighter spots that glinted in the faint moonlight.

The boy ceased trembling and forced himself to meet
the eagle's gaze. Should he ask a question? Overwhelmed,
he waited, saying nothing.

The eagle continued to regard him. Finally, the boy felt
words forming in his mind and heard his own voice in the
silence.

"Welcome, Tunkaśila, Grandfather. I am honored that
you have come. What can I, a man born to the white eyes,
learn from you, Wambli Gleśka, the Spotted Eagle?"

As soon as he had spoken, he wished he hadn't. He
sounded so young, so weak. But the eagle seemed pleased
and answered the boy.

"Wakantanka, the Great Mystery, knows you, Iśte Śkan
Niyapi, you who have eyes that are alive with the sky,
and I have come as a messenger. I will show you things
you will need to know to serve the Lakota. Come with
me."

The words died away, and the boy felt himself drawn
up into the air with the eagle, sweeping ever higher into
the night sky, until he thought they would brush the very
stars. High and far they flew, into the east. The boy saw
the great rivers below them shimmering like ribbons. As

the sun lifted over the distant horizon, throwing a pale yellow light into the sky, they reached a land of rolling hills and low mountains covered with dense forests. Among the trees were farms and fields, and along the rivers were towns, white people's towns, and many, many white people. The boy had seen these places years ago, when he had traveled through them with his father, before they had met the Oglala. Yet something was different about the hills and towns. Looking closely, the boy saw an ugly pall of smoke overtaking the land and flashes of fiery light glinting red through the trees. The eagle drifted downward on the wind currents, and soon the boy heard terrible sounds. People were crying everywhere, and explosions and gunfire erupted all over the land. Then the noises faded, and he and the eagle kept flying toward the east, finally reaching a city that the boy recognized as the place where the White Grandfather lived, the laws were made, and the white councils met. He had visited this city with his uncle once when he was very young, perhaps five or six. It seemed very strange and frightening now. He wondered why the eagle had brought him here.

In answer to the boy's thoughts, the great bird swept low over the city, so close that they could hear people talking. There was talk about the war, and about the need for land, more land in the west. People talked of cattle and railroads and gold. And they spoke of the Indians.

The boy listened hard to hear what was said about the Indians, and his heart grew cold at the words he heard. *Savages. Animals. Murdering heathens. Let the army take care of them after the war is over. They're sitting on land we need. Push them off. Eliminate them. Make room for good Christian people.* The boy was ashamed that he was of the same race as these callous men, and he was shocked by their ignorance. Indignation and fear burned his spirit. Their own country in war-torn ruins, they calmly spoke of taking the Indians' country and carrying their ugliness onto the plains, bespoiling them forever. There were men who defended the Indians, but they were few, and even they did not seem to understand the horror of what the others said.

Then he heard the eagle's voice in his ear. "You will be able to help the Lakota. You know this world, and they do not."

The eagle bore him high above the city again, and they turned back toward the west. The boy thought about what the eagle had said. He didn't feel as if he knew this world at all. He knew the prairies and hills of Dakota and the Powder River country. He knew horses and hunting and how to survive on the high plains. He had been a child in the white man's world, but he didn't know it any longer. He was becoming a man in the world of the Lakota, and he was happy there. He didn't wish to return to his old life. Would he have to? Was that what Wakantanka wanted him to do?

The dawn caught them again, and the eagle carried the boy back and forth above the earth between the Missouri River and the Bighorn Mountains. He showed the boy the bands of people traveling with their horses and their travois from camp to camp, from south of the Platte River to the Canadian border. The land was wide and lovely, full of game and wild fruits and herbs. Buffalo blanketed the prairies, moving like a dark cloud through the broad valleys and across the hills, and the people were happy.

But each time the boy and the eagle crossed the land, they didn't go as far as they had the time before. Soon they didn't go as far south as the Platte. They didn't go as far west, or north or east, either, and the people didn't travel as much from place to place. There were large camps along the Missouri that never moved, and the people were not so happy. The buffalo and the other animals began to disappear, and the people grew weary. When the boy and the eagle flew only between the Black Hills and the Missouri, the people were starving. Then the boy caught his breath. There were white people in the Black Hills! The Lakota were being chased away, sent to the river to die of white men's diseases and grief. Everywhere now there was the sound of mourning. Hunters returned with empty hands, and children and old people cried because their stomachs were empty and their hearts remembered better days. The land itself sighed with sorrow for the people and all the relatives, the buffalo, the elk, the birds, and all who were disappearing.

The eagle flew back toward the Hills, where the boy saw a single buffalo cow below on the prairie, trotting toward the Hills. The eagle followed it.

The buffalo picked its way through the trees, sometimes lost to sight in the narrow gulches it followed. After a long time, it disappeared into a thick grove of pines and spruce in a meadow and did not reappear. The eagle soared above, and the boy looked down on a small waterfall and a pool. A tall pine rose like a spire next to the falls. The eagle glided down to perch in its uppermost branches, and they waited, looking for the buffalo. It was so beautiful and peaceful in the meadow that the boy forgot the suffering he had seen.

There was a sudden movement below. The boy and the eagle looked down immediately, but instead of the buffalo, a woman walked from beneath the trees. At least the boy thought it was a woman. He couldn't see her clearly; a cloud of mist from the falls obscured her from view. The eagle lifted his wings, and they dropped to the earth before the woman, yet still the boy couldn't see her. Then the mist cleared, but only for an instant. All the boy saw were her eyes, the most beautiful, mysterious eyes he had ever seen, as brown as the moist earth below his feet, and as green as the dark pine boughs above him; eyes that beckoned him with expectation and the warm promise of invitation. His heart leapt into his throat as he instinctively reached toward her, his hand grasping for hers through the tattered wisps of clouds and fog. Then the mist wrapped around her once again, as quickly as it had cleared, and he felt the powerful thrust of the eagle's wings as they rose into the air together. He strained his eyes, hoping for another glimpse of her, but he was too far away. She was gone.

Soon he saw the familiar shape of Bear Butte below, and he was falling, falling back to the ground, back onto the bed of sage within the square marked out by the four poles and colored flags. He hit the earth facedown and knew no more.

"Father!" Black Wolf shouted. "I think we'd better bring my brother back. I just checked on him, and there was an eagle perched on the buffalo skull. My brother was on the ground at its feet, not moving."

"I told you not to disturb him, *cinkś,*" Long Feather said with a frown.

"I didn't go close. Only on the hill there where he couldn't see me."

"But maybe close enough to disturb the spirits," his father warned.

Concern lit the boy's dark eyes. "I'm sorry, but really, I think he needs help now. Please come," Black Wolf pleaded.

"All right, *cinkś.* Get his father and we'll go."

A few minutes later, the two men and the boy stood on the promontory where they could see the sunburned boy stretched out on the ground about two hundred yards away from them. There was indeed an eagle sitting atop the western pole, above the black flag and the buffalo skull that Long Feather had placed there when he had left the boy four days ago. The holy man lifted his arms to the four directions, to the earth and the sky, then to the bird, murmuring a prayer as he did so. Then the eagle gave a shrill cry and pushed himself up into the air, his powerful wings pumping smoothly until he was high enough to ride the wind. They waited until the bird was out of sight. Then they walked to the boy, now a young man, and carried him back to the camp.

When Iśte Śkan Niyapi told his father and Long Feather what he had seen, his Indian father leaned back his head, closed his eyes, and was silent for many minutes. The boy exchanged a worried look with his natural father, who smiled at him encouragingly and shrugged. They had been with the Oglala for four years now, but the white man knew he would never be Lakota. He didn't understand what had happened to his son out on the lonely hill, but he accepted that his son was Lakota now, despite his birth into an Eastern family of means and influence. Long Feather had recognized it the first time he had seen the boy, and in some ways Andy Rutledge felt that he had lost his son to the Indian holy man in that brief moment years ago. It didn't trouble him overmuch because the boy was strong and happy. He belonged with the Oglala, and he would be a good man, brave and generous. It was enough.

Long Feather opened his eyes suddenly, his gaze boring into the fourteen-year-old boy in front of him.

"You will return to the *wasicus,* the white men, my son, when the time is right," Long Feather said, his voice soft but resonant. "Thus you will learn their ways as well as you have learned the ways of the Lakota. As you've seen, hard times lie before us, and you will be called upon to aid us in the struggle to maintain our way of life when the white men come. We'll need your help, boy. But don't worry about this too much now. It won't happen for a while yet. Our moon hasn't sunk below the horizon yet."

"What about the woman at the falls?" the boy asked, remembering her beautiful eyes. "What did that mean?"

"I don't know," the man told him honestly. "Maybe she is a spirit that will help you in a time of need. Maybe she is a real woman you will meet someday. You'll understand when you see her again."

When would he see her again? he wondered. He would remember those eyes, so he would recognize her.

No matter how long it took.

Chapter 1

Deadwood, Dakota Territory, July 1880

"**Y**our brother ought to be along right soon, Miss Parker. I'm just sorry you have to wait on such a hot day," Elias Pratt, the stage agent for the Cheyenne to Deadwood line apologized to the pretty blond woman who had arrived that morning. He rambled on, enjoying his captive audience. "It don't usually get so hot up here in the Hills. Of course, we do get an awful lot of thunderstorms this time of year. The weather could be completely different by this evening if—"

A sudden commotion in the street outside the stage office interrupted the man's monologue. Emily Parker heard feet running along the wooden sidewalks, then several shouts. She stepped through the door, the elderly stage agent close behind her, stopping short at the sight of three men aggressively circling one another in the dusty street. Onlookers poured from the surrounding buildings, forming a ring around them. Emily noted with surprise that two of the men, whose backs were to her, were Indians, dressed similarly in buckskin shirts and trousers. The third man was huge, standing several inches over six feet and wearing black trousers, a white shirt stained with sweat, and the heavy boots of a miner. From her position in front of the stage office, Emily could see his face clearly. He had curly red hair, and his complexion was flushed to match, hatred blazing across his features.

Moving with surprising speed for a man of his size, the

8

red-haired man lunged at one of the Indians, grabbing his
head and slamming it into a beefy fist. At the same time,
he drove his knee into the Indian's stomach. The Indian
doubled over, falling to his knees in the street. Before his
companion could come to his aid, the miner pushed the
Indian's face into the dirt and viciously kicked the back
of his head. The Indian collapsed, unconscious, and a dark
stain appeared in the dust beside him. Emily's hand flew
to her mouth in horror, her eyes riveted to the violent
spectacle before her.

The miner now stood opposite the second Indian, but
for some reason he didn't attack, though he clearly held
the advantage of size and strength. A flicker of uncertainty
entered his eyes as he looked at the smaller man, and the
atmosphere crackled with tension. Emily shifted her gaze
to the standing Indian. With a start, she saw that his hair
was a light golden brown, and it was not braided as was
his companion's, but tied back with a leather strip. She
remembered hearing that the legendary Crazy Horse, killed
three years ago at Fort Robinson, Nebraska, had been fair
with sandy-colored hair. She wondered if this Indian was
related to him. Was that why the miner was afraid?

Her speculations ended when the light-haired Indian
dropped to one knee, pressing his fingers to the fallen
man's neck. His eyes remained on the miner's face above
him. When he rose, his spare movements reminded Emily
of a great, tawny mountain lion stalking its prey. His right
hand hovered close to the knife sheathed against his muscular thigh, but he made no move for it. Instead, he spoke,
his voice low and vibrant in the suffocating July air.

Emily heard only the cold tone of his voice, his quiet
words swallowed up in the heavy atmosphere, but she was
surprised by his fluid intonation. She had heard on the long
stage ride that few of the local Sioux and Cheyenne Indians spoke any English. Again, however, her curiosity
about the strange Indian was curtailed by the reaction of
the miner to whatever he had said. The bigger man's face
went from crimson to sickly white in less than a second,
and he couldn't hide the fear that flashed through his eyes.

Then his temper flared again, and he stepped toward the Indian.

A man with a huge walrus moustache pushed his way through the crowd and put a hand on the miner's arm. He wore a tin star on his leather vest.

"That's enough, Jack. It's too hot today for this kind of bullshit. Why don't you just head back in to your game before I have to do something none of us'd be too happy with. You." The sheriff nodded curtly to the Indian. "Collect your friend and try not to cause any more trouble here."

The crowd broke up quickly, people slipping back into shaded doorways, up alleys, and down side streets into saloons, stores, and hotels, no one caring to linger in the sun once it was apparent the show was over. Heat waves shimmered off the roofs on the opposite side of the street, and the dust settled once more into the rutted dirt surface.

Emily remained on the sidewalk, watching in fascination as the Indian stooped to pick up his injured companion. Something about him held her attention. What on earth had he said to the angry miner to get such a wild reaction? She was sure the miner had been terrified, even though he was taller and at least fifty pounds heavier than the Indian. All the stories her fellow travelers had told about vicious Indian attacks were fresh in her mind, and while she knew from the Eastern newspapers that these were largely exaggerated, it was apparent that there was a great deal more antipathy between the white settlers in the Hills and the Indians than she had realized.

Rarely having seen western Indians at such close range, Emily looked carefully at the man as he raised his friend from the ground and positioned him across broad shoulders. Now that he was not standing next to the huge miner, she saw that he was himself quite tall and well built. The powerful muscles in his arms and back rippled under the weight of the unconscious man as he shifted to accommodate his burden. Emily felt a curious tightening in her chest, and a disturbing image flashed unbidden through her mind as she wondered what it would feel like to be held in such strong arms. She blushed instantly, faintly shocked by the flutter in her stomach. She dismissed it promptly, attributing her reaction to the strain of her journey and the uncharacteristic excitement of the fight.

The Indian turned toward the stage office suddenly, and Emily looked away, embarrassed by her thoughts. Out of the corner of her eye, she saw him pause for a second, then move off down the street, his back to her once again. Her eyes followed him.

"Now, I'm right sorry you had to see that, Miss Parker, especially when you just got to town and all," Mr. Pratt said, mopping at his forehead with a large white handkerchief. "Are you all right? This ain't the sort of thing ladies should have to put up with."

Emily felt a bit shaky, but she smiled weakly at the stage agent.

"I'm fine, Mr. Pratt. Is fighting in the street still a common occurrence in Deadwood? I had the idea from my brother's letters that the community had become quite respectable," she said.

"Oh, yes, for the most part Deadwood has simmered down. It surely ain't like it was in '76, during the Gold Rush. No ma'am. But we're still a little rough around the edges," the agent told her, chuckling. "See those houses up there?" He pointed at the steep hill that rose a few streets away from them. "That's Forest Hill. All the respectable merchants and businessmen have their homes up there. We're mighty proud of the way we've recovered from last year's fire. Why, your own brother built several of those houses. Now, Miss Parker, if you're up in Forest Hill, Deadwood is as respectable a town as any back in the States. You just want to be watching out a little in some other neighborhoods. It all depends on where you go."

"That could be said of most anywhere, I believe." Emily laughed in response.

"That it could," the stage agent agreed with a warm smile. "Why don't you come back inside and sit down out of the sun to wait for your brother," he urged, stepping into his small office.

"If you don't mind, I'd like to sit out here for a while,"

Emily said, gesturing toward the bench in front of Mr. Pratt's window.

"Fine with me," he replied, dabbing at his brow again. He disappeared into the building.

Emily sank down onto the wooden seat with a sigh. It was dreadfully warm, and she was exhausted. She had left her mother's home in Elmira, New York, ten days ago and journeyed by rail and stage to meet her oldest brother, Sam, in Deadwood. She was covered with dust and grime from the stage road, and she felt a trickle of sweat slide down her spine underneath her chestnut-colored traveling suit. Where *was* Sam? In his last letter, he'd assured her that he would be on hand to meet her when the stage arrived, but she'd already been waiting for nearly an hour. Mr. Pratt had told her not to worry, however, that thunderstorms the night before had likely raised the level of one of the creeks Sam had to ford on his way in from his ranch at the edge of the Black Hills, slowing him down. Emily felt a twinge of guilt for her impatience over his tardiness, for she knew he would never intentionally keep her waiting.

Leaning her head back against the warm panes of glass, Emily smiled at the thought of seeing Sam and his family again. It had been five years since his and Maggie's last visit to Elmira, and Emily had not yet met her youngest nephew, Daniel, who was only a toddler. In spite of the heat and her lack of energy, she was excited about being in Dakota Territory and seeing her brother and his family.

And she was thrilled to be away from Elmira and George Parks, her brother Henry's partner at the bank. George had fancied himself her fiancé, as had her mother and her brothers Henry and Charles, all despite the fact that she had resolutely refused to marry the man. Their united insistence that George was the perfect mate for her had become intolerable, and her frustration with them for paying so little heed to her own wishes had finally compelled her to take matters into her own hands. Emily's smile deepened as she remembered George's chagrin when he had learned that she had resigned her teaching position at the Elmira Senior Academy and arranged a trip to the wilds of Dakota. He'd very nearly had a fit in front of her mother, a most unseemly thing, and wholly out of character for him. His pencil-thin moustache had quivered on his upper lip as he had informed her that she would do no such thing. Then her mother had told her she would not go; Henry had told her she should not go; Charles, and even his wife, Lucy, had told her she should not be ridiculous. She simply could not go gallivanting off into the uncivilized and unpredictable West. Yet, here she was, sitting on a bench in Deadwood. Emily chuckled to herself in satisfaction as she surveyed her surroundings.

Deadwood lay in a narrow gulch, surrounded by steep hills that were sparsely covered with evergreens and bushes, and the hot air was dusty, smelling of livestock and something acrid that she supposed was a result of the mining in the area. She found it hard to believe that the town had only been in existence four short years, and that before Custer's famous expedition into the Black Hills in 1874, when gold had been discovered, there had been nothing in the Hills save a few Indians, trees, animals, and the rocks themselves. Sam had estimated in one of his letters that there were over ten thousand people in the Deadwood area alone now, and there was even a telephone line connecting Deadwood with the nearby community of Lead. It was astounding how rapidly the town had grown from a rough-and-tumble mining camp into a bustling little city. Thinking of Indians, however, reminded her of the fight she had seen and that Deadwood still was a far cry from Elmira.

Shifting uncomfortably, Emily removed her jacket and set it on the bench beside her. As she sat forward, the dry air hit her back, giving her a blessed moment of coolness as the moisture evaporated out of the fine cotton of her shirtwaist. Not for the first time on her journey, Emily was thankful that she had dispensed with wearing her hated corset. Her mother would have been positively scandalized at the thought of her daughter brazenly appearing in public without the constraining benefits of the heavy, uncomfortable undergarment, but Emily only grinned wickedly at the thought. She probably would have swooned long ago in this heat had she not left the cursed thing in her trunk. As it was, she was quite miserable enough. Finally, she loosened the buttons at her cuffs and shoved her sleeves up to her elbows, then released the top two buttons at her throat. After a minute, she released a third. Hurry up, Sam, she thought impatiently.

Elias Pratt pulled his gold pocket watch from his trousers and glanced at it. He really didn't need it to tell him the time, for his stomach had already done that, and it was long past dinnertime, no doubt about it. With a regretful look out the window at the blond head leaning back against the dusty glass, he locked his cash drawer and checked the safe to make sure it was still locked. Then he stepped out onto the sidewalk.

"No sign of your brother yet," he announced, stating the obvious.

"No, I'm afraid not," Emily responded glumly. "Perhaps I should take a hotel room and wait for him there."

"No, he'll be along shortly, sure's shootin'."

"I certainly hope so."

There was a brief silence. Emily realized that Mr. Pratt had something more to say by the way he shifted uneasily from foot to foot, but he seemed to be waiting for her to speak first. Suddenly, it dawned on her. It was almost one o'clock, and he hadn't gone for his dinner yet. She made a show of looking at the watch pinned to her shirtwaist.

"Oh, my goodness! Will you look at how late it's gotten!" she exclaimed. "It's past dinnertime, and here you've been patiently waiting with me, missing your meal. Mr. Pratt, I insist that you leave this instant. I'll be perfectly fine while you're gone."

"You sure about that, Miss Parker? After that fight and all, I didn't know if you'd want to wait alone, so I was wondering if you'd like to join me. You look like you could use a bit of refreshment."

"Oh, dear, do I look that bedraggled?"

"Not at all, you look just fine, miss," he answered a little too quickly. "I was only referring to the heat."

Emily smiled gently at the station agent's gallant reassurance, fully aware that she must look an absolute mess. She could feel wisps of hair on her neck and face where they had escaped the knot at the back of her head, and she knew she was filthy. She had wiped her face and tried to shake as much dust as possible from her clothes, but she doubted it had done much good.

"To be honest, Mr. Pratt, I'm simply too exhausted and far too warm even to think about eating." A glass of water would have been nice, but she didn't want to chance missing Sam. "I think I'll just wait here, Mr. Pratt. Thank you for your invitation." Emily smiled again.

"Well, if you're sure, then I'll lock up and be on my way. I should be back in an hour. Say hello to your brother for me, and if I don't see you, it's been a pleasure to meet you. Now don't go wandering off, and you should be just fine," the agent told her, turning the key in the lock and starting across the street. "I'll be seeing you," he said, tipping his hat.

"Goodbye, Mr. Pratt," Emily called after him.

Drew Rutledge carried Black Wolf down Sherman Street to the corner of Main and then up the back staircase of the seedy-looking hotel where he kept a room. It was the only place in town where he could bring his Lakota relatives and friends if he had to, so he didn't complain if the other upstairs rooms were used for less than moral pursuits. At this time of day, the corridor was empty, and an eerie silence reigned in the dim light. The girls wouldn't be up until late that afternoon, and with the unpleasant heat, he doubted that there would be many folks downstairs until after sundown.

Drew managed to unlock his door without dropping Black Wolf, then crossed the small room and laid his adopted brother on the narrow bed. The Indian was still out cold, but he groaned when his head fell back against the pillow. Drew stripped off his own leather shirt and opened the window, though the blast of hot air that hit him in the face did little to relieve the stifling mustiness in the room. He picked up a pail from the floor beside the washstand

and walked back to the hall, where a small boy met him at the top of the stairs.

"Sheng-li! Just who I was looking for! How you been?" the man greeted the boy. "Black Wolf's hurt. Can you take this downstairs and fill it at the pump?" The boy nodded happily, then ran quickly down the stairs.

Drew returned to the room and sat down on the bed next to Black Wolf, turning the man on his side so he could get a better look at the wound on the back of his head. It was still bleeding and had swollen up to the size of a goose egg. Drew raised the shade to let more light into the room and rose to find a razor and something to wipe away the blood and bandage the wound. By the time he had located some old shirts in the bottom of one of the bureau drawers and ripped them up, Sheng-li had returned, staggering slightly under the weight of the full pail. Drew took the basin from the washstand, set it on a chair beside the bed, and poured water into it. He eased the Indian's shirt over his head, then unwound Black Wolf's braid and cut away his brother's hair in a circle around the wound, cleaning the ugly cut and probing the bone underneath to make sure it was solid. He picked up a leather parfleche from under the bed and extracted a horn container filled with greasy ointment. He smeared it on the wound, then pressed a pad of clean shirt strips to it, securing the bandage with a strip of cloth that looped up over Black Wolf's forehead. He turned the pillow so that the blood on it was against the mattress, then laid his brother back on it.

Drew turned to Sheng-li and smiled.

"Is he hurt bad?" the boy asked solemnly.

"I don't think so, but he needs to sleep for a while," Drew said, setting the basin on the floor and moving into the chair.

Sheng-li moved close to him, and Drew lifted the boy onto his lap. He liked children. They never seemed suspicious of him as adults did—white adults, at any rate. He chatted with the boy for a few minutes, then sent him on his way back downstairs to the washroom where his mother worked, doing the laundry for the house girls. Drew carried the pitcher to the washstand and looked at his face in the rectangular mirror with its cracked glass.

For an instant he didn't see himself; instead, the image of a trim figure in a reddish-brown skirt and jacket, with blond hair pulled into a spinsterish bun, flashed before his eyes. She had stood very primly by the stage office, studiously avoiding him when he turned toward her. She was fairly attractive, but that wasn't why he had noticed her. Something about her seemed familiar to him, something he couldn't quite place. Then he remembered. Sam Parker's schoolteacher sister was due to arrive soon. That woman had schoolmarm written all over her, he thought with a grin, with her chin high and her back stiff as if she were about to rap some poor kid across the knuckles for a minor transgression. Besides, she had the look of Sam, now that he thought about it, though it must have been something in her expression, for her coloring was completely different. He dismissed the image and dipped a cloth into the clean water and scrubbed at his face. A bath would have been better, but there was no one around to haul the water, and he didn't feel like doing it himself. It was too damn hot to do anything.

When he was sure that Black Wolf was sleeping peacefully, Drew pulled on a clean leather shirt and slipped out of the room, heading downstairs for the post office and a quick meal at one of the lunchrooms on Main Street.

Mr. Pratt had been gone nearly forty-five minutes, and there was still no sign of Sam. Emily's mouth felt as dry as the dusty street in front of her, and she knew by now that she simply had to have a drink of water. She looked across the street dubiously. The miner who had been involved in the brawl had gone into one of those doors, but she wasn't sure which one. She didn't care to venture into any of them and find out. Her eyes lifted in consideration to the steep slopes of Forest Hill. Perhaps the businesses at the base of that hill would be more reputable, and there would be a respectable restaurant or hotel in that direction, she reasoned, rising to her feet. She looked up and down the street uncertainly, hoping Sam would appear at any

minute, still afraid that she would miss him if she left the
stage office.

When he didn't appear, Emily collected her purse and
started off down the street toward Forest Hill. She crossed
a wooden bridge and looked down into the murky waters
of an unpleasant-smelling creek. Wrinkling her nose, she
continued until she saw a street sign that informed her she
had reached Main Street. Confident that she was approaching the better part of town, Emily turned down the street
and immediately saw what she was looking for. Swinging
from a bracket was a green and white, hand-lettered sign
that advertised the Sheridan Hotel. She strode purposefully
toward the door, her heels echoing on the dry sidewalk
planks.

She stopped just outside and peered into the dim interior
of the hotel, blinking as her eyes adjusted to the gloom.
There was a long desk along the far wall, she thought, and
several tables scattered around the room. Then she heard
the sound of liquid being poured into a tall glass, and her
decision was made. She glided across the worn floorboards
until she stood before a high bar. A fat man with a thick
black moustache stood behind it, eyeing her speculatively.
Emily glanced around her apprehensively, but decided that
she simply had to have some water. If this was one of the
more reputable parts of town, she hated to think what the
disreputable areas must be like.

Stepping up to the bar, which came to the middle of her
chest, Emily cleared her throat and spoke.

"Excuse me," she said, addressing the man behind the
bar.

The bartender stepped forward and smirked at her.

"What can I do for you, little lady?"

"I'd like a glass of water, please," she replied, trying
to sound businesslike.

"Would you, now?" the barman said. "Are you sure
that's all you want?"

"Yes." Emily said firmly, looking him straight in the
eye.

She thought she detected an underlying threat in the

man's tone. Just as she was about to turn on her heel and flee, the man reached under the bar and produced a pitcher of water and a smudged glass. She hesitated.

Pushing the water and the glass across to her, the bartender laughed. Her hand shaking somewhat, Emily ignored him and poured herself a glass of water. She drank it in one long draught, and though it was warm and the glass was far from spotless, it tasted as good as any drink she'd ever had. She lowered the glass and filled it again, drinking more slowly. She felt much better as she looked back at the barman.

"What do I owe you?" she asked curtly.

"Oh, I don't know. What ya got to give, missy?" There was an unpleasant glint in the man's eyes.

Emily looked at him warily, then reached into her purse and extracted a dollar. It should be more than enough for a bottle of whiskey, much less two glasses of water, and she laid it on the counter, then turned to leave. She found her way blocked by four dirty, sweaty men, all of them leering at her through the gloom.

"Excuse me, gentlemen," she said icily, stepping forward.

The men didn't move. One of them bared yellowed teeth in a grotesque smile. She noticed that he had on soiled corduroy trousers and a worn leather vest with no shirt beneath it. He grabbed her jaw in his hand, gripping tightly so that she couldn't pull away. Fear shimmied up her spine and stuck in her chest, making her breath come in shallow gasps before she forced indignation to overcome the numbing trepidation.

"Hey, Joe," he said in a gravelly voice. "I think this pretty lady's got all sorts o' treasures she could share with us. I wouldn't settle for no dollar from this one. Where you workin', girl?"

"Let go of me, and let me pass," Emily insisted quietly, her voice shaking now with anger as much as fear. She jerked her chin from the loathsome man's grasp.

Another of the men spoke up. "Looks like she don't like you too much, Hank. Why don't you let me talk to her. She's probably waitin' for a real man to show her a good time. What's your name, sugar?'' The man pulled her into his arms.

Emily nearly retched at the sour smell of the man's unwashed body and his whiskey-tainted breath. She pushed against him with all her might, and he toppled backward, stumbling over a chair. The entire company laughed loudly while Emily looked quickly around the room, seeing no one else there, no one to appeal to for help. She forced her fears down again and tried to think what to do.

A third man stepped toward her, his stringy blond hair falling across bloodshot eyes. He looked as if he was barely twenty years old, yet there was a cruel cast to his stubble-covered features.

''Now why're you being so hard on us, darlin'? We just want to get to know you better, that's all. Isn't that what you do? Get to know men? What's the problem, darlin'? Maybe it's the heat,'' he said with a knowing grin. ''She probably knows I aim to get her a whole lot more hotted up than she is now.''

The others laughed again, and the man reached out to touch the open neckline of her blouse, sliding his grimy fingers inside her collar, where they brushed her skin.

Emily slapped his hand away furiously as understanding dawned on her. These men thought she was a whore! And they were all drunk, hardly likely to listen to reasonable arguments. The seriousness of her predicament impelled her to action. As the man before her moved closer once again, lowering his head toward her mouth, Emily waited until he was only inches away. Then, with sure swiftness, she brought her knee up sharply, slamming it into his groin. She wondered how she could get away from the other three men and the bartender as she watched the blond man crumple onto the floor, clutching himself. He yelped and cursed, writhing at her feet.

Once over their surprise, two of the men simply laughed, but the first, the one called Hank, turned on her with an expression of outrage. He reached for her arm, but suddenly catching sight of something behind her, he released her and took a step backward. Emily saw fear in his eyes. The other men's laughter died as they stared over her shoulder.

Emily turned slowly to see what stood behind her.

Chapter 2

Emily looked up and found herself caught in the bluest, most penetrating gaze she had ever encountered. For an instant, it was as if the others in the room evaporated like fog in the sunlight, and she felt as if she were looking into the clearest, deepest October sky she could imagine, and then deeper still. Her pulse quickened, and her eyes widened in panic as she recognized the light-haired Indian she had seen earlier that day. The angry expression on his face was frightening, but as his eyes met hers, there was a brief flicker of something else. Was it surprise? It was gone as soon as it came, and Emily held her breath.

Looking at him now, she realized that he couldn't possibly be an Indian, though he was dressed like one. He was taller than the other men in the room, and his broad shoulders tapered to lean hips and powerful thighs, heightening his aura of strength and dangerous vitality. He was devastatingly handsome, wild and disturbing, blending the classic face and body of an ancient god with the raw, unadorned grace of a Lakota warrior. He appeared to have as unsettling an effect on the men harassing her as he did on her; they stood as if thunderstruck.

He moved smoothly to her side, standing so close to her that she had to tilt her head back to maintain his gaze. He looked down into her face, scrutinizing every feature, from the thick blond hair falling around her face to her small, straight nose and generous mouth. Then he looked into her dark, green-brown eyes. There was a searching question in his own eyes to which Emily had no answer. She felt invaded by his look, and she realized that she was shaking, though with fear, anger, or something else, she didn't know.

A strong hand caught her elbow, drawing her closer to him, and she didn't resist. Then she heard his voice, soft and confident.

"If you boys don't mind, I think I'll take this lady for myself."

Emily was surprised to hear the deep, resonant timbre that she associated with Eastern gentlemen of the upper classes, but she found nothing at all gentlemanly in this man's statement, and she most certainly did not like the way his eyes swept down her body, taking in the arch of her neck, her slim waist and flaring hips, then lingering on the full curve of her breasts. She strove to control the flush that spread upward from her neck.

"Oh, you will, will you? We'll just see about that, mister," she replied, finding her tongue at last.

She swung quickly away from him, but his hand captured her wrist in a bruising grip. She tried to free herself, twisting and wrenching her arm away from his grasp, but he didn't let go. Instead, she found herself pulled roughly against his chest, her hands trapped uselessly between them. Emily gasped with shock and rage, painfully aware of the feel of his muscled body pressing against her breasts through the thin cotton of her shirtwaist. Appalled, she felt her nipples contract in reaction to his close embrace. Her flush deepened, born in equal parts of furious resentment and embarrassment.

"Get your hands off me!" she hissed, struggling impotently against his iron grip. If anything, his arms tightened fractionally.

He chuckled softly, his voice close above her ear, and she felt the vibration of his mirth under her hands and chest. Enraged, she took as deep a breath as her constricted lungs would allow and opened her mouth.

"Why, you filthy bastard, get your da—! Ow!" she screeched as he jerked her head back by the bedraggled knot in her hair.

For a split second, she caught a blaze of white light

shooting through his blue eyes, then she clamped her mouth shut as he lowered his head toward hers. She squirmed wildly, but he held her immobile and quickly covered her mouth with his own. She tried to turn away, but the painful pressure of his fingers at the back of her head and his punishing lips left her no escape. She set her mouth tightly against him and struggled for breath. Her lungs felt as if they would burst, and try as she might, Emily could not elude his lips as they moved upon her own. She had never been so humiliated and angry in her life, but there was nothing she could do. He was too strong, and she couldn't evade him.

Gradually, she ceased to struggle. The pain at the back of her head subsided, and Emily felt an easing of the intensity of the man's assault, though his lips didn't leave hers. She stood quiescent finally, hoping that he would soon finish. She didn't think beyond escaping his embrace.

Drew felt her resistance lessen and relaxed his grip on her head so that he merely held her face to his. He didn't need to prolong the kiss; she'd calmed down, and he'd made it more than clear to Hank and his friends that he didn't need their help to handle the woman. He could feel her fear and anger, and he knew she was repulsed, but for some reason, he didn't want to pull away. One of his hands slid over her back, roaming freely, dropping to the curve of her hip, feeling her form through her heavy skirts. Her silky hair and the yielding quality of her soft flesh beneath his sliding hands entranced him, though he didn't forget for a moment where they were and that they had a most interested audience.

Emily felt the change in him. The tension in the taut muscles of his shoulders shifted almost imperceptibly, and the pressure of his mouth eased a fraction. In her confusion and anger, compounded by a dizzying awareness of his lean body pressed so close to her own, a quiver of angry response threatened to break through her will to remain passive in his arms. Though she strove to control it, a tremor of reaction shook her from her innermost being. A defeated whimper caught in her throat.

Drew ended the kiss abruptly. He straightened without releasing the woman in his arms, looking over his head at his gawking audience. He was breathing heavily, more affected by the kiss than he had thought possible, but he forced a challenging glint into his eyes. The man named Hank met his gaze directly.

"You reckon the rest of us'll enjoy the lady's charms as much as you seem to be doin'?" he asked with a lascivious wink.

Emily flinched at the words. She closed her eyes and sagged against the man's chest, willing herself not to give in to the despair she felt. If only Sam had come! This had to be the worst experience in her entire life.

"You're not going to get the chance, gentlemen," the man holding Emily announced. He grinned broadly. "If first tastes are any indication, it's going to be a good long while before I part with this little morsel. You boys got any objections to that?" There was a thinly veiled threat in his voice.

Emily tensed and gritted her teeth, then decided to wait until she was alone with the man before attempting to escape. It would be far easier to deter one than five or six.

"Hey, that ain't fair!" the young blond man called from the chair where he set nursing his pride.

"You aren't likely to be needing a woman for at least a few hours, so don't trouble yourself any, if you know what I mean," Drew said with slow emphasis. "I don't take very well to trouble. It reminds me of the Little Bighorn."

He watched the man blanch, and the others edged away. Drew hadn't been at the battle of the Little Bighorn, but the idea of a white man fighting with the Indians against Custer tended to have a deleterious effect on even the most hardened outlaws. The lie had served him well on more than one occasion; it had worked twice that day alone.

"Take yer time," Hank said amiably, holding up his hands in concession. "Enjoy yerself. Hey sugar, ya know where to find us when he gits tired of ya. More'n one man can show ya a good time."

Emily stiffened. She'd be damned if she ever let one of

these foul beasts set eyes on her again, much less touch her.

"Don't wait around, boys. It'll be a long time before she gets tired of me." The words spoken above her ear were too much for Emily.

"You arrogant ass! Who do you think you are? When the sheriff finds out about this, you're all going to be sorry! I'm going to—! Hey! Put me down this instant, you beast!"

Drew lifted Emily smoothly onto his shoulder, pinning her legs so that she couldn't kick, and headed for the stairs at the back of the room. Her indignant protests fell on deaf ears as he carried her up the stairway.

For the second time that day, Drew carried someone into his room. This time he kicked the door shut behind him, turned the key, and pocketed it before he put down his squirming burden. He let the struggling woman in his arms slide down the length of his body, grinning rather wickedly as he did so, then held her with her arms pinned behind her, her breasts thrust forward into his chest. Her twisting movements only succeeded in making them both aware of their bodies to an alarming degree. Finally, she stood still, breathing heavily. His intense gaze bored into her, and Emily caught her breath at the anger she saw reflected in his blue eyes.

A taut silence stretched between them. The room was miserably hot, and Emily felt as though she would suffocate if the man didn't let her go. At the same time, she was conscious of an unfamiliar flutter in her stomach that was not exactly unpleasant.

"Now what?" she inquired with asperity. "I suppose you intend to rape me. Well, you can think again, you—"

The man shook her hard, the little flecks of silver light flaring suddenly in his eyes. Hair pins tumbled from her disheveled hair, clattering to the bare wooden floor. Her long golden tresses slipped down her back and over her shoulders, framing her face with soft curls.

Drew swore under his breath and released her so abruptly that she stumbled.

"I have no intention of raping you, Miss Parker, although I'm sure the experience would prove most diverting, and *not* only for me. It's a bit too warm a day to be deflowering virgin schoolmarms who don't have the sense to stay out of brothels.''

Emily gasped. Color once again flooded her face. How did this man know her name and that she was a schoolteacher? And that she was a virgin, for God's sake? And this was a brothel? Good Lord, what had she walked into? Who *was* this odious man? She stared at him, unable to voice even one of her questions before he spoke again.

"I hope you realize how lucky you are that I happened to go downstairs just as your little escapade was getting out of hand. Those men are not what you're used to dealing with, and they would have raped you without a second thought. Most likely they thought you were a new upstairs girl, with your hair falling down like that and your shirt unbuttoned. They spend their days too drunk to be able to tell the difference between a lady and a whore, so I'd advise that in the future, you stay south of Wall Street. If you go wandering off around here by yourself, you're not likely to escape with your virtue intact.''

"Please forgive me if I was an imposition,'' Emily snapped indignantly, "although I do not recall asking for your assistance, such as it was.''

"Fine, don't thank me. Lovely manners, I must say. They match your language. Would you rather I'd let you handle things on your own?'' His blue eyes mocked her. "What were you planning to do? Tell the lot of them what bad boys they were being, slap them on the wrists, and waltz out the door? Just where exactly do you think you'd be right now if I hadn't intervened? No doubt having a similar argument with the five gentlemen downstairs.'' His cutting voice dripped sarcasm.

"I would have thought of something!'' Emily retorted angrily. "You certainly have a high opinion of yourself! If you call your assault on me help, then I'd dearly love to see what you do when you set out to harm!''

The man moved a step closer to her. "Believe me, you wouldn't. You can thank God for my help when you say your prayers tonight if it'll save your pride to refrain from thanking me in person.''

"You are an insufferable cad, a conceited boor, and a . . . a . . ." No words seemed strong enough. "A beast!" she finally shouted at him.

"Yeah, so you said." He had the audacity to grin at her mockingly, as if she were of no more consequence than a buzzing mosquito.

At that moment, a deep voice spoke quietly from behind a painted Chinese screen.

"Iśte Śkan Niyapi? Is that you?"

Drew immediately stepped farther into the room, went to the side of the bed, and sat down on the edge of the mattress. Emily stood still for a moment, the interruption puncturing her expanding indignation, then marched after the man to peer around the edge of the screen, stopping when she saw the half-dressed Indian lying on the bed. He wore a bandage around his head and looked disoriented. It was the man she had seen kicked in the head by the belligerent miner.

Emily glanced at the man who had carried her upstairs and was startled by the sudden change in him. He was smiling tolerantly now, handing the injured man a glass of water and helping him drink. He asked the Indian a few questions in a language Emily couldn't understand and received a few brief answers. When he looked up at Emily, she could hardly believe how handsome he was now that he wasn't angry. He astounded her by giving her an almost pleasant look. The Indian on the bed looked at her as well.

"Is he all right?" she asked at length, concern finally overcoming her anger. "Surely you should call a doctor."

Her eyes darted back and forth between the two men. They didn't look at all alike, yet there was an uncanny resemblance between them. Emily realized she was staring.

The Indian made a comment she couldn't understand. The other man smiled and answered, whereupon the Indian said a few more words and then closed his eyes, making every appearance of going back to sleep. Relief showed on Drew's face, and he relaxed his jaw noticeably.

"Is he all right?" Emily repeated.

"He will be. He's got one hell of a headache, and he'll probably sleep straight through to tomorrow, but otherwise he's fine. He's lucky he's got such a hard head. He did ask me to keep it down, though, so I promised to withhold my lecture on the evils of walking the Badlands unescorted until later. Not that I've any faith I'll be listened to," he added wryly.

"Has a doctor seen him?" Emily persisted, refusing to rise to the bait dangled before her.

"No, and one isn't likely to. It could ruin a man's practice to be seen doctoring an Indian."

"But that's scandalous! How could a doctor refuse to help an injured man?"

Drew looked at Emily carefully. "A lot of folks don't think the Indians are people, Miss Parker. They think they're savages, animals, with no more feelings than a dog or a horse. Maybe less." His voice was neutral.

"You don't sound terribly upset by that," she noted, her eyes troubled.

"It upsets me plenty, but I'm used to it. Anger doesn't help the situation any. Did you know that the white folks around here are so fond of the Sioux that three years ago they got the county to offer two hundred and fifty dollars for any Indian brought in dead or alive? Things are better now, but what you saw this morning isn't unusual. The only reason the miner started that fight was because we're Lakota."

"Anger isn't helpful in many situations," she couldn't resist pointing out. He looked up at her sharply, but before he could interrupt, she asked, "Are you really an Indian?"

"Not by blood, but in spirit."

Emily waited for him to say more, but he remained silent.

"What tribe is your friend—I mean, what tribe are . . . you . . . from?"

Drew didn't answer immediately. He assessed the woman before him cooly; she was beautiful, with her hair loose and her expression clear now, her anger and fear almost vanished. But it was her eyes that drew him. They were large and set wide apart in her delicate face, their color a perfect mixture of green and brown, like a woodland glade. They were fringed with long lashes that were darker than her hair. Drew had never before met a woman with eyes like that, and a peculiar excitement rose inside him. Could she be the woman from his vision? What was it Long Feather had said? That he would know when he finally met her. Years ago, he'd ceased looking for the mysterious woman, and he hadn't thought of those eyes for a long time, yet now they were before him. Was this the woman the eagle had shown him? He realized with some disappointment that he wasn't sure. And what if she was? What would that mean?

He heard her repeat her question.

"Sorry," he apologized for not responding. "We're Oglala. One of the Lakota tribes. We camp with Red Cloud."

"When you aren't patronizing Deadwood brothels," she observed dryly.

"I keep a room here because no one else will tolerate Indians," he said quietly. He rose to his feet and walked toward her.

Emily took a step back. "Did you really fight at the Little Bighorn against the cavalry?" she asked, a frown creasing her brow.

"No; I didn't."

"Oh." She took another step back as he approached. "How do you know who I am?"

"I know a lot of things," he answered with a lazy grin. He walked past her to the door.

"I can see that, but you didn't answer my question."

Drew fished in his pocket for a minute and recovered the key to the door. He unlocked it and poked his head out into the corridor.

"You stay here. I'll be right back," he told her, ignoring her question and pulling the door shut. She heard the lock turn on the other side.

"Of all the rude, impossible people I've met in my life,

that man takes the prize!'' she exclaimed loudly. Then she remembered the sleeping man and fell silent.

Drew returned several minutes later, slipping quietly into the room. Emily stood by the window, looking down into the street through the crack in the shade. Her mouth was set in a grim line when she looked up at him.

"Someone's watching for your brother. As soon as Sam gets to town, we'll take you out the back. In the meantime, I suggest you gather up your hairpins and make yourself more presentable. There's a comb in the washstand," he said, gesturing to the pins spread across the floor.

"I asked how you know who I am and you never answered me," Emily replied with quiet determination. "And who are you?"

"There's some clean water in the pitcher and a washcloth there if you'd care to wash your face," Drew said, again ignoring her questions.

Emily threw him an exasperated look, then dropped to her knees to gather her pins.

"You grab me and assault me in public. You carry me up a flight of stairs and then lock me in your room with an unconscious man. You won't answer simple questions. You complain about my manners and my language, even though you meet me just as I am about to be sorely used by a band of disreputable good-for-nothings. Then you criticize my poor appearance, for which, I feel compelled to point out, you are partly responsible. Such a paragon of manners *you* are, sir!''

Snatching up her last hairpin and jabbing it into her fist, Emily sat back on her heels and looked up at the man standing above her, only to discover an amused smile playing across his mouth. With a most unladylike snort, she rose to her feet and spun toward the washstand, her skirts swirling. She slammed the pins down next to the white ceramic pitcher, yanked open the drawer, pulled out the comb, and began tugging it through her tangled hair. In the unframed, cracked mirror above the washstand, she saw wide shoulders and a sunstreaked head move into the space behind her. Her resentful gaze caught his in the glass.

"I wasn't criticizing your appearance," he told her calmly. "In fact, you look quite alluring this way." His fingers caught gently in her hair, fanning it out on either side of her face. "Such a lovely color, like autumn grass in the sunlight, and so soft." His voice was barely more than a whisper.

Emily felt a queer contraction in her belly as she watched him in the mirror, and her heart hammered against her ribs.

"Unless, however, you want to tempt every man in this godforsaken place to carry you off to his bed, you'll have to make a few adjustments," he continued, his voice silky.

He let the golden strands fall as he slid his bronzed hands to the lowest undone button of her shirtwaist. Emily felt the warmth of his body as he stood close, not quite touching her. She felt the light caress of his fingers against the fine white cotton of her blouse, a fleeting pressure against her breast. She watched their reflection in the mirror, his head bowed over her shoulder, and a curious languor crept over her.

Ever so slowly, almost impersonally, he began to button her blouse.

Embarrassment flooded through Emily, staining her cheeks with color. What was she doing allowing such an intimacy to a stranger? With self-loathing, she acknowledged that she was not repulsed by this man's touch. Far from it; it excited in her a response she had not known herself capable of. She cursed herself for ever wishing to be held in his arms and angrily shrugged away from him.

"What? Disappointed that I decided not to play the wolf after all?" he teased, enjoying her discomfiture.

"Don't flatter yourself," she returned, striving for a note of worldly unconcern. He moved away from her, and she finished the buttons herself, then set to work on her hair.

As Emily pushed in the last pin, there was a soft knock on the door. Drew opened it and admitted Sheng-li. Emily looked at the boy in surprise.

"This is Sheng-li. He'll be your guide back to the stage office. *Don't* let go of his hand," Drew ordered. He opened the door a crack and looked down the hall.

"Why do we have to be so secretive?" she demanded.

"Do you want to run into any of your friends from downstairs?"

"Oh. I hadn't thought of that."

"That and a lot of other things. All right, go ahead." He swung the door open and pushed them out.

Emily paused briefly. "I guess I should, uh, thank you. For your help," she said awkwardly.

"Yes, you should, and sometime I'll see to it that you do it properly," Drew replied with a rakish grin. He patted her posterior as he pushed her down the hall.

"Why, of all the—!" she sputtered.

"See you later, Miss Parker. By the way, I like that new Eastern fashion you're sporting," he called after her softly.

Emily flung a startled, questioning look back at him.

"No corset," he mouthed, lounging insouciantly against the door frame, chuckling with pleasure when she turned her head haughtily and marched away from him, chin high in the air.

It was with inordinate relief that Emily saw Sam approaching, driving a wagon drawn by four black horses. She turned to the boy at her side.

"Thank you for your help, Sheng-li," she said, her eyes shining. The child smiled happily and ran back down the street before she could say another word.

She turned back to watch her brother bring the horses to a halt beside the stage agent's office, barely able to stand still. As soon as Sam jumped down from the high buckboard seat, Emily catapulted into his arms.

"Sam! I'm so glad to see you! It's been so long," she exclaimed, tears forming in her eyes.

Her brother swung her around in a bear hug, laughing merrily. "It's good to see you, too, Emily." He put her down and held her away from him for a long look. "I can see that I'm going to be fighting all the eligible bachelors in the Hills for your company, Emmy. You're even prettier than I remembered."

"Sam!" she reproved, blushing. She hoped he was wrong. She'd already had about enough of Black Hills bachelors to last her a lifetime.

"I'm just teasing you. Don't look so worried. I'm sorry I'm so late. I had a problem with the load I was hauling, then the creeks were high, and that slowed me down."

"It doesn't matter. I'm so glad to see you!" she said, giving him another hug. "And I can't wait to see Maggie and the children."

"Then let's get your trunk and get going. I'm sure you've got plenty of stories to tell, what with traveling alone all this way. The first one I want to hear is how you happened to be racing hell-bent-for-leather out of the Badlands as I was driving up," Sam said, shooting her a piercing glance.

"What are the Badlands?" Emily asked innocently.

"The lower end of town where all the drinking, gambling, and dissolute activities take place," Sam informed her, his curiosity more than aroused.

"Oh, that was nothing, just a little mistake. I'll tell you all about it later. I have a letter here from Mother for you and photographs of everyone. Wait 'til you see how proper Charles has gotten since he married. All of his clothes even match now." She giggled, hoping Sam would forget about the Badlands.

"I don't believe it." Sam hooted. "Come on, girl, let's get your things. If we don't get a move on, Maggie's going to think wild Indians have got us."

Emily pointed out her trunk and collected her jacket and smaller possessions, thinking rather grimly that wild Indians, or at least one wild, sort-of Indian, very nearly had gotten her. But she wasn't going to think about that now. Sam was here, and there was so much to catch up on.

Sitting next to her oldest brother in the wagon, Emily looked at him, noting the changes the years had wrought in him. His dark hair was longer, curling thickly over his collar, and she noticed one or two silver hairs at his temples that had not been there before. There were more lines at the corners of his eyes, but otherwise he looked little different from the last time she had seen him.

Sam was ten years her senior, but they'd always been close despite the difference in their ages. When Sam had left the family home in New York state ten years previously, Emily had been only fifteen, and she had missed him dreadfully in between his sporadic visits home.

When the Black Hills were opened to white settlers after the 1876 Gold Rush, Sam and his young family had gone west, lured by the promise of good land and a booming economy. Emily envied him his initiative and courage in pursuing his dreams. Her other brothers were far more staid, preferring the comfortable life they had grown accustomed to in Elmira. Only she and Sam had inherited their late father's thirst for challenge and adventure, and, she thought sadly, only Sam had done anything with it.

Until now. Smiling, Emily felt a great satisfaction at having journeyed all the way to Dakota Territory alone. Maybe she was more like Sam than she had thought.

She questioned Sam about Maggie and the children. Everyone was doing well. Joshua was now eight and fascinated with hunting, tracking, geography, and Indians. Sarah was six and learning to read. Daniel, the baby, at eighteen months was already more of a handful than any four other children, according to his father. And Maggie loved the hills and wild prairies. Emily drew more details from him, listening eagerly to every word. Suddenly, he stopped in mid-sentence, allowing his eyes to follow Emily's as she gazed at the mountain wilderness around them.

"I've come to love this land, Emmy," he told her with quiet feeling. "I never got too attached to places before. All I ever cared about was designing and building things, and as long as Maggie and the kids were with me, I figured it didn't much matter where I was. That's changed now. I've found a part of my heart here."

Emily heard the reverence in his voice.

"I guess you've found your home," she said softly. A deep longing came over her, a sudden yearning to belong somewhere. "It is beautiful," she added wistfully.

"That it is. You never know what will happen to you when you go to a new place, Emmy. You just might get caught in the spell these hills cast yourself."

The picture of vivid blue eyes, dancing with white lights, flashed unbidden through her mind—eyes that cast a spell of their own.

She laughed out loud, dispelling the image. Her clear voice carried across the sylvan park. Sam met her gaze, his eyes, so similar to hers, reflecting her laughter.

"Maybe," she agreed lightly. "You never know."

Chapter 3

It was a long ride back to the Parker ranch, but neither Sam nor Emily minded as they continued to chatter happily. As they entered Boulder Park, a long mountain meadow, they both laughed aloud as Emily told how Clara Anne Bundy, the Presbyterian minister's wife in Elmira, had come to the June Ladies' Aid meeting in a fancy new dress from New York City. It was tighter than a corset practically, and she was as proud as a peacock in it, only to have it split at the seams after her second glass of lemonade. As their laughter faded from the mountain air, it was replaced by the sound of hoofbeats. Casually, Sam reached for the Winchester rifle that was propped against the wagon seat and laid it in the crook of his arm.

"Is that necessary?" Emily asked, frowning.

"Most likely not, but there are so many road agents in these parts that it never hurts to be prepared," Sam answered.

A lone rider came into view astride a magnificent sorrel stallion. Sam relaxed as soon as he saw the man, pulling the wagon to the far side of the track.

The rider slowed to a walk as he approached, his hat pulled low over his brow, giving him a faintly menacing look. Upon reaching the wagon, he pushed the hat back and smiled in greeting, immediately dispelling that impression. His face was open and friendly, and Emily saw that he was tall and perhaps a few years older than herself. He had wavy black hair and a neat moustache that contrasted with his fair skin. Soulful dark brown eyes regarded her with open curiosity.

"Howdy!" he called. "What do you know, Sam? I'm almost finished with that spruce for you, and we'll be bringing it down in a couple of days. I don't believe I've met the lady, Sam." His voice was pleasant.

"Nice to see you, Zach. Zachary Stevens, meet my sister, Emily Parker. Emily's come to visit us for a while," Sam said amiably.

"Well, Miss Parker, it's a pleasure," Zachary Stevens said with a slight bow from the waist as he removed his hat. "I'm sure I speak for all the men in the vicinity when I say that I hope your visit is a long one."

"It's a pleasure to meet you, too, Mr. Stevens," Emily responded with a smile.

"Call me Zach, please. We're not too formal around here generally," Zach urged.

"I have to warn you, Emily, this man is the most notorious heartbreaker in the Hills," Sam interjected. "He's got girls pining for him from Custer City to Spearfish. He also runs one of the best sawmills around, so we see a lot of him at the ranch. Somehow, I've got the feeling we may be seeing even more of him than ever now." Sam shook his head.

Zach laughed. "You malign me, sir," he protested. "For now, though, you'll have to excuse me, much to my regret. I've got an appointment in town that can't wait, and I know you must be anxious to get home after such a long journey. Perhaps I'll see you soon, Emily."

"That would be lovely," she replied warmly.

"See you in a few days, Zach," Sam said, gathering up the reins again.

With a wave, they proceeded down the track. Zach didn't go immediately, but spent a moment looking back at the pretty blond woman. When the wagon disappeared around a bend, he replaced his hat, shoving it low over his ears, and galloped off, a satisfied smile playing across his handsome face.

"I guess all Dakota men aren't rough scoundrels, after

all," Emily declared as they left Zachary Stevens behind. She regretted the words instantly.

Sam pounced on them. "Ah, yes. Thanks for the reminder. Now, what exactly happened back in Deadwood, Emily? That little mistake you mentioned earlier. We have about enough time before we get home for you to tell me all about it."

Sam's tone let her know in no uncertain terms that he wouldn't let her off the hook. She tried anyway.

"Sam, you don't have to play the big brother routine anymore. I can take perfectly good care of myself. Nothing out of the ordinary happened," she insisted. She didn't want to tell him how foolish she had been, and she didn't want to think about that man with the blue eyes. She especially didn't want to think about her embarrassing reactions to him.

"Come on, Emmy. Out with it. If it was no big deal, then you won't mind telling me. If it was, I'll hear about it sooner or later anyway."

"Honestly, it was nothing." There was a bit too much emotion in her voice.

"Talk!"

"Oh, all right! If you promise you won't tell Mama, or anyone, except maybe Maggie." She glared at him. Older brothers never changed, it seemed.

"I promise. Now talk, for God's sake!"

Taking a deep breath, Emily told him about the fight between the miner and the Indians, and how hot she had been, and finally about going in search of water. Sam didn't say anything, but as she talked, she watched his hands grip the reins tighter and tighter until, by the time she got to the part about walking into the Sheridan Hotel and being surrounded by several drunken men, his knuckles were positively white. Emily paused.

"And?" Sam demanded.

Emily decided to omit the details.

"And then this rather peculiar man helped me out and I went back to the stage agent's office," she said with a fair amount of disgust. Again, she cursed herself for not watching her tone more carefully.

Sam looked at her appraisingly for a moment.

"You don't sound too thrilled about that," he observed far more mildly than Emily had expected.

Emily looked down at her lap, absently plucking at the folds of her skirt. She would not tell Sam how she'd allowed herself to be carted upstairs to the man's room.

"I was quite angry at the time. Now, of course, I am thankful for his intervention," she said primly.

To her astonishment, Sam threw back his head and laughed.

"You're thankful for his intervention? The man saves you from four or five drunken cabbageheads who think you're a prostitute and that's all you can say? I think you've been a teacher too long, Emmy. You got out here just in time. What did you say to him?"

"Not much. I wasn't thinking very clearly by that time."

"No, I suppose not. By any chance, Emily, do you know this man's name? You really should thank him." He was still chuckling.

"No, I don't know his name, and I doubt if I shall ever see him again, so it doesn't matter. Besides, I did say thank you." She was disconcerted, then annoyed by Sam's amusement. The situation hardly seemed funny.

"And I'll bet you were grace itself, weren't you?"

She rolled her eyes.

"That's what I thought. This wouldn't happen to have been a tall fellow with real blue eyes, dressed like an Indian, would it?"

Emily's incredulous expression was all the answer he needed. He chuckled again.

Emily sputtered with annoyance that Sam was laughing at her. She'd had a frightening experience, and she thought he could do better than laugh. She forced herself to calm down.

"Do you know this man? Who is he?" she asked rapidly. "Personally, I wasn't terribly impressed with him. He seemed quite a rogue to me, and playing at being an Indian to boot!"

"I know who he is, Emily, and he's not exactly what

I'd call a rogue. Some people around here call him Sky in the Eyes, which is a corruption of his Sioux name. And he doesn't play at being an Indian. He grew up with one of the Oglala bands, and for all intents, he might as well be one of them."

"That's a stupid name." Emily realized she sounded petty and childish, but she didn't care.

"Emmy, I'm sorry I laughed. It's just that you had pretty good luck running into that man, considering your predicament. I can't think of anyone, not even the sheriff, that you'd have been safer with. As near as I know, he's never hurt anyone who didn't more than ask for it, and most folks in these parts are more scared of him than they are of the Indians. Why, those hoodlums would no more have crossed him than they would a rabid grizzly bear."

Emily wasn't sure she entirely believed this, but her brother's apology mollified her slightly.

"I'm sorry, too, Sam. I'm sure I'm overreacting because of the journey. I'm not angry with you at all, it's just that that man was so arrogant and difficult and I was already scared half to death before he even showed up. It was all a bit much to take. Will you forgive me for snapping at you?"

"Of course I will," Sam assured her affectionately. He put his arm around her and gave her a quick hug as the wagon pulled out of the canyon and into the open valley that encircled the Black Hills. "We're almost there, Emmy. Promise me one thing." His voice was serious now.

"Anything."

"Don't go wandering around in Deadwood by yourself until you know the place a little better."

"I promise."

"Good. Let's get on home, then," he said, turning the team to the south, toward his ranch. "Your journey's almost over, Emmy."

"Thank God." She sighed.

That evening, a groggy Indian awoke, his headache nearly gone, and the heat of the day dissipating as the sun sank behind the hill that rose across the street from the Sheridan Hotel. He raised himself on one elbow and saw his companion working at a table across the room.

"Well, *misun*," he said quietly in Lakota, "I think I'm going to live. I had a strange dream, though, that there was a woman here, a pretty blond woman. What do you think that means?" He grinned at the man's back.

Without turning, the other man answered. "It means Sam Parker's sister arrived today and got herself into some trouble downstairs. Fortunately, I managed to get her out of it." He paused to dismiss the topic. "How do you feel?"

"I've felt worse, and I've felt better. Tell me the whole story, *misun*," Black Wolf prompted. "I seem to remember you weren't so happy with Miss Parker, nor she with you. I'll recover faster for a good tale." He chuckled softly.

Drew turned in his chair and frowned when he saw his friend's grin.

"I don't suppose you'd just let it alone, would you?" he asked, knowing the answer he would receive. He didn't want to talk about the woman. He had letters that needed immediate attention.

"You're my adopted brother. My father took you and your father into his tipi as family more than twenty years ago. This is how you repay me? You won't even tell me a little story to pass the time while I'm forced to lie abed because a stupid miner hates the Lakota? You're a hard man," Black Wolf chided with a half smile.

"You're not going to give up, are you?"

Black Wolf only grinned.

"All right." Drew pushed away from the table and turned his chair to face the bed. Quickly, he recounted the afternoon's events.

"How did you know who she was?" Black Wolf asked.

"I remembered Sam telling me a few weeks back that his sister was coming. He said she was a schoolteacher, and this woman just had the look of a teacher, in spite of being prettier than most of them."

"She's prettier than most women, not just schoolteachers," Black Wolf said authoritatively. "Most white women," he amended.

"I'll tell Red Eagle Woman you think so," Drew replied, referring to his brother's wife.

Black Wolf merely looked patiently at him. He and Red Eagle Woman had been trying to find a woman for his adopted brother for years, and the whole camp wondered when he would take a wife.

"Besides, I recognized her eyes," Drew added pensively. He hadn't meant to say it like that.

The Indian's sudden attention was obvious in his now serious countenance.

"How so?' he asked.

Drew appeared lost in thought for a moment. Then he shook his head briefly. "They're exactly the same color as Sam's. Kind of brown and green at the same time. I never met anyone else with eyes that color, so I figured it must be his sister. Lucky guess, as it turned out."

His voice sounded as if he were trying to make light of the matter, but Black Wolf knew better. He knew Drew better than he knew anyone else alive. He knew all his secrets and most of his dreams. They had first met when they were ten years old, and Drew and his father had wandered into the Bad Faces camp. Black Wolf's father, Long Feather, an important holy man, had taken a special interest in the white boy with the strange eyes. The Indian shaman adopted him and his father both in the *hunka* ceremony, and they had lived as a family for almost ten years. The boys had grown to manhood together, learning to hunt, track, and do all the other things that made a man Lakota.

Then, after the white men's war was over, the white boy's uncle had journeyed from his home in Boston to find them. He had convinced Drew's father to return and take over the family shipping business so that he could enter politics. Reluctantly, Drew had also returned. Black Wolf went with him and spent a couple of years living with the Rutledges in a big brick house in Boston. The two men knew each other as friends and as brothers in both their worlds. They understood each other, and they worked together to save what they could of the Indian way of life from the encroachment of the white men around them.

Right now, Black Wolf knew that this woman his brother had met was not just any woman. She could be the woman from Drew's boyhood vision.

"You don't know her eyes from somewhere else?" he prompted, his dark gaze piercing.

"It might be the woman by the pool," Drew replied at length, avoiding the other man's eyes.

Excitement crackled between them.

"You think it's possible?" Black Wolf asked seriously.

"I don't know," Drew answered impatiently, shaking his head, staring at the uneven floorboards. "I certainly never expected her to be an old-maid schoolteacher from Elmira, New York. It doesn't seem likely."

"Wakantanka is the Great Mystery. We don't understand the ways of the Grandfathers, *misun*. Was there anything unusual about her? Besides being so pretty." He smiled.

"She wasn't afraid of you. She seemed concerned, in fact. But a lot of Easterners would have been. I don't know. I can't even think about it right now." Drew gestured to the pile of papers on the table, his voice grim. "I've got some pretty disturbing messages here. I think I'm going to have to clear on out of Deadwood and spend more time at the cabin. Looks like I may have my hands full keeping an eye on things there for a while. There are several shipments due, and I don't want to lose them."

"I'll come with you," Black Wolf told him. "But don't forget about this woman. You should find out soon enough if she's your vision woman or not."

"Yeah, I expect I will," Drew replied absently, his thoughts already elsewhere. "Take a look at this wire from the commissioner and tell me what you think."

Their conversation turned to urgent business.

Two days later, Emily stood just outside the kitchen door, watching the summer sun climb high into a cloudless blue sky. She looked south toward the creek that rippled merrily along, fed by last night's thundershowers in the hills. A feeling of warm vitality spread through her as she stepped off the porch for a walk around the neat yard. She loved being with Sam and Maggie, she had no cares or responsibilities for the moment, and it was going to be a glorious day. She had been right to leave Elmira. A change of pace was exactly what she needed.

Emily had been quite impressed with Sam and Maggie's ranch. When they first drove up, she had looked at Sam in astonishment, never expecting the elegant two-story house that wouldn't have been out of place in a stylish Eastern neighborhood. In addition, there was a bunkhouse nearby for the two young men who worked as Sam's apprentices and his hired man. A big red barn stood a few hundred yards from the house, with a chicken house and Sam's workshop behind it. Enjoying her surprise, Sam had modestly told her that business had been pretty good. To Emily, it looked as if business had been excellent.

The location of the ranch had much to do with its charm. Sam had chosen land that was right on the edge of the Hills, part mountain and part prairie. The house itself was tucked up against the last of the Hills proper, the dark pine forest rising behind it, the broad meadow of the red valley that ringed the Hills stretching away before it. Across the valley was a final ridge of smaller, pine-dotted hills, then the open plains beyond. The house was situated to take full advantage of the southern sun, and the garden and a small apple orchard had been planted south of the house. Beyond them, the creek flowed clean and fast, its banks lined with cottonwoods, aspens, elms, willows, wild plums, and chokecherries.

The barn where Sam kept his horses and a few head of cattle, when they weren't grazing in the pastures, was spacious and clean. A corral was hidden from view behind it, as were some of the smaller outbuildings and Sam's workshop. In showing her the workshop, Sam's modesty had evaporated. With obvious pride, he'd pointed out the latest machinery and equipment that he'd had freighted in from the East, via the Missouri River steamboats and then by wagon train from Fort Pierre. Sam did some cabinetry work and furniture making here, mostly for his own home and for special friends, and it was this work that he loved best. He had, however, found far more profit in the Black Hills in raising houses for the rapidly growing population, and this work occupied the greater part of his time. Emily was proud of her brother's success, and she could see that he was liked and respected by the men who worked for him and in the community. He'd made a good life for his family in the Dakota wilderness, and Emily understood why he was happy here.

Facing the south, the dark line of the hills stretching away to the right, Emily closed her eyes and breathed deeply of the warm air. It smelled of pine and mown hay. A meadowlark's song rose into the morning sky, and the stream babbled softly. Maybe this is a paradise, Emily thought contentedly.

As she stood with her back to the house, she heard the kitchen door burst open, then slam shut with a bang.

"Aunt Emily!" the little girl's high voice called. "Aunt Emily! Are you out here?"

"There she is!" her brother proclaimed. "In the garden. Race ya!"

The dark-haired boy was off before his younger sister, who bellowed a protest at the headstart he took, but she lit out on his heels. They reached Emily at almost the same instant, both loudly claiming victory. Emily smiled happily at them.

"My word, but if you two aren't the fastest children I ever saw, then my name must be Murgatroyd," she told them, her eyes dancing. "How'd you learn to run so fast?"

"We race a lot," Joshua informed her, emphasizing the last word.

"Are we really the fastest, Aunt Emily?" Sarah asked, beaming under the compliment. Her fair curls bounced as she skipped through the garden.

"Yes, you really are. And remember, I'm a schoolteacher. I've seen a lot of children, so I should know."

Both children were thrilled. Then Josh remembered his errand.

"Ma wanted to know if you'd like to go into town shopping with her today. She was on her way out to ask you when Daniel knocked over the sugar bowl, so we came instead.''

''Oh, dear, maybe we should go in and help clean up,'' Emily said, starting for the house.

Both children agreed, and each grasped one of their aunt's hands as they skipped back across the grass.

In the spacious kitchen, Maggie had just finished cleaning up the spilled sugar when Emily, Josh, and Sarah entered.

''Just in time,'' she announced. ''Joshua, will you take your brother outside for a bit? Stay inside the fence, and don't leave him alone, all right?'' the pretty woman asked, handing the pudgy toddler to his older brother. ''Thanks a lot, Josh.'' She smiled after her sons as they exited. Sarah followed them out.

''I don't know how you do it,'' Emily told her sister-in-law.

Maggie's brown hair was tied back with a piece of blue ribbon that matched her wide eyes. She looked calm and happy in her bright red and white print cotton summer dress with a full skirt and loose sleeves, not at all like the mother of three active children, one of whom had just made a colossal mess for her to clean up.

''Whatever do you mean, Emily?'' Maggie asked her in puzzlement.

''You never seem to get flustered, and I haven't heard you become cross or raise your voice once to the children in the two days that I've been here. And there has been plenty of provocation,'' Emily answered with a smile, her eye on the empty sugar bowl.

Maggie laughed.

''Oh, I yell at them as much as anyone. You'll see. It's just that I'm in a particularly good mood lately. I love this time of year, and I'm so happy that you've come, Emily. I'm having far too good a time to spoil it by being cross with the children. I had the most wonderful idea,'' she continued. ''Mary Guthrie, John and Hannah's oldest daughter, is coming over in about an hour or so. She comes several times a week to help with the children and the housework, and I was thinking it might be fun if we had Frank drive us into Deadwood in the new buggy to do some shopping. Sam told me the Big Horn Store has some new summer fabrics," she finished temptingly. "Would you like to go?"

"Yes, I'd love to," Emily told her warmly. "That is, if you promise you'll tell me exactly where the reputable businesses are."

"Of course I will. Where else would we be going? Let's see if we can find Frank," Maggie said over her shoulder, already heading for the door.

Where else, indeed, Emily thought to herself.

Chapter 4

ᔓᔓ

They found Frank Snyder, the hired man, in the barn currying a new bay mare that Sam had recently purchased. He was amenable to a trip into town, and within an hour, Mary had arrived and received her instructions. The children were disappointed that they were not included in the trip, but Mary consoled them with plans for a picnic in the garden.

On the drive to Deadwood, they skirted the newer town of Sturgis and Fort Meade, while Maggie told Emily about the history of the area. Ever since white settlers had first started coming to the Black Hills, they had petitioned the army for a fort to protect them against the Indians. The government had at first been loath to establish a permanent post because the settlers were in the Hills in violation of the treaty signed with the Sioux at Fort Laramie in 1868. Finally, the army had given up trying to keep newcomers out and acknowledged that some protection was needed from the periodic Indian attacks. Fort Meade, named after the Civil War general, was established on the northern edge of the Hills, near Bear Butte, in 1878. The little town of Sturgis had grown up in the valley alongside it. It was still small, without the developed commercial center that Deadwood possessed, but with all the vices that could be found in lower Deadwood, catering to the large soldier population. Maggie preferred to avoid it if she could.

About a mile north of the ranch, the trail wound up Boulder Canyon toward Deadwood. Emily and Maggie chattered happily, drawing Frank into their conversation when they could. Emily found out that he had come to the Hills from Vermont during the early days of the Gold Rush, but he had soon tired of a miner's grueling existence. He'd been with the Parkers ever since Sam had moved from Deadwood out to the ranch, and he was accepted as one of the family.

Emily and Maggie were examining bolts of brightly colored calico at the Big Horn Store's counter, debating the merits of the various prints as dresses for Sarah and shirts for Joshua and Daniel when an excited voice called Maggie's name.

"Margaret Parker! Where have you been keeping yourself?"

The speaker was a young blond woman, about Maggie's age. She was accompanied by a young, blue-uniformed soldier who was struggling beneath a number of packages.

"Caroline! How nice to see you!" Maggie answered. "I've been busy at the ranch lately, but today seemed like the perfect day for shopping, so here I am."

Maggie introduced Emily to Caroline Reynolds, whose husband, Colonel Matthias Reynolds, was the commanding officer at Fort Meade. Emily took an immediate liking to the petite woman. Despite her fragile, china-doll appearance, Caroline was lively, outspoken, and full of merriment. Caroline helped them pick out their material, then added a few more packages of her own to her escort's burdens.

All their purchases completed, the three ladies stepped outside just as Colonel Reynolds reached the shop's entrance. He was a tall, thin man who smiled instantly at the sight of his pretty wife. With a quick glance at his subordinate's overflowing arms, he rolled his eyes skyward and shook his head in mock despair.

"Lord, Caroline, it looks like you've cleaned out every shop in town, along with my purse," he mourned. He took a few parcels from the younger man. "Hello, Mrs. Parker," he continued, nodding and removing his hat.

Caroline interrupted him to introduce Emily. After a few minutes of polite conversation about Emily's journey and the weather, a topic Emily found held untold fascination for Dakotans, the foursome wandered down Main Street to the Grand Central Hotel. The colonel left the ladies there, excusing himself to attend to business.

"Well, shall we go in and have some tea?" Caroline asked. "I want to tell you all about the plans for the dance this Saturday night. I do hope you're coming."

"Oh, my goodness!" Maggie exclaimed, her hand flying to her mouth. "With all the excitement of Emily's arrival, I've completely forgotten to tell her about it!"

"Then I will be glad to," Caroline said. "And perhaps you both can give me some good suggestions for the decorations. It's so difficult to come up with anything new." With that, the three women proceeded into the hotel parlor to discuss the dance over tea.

The next morning, Zach Stevens delivered his load of lumber to Sam's shop. When he was finished, he and Sam came up to the house where Emily and Maggie were sitting on the porch shelling peas, while the children were pretending to dig for gold in a corner of the yard given over to their purposes. It was a pleasantly warm day, the sky full of puffy white clouds. Zach greeted the women.

"Howdy, ladies," he said with a warm smile. His eyes rested appreciatively on Emily. Sam and Maggie exchanged a knowing look.

Maggie answered him. "Good morning, Zach," she said. "Would either of you be interested in a glass of lemonade?"

"That's why we're here," her husband answered as she set aside her bowl of peas and rose. "I'll help you," he said, following her into the kitchen.

Emily was left alone with Zach. She continued shelling peas while he stood with one foot on the porch steps, a hand resting against an upright post. When Emily looked up at him, she was startled somewhat by the intensity of his gaze. Almost immediately, he smiled, and his brown eyes lost the deep look they had held a second before. Stepping up onto the porch, he commented on the weather.

"It's a right nice day," he said.

Emily smiled, wondering if every conversation in the hills began with a comment on the weather.

"Yes, it is," she agreed. She decided to try a new subject. "How long have you lived here, Zach?"

He immediately lost his reserve and told Emily that he had been in the hills for three years. She found out that he was from Illinois, as was Maggie, and that he'd had quite a few different occupations before opening his sawmill. He continued talking for a few minutes, then fell silent. After a moment, he spoke again.

"Sam tells me you all are going to the Fort Meade dance Saturday," Zach began. He paused again and ran his hand up under the open collar of his shirt.

"Yes, that's right," Emily answered. "I'm looking forward to it." She wondered why Zach seemed so nervous.

"Well, ah, I . . ." he stammered.

Emily realized in a flash what he wanted and smiled down into her bowl of peas. She was a little surprised that this confident young man was having difficulty asking her to the dance.

"I, uh, was wondering if you would like to go with me? It would be an honor," he finally said.

"It's very kind of you to ask," Emily responded, not completely sure she wanted to go to the dance in one man's company. She didn't want to land herself in another situation like she'd been in with George Parks. She needed time to think about what she wanted from a man before she got involved again.

For some perverse reason, her mind recalled the picture of the man Sam had called Sky in the Eyes standing behind her in the mirror, his hands in her hair. She pushed the image from her and concentrated on the man in front of her. She didn't want to hurt his feelings.

"Why don't I meet you there?" she offered.

"May I have the first dance with you?" he asked, accepting her suggestion gracefully.

"It would be my pleasure, Zach."

Sam and Maggie returned just then with a tray of glasses, a pitcher of lemonade, and a plate of sugar cookies. The children came running over from their "gold" field, and Sam and Zach began telling Emily how rich the land in the Black Hills was. Many different kinds of lumber were abundant, there were good water supplies, game in the hills, and fertile land surrounding them. The conversation went from topic to topic. Emily and Maggie soon finished the peas, and the children finished their refreshments and returned to their games. Zachary brought up a new subject.

"I heard there was some Indian trouble last week down by the Buffalo Gap," he announced grimly. "Seems a couple of Sioux surprised a family on their way to Custer City. They didn't kill anyone, but they took their horses and left the family stranded on the trail. It's got folks down there riled up. I wish the army would either keep those redskins at the agencies or get rid of them. They're a bloody menace." His voice was matter-of-fact, with no apparent emotion.

Emily was shocked at his coldbloodedness. She knew that Westerners' attitudes toward the Indians were almost uniformly hostile, and she'd seen evidence of this, but she hadn't realized *how* hostile until this moment. She had assumed that educated, intelligent people could see that the Indian tribes had lost their way of life and that some problems were to be expected. It was a price to be paid for settling their lands. Besides, it wasn't as if the white people never did horrible things to the Indians. She considered saying something to Zach, then decided against it. She didn't wish to start an argument, but she was suddenly glad she hadn't committed herself to attending the dance with him.

Neither Sam nor Maggie made any comment, causing Emily to wonder if they agreed with Zach, or if, like her, they held their tongues. She'd have to ask them when Zach left. Sam interrupted her thoughts with an observation about the children's activities, and the tenseness that Emily felt eased as they all chuckled over the pretend goldmining operation. After a few more minutes, Zach excused himself, refusing an invitation to stay for dinner, said his goodbyes, and left.

"See you Saturday night," he called to Emily as he walked toward his team.

"Yes, goodbye," she said, waving.

Maggie shot Emily a quick look. "Are you going to the dance with Zach?" she asked with one eyebrow raised.

"No, I'm going with you and Sam. I'm dancing the first dance with him," Emily returned easily.

"Do you like him?" Maggie asked with a small smile.

Emily laughed. "Now whatever do you mean by that?"

"You know what I mean," Maggie said, smiling more openly. "Do you?"

"Did my mother write to you asking you to introduce me to one of your nice gentleman friends?" Emily asked suspiciously.

"Of course she did," Maggie said airily. In a more serious tone, she added, "But that's not why I'm asking, Emily. Zachary Stevens seems awfully interested in you. He's a flirt, to be sure, but he acted a bit different with you from what I've seen before with other girls. Definitely more serious. I thought you might not be wanting that right now, after what happened with George, that's all."

Emily breathed a sigh of relief at her sister-in-law's understanding.

"Thank you, Maggie," she replied. "Zach seems nice enough, and he's certainly handsome, but you're right. I'd rather not worry about men for a while."

Unbidden, the memory of wide shoulders covered in soft leather beneath her hands leapt into her mind, causing her heart to race momentarily.

"Any man," she reiterated thoughtfully.

Maggie looked at her, wondering what had caused the sudden faraway look in Emily's eyes, followed so quickly by set determination.

"If you ever need any excuses to put Zach off, you can count on me to back you up," she offered. "Now, we'd better get supper going, or I know at least three children and four men who are going to be mighty put out!"

Laughing, the two women gathered up the peas and returned to the kitchen.

* * *

That evening, after the children had been put to sleep, Emily sat on the porch with her brother and his wife, enjoying the summer twilight. The first stars were peeping out in the deepening sky. The color reminded Emily of something, though she couldn't think quite what. In a rush, she remembered eyes that color, deep, alive with lights, drinking her in. She felt herself blush and hoped Sam and Maggie wouldn't notice in the dusk. She decided to ask Sam about Zach's earlier comments regarding Indians.

"Do you remember what Zachary Stevens said this morning about that Indian attack?"

"Are you worried about Indians, Emmy? You don't have to be. We're too close to Fort Meade to have much trouble up here," Sam reassured her.

"No, I wasn't worried about our safety. But I didn't like what he said about killing them off to protect the white settlers. I understand that's quite a popular opinion locally."

"That it is," Sam agreed, resignation in his voice. Emily was relieved to hear it. "Unfortunately, most of us don't know a thing about the tribes except the horror stories of battles and raids, and that they are very different from us. They see the world differently than we do, and that breeds misunderstanding and hatred."

"Back East, there's a lot of support for the Indian cause. I thought the government was trying to take care of them," she commented.

"Some of the folks in Washington are sympathetic to the Indians, but that might not last, Emily. The army, however, is not exactly what you could call pro-Indian. People out here get real annoyed when they hear Easterners defending the Indians. That's why we didn't say anything to Zach. A lot of our friends and neighbors are scared to death of them. They're just wild, murdering savages in most folks' eyes."

"But not yours?"

"Not mine, Emily," Sam said quietly. "I worry a hell of a lot more about the white outlaws and road agents that prey on folks in these hills."

"Sam!" Maggie interjected softly. "Your language."

He smiled at his wife's gentle reprimand. "Emily's a schoolteacher, Mags, not a nun. I'm sure she's heard worse."

The conversation drifted off in other directions as the last light faded and night fell.

The Parker family spent most of Saturday getting ready for the dance. The children were all given baths, Sunday clothes were pressed and hung out of reach of grubby hands, hair was combed and curled, and food and bedding were packed into the wagon. Finally, late in the afternoon, the children were dressed, and everyone climbed into the wagon. Eddie Dillard and Sam's other apprentice, Kenny Carroll, rode alongside. Frank stayed behind, claiming that dances only brought out the devil in him.

When Sam saw his wife and sister, he let out a long whistle.

"My word, you two look handsome," he said with admiration. "I'm going to be the envy of every man at the dance."

Emily and Maggie did look lovely in their prettiest dresses. Maggie's was a full-skirted light blue muslin trimmed with fine white lace at the throat and wrists. On her bodice, she had pinned the cameo that Sam had given her for their wedding, and the lace of her finest petticoat peeked out below the billowing, blue skirts that exactly matched her eyes. Emily wore a deep green silk gown, cut according to the latest fashion in the East. It fit snugly through the bodice, so snugly, in fact, that Emily had had little choice but to resort to her corset. Then the dress nipped in even tighter at the waist and fell in a dramatically narrow skirt. Emily had been afraid the dress would make dancing difficult, but she found it did not restrict her movements as much as she had thought it would. It was warm, though, with its high neck and close-fitting sleeves. Emily hoped the evening would bring a cool breeze to the fort.

The drive to Fort Meade took less than an hour. The fort sat just below the last ridge of hills, on the edge of the great plains along Bear Butte Creek. To the northeast loomed Bear Butte, a lone outrider of the hills, rising high above the surrounding plains. Emily had not seen it before, for it was hidden from view at the Parkers' by the hills on the outer rim of the red valley. She thought it had a mysterious air about it, especially when Sam told her that there were legends that it was sacred to some of the Indians.

Emily would have liked to have asked more, but they had arrived at the fort, and she was needed to help Maggie unload the food into the dining hall. Caroline Reynolds had managed to find paper streamers to drape from the rafters, and bouquets of wildflowers decorated the long tables, fast filling up with food. The dance itself would be held on the parade ground, where a bandstand had been set up to accommodate the Seventh Cavalry Band. Emily made her way across the room to congratulate Caroline on her festive decorations.

Looking dainty in a pink gown with ruffled sleeves and flounces, Caroline was busily ordering young members of the Seventh Cavalry hither and thither with plates of chicken, ham, potato salad, hardcooked eggs, assorted fruits and vegetables, and large pitchers of lemonade. When she caught sight of Emily and Maggie, she waved her hand wildly and bustled over.

"Hello! I'm so glad you're here a little early," she exclaimed. "Emily, that dress is simply gorgeous! Maggie, you look stunning! *Très chic,* as they taught us at Miss Lucinda Culver's School for Young Ladies. There I go babbling again," Caroline apologized. "I do that when I get nervous. I was wondering, Maggie, if you would help me with a few last-minute details. Emily, you must meet some of our young officers. Why, here's one of them now."

A pleasant-looking young man about Emily's age was passing by. Caroline introduced him as Lieutenant Avery Smith from Lansing, Michigan, and instructed him to show Emily around a bit before supper. The lieutenant, a quiet man with long, curling brown hair, was delighted with the unexpected duty and promptly steered Emily back outside to show off with her for a while. Pretty soon, a small circle of young cavalrymen had gathered around them. It appeared that there were nowhere near as many young women in the Dakotas as there were young men, and even fewer real ladies, guaranteeing the popularity of any young woman with passable looks and a tolerable manner. Emily, no stranger to attentive male companions, faced a barrage of eager masculine faces that was unparalleled in her experience. She chatted happily with them, asking them about their homes and their families, enjoying their bantering conversation and the constant stream of flowery compliments they paid her.

Gradually, guests arrived from the surrounding ranches and towns, including quite a few prominent citizens from Deadwood. Soon, Emily was joined by several other young women, most of whom were quite a bit younger than she was. Small groups of the young people stood outside watching the sun set behind the hills, talking noisily until the supper call sounded. On the way into the dining hall, Emily heard a familiar voice.

"Emily!" Zach Stevens called to her across the throng.

She had completely forgotten that he would be there, so involved had she been with her companions. He elbowed his way through the crush of blue uniforms and Sunday dresses to stand at Emily's side. He wore a fashionable dark suit and smelled faintly of cologne as he leaned close to Emily.

"You look beautiful!" he said quietly, his gaze intense for an instant, then quickly veiled.

Emily felt vaguely uneasy. There was a fleeting possessiveness in his eyes that she didn't welcome. She controlled her involuntary desire to take a step back and forced herself to smile back at him. She told herself that she was simply overreacting, still affected by her experiences at the Sheridan Hotel.

"Zachary, how nice to see you again," she said pleasantly. "I believe you're just in time for supper."

"Will you join me?" he asked politely, offering her his arm.

"Certainly," she answered.

There was a chorus of groans from the Seventh Cavalry

officers encircling them. Zach laughed, his face glowing
with pride as he escorted her in to supper.

The dining room was noisy and crowded. Children raced
back and forth, playing tag and grabbing choice pieces
from the platters of food. Mothers tried in vain to settle
them down as they exchanged the latest gossip with their
neighbors and friends. The older men congregated to discuss politics, business, and, of course, the weather. The
single young men and women ate together with a few older
folks who jokingly chaperoned them. Emily caught sight
of Sam and Maggie sitting with Colonel and Mrs. Reynolds and moved to join them. Over the din, Maggie asked
if she was enjoying herself. Emily's wide smile answered
that she was.

After supper, the women helped clear up the food and
then packed the smallest children off to bed in a loft set
aside for that purpose. The men went outside to smoke
and light torches to place around a circle on the parade
ground to provide light for the packed-earth dance floor.
Chairs were carried out and set around the edges of the
circle while stray notes from horns and strings drifted with
the breeze as the band members began warming up in the
open air of the Dakota night. The moon was nearly full,
bathing all in a silvery glow, and the stars shone like diamonds against the black sky. Emily and Caroline walked
across the grass to join the crowd, where they found Sam
and Colonel Reynolds. Zach was nowhere to be seen. The
colonel smiled affectionately at his wife.

"My dear, you've done a splendid job tonight. Rarely
have I seen the men enjoy themselves so much, and I think
everyone else is having a wonderful time as well," he told
her approvingly.

"Thank you, Matt, but I'm afraid we should thank Emily for your officers' having such a good time. I think she's
singlehandedly turned them into as docile and polite a
group of gentlemen as the Seventh has seen in many a
year," Caroline teased. "I hope you wore comfortable
shoes tonight, Emily, because I doubt if you'll sit for a
minute once the music starts."

As if on cue, the band director signaled to Colonel Reynolds that they were ready to begin. He and Caroline went forward to lead the first dance. Emily looked around and found Zach at her elbow.

"You didn't think I'd miss our date, did you?" he said merrily, taking her hand. "Shall we?"

"With pleasure, Zach," Emily replied.

The crowd grew quiet and the band struck up the first tune, a fast waltz. After the colonel and Caroline had completed a turn, the parade ground-turned-dance-floor filled with couples. As she spun around the circle with Zach, Emily caught sight of Sam dancing with Sarah. She laughed when she saw Josh and another boy the same age dancing together in mimicry of the adults, mincing and bowing, then stumbling all over each other, giggling gleefully all the while. Zach was a good dancer, and he didn't hold her too close as she had feared he might. When the waltz was over, she was swept out of his arms and into a freewheeling polka by her brother. Emily was flushed with excitement, her eyes dancing as well as her feet, but she got no chance to catch her breath. Caroline's prediction appeared to be coming true, for as each dance finished, there was ever yet another young man at Emily's side, claiming the next dance.

After several numbers, the band took an intermission, promising to play a couple of popular numbers when they returned. Emily thanked her partner, a young cavalry officer, and sought her family. She found Maggie among a group of ranchers and their wives along with a few uniformed men. Emily was introduced to those she didn't yet know, thinking that she would never remember all their names. She couldn't count the people she'd met that night.

"I had a real good alfalfa crop this year," one rancher was saying. "If we get a late freeze, I may be able to cut a second time."

Two other men offered comments on their crops, then began to discuss horses. One of the officers was looking to purchase a new mount and wondered if they knew of any good animals for sale. At that point, Maggie saw someone she knew and excused herself.

"Wait right here, Emily. I've just seen someone I want

you to meet," she said in Emily's ear, disappearing into the milling crowd.

Emily was talking to one of the rancher's wives about new dress patterns when the woman's husband's voice interrupted their conversation.

"There's that damn Rutledge." The man practically spat the name out.

"What the heck is he doing here?" another rancher asked with ill-disguised distaste.

Emily wondered who they were talking about. She followed their eyes but couldn't tell who they were looking at in the dim red light of the torches. She asked the woman beside her to point the man out.

"He's that tall fella, with his back to us, next to the bandleader," she told Emily.

Emily picked him out, his broad shoulders rising above the crowd. Something about him seemed familiar, but she couldn't see his face. She tried to remember if she'd met him earlier that evening, and could not. She turned back to the little circle around her.

"What's he done to become so unpopular?" she asked the woman quietly.

Her husband heard the question and answered.

"He's an Indian lover, Miss Parker. He's got some fancy law degree from back East, and he's set himself up as the Indian advocate in these parts. He's got a rich family, so he don't got to work for a livin' like the rest of us."

"That's right," added another rancher. "He don't take no regular cases, like a normal lawyer. Instead, he goes gallivantin' across the territory inciting the damn Indians, if you'll excuse my language, yakking at them about treaty rights and other nonsense."

"Yup, and he's even been known to haul a couple of 'em back to Washington to try and soften up the federal government toward 'em. He wants to protect their land and their rights," the first man sneered. "As if they had any rights. The man's a traitor to his race."

"I heard some rumors that he smuggles stolen supplies out to the reservations," one of the officers volunteered.

He was a pale, black-haired man with watery blue eyes. Emily thought his name was Lieutenant Logan.

"He ought to be shot along with every one of those heathen, bloodthirsty savages," the second rancher stated flatly.

Emily listened with growing indignation. Her sense of justice would not allow her to remain silent, in spite of Sam's warning that defending Indians was a wasted effort in Dakota.

"Really, gentlemen," she began, trying hard to keep the disapproval out of her voice. "I fail to see that the Indians have no rights. The government did sign treaties with them, and we *are* all here in direct violation of them."

The people around her looked at her in surprise.

The army officer spoke. "Miss Parker, you haven't been here long enough to know that the Sioux are also in violation of their end of the treaty agreements. They've continued hostilities against white settlers. Many of them won't even stay put on the reservations." There were nods and grunts of assent.

Emily's temper rose at the condescending tone the officer used.

"Lieutenant, I assure you that I am aware of what you call treaty violations on the part of the Indians. I can also assure you that if I had a legal document guaranteeing my right to my ancestral lands and someone decided to disregard that and take over my land, I might well be inclined to break a few rules myself." Emily's eyes were flashing now in the torchlight, reflecting the green of her dress. "Furthermore," she continued, all pretense of neighborly tolerance now vanished, "while I can understand your concern for the safety of your families and your property, I do not at all comprehend this barbaric desire to exterminate an entire race, whether by starvation or out-and-out murder."

Emily was aware that the group had become very still. One rancher straightened his shoulders and cleared his throat, but she didn't give him the chance to speak.

"If this is an example of contemporary Christian values, I would sooner trust myself to the Indians!'' she declared hotly, glaring at the ranchers and the officers.

No one spoke. She was suddenly aware that they were not looking at her. Their eyes were focused on a point behind her, and she experienced a brief sensation of déjà vu.

"And you would most likely fare considerably better than in present company," a familiar voice drawled.

Chapter 5

The skin on the back of Emily's neck prickled and her heart lurched. For an instant, the torch-lit parade ground receded, and she was back in the Sheridan Hotel in Deadwood. With an effort, she cleared her mind. What on earth was *he* doing here? At a *dance,* of all places? Color flooded her face, staining her cheeks crimson. Then Maggie's voice sounded close, and there was a touch on her arm.

"Excuse me, Emily," she said gently, almost hesitantly. "There's someone I'd like you to meet."

Emily turned slowly. The ranchers and their wives drifted away, mumbling excuses. Looming above her, next to Maggie, was the man who had rescued her in Deadwood, but he wasn't dressed like an Indian now. His hair had been cut to just above his collar, and he wore an elegantly tailored black coat with a gold watch chain glittering across his matching waistcoat. Through the pounding blood in her ears, Emily heard Maggie's voice.

"Emily, this is Andrew Rutledge, our closest neighbor. Drew, this is Sam's sister, Emily Parker."

Neighbor? Emily's first thought was that she was going to kill her brother. Why hadn't he told her? She held her breath, wondering if the man would say something to reveal that they'd already met, praying that he wouldn't. It would be most embarrassing. Feeling as if she would choke, Emily struggled to produce a smile.

"A pleasure, Mr. Rutledge, I'm sure," she said in a strangled voice.

"The pleasure is all mine, Miss Parker."

His voice was deep and resonant, and she recalled the feel of it vibrating in his chest, under her hands. This has to stop, she told herself. She waited for him to speak again, but, to her relief, he said nothing. Apparently, he wasn't going to say anything about their previous meeting, though, glancing up at him, Emily saw a threatening gleam in his blue eyes. He caught her gaze and held it for a long moment, saying without words that he'd do as he pleased and that for now it pleased him to indulge her sense of propriety. He exuded power and confidence, and his civilized clothes did little to mask his untamed spirit. His expression was inscrutable, but Emily thought she detected a flicker of amusement before he smiled politely. She tore her eyes away and sought Maggie's.

"Did you say neighbor, Maggie?" she asked with a note of alarm.

Maggie's sharp eyes had missed little of the tension between her friend and her sister-in-law.

"Yes, Drew owns the land that borders ours on the west, in the hills. Although he doesn't spend much time there," she offered pleasantly.

"Actually, I'll be spending more time in the area soon," Drew informed Maggie, turning his glance toward her. "I've spent the last few months traveling, and it will be a welcome change to stay in one place for a while. I've finally moved my things permanently to the cabin."

Emily heard his words with trepidation. What would she do if he were a regular visitor at the ranch? Why was she even worried about it? Her mind whirled with confused thoughts.

Maggie laughed. "If I know you, that means you'll stay put for all of two weeks, then take off again."

Andrew Rutledge smiled in agreement. "You're probably right. But you never know," he added, looking meaningfully at Emily.

Unwittingly, Emily took a small step backward, her eyes widening under Drew's intimate regard.

At that moment, Sam and Zach approached bearing cups of punch for the ladies. Emily accepted hers gratefully from Zach, who noted Drew Rutledge's presence evenly.

"Howdy, Rutledge," Zach greeted him. "Enjoying yourself?"

Zach's tone was friendly, but he didn't look happy to see the man. His eyes darted quickly between Drew and Emily, and he took a step closer to Emily.

Sam greeted Drew warmly, shaking his hand. The band returned to play the rousing numbers they had promised while everyone listened attentively, and when they finished, the dancing commenced afresh. Emily turned immediately to Zach, seeking to avoid dancing with the disturbing newcomer. Zach was only too glad to sweep her onto the dance floor.

Emily found relief in Zach's polite embrace. Drew Rutledge hadn't even touched her, yet she felt violated by his intense gaze. Worse, she couldn't forget the memory of his warm hands on her back, in her hair, around her waist. She blushed at the unsettling direction her thoughts were taking. She didn't think she could stand to be close to him in a public place where onlookers must surely see that she was mesmerized with his tawny good looks. And she shouldn't feel this way. It was positively indecent and unladylike.

She heard her name through a fog.

"Emily?" Zach was saying. "Are you feeling all right? You're a little flushed. Would you like to sit this one out?" Zach hoped it was only the exertion of the dancing that was affecting her.

Emily cursed the fair complexion that betrayed her every feeling, shook her head, and smiled up at Zach.

"I'm sorry. I'm not used to so much exercise," she lied. "I'm feeling much better now though, so please, let's continue."

Zach smiled at her in return, and they finished the dance.

Emily danced once with Eddie and Kenny, once with Lieutenant Smith, and once more with Zach, and then with Sam. She didn't allow herself to search the dance floor for a tall figure in black, forcing herself to attend fully to each of her partners in turn. Finally, at the end of a reel with Sam, she decided she needed a break and slipped away from the torch-lit circle of dancers, wandering out into the velvet darkness, the music following her. Soon her eyes adjusted to the moonlit night, and she could see the ground in front of her well enough to walk easily.

Emily breathed deeply of the clean air away from the smoky dance circle. It was a warm evening, but there was the light breeze she had hoped for. It fanned her face and neck pleasantly as she looked up at the multitude of bright stars. Ahead of her, she could see the outline of Bear Butte, dark against the starry sky. She remembered Sam saying it was a sacred mountain as she contemplated it silently for several minutes.

"What are your secrets, mountain?" she asked out loud, her voice barely a whisper.

"Do you really want to know?" a man's voice asked, equally soft.

Emily started and turned toward the sound.

"I didn't mean to frighten you," Drew said. "I did think you might have learned not to wander off by yourself in strange places, though."

He moved a step closer, soundlessly.

"Thank you for your concern," she replied icily. "I should be returning to the dance, if you'll excuse me."

She tried to move past him. Broad shoulders blocked her escape.

"Are you really interested in the Butte?" he asked again, as if she hadn't spoken.

Curiosity got the better of her.

"Yes, I am," she said warily. "Sam told me earlier that it was sacred."

She turned back to look at the dark mountain.

Drew stood close behind her, and Emily was acutely aware of him. She should leave, she knew, but she was drawn by both the man and the story he had to tell. His low voice was soothing, impersonal, as he told her about Bear Butte.

"The Sioux call it Mato Paha. *Mato* means bear and *paha* means mountain or hill, as in Paha Sapa, the Black

Hills. But the mountain is most sacred to the Cheyenne. It's where their prophet, Sweet Medicine, received the sacred arrows. They call the butte *Noaha-vose*, and there's a cave on the mountain where Sweet Medicine lived for many years. He was a wise prophet. In fact, he foretold the coming of the *wasicus*, the white men, and that they would foul the land. The Lakota and the Cheyenne both come to the Butte to seek visions and to pray, for it is indeed a sacred mountain where the spirits speak to us."

Emily looked at its outline against the night sky. White men would foul the land, he said. She thought of the creeks that now ran gray with mining wastes, the piles of slag that rose in what were once pristine forest glades. A feeling of melancholy descended on her, and she stood silently.

After a few minutes, she asked him a question. "Were you here before the settlers and miners came?"

"Yes. I first came when I was ten years old, with my father. That was before the war." He answered easily, without the reserve she had expected.

Tentatively, Emily began to question him. "Why did you come?" she asked quietly.

Drew sighed a little.

"My mother had just died, and my father was heartbroken. He lost interest in his business and life in general. We left our home in Boston and gradually worked our way west, wandering without any real purpose or destination. We ended up with a band of Oglalas who took us in, and we stayed."

"Oh. I'm sorry about your mother. My father died when I was ten. In the war." Emily was silent for a minute. "What was it like here then?"

"It was different than it is now. The buffalo and other game traveled freely across the plains. The people followed them in the summer, and camped in the valleys in the winter. There were no cattle, no fences, no mining. It was cleaner, safer, and happier for the Indians. There was usually enough food. The winters were still hell, though, and the weather's always been as changeable as a rich lady's mind. It wasn't completely different."

Emily could hear the smile in his words.

"Ah, yes," she chuckled. "The ubiquitous weather. Perhaps you can tell me why everyone talks incessantly of it?"

"Look at the sky, Emily."

She liked the way he said her name, making it sound like a caress. She immediately cursed herself for thinking so, then looked up.

The sky formed a glittering dome overhead, from the hilly western horizon to the gently rolling prairies in the east. It was so big and so close that she felt lost in it.

"Have you noticed it during the day? The way you can see clouds for miles? It's the most present element here, especially out on the plains. The land is more static, but the sky is always changing. And the sky brings the weather," he finished. The breeze carried the fresh scent of her hair to him.

"I hadn't thought of it that way," Emily admitted, but her mind was only half on their conversation. Her senses quivered with awareness of the man behind her. Every shift, every movement registered deep in her being. He stepped to her side.

Emily remembered that she had never properly thanked him for his help her first afternoon in Deadwood. She wasn't sure how to begin.

"Mr. Rutledge, I want to, uh, thank you for your . . . help." She practically choked on the word. "You know, last week," she finished lamely.

Honestly, she thought, that was the most ungracious thank you she'd ever uttered.

"Well, I suppose I'd best return to the dance," she mumbled, moving away from Drew.

A firm hand reached out to take her arm. Emily looked up at him, her eyes wide, her lips parted in exclamation.

It was all Drew could do not to take her in his arms and kiss her.

"Do you really want to thank me? Properly?" he asked softly.

Panic beat through Emily's veins. She didn't understand

why her legs suddenly felt like jelly or why she couldn't summon her voice to answer him.

"I . . ." Words failed her.

"Dance with me here," he said abruptly, persuasively.

She hesitated.

"Come on. We can hear the music."

He was right. A soothing melody drifted over from the distant bandstand. His warm hand slid to take her fingers in his as he bowed before her.

"Miss Parker?" he asked quietly. "May I have this dance?"

It would be churlish to refuse, though she knew it was folly to accept. The man was altogether disreputable despite his gentlemanly appearance. He lived in a brothel and his manner was far too intimate, arousing exceedingly unconventional responses in her. He wasn't at all proper, she thought with alarm, but she did owe him thanks for his help last week. The warm strength of his fingers on hers presented an invitation one part of her hesitated to decline.

"All right, Mr. Rutledge," she answered after a long moment.

Emily was swept instantly into his arms, drawn up close against him. She could faintly smell soap on his skin, and she felt the strength of his thighs through her skirts. His embrace was far too intimate, she knew, and had she been on the dance floor, surrounded by dozens of onlookers, she would have been mortified. Yet, here, alone in the night with this man, she succumbed to the temptation. What harm would it really do? It was only one dance.

She began to enjoy the pleasant music and their swirling movements through the darkness. They moved well together, each attuned to the other and to the rhythm of the music. Emily found that she liked the strength she felt below her hand where it rested on Drew's shoulder. His hand lingered at her waist, and he breathed deeply to inhale her perfume, his heart pounding when she smiled up at him, her dark eyes aglow in the moonlight. Without realizing it, they stopped moving, clinging to each other, staring into each other's eyes.

Emily felt a tightening in her lower body as she gazed into the face of the tall, unfathomable man who held her. Guiltily, she acknowledged that she didn't want him to release her. She watched his eyes drop to her mouth, and she knew that he was going to kiss her. Her mind told her to flee, but her body betrayed her, and she sighed with pleasure when his lips finally brushed hers. A small sound of contentment escaped her throat as she pressed herself more closely against his hard chest, twining her arms around his neck.

Her lips moved against his, inviting the tip of his tongue to probe the soft contours of her mouth. She parted her lips, accepting the bold advances of his tongue. Tentatively, she touched her tongue to his, wondering at the taste of him and the beguiling sweetness of his kiss. As she responded to him, a fire sprang to life within her. Drew's arms tightened possessively around her, and she felt the same fiery need in him. She buried her fingers in his thick hair and leaned shamelessly into him, caressing his hard body with her soft curves.

Suddenly, his hands gripped her wrists and he set her firmly away from him. She felt a sense of keen disappointment, then shame flooded through her. She looked at him accusingly, ready to turn and run, when she heard light footsteps approaching. Her hands flew to her throat, and she turned away from Drew.

"Emily?" Zach's voice sounded concerned. "Emily? Is that you?"

"Yes, Zach. I'm over here."

Oh, Lord, how much had he seen? Zach came to her side, his eyes searching hers in the dim light. She met his gaze steadily and smiled. He relaxed a bit.

"Rutledge." He nodded belatedly to Drew.

"Mr. Rutledge was just telling me some of the Indian legends about Bear Butte," Emily said conversationally, amazed at how casual she sounded. "It was most interesting. Thank you very much, Mr. Rutledge. Good evening," she called over her shoulder as Zach steered her back toward the dance.

"My pleasure, Miss Parker," Drew said lazily. "See you again sometime."

His voice was low and vibrant. Emily wasn't sure if his words were spoken as a promise or a threat, but her heart leapt at them. Damn! she swore at herself. What is happening to me?

Throughout the rest of the evening, Emily danced with soldiers and ranchers until she thought she would drop from exhaustion. She didn't see Drew again, and she told herself that she wasn't looking for him. When the band finally stopped playing, a young cavalryman from Kentucky produced a fiddle, and the dancing continued past midnight. When it was time to gather the children and head back to the ranch, Emily was thankful. She could hardly wait to get back to her room and collapse into sleep.

Later, riding home in the wagon, her sleepy mind wandering, Emily's thoughts turned to Indians and to wondering what their lives had been like before the white people had come. Looking at Sam driving the team, Maggie leaning against him with Daniel asleep in her arms, listening to their quiet voices, the plodding horses, and the creak of leather harnesses and wooden wagon wheels, she had trouble understanding that they and people like them were a threat to anyone's way of life.

Then her mind filled with the image of a tall, tawny-haired man, his blue eyes catching and reflecting the silver moonlight. Instantly, Emily was wide awake, her pulse singing in her ears. This time she didn't push him from her thoughts. For a few moments, she savored the memory of his arms around her and his breath against her temple, and the dangerous excitement that he stirred in her. It wasn't right, she knew. The things he made her feel were frightening. She hadn't known herself capable of such wantonness, and she was ashamed. Emily had been raised a proper young lady, and proper young ladies didn't behave the way she'd behaved with Drew Rutledge that night, especially when they were trying to avoid involvements with men. She acknowledged that she'd utterly abandoned herself to the sensations he'd aroused, and she couldn't think how she might have done so. She must have lost her mind! Who knew what would have happened had Zach not appeared when he did?

It occurred to her that if she'd felt half as excited when George had kissed her as she had when Drew had kissed her tonight, she'd have married George without a backward glance. But then she'd known George for years and knew exactly what sort of life they'd have had together. A beautiful home, three children, a cat, and standing in the community. This attraction to Drew Rutledge was something else entirely. All she really knew about him was that he was completely beyond her experience. She couldn't imagine *any* sort of future with him, yet she was still fascinated. And to her thinking, a physical attraction without love and the stability of a commitment smacked of immorality.

She didn't like to think of herself as immoral, but she had to face it. Perhaps the wild, beautiful landscape about her had awakened a deep, hitherto unknown facet of her character. Well, she thought with grim determination, if that was the case, then she'd simply have to be on guard against it and not allow herself any more opportunities to indulge her baser instincts. If Drew Rutledge brought out that undesirable part of her, then she'd have to avoid him. Forming a liaison, however brief, with such an unpredictable man was out of the question.

After returning home, caring for the horses, and settling the children in bed, Sam and Maggie lay awake in the dark. The soothing sound of crickets floated in through the open window, and a light breeze lifted the sheer summer curtains. They lay atop the sheets, the quilt and blankets draped over the cherrywood footboard. Sam had built the furniture in the room as a gift for Maggie when Daniel was born, making the bed extra long to accommodate his long legs. There was a trundle beneath it where the children slept when they were sick or during the bitter cold spells in winter when the upstairs was closed off and the family spent their time in the warm kitchen and slept in the downstairs bedroom, with its big fireplace with a carved cherry mantel that matched the other furnishings. Now, in the summer, the fireplace was cold and the door into the kitchen remained open to catch the cross breeze.

Maggie nestled close to her husband, resting her head in the hollow of his shoulder.

"Sam," she said softly. "Are you still awake?"

"Just barely," he answered, drawing his arm around her.

"Do you think Emily had a good time?" There was doubt in her voice.

"Yes, I think she did." He chuckled. "I can't remember when anyone created quite as much of a stir as she did tonight."

"Yes, but she was so quiet on the way home. She didn't say two words."

"She was probably tired from so much dancing and meeting so many new people."

"Maybe. Though I noticed a change in her after she got into that argument with those ranchers and that unpleasant Lieutenant Logan. He's that bandy little officer with the pale eyes."

"Mmm-hmm, I remember him," Sam told her sleepily. "What did they argue about?"

"Drew had just appeared, and the men saw him and started complaining about what an Indian lover he is." Maggie sighed. "The usual."

Sam smiled in the darkness. "I can imagine Emily's response."

"Yes, she was quite irritated. But that wasn't what struck me most, Sam. I only heard the end of the argument because I had gone to get Drew to meet Emily."

"You mean she didn't recognize him?"

"What do you mean?" Maggie asked quickly.

"Nothing, nothing. Go on. Tell me what was so strange?"

"Well, she acted so uncomfortable with him when I introduced them, nervous and almost embarrassed. I was so surprised. At the same time, there was a certain tension between them. For about half a minute, I could swear they weren't aware there was anyone else around. Then later when I was dancing with Drew, all he could talk about was Emily. He asked question after question, just like a little boy. Honestly, I've never seen him like this. But then he never danced with Emily or said another word to her. It was odd." Sam recognized a familiar excitement in Maggie's voice. "Wait, you said *recognized*. Had they already met? But where? Sam, what aren't you telling me?" She pushed herself up into a sitting position.

Sam groaned. "This couldn't wait 'til tomorrow?"

"No!" she exclaimed. "I'll never sleep if you don't tell me."

"All right," Sam said with exaggerated resignation.

He related the story Emily had told him about her first meeting with Drew Rutledge. Maggie listened attentively, interrupting occasionally to ask questions. When he finished, she was silent for a moment. Had there been enough light, Sam would have seen a small smile play upon his wife's lips. A thought occurred to Sam.

They spoke in unison.

"You don't think—?" Sam began.

"Do you suppose that—?" Maggie giggled. Sam was laughing as well.

"Emily wouldn't appreciate our meddling in her affairs," Maggie continued lightly.

"Nor would Drew," her husband observed. "But . . ." He left the thought hanging.

"Sam, we shouldn't try to play matchmaker." She spoke with little conviction.

"I think the interest is already there, so it wouldn't exactly be matchmaking. It would be more like providing opportunities for love to blossom and grow." He chuckled.

"I don't know, Sam," Maggie said merrily. "I don't think Emily has any idea what she feels for Drew," she added more seriously. "He's so terribly unconventional, and you know Emily has a lot of spirit, but she's rather a prude at heart. It may take a long time before she's comfortable with him at all, much less as a prospective suitor."

"Yes, but we can't forget about Stevens, Maggie. He's

clearly interested in Emily, and he can be awfully persistent. Drew needs to get on the stick.''

"Mmm." She considered. "I don't think Zach is Emily's type. She didn't like some of the things he said the other day.''

"I think we should see if we can't get Drew over here more often," Sam said with finality. "You try to find out how Emily feels about him, but don't make her suspicious or scare her off. I'll work on Rutledge. You know, I can't think of a man I'd rather see marry my sister," he added with satisfaction. "Now that that's decided, let's get some sleep."

Smiling conspiratorially to themselves, Sam and Maggie closed their eyes and were sound asleep within minutes.

Emily awoke late the next morning, the tantalizing smell of freshly brewed coffee beckoning her downstairs to the kitchen. She stretched luxuriously, then threw back the white linen sheet and rose. Padding across the soft green rug to her dresser, Emily thought how pretty the room was. Sam had made the bedstead of light oak to match a low dresser and a high chest of drawers. A large oval mirror topped the dresser, reflecting the pink and white flowers on the porcelain washbasin and pitcher that sat on it. Delicate lace runners topped both dressers, and a soft white quilt embroidered with pink flowers and green leaves covered the double bed. A dressing table and chair stood to the left of the bed beside one of Sam's newfangled built-in closets, and tall windows let in the late morning sun on the south and east walls of the room through sheer, white-lace curtains. Mingling with the smells of breakfast cooking below was the sweet perfume from a bouquet of pink and red garden roses that Emily had placed on her dressing table the day before.

Emily washed quickly, pinned her hair in a loose knot, and dressed in a simple blue and white checked gingham dress. She glanced at her reflection one last time in the mirror. Satisfied, she left her room and walked quickly down the hall past the children's rooms to the stairs, then down into the front hall.

Passing the parlor on her left, Emily had to cross the empty dining room to get to the big farm kitchen where the Parkers took their breakfast. Her hand was poised to push open the swinging door between the rooms when Sam's voice stopped her.

"Apparently the colonel is pretty worried about a shipment of rifles and ammunition that was stolen last week. He seems to think there may be more involved than a simple theft. They brought back one of the teamsters, the only one that wasn't dead when they found them, and before he died he said something about Indians accompanied by at least one white man. He was raving about how they said they were going to smuggle the guns up to Gall and Sitting Bull's people up in Canada, and then take back the Hills."

Emily felt a cold shiver descend her spine. How many white men in the area were closely associated with the Indians? She knew of only one: Drew Rutledge. She heard Maggie speaking now.

"Oh, dear, do they think Drew was involved?" she asked with concern.

Sam answered. "There's no proof. The teamster was delirious with fever by the time they got him into the fort. There's no telling what really happened, but you know how easy it is to arouse suspicions when Indians are involved. Reynolds is trying to keep this under wraps until after next week when Red Cloud and some of his warriors are due to testify at that trial in Deadwood. Only a couple of the officers and the doctor know so far. Reynolds didn't mean to tell me, but he was asking me about Rutledge's movements, and he knows I'm about the only man around that Drew talks to. Anyway, I figured a few things out, then he told me the rest. I agree that letting the news out could be dangerous. It could get ugly if folks thought Indians were involved in the shipment theft, and since there isn't any clear evidence that they were, it's better not to say anything."

No proof, Emily thought. But Drew Rutledge was a

smooth talker, and he was smart and dangerous. She wondered if he really was involved. For some reason, though, he had her brother's respect and trust, and Sam was not usually fooled by people.

"Does Drew know about this?" Maggie asked.

"Well, you know him, he wouldn't say if he did, but I reckon he does. That's probably why he was at the dance last night."

"I don't believe for one minute that Drew was involved, Sam. Do you?" Her voice was firm.

"No, Mags, I don't. I'd sure like to know what's going on, though, and I hope Rutledge hasn't gotten in over his head this time. That man runs a mighty fine line with the law as it is, and I don't know that sometimes he might not cross it." Emily could almost see her brother shaking his head as he spoke.

What did Sam mean about Drew running a fine line with the law? She recalled Lieutenant Logan's accusation that Rutledge smuggled stolen supplies to the reservations, but she wondered how serious a crime that could be when the U.S. Government had been supplying the Indians for decades, even during the years of their armed conflicts with the cavalry. Was Drew involved in illegal activities? Questions whirled rapidly in Emily's mind, but Maggie's voice curtailed them.

"Breakfast is ready now, Sam. Why don't you see if Emily's awake yet, and I'll call the children."

Not wishing to be caught eavesdropping, Emily ran back across the dining room into the hall. Just as Sam started through the door from the kitchen, she swung back through the hallway door. For just a moment, Emily saw a look of grave concern on her brother's face. As soon as he saw her, he burst into a wide grin, and the concern was gone.

"Well, if it's not the belle of the ball! I was just coming to see if you'd danced your feet off last night and might need carrying downstairs," he teased.

"My feet are none the worse for wear, thank you," she responded lightly, forcing a smile in return. "It smells as if I'm too late to help Maggie with breakfast. Can a lazy woman get a cup of coffee around here?''

"You bet you can," Sam answered, holding open the kitchen door for her.

Emily walked past him, musing on the irony that had brought Drew Rutledge to her thoughts so soon after she'd decided to banish him from her mind for good.

Chapter 6

The next week was one of constant activity, so Emily had little time for her own thoughts in the flurry of picking berries, harvesting vegetables, and putting up jams, jellies, and canned vegetables for the coming winter. She picked blackberries and chokecherries from bushes along the creek, the first few wild plums from bushes in the Hills, and the last of the strawberries from Maggie's garden. The garden also produced green beans, cucumbers to make into pickles, summer squash, tomatoes, beets, carrots, and many herbs that Emily helped tie in bundles to dry in the pantry. Sometimes Emily entertained Daniel while Maggie canned the seemingly unending array of produce brought in by Josh and Sarah. Sometimes she worked in the hot, steamy kitchen while Maggie took a break. Mary came several days to help as well, and every day the shelves in the cellar and pantry held more filled and neatly labeled glass jars than they had the day before.

Although she worked hard, Emily felt a sense of accomplishment watching the shelves fill, and she threw herself willingly into the work that left her little time alone and even less to dwell on the man she didn't want to think about. Nevertheless, she found her thoughts straying to things Drew Rutledge had said about the Indians and the land, and to the silver lights that flashed in his deep blue eyes. She wished that he was not quite as wild a character as he seemed. He was terribly attractive and exciting in a dangerous fashion, but he clearly wasn't dependable husband material, and at her age, that was a consideration. It would be better to forget the man existed.

Maggie had tried to question Emily about him once, but Emily's vague replies let Maggie know that, for whatever reason, she didn't wish to speak about him. Maggie was puzzled, but she didn't press Emily. Clearly, Emily wasn't going to confide. She felt sure that if Emily spent more time with Drew, she would be more open about her feelings. After all, he was a bit overpowering and intimidating on occasion. Some time alone was probably all they needed.

Before Sam and Maggie had a chance to invite Drew to the ranch, he showed up on his own. From the garden, Maggie saw him approach on a buckskin Indian pony. He waved to her, asked if Sam was around, then continued on to the carpentry shop where Sam was supervising the loading of some hand-carved mahogany panels for a new hotel in Deadwood. Maggie hurried into the kitchen, where she found Emily chasing a squealing Daniel, a handful of butter cupped in his small hands.

"Emily, I just remembered that I forgot to—" she began, then caught sight of the toddler. "Oh, honestly, Daniel, you make the biggest messes!" she interrupted herself, intercepting the child as he headed for the door. Holding him with his back against her, greasy arms stuck out straight in front of him, Maggie made for the sink. She removed the yellow mass from Daniel's hands and proceeded to soap his arms.

"That was a timely entrance, Maggie. He was almost out the door," Emily said, marveling again at Maggie's calm in dealing with her younger son.

"I'm hoping this wild stage runs its course quickly, but I'm afraid with Daniel it may be permanent," Maggie responded, pumping water over his chubby, outstretched arms. "Emily, I was going to send a jar of plum jelly in to Mrs. Sherman with Sam. That's Kenny's aunt, and he said she's been ill. Would you mind running it down to Sam before he leaves? Kenny or Eddie can deliver it."

"No, of course not," Emily replied, going to the pantry for the jelly.

"Thanks a lot," Maggie called as Emily stepped out the door. "Take your time."

She smiled merrily at her baby as she dried his clean arms on a length of toweling. "Both of us are up to mischief this morning, aren't we, Daniel?" she asked him laughingly.

Emily walked quickly past the barn down to the workshop, where she found the wagon loaded and ready to go, but Sam nowhere in sight. She heard a horse nicker from the direction of the creek and followed the sound, taking a narrow track through the bushes and trees that lined the creek. She gathered her brightly colored cotton skirt in her left hand, along with the jelly jar, to keep it from catching on low branches and picking up foxtails. As she rounded a turn, the bank rising on her left, the creek came into view. Beside it stood an unfamiliar buckskin horse, drinking from the clear water. Next to the animal, one hand resting casually across its back, stood Drew Rutledge.

It was the first time she had seen him since the dance, the first time since realizing that he was capable of flouting more than convention and that he might well be involved in illegal doings. For a brief moment, she drank in the virile picture he made, his buckskin Indian clothing nearly the same color as his horse, the sun picking out the shining highlights in his light brown hair and his eyes. Oh, what eyes, he has! she thought. Even from twenty feet away, she could see their deep color clearly. Then she remembered her purpose. Sam must have gone for a walk away from the shop to talk to Drew. Where was he now? Warily, Emily took a step forward.

Standing very straight, she cleared her throat.

Except for her skirts balled up in her left fist, she looked exactly as Drew imagined she might when interviewing the parents of a particularly difficult pupil. Polite, formal, commanding, yet distinctly uneasy, all at the same time. He was used to a wide variety of reactions from women of his own race, but none intrigued him as Emily's did. His gaze swept her approvingly, lingering for a second on her left calf, exposed where her skirt and petticoat were lifted clear. A lazy smile spread across his sensuous mouth.

Emily stared back at him challengingly. When his eyes touched her legs, she remembered that her skirts were hiked up, and calmly dropped them back into place. Only the mounting flush on her high cheekbones belied her embarrassment. She cleared her throat again.

"I'm looking for my brother," she announced.

"Go right ahead," he replied. "Don't mind me."

He continued to smile at her, making her feel that he was laughing at her. The man had insufferable manners.

"I thought you might have seen him," she suggested, her voice firm, but cool.

"I might have," Drew agreed evenly.

He paused. He saw Emily clench her fists, but her expression changed not a whit. He didn't know why he felt tempted to tease her so, but he couldn't help himself.

"But," he added, his conscience prodding him to more amenable behavior. "I don't know where he is now. You might try the shop."

"I've just come from there," Emily snapped.

She walked toward him, stopping a few feet away, her hands planted on her hips. The horse stood between them, its head still lowered to the stream.

"What are you doing here, anyway?" she demanded.

The smile left Drew's face, and he began to feel annoyed with her unexpectedly suspicious tone of voice. It was a tone with which he was all too familiar.

"What do you think I'm doing here?" he asked her, his eyes narrowing.

Under his scrutiny, Emily quailed for a long moment, though she returned his gaze directly.

"I'm sure I have no idea, Mr. Rutledge. I did ask, didn't I?" she said with mock sweetness. "However, since I rarely seem to get straight answers out of you, I'm no longer surprised by your evasiveness. Why, one would think you had something to hide, the way you so often answer questions with questions of your own." Her words were soft, but her regard remained challenging.

Drew was surprised and irritated by the change in Emily. He'd known she would hear sordid tales about him, but he had relied on Sam and Maggie's friendship and on the powerful physical attraction between him and her to balance her fear and distrust of him. Clearly, he'd been wrong. He'd been foolish in thinking that she might be the woman from his vision. Disappointment, then anger, surged through him.

"I don't answer to you." He spoke softly, with deceptive calm.

Emily searched his face for any hint of his thoughts, finding none. He remained impassive, yet she was aware of a violent tension in him. Did he suspect she knew the truth about him? She couldn't tell, but suddenly she was no longer angry. She glanced around her. A cloud drifted across the sun, casting them into shadow; nothing stirred. Her green-brown eyes lifted to his. He saw disappointment where only moments ago he had seen promise. Emily saw no emotion, but she felt his fury, far greater than what she had seen the first day she met him.

"Do you answer to anyone?" she whispered.

Then she turned and fled back through the trees.

Drew stared after her for a long minute, the angry light in his eyes fading to sadness. He shook his head. Some things never changed, it seemed.

Emily returned to the house, trying to put her meeting with Drew out of her mind. The man disturbed her profoundly for despite the knowledge that he promised nothing but trouble, she still found herself drawn to him. It wasn't just that he was an attractive man, either, she knew. There was definitely more to her feelings for Drew Rutledge than that. A deep part of her longed to know him better, to know his thoughts and his spirit, but she told herself it was impossible. It was better to forget the man existed.

Maggie looked at Emily questioningly, eyes bright, when she returned to the kitchen. Emily had been gone half an hour, so Maggie assumed she had spoken to Drew. She was dying to know how it had gone, but one look at the grim set of Emily's mouth told her it hadn't gone well.

She decided to wait. Perhaps Emily would talk about it in her own time.

Emily didn't say a word about Drew all day, but he was often in her mind as she weeded vegetables with Sarah, mixed biscuits for dinner with Maggie and Mary, dressed chickens for supper, and read from *Tom Sawyer* to Josh and Sarah. Late in the afternoon, when the sun was slowly dropping behind the hills in the west, Zach Stevens rode up on his beautiful sorrel stallion. Emily was in the garden cutting a few blooms for the supper table. He called her name, and she turned toward him with a smile.

"Zach, it's nice to see you," she said sincerely. "Where have you been keeping yourself lately?"

His warm brown eyes smiled at her in return. "I might ask you the same thing," he said. "I'm going to have to talk to your brother about keeping you cooped up out here on this ranch. If I know him, he's probably got you working so hard you don't have any time left for taking pity on the local swains who would die for but an hour of your company." His tone was gently teasing.

Emily laughed. "I'm not sure Sam would appreciate your perspective. Actually, I have been working rather hard, but I have been enjoying it tremendously. Back in Elmira, I was always busy with lessons and tutoring, and Mother has enough help that I didn't do much gardening or housework. I find it quite satisfying."

She finished cutting the marigolds and looked up at Zach. "Why don't you come in, and I'll get you something to drink?" she invited.

"Thanks, Emily, but I really can't stay. I just stopped to ask if you might like a little break tomorrow. I know you seemed kind of interested in the Indians the other evening, and Red Cloud and some of his tribe are coming into town tomorrow to testify at a trial. There's word that they're going to put on a dancing exhibition, and I was wondering if you might like to go with me to see it."

Zach was rewarded by Emily's obvious excitement.

"Oh, that would be wonderful! I haven't seen but one Indian since I've been here, and I really am interested.

Thank you for asking me, Zach.'' Her dark eyes glowed with anticipation.

Zach smiled beneath his neatly trimmed moustache. ''Good! I was planning to ride so we'd have more time in town. Is that all right with you?''

''Oh, yes, that's fine. I'm sure Sam has a horse I can use.''

''Then I'll see you tomorrow morning. I'll be by about nine.'' Zach turned toward the gate. ''Goodbye,'' he called back over his shoulder.

''Yes, I'll be looking forward to it,'' Emily called after him.

That evening when the Parker household was finishing supper at the big oak pedestal table in the dining room, Sam made an announcement.

''Okay, everybody quiet. Big news here,'' he said, his voice booming.

Everyone fell silent and looked at him. His expression was almost serious, except for the telltale twinkle in his eyes.

''Tomorrow,'' he intoned formally, then paused. ''Tomorrow,'' he repeated, ''is going to be a holiday!''

Josh and Sarah squealed with delight, squirming in their chairs. Eddie and Kenny grinned broadly. Frank didn't look up from his blackberry pie, but a smile creased his weathered face.

''What holiday, Pa?'' Josh asked breathlessly. ''What holiday is in August?''

''This is a one-time-only holiday. Drew came by today to tell me that Red Cloud and some warriors are in Deadwood for a trial, and tomorrow they're going to demonstrate Indian dances. He asked if we'd like to go in with him and meet the Indians.''

The excitement on Josh's face was intense. He looked as if he might burst.

''I told him I wasn't sure . . .'' Sam paused meaningfully and looked at his older son, trying hard not to smile.

Josh fairly screamed, ''Oh, yes, Pa, we want to go! All of us do, don't we?''

Sarah was nodding vigorously. Kenny looked almost as excited as Josh, and Eddie was smiling. Maggie laughed, and Daniel strained in his high chair, waving his arms and chattering to himself. Frank even looked up with interest. Only Emily was restrained. She couldn't believe her brother would allow his children to be influenced by a man who might well be a criminal!

"Well, that's good," Sam said slowly. "Because that's what I told him."

There were cheers from the children.

"He'll be here to ride in with us pretty early in the morning, so you all had better get a good night's rest tonight," he cautioned his children.

As they rushed to clear their plates from the table, Emily thought her brother gave her a questioning look. Eddie and Kenny excused themselves as well.

"Aren't you interested, Emily?" he asked quietly, noticing her lack of enthusiasm.

"Yes, of course I am," she said forcing a smile to her lips. "It's just that when Zach stopped, he asked me if I'd like to go with him, and I accepted. I didn't realize it would be a family outing." Emily didn't see the impatient look that Maggie directed at her husband.

Sam hesitated a moment, watching his wife. Looking back at Emily, he spoke in a carefully neutral tone.

"If you'd rather go with Stevens, then by all means, do. If I'd have known what he was intending, I'd have said something sooner, as you'll learn a lot more and get a chance to meet Red Cloud in person if you go with Drew."

Emily had the impression Sam was trying to convince her to change her plans, but she knew it would never do for her to spend a whole day in Drew Rutledge's company, even with other people around.

"It's a shame you didn't say something earlier, but I think I should go with Zach. I would feel terrible if I had to disappoint him." Emily looked at the plate in front of her as she spoke.

"He'd get over it," Sam said brusquely, pushing himself away from the table. He didn't attempt to sway her further, but he wondered what had caused his sister to have such cold feelings toward his best friend.

"Sam," Emily spoke hesitantly. Her brother stopped and faced her. "Are you sure you should let the children go tomorrow?"

She'd meant to ask if it was safe to trust his children in Drew Rutledge's company, but the fierce expression in Sam's eyes warned her that he wouldn't appreciate her concern where his friend was involved.

For his part, Sam couldn't understand Emily's attitude toward Drew at all. The man had saved her from being raped by a gang of hooligans, for God's sake!

"Emily, I already told you once that Rutledge is probably the most trustworthy man I know. Nothing is going to happen, and the children will be perfectly safe. Joshua practically idolizes that man and lives for the time they spend together. He'll remember tomorrow for the rest of his life."

Emily felt chastened, but she couldn't help worrying.

"I'm sorry, Sam," she apologized. "I'm sure it'll be a special day for everyone," she said, trying to sound cheerful.

"I don't understand why you dislike Drew so much, Emmy, but if you ever want to talk about it, either Maggie or I'd be glad to listen."

"Thanks, Sam. I'll remember that," she replied softly. But she knew she couldn't talk to them about it.

The next morning, the Parkers left early in the wagon, accompanied by Drew on his buckskin. Emily stayed inside the house when he arrived, arranging her toilette so that she wasn't yet dressed and didn't have to meet him. She put on an especially pretty yellow and white sprigged cotton dress and a new straw hat trimmed with daisies to protect her fair skin from the summer sun. Then she sat down on the porch with a book to wait, enjoying the rare solitude. A couple of hours later, Zach rode up and helped her saddle the sweet-tempered bay mare that Sam had offered for her use. When the horse was ready to go, Zach looked at Emily appraisingly.

"You look real nice in that dress, Emily," Zach complimented her. "You'll be the prettiest girl in town, that's for sure. I'll have to pay close attention or some other gentleman may steal you away from me."

Emily smiled, but inwardly felt a twinge of annoyance at the proprietary tone in his voice. She thought of Zach as a friend and didn't welcome the intensity of his gaze as he spoke to her. She felt a momentary regret that she had accepted his invitation.

"Really, Zach," she reproved lightly. "I'm sure you say that sort of thing to all the girls. No wonder you're so popular." Before he could respond, she tightened the cinch a final notch and offered her hand to Zach. "Shall we go? I don't want to miss anything," she said with a bright smile. Zach helped her into the sidesaddle and led her horse out into the yard where his sorrel stood waiting. He mounted smoothly, and they trotted off.

The morning air was still cool when they set off for Deadwood, meadowlarks singing in the pastures, the smell of earth and grass rising where the horses' hooves bruised the ground. It promised to be a lovely day. Looking over at Zach, dashingly handsome in dark broadcloth trousers and a crisp, white linen shirt, his well-fitting jacket emphasizing his broad shoulders, his black hair glinting in the sunlight, Emily wondered why she didn't feel the curious flutter in her stomach that she did when she was with Drew Rutledge. Why couldn't she have been attracted to this kind, polite, upstanding man who so obviously liked and respected her? Perhaps if she got to know Zach better, she'd learn to care more deeply for him. She might even be able to convince him that Indians were not the terror he thought them to be. Yet something would still be missing, namely the excitement she felt when she was with Drew. Emily was realizing that she wanted both stability and a certain amount of passion, and she wondered if she'd ever find both with one man.

The ride into Deadwood took two hours or so. Other wagons and riders were on the road, all heading in to see the Indians dancing. There was a holiday atmosphere, and Emily's excitement grew as they approached the little town. When they arrived, Zach left their horses at a livery stable, and the two of them walked out onto upper Main Street. They strolled through town for an hour, stopping often to talk with friends and acquaintances, Zach performing introductions when necessary. At noon, they went to the Merchant's Hotel for dinner. The popular restaurant was crowded, but when the maitre d' saw Zach, he ushered them to an intimate corner table immediately.

During the meal, Zach proudly described the many sophisticated and elegant entertainments that were available in Deadwood. He promised to take her to the opera house and Jack Langrishe's theater, where traveling performers regularly showcased their talents. Emily listened attentively, but she was more interested in viewing that afternoon's more exotic performance. She was glad when the meal ended and it was time to go outside and find a vantage point from which to view the dancing.

The street filled rapidly with interested townspeople, miners, and ranchers who had come from outlying areas with their families. Eyes wide with excitement, small children darted to and fro among the crowd. The adults were nearly as eager to see the Indians as the children were. It was rare for the white settlers in the Hills to see the local Sioux tribes up close, and rarer still to witness their traditional dances and ceremonies, despite the Indians' close proximity. Indians met alone on an isolated homestead or trail were regarded with fear and distrust. They were the enemy. Met on the Main Street of Deadwood, however, surrounded by friends and neighbors, as well as numerous soldiers from Fort Meade, they provided an exciting diversion.

Emily and Zach managed to wedge themselves into a narrow space right in front of the circle where the dances were scheduled to take place. Emily saw Josh race into the mass of people opposite them, chased by several boys his own age. She looked around for Sam and Maggie, catching sight of them across the street and to her left. The colonel and Caroline Reynolds were with them. Sam saw her and waved. She waved back cheerily, but she couldn't help noticing that Drew Rutledge was nowhere in sight.

People continued to press into the crowded streets when, suddenly, a hush fell over the excited throng. Jack Langrishe stepped out into the open street, followed by the Indian Emily had seen in Drew Rutledge's room at the Sheridan Hotel on her first day in Deadwood. He looked different today, savage and foreign, dressed only in a leather breechcloth and moccasins, his face and body brightly painted. Half of his face was red, the other half black, and long yellow streaks were painted on his chest in a vee and down each of his arms and legs. His long hair was braided, falling well below his shoulders, and around his neck he wore a necklace of wolf's teeth. Bright earrings dangled from his earlobes, and two painted feathers stuck up straight at the back of his head. On his feet were beaded moccasins, and sleigh bells sewn to leather strips were tied just below his knees. He carried a lance decorated with buffalo hair and more eagle feathers; the effect was startling. Many in the audience took an involuntary step backward, and Emily heard gasps in the crowd behind her.

Langrishe, Deadwood's premier impresario, instantly had everyone's attention. His voice boomed in the warm afternoon air, announcing that Red Cloud and members of his tribe would perform traditional Sioux ceremonial dances. He introduced the Indian at his side.

"Ladies and gentlemen, boys and girls, beside me here stands Šunkmanitu Sapa, otherwise known as Black Wolf, an Oglala warrior. He has learned the white man's tongue and has agreed to translate the mysteries of his tribal dances for the good citizens of the Black Hills. Before I turn the afternoon over to him and his fellow warriors, I must ask you to remember that we are privileged to behold these sacred Sioux ceremonies that few white men have ever seen and lived to tell about."

Emily thought she detected a flicker of annoyance cross Black Wolf's painted face.

"Please stay back and remain quiet, so that you can experience the full effects of these pagan rituals."

Langrishe paused. Seeing that the crowd was transfixed, all eyes expectantly on Black Wolf, he stepped back.

"Ladies and gentlemen, I give you Black Wolf and Red Cloud's Oglalas."

As Langrishe melted into the background, Black Wolf stepped forward. An unseen drum began a slow, rhythmic beat. Black Wolf began to speak, his softly accented voice carrying clearly.

"The Lakota dance to celebrate victory in war and in love. Today we will share with you our scalp dance and some of our war dances. These are performed by the warriors of our camp for the enjoyment of the people."

So saying, Black Wolf began a series of steps in a circular motion. The drumbeat grew louder, and rattles and bells began to shake, creating a melody of percussion. A file of fiercely decorated Sioux warriors joined him, their painted faces alarming in the bright afternoon sunlight. There were more gasps from the audience, and all eyes were riveted on the striking spectacle of Indian warriors in full regalia right on the Main Street of the largest town in the Black Hills. The drum was carried into the street and was quickly surrounded by a group of singers, beating on it as their voices lifted in high-pitched song. A haunting melody rose, and the dancing began. At intervals, the music quieted, and Black Wolf briefly explained the significance of the dances.

Emily was transported into a different world. The music, the movement, the brightly painted faces, the dust rising from the dancers' feet as they hit the ground belonged to a more ancient way of life. She was deeply moved by the simple beauty of the dances and the rhythmic cadence of the drums, bells, and rattles. She imagined how dramatic the scene would look at night, the red flames from campfires throwing the dancers moving limbs into sharp relief. As the dancing progressed, she became oblivious to the press of people around her and the handsome man at her side. Her keen eyes noted every detail in every moment, her ears attuned only to the music and the movement, and all sense of time fled. Emily was lost in the swirl of dust, the beat of the drum, the flash of glittering eyes in wild faces, and the rapid movements of painted flesh.

All too soon, the drum ceased. A taut silence hung in the air. Then the crowd erupted into thunderous applause. Emily squeezed her eyes shut, trying to recapture the elusive thread of connection she felt watching the dances, to what she did not know. If only it had continued a little longer, she might have grasped it! A wistful longing flooded through her as she realized that it was lost. The dancing was over.

With a soft sigh, she opened her eyes. The feeling of oneness and recognition, of knowing and being known, surged through her once again as she found herself staring across the street into the electric-blue depths of Drew Rutledge's searching eyes. Her own eyes widened in surprise. Then she quickly looked away.

Drew had been standing in the shadows leaning against the wall of the Big Horn Store. He was dressed inconspicuously in jeans and a gray cotton shirt. On his feet he wore simple, undecorated leather moccasins. He had planned to watch the proceedings from there, not feeling it necessary to have a front row spot for dances he knew as well as he knew the waltz. Then Josh Parker burst through the line of townspeople in front of him, grabbed him by the hand, and began pulling him through the row of disgruntled onlookers. Josh was hopping up and down, pointing excitedly as Jack Langrishe made his way into the street with Black Wolf. They listened to the introductory remarks and then, as Langrishe exited, Josh pulled on Drew's sleeve.

"Look, there's my Aunt Emily and Mr. Stevens, right across the street!" he exclaimed.

Before he could call or wave, however, the drum began, and Josh's attention was given solely to the approaching warriors.

Drew found himself staring at the beautiful blond woman across from him. He felt a surge of jealousy as he saw her standing next to Zach Stevens, obviously enjoying herself. Why he felt so irritated, he had no idea. The woman was not worth the effort; yesterday she had made it clear that she had judged him without knowing anything about him. Yet today she looked radiant, her expression rapt as she watched the dancing before her. She was swaying slightly with the pulsing rhythm, the light yellow material of her skirts outlining her hips as she moved. He was captivated, and he remembered the feel of her soft curves beneath his hands, her full lips against his own, and he cursed himself for allowing the woman to affect him so. It was becoming a hindrance. He had work to do, dangerous work, and he couldn't afford to be encumbered with these foolish schoolboy reactions to a beautiful woman. Especially one who was not interested in him.

But when the performance finally ended, he was still watching Emily. As the applause burst around them, Drew didn't see Zach's dark eyes narrow as he noticed Drew gazing intently at her. Emily's eyes were closed, a curious expression of both wonder and loss on her face, and she was unaware of either man. Zach reached to place his hand on Emily's elbow, and her eyes flew open. Drew found himself looking directly into her dark, green-brown eyes, eyes like green grass over dark earth, and he felt a momentary sensation of completion. He couldn't fight the feeling that somehow this woman belonged with him.

She looked away abruptly, and he told himself he was a fool.

"Can we meet the Indians, now?" Josh asked excitedly.

The boy was once again tugging at his fist, pulling him down the street after the departing warriors. Drew continued to stare across the street for a moment, reluctant to lose sight of Emily. Then he shook his head and clapped a hand on the boy's shoulder.

"That's where I'm headed. You coming?" he said, warmly smiling down at the boy.

"You bet!" Josh exclaimed. "Let's find my folks!"

Emily realized that Zach's hand was on her arm and that he was looking over her head at Drew Rutledge.

Glancing up at him, she was taken aback by the smoldering fury she saw there. In response to her movement, Zach turned his gaze to her, his expression immediately one of polite concern.

"What did you think?" he asked conversationally. "I found it rather pagan, but also intriguing. Those costumes are quite something, aren't they?"

"I thought it was wonderful," Emily replied, very quietly. She didn't wish to dissect the performance; it had been far too powerful an experience for her to talk about casually.

Zach didn't appear to notice her withdrawal.

"Shall we get something cold to drink before we start back?" he suggested. There was the slightest trace of impatience in his movement when Emily didn't respond immediately.

At that moment, she caught sight of her nephew, now standing beside her brother and Maggie. The Reynoldses had disappeared, but Drew Rutledge was guiding her family down the street in the direction the Indians had gone. Suddenly, an urgent desire to meet the dancers overcame her. She spun to face Zach.

"I know you were planning to go back soon, but before we leave, would you mind if we followed Sam and Maggie? I know they're going to meet Red Cloud and the others, and I would *so* like to meet them," she implored, her eyes shining.

"Are you sure?" he asked doubtfully. "I'm not certain you'll like what you'll see," he warned.

"I'm sure, Zach. Come on," she urged, smiling now. "If we don't hurry, we'll lose them," she said as she turned and started down the street after them. Zach followed reluctantly.

Emily and Zach trailed the Parkers down Main Street for a couple of blocks and then turned right around a corner. Ahead of them about half a block, the group of Indians were washing off the remains of their paint at a horse trough. Emily wondered why they didn't go into a hotel to their rooms to wash, then realized that it was doubtful that a hotel in town would accept them as guests. They were most likely camped someplace nearby. A few of the warriors lounged in the shade of the sidewalk awnings and between the woodframe buildings. Emily stopped when she saw Drew Rutledge leading her nephew up to a tall, stoic Indian with a mahogany face.

It was Chief Red Cloud.

Chapter 7

Emily could tell by his bearing that Red Cloud was a powerful man. She had read about him in the newspapers ever since she was a girl. He had waged a successful campaign to oust the army and the hordes of settlers traveling the Montana Road through the Powder River country in the late 1860s, culminating in the horrible Fetterman fight. Eighty-one soldiers had ridden into an ambush where they were attacked by thousands of Indians. No soldiers survived, and, at length, the army gave up and left the important hunting grounds that were so vital to the Sioux alone. For the past two years, Emily had read about the troubles on the recently established Pine Ridge reservation and earlier that summer, Red Cloud had visited Washington with several other chiefs, stopping at the new Indian boarding school at Carlisle, Pennsylvania. He had been present when Spotted Tail, chief of the Brulés at the Rosebud Agency, had defied the government and removed his children from the school, an incident that had caused quite a stir in the Eastern press. Emily found it hard to believe that she now stood less than fifty feet away from this famous Sioux leader.

He was tall and thin, and his face looked as though he did not smile easily. Deep lines creased his face, and he had a prominent nose. His long hair was pulled back into two braids that fell below his shoulders, revealing a high forehead. He wore a buckskin shirt and leggings, decorated with colorful beads and quill work. Intelligence snapped in his heavy-lidded, dark eyes. Emily hung back, watching and listening, as Drew introduced Joshua and then little Sarah to the great chief. The children fell silent, their chattering stilled for once as they stared in awe at the tall Indian as he sat down in a straight-backed chair. With amazement, Emily saw Drew crouch between Josh and Sarah, a supporting arm around each of them. Gradually, he drew them out, translating between English and Lakota, and within a few minutes, both children had relaxed and were busily asking Red Cloud questions.

Emily wondered at Drew's gentle, reassuring manner as he spoke with the chief and her niece and nephew. It was a side of him she wouldn't have suspected existed, though this must be the behavior that Sam and Maggie had seen that caused them to trust him so implicitly.

Black Wolf approached the small group in front of Emily. Drew stepped back to include Sam and Maggie in the conversation with the old chief, and one or two other warriors walked up and stood listening. To her surprise, Red Cloud reached out for Daniel, and Maggie handed the boy to him. Zach drew in his breath sharply, though he said nothing. She had almost forgotten he was there. Emily thought uncharitably that there would be little Red Cloud could do to win her escort's approval.

At that moment, Black Wolf looked down the street and saw Emily. The Indian said something to Drew which caused his relaxed smile to vanish instantly. Sam turned immediately, hailing her and inviting her and Zach to join them. The set expression on Drew's face almost stopped her, but she thought again of the thrilling dances and marched resolutely forward. She was not going to let him intimidate her. Zach tagged along, clearly uneasy.

Upon reaching the circle where her family and the Oglalas stood, Emily noticed that everyone, including her brother and Maggie, was looking back and forth between her and Drew. Even the children were looking at her curiously, and she had the distinct impression that they were trying hard not to smile. Attempting to maintain decorum, Emily felt a flush creep under her skin. She glanced quickly at Drew, but he was looking stoically at a point beyond

Red Cloud's head. In consternation, she looked at her brother, her eyes questioning.

"Hello, Emily. Your timing was perfect!" he announced cheerfully. "Black Wolf was just telling about how a couple of weeks ago, he came to from a nasty bump on the head, only to find Drew hollering at a lady who was hollering right back at him. He thought for a minute he was at home listening to his parents argue, then he realized the hollering was in English, so that couldn't be. Says he never heard Drew yell like that at any woman. He figures you must be pretty special." He was chuckling merrily, as was everyone else. Everyone except herself, Drew, and Zachary.

Emily was mortified. She couldn't imagine what Zach must be thinking, and she couldn't bring herself even to look at Drew. To her dismay, she noticed that the Indians were getting quite a laugh out of the situation and had passed the little story among themselves. Several of them wandered over to take a look at her, chattering and joking in their language, and Emily did not need a translation to understand the gist of their comments. She wished that she'd never come. She should have let Zach take her home.

Black Wolf seemed to sense her acute embarrassment and said something in Lakota that brought a general laugh, after which the warriors dispersed. Emily noticed the ghost of a smile hovering about Drew's mouth now. She wondered what had been said, but not badly enough to ask. She felt Zach stiffen behind her.

Stepping forward, Black Wolf introduced himself in English.

"Please forgive us. We are having a little fun at my brother's expense, and I fear we have caused you discomfort. I believe we've met once before, although I wasn't at my best at the time. I am Śunkmanitu Sapa. You may call me Black Wolf."

Emily was struck again at the similarity between Drew and this Indian. He had referred to Drew as his brother—could that be? She glanced quickly back and forth between them. It was not their features, but the way they moved that was so alike.

Black Wolf followed her look. "No, we weren't born brothers," he said in answer to her unspoken question. "My father adopted Ista Ŝkan Niyapi's father as his brother and Ista Ŝkan Niyapi as his son. We are *hunka* brothers and I call him *misun*, my little brother."

He used the Indian name he had used before when addressing Drew. Sky in the Eyes, Sam had said. Black Wolf smiled easily at Emily, and she relaxed a little.

Red Cloud interrupted, speaking rapidly in Lakota. Black Wolf spoke again when he had finished. "My uncle says that I am rude for not introducing you to him. Miss Emily Parker, may I present you to the great chief of the Oglala Sioux, *Mahpiya Luta*, called Red Cloud by the white men." Then he said something in the Indian tongue to the chief, presumably explaining who she was. Then Sam introduced Zach. Red Cloud looked at him only briefly, turning his attention to Emily.

She asked Black Wolf to translate for her. "Would you tell the chief that it is a great honor for me to meet him, and I thank him for bringing his people to dance for us. I'm very interested in Sioux traditions and lore, so for me the dancing was a gift that I will remember always." She spoke solemnly, her dark eyes glowing.

Black Wolf spoke in Lakota when she had finished, and the chief and the men standing beside him nodded their acceptance of her thanks. Red Cloud said something in response. Out of the corner of her eye, Emily saw Drew impassively staring at the street.

"Red Cloud is glad you appreciated the dances. He says that if you're very interested in our people you should come visit us at the agency. There you could see more dancing, meet our women, and learn much." Black Wolf paused. "I speak for myself that if you would come, you would be welcome in my wife's or my mother's tipi," he said smiling.

Emily saw Drew's head jerk up. He cast a malevolent look at his adopted brother, then took a few steps away and leaned against a hitching post. It amused Emily to see him annoyed.

"Thank you for the invitation," she replied warmly. "It's most gracious of you."

Zach interrupted. "It's not safe for women to travel to the agencies." Several pairs of dark eyes turned on him, their expressions unreadable. "There are too many road agents along the way," he amended smoothly.

Josh broke the momentary tension. "If you go, Aunt Emily, you have to take me with you!" he announced, fearful that he might be forgotten.

"Me, too!" Sarah chimed in.

The adults smiled indulgently at the children's excitement. Josh began to describe all the things he wanted to do when he visited the agency, and soon the group was conversing freely with Black Wolf's help. Drew pointedly remained apart and said not a word. Sam and Maggie exchanged worried glances, but there was nothing they could do. Zach stayed close to Emily but didn't say much, either.

Josh was fixed on the idea of visiting the reservation, and he began to plead with his parents to allow him to return with Red Cloud and his band. He thought he could stay for a few months, polishing up his hunting and riding skills, then come back.

"I think you're forgetting about something," Maggie cautioned him, her eyes twinkling. "What about school? Don't you want to go back in the fall?"

Josh had forgotten about school. He groaned, but not because he didn't want to go. He loved school, especially history lessons. But if he went to the reservation, he couldn't go to school, and if he stayed home, he would never learn to be an Indian warrior. He was in torment, and his face showed it. He explained his quandary through Black Wolf.

The Oglala chief listened as Black Wolf translated Josh's words. Then he asked the younger man a few questions and Black Wolf answered in Lakota. Red Cloud thought for a minute, his stern brow furrowed with creases as he drew his eyebrows together. Finally he spoke at length. When he finished, Black Wolf began.

"Red Cloud was interested to hear the boy say he likes

school, though he realizes that white men's schools teach their children about their history and their ways. He had only heard adults tell him children must learn these lessons, and he assumed that the children would hate the schools because they must sit indoors all day. The Indians teach their children also, but not in schools. Indian children don't need to know the same things that white children must know. Therefore, they don't need to go to white men's schools. He thinks the boy should come stay on the reservation for a time, but that he should also go to school.''

"Is there a school at the agency?" Josh asked hopefully.

Black Wolf looked warily at the chief as he translated the question. Red Cloud's scowl deepened considerably, and he practically spat out his words. Turning back to the interested circle, Black Wolf wore an expression of regret.

"Unfortunately," he told them, "there has been much argument over the establishment of schools at the agency. McGillycuddy, the agent at Pine Ridge, has built a school and has plans for many more. And, of course, many of our children were sent away to Carlisle and are not happy. Schools are used to take our traditions and our way of life away from our children, and Red Cloud is opposed to having schools on the reservation. He feels most strongly about it. He said he will never willingly accept a school at the agency.''

Emily wondered what had happened at the school at Carlisle and in the agency schools to create such antipathy. As a teacher, she had always thought of education as an enlightening influence, one that bestowed great benefits on those lucky enough to receive it. She knit her brow in concern, but before she could formulate a response, Zach spoke.

"If those Indian children are going to live in a white man's world, they need to learn how we do things. If they don't go to school, where are they going to learn?" His tone was mild, but the Indians bristled as Black Wolf translated his remark. One of the men standing next to the chief spoke.

"Yellow Thunder says that the Oglala do not wish to live in the white man's way, and that schools and teachers are an evil presence among our people," Black Wolf said, keeping his voice even. He shot a worried look at Emily.

Emily bit her lip, deciding to say nothing about being a teacher. She tried to think of some way to change the subject before one of the children brought it up. Once again, she wasn't quick enough.

Drew chose the moment to rejoin the conversation. He spoke in Lakota, but he looked straight at Emily The Indians all turned to stare at her, leaving not a shred of doubt in her mind as to what he had said. She glared at him angrily. He really was the most impossible man! Why couldn't he have kept quiet? He was deliberately trying to make the Indians dislike her, trying to make her look bad. And there he stood, gazing blankly into the street again, one foot resting casually on the hitching post, as if nothing were wrong. She wanted to kick him.

Instead, she faced Red Cloud. She had expected him to be cold as a result of Drew's disclosure, but she beheld only curiosity in his eyes. She ventured a smile and looked to Sam and Maggie for help, not knowing what to say. Red Cloud began speaking to Black Wolf. By the time the chief finished speaking, he seemed to have thought of something quite funny, for he broke into a wide smile, leaving Emily at a loss.

"Red Cloud says you don't look evil, and he's sorry if our friend's remark unknowingly insulted you. He hasn't met many lady schoolteachers, and certainly none that were as kind, or as interested in our people, as you are. Because you are interested in our people's ways, he wonders if you would explain some things about schools to him, as a friend. He hasn't met many teachers that he wished to talk to before, but he thinks you are perhaps a little different."

Drew made an impatient motion at this, as if he didn't agree. Black Wolf ignored him and continued speaking.

"The chief has asked me to invite you again to visit us. He says if he issued the invitation formally, McGillycuddy would refuse to let you come, but if I ask a schoolteacher to visit for a few days, the agent will think it a coup against

Red Cloud. McGillycuddy knows how much Red Cloud dislikes anything connected with schools. Maybe the agent will even put on a feast for you. Red Cloud likes the idea of putting one over on McGillycuddy very much,'' he finished with a grin.

Emily hadn't expected such a turn. Glancing at Drew, she could hardly miss the black look on his face as he continued to stare at the street. She felt a triumphant satisfaction that his little trick had backfired. At the same time, she wondered how she could manage to get out to the reservation, which was several days' travel from Sam's ranch. Sam was too busy to take her, and she knew of no one else she would dare impose upon for such a favor. It hardly seemed feasible, and yet the chief seemed intent on her coming.

"I'm flattered by your invitation," she began earnestly, "and I would love to come, but I'm afraid I don't know if it will be possible. I don't know anyone who could take me," she explained, hoping Red Cloud would understand.

Drew abruptly removed his foot from the hitching post and stepped closer. His blue eyes bored into her.

"What you mean is that you have no intention of setting foot in an Indian camp. Indians are interesting when you're in town, and their stories are entertaining when you're standing safely in an army fort, but making the effort to visit them at their camp might be too much for your gentle sensibilities, mightn't it, Miss Parker?" His tone was scathing.

Emily was flabbergasted by his attack. She would have loved to visit the agency, and the injustice of his remarks galled her.

"I have no idea what you are talking about," she retorted crisply. She took a deep breath to continue, but was cut off.

Zach stepped forward aggressively. "Now see here, Rutledge," he said angrily. "You're entirely out of line!"

Emily was becoming more embarrassed and angry by the second. She hardly cared what she did or said as she grabbed Zach's arm.

"Thank you, Zach, but I'll handle this myself," she told him softly.

Zach looked down at her for a long moment, then shook his head. He said no more, but he was obviously furious. Maggie watched with concern, while Sam and the Indians looked on with interest. Drew spoke again, picking up right where he had left off.

"Come now, Miss Parker, we've had lots of Easterners out here checking on the agency conditions for their various benevolent societies, all of them spouting righteous speeches about the plight of the poor savages. Wouldn't you care to join the parade? We haven't scalped too terribly many of them in their beds. Have the white Dakotans already convinced you that the Indians are nothing more than a pack of begging, thieving leeches? That wasn't what I heard the other evening," he reminded her caustically. "What happened to the humanitarian young woman who would rather trust herself to the Indians than her Christian countrymen? It's all very well to support the Indian cause from a distance, but when you have the opportunity to do something that might actually help, you find that it's inconvenient and you can't do it." His voice was contemptuous.

"That is not true!" Emily cried in outrage. "I wouldn't be here if I didn't care, and I am not the kind of person who is deterred by difficulty. Not," she added furiously, "that you would know." She folded her arms across her chest and stared challengingly at him. "I fail to see what gives you the right to pass judgment on me."

"I just call them as I see them, lady," he said, his eyes never leaving hers. "And I heard you were in the territory to avoid an overzealous lover, not to give aid and succor to the beleaguered Indians."

Emily turned an accusing eye on Sam. How could he have discussed her personal life with this recalcitrant hoodlum? She felt betrayed, and her anger burned even hotter. Rutledge made it sound so sordid. George had not been a lover; she'd hardly even kissed him. That is, not a real kiss, not the way she had kissed Drew Rutledge. Now why had she thought that? She looked away in consternation, lest her eyes give her thoughts away. She was so angry she wasn't thinking straight.

Drew went on.

"Now *that* was true charity. You probably led the poor sop on, then got scared and ran when he responded to you. Then you try to cover up your fears with a nice display of compassion for the Indians. Something diverting to take your mind off dealing with men. How generous! What are you so scared of, Emily?" he asked insinuatingly.

He had gone too far, and he knew it. Sam threw him a warning glance, and Black Wolf moved to his side. Zach's hand was moving a little too close to the gun holstered under his shoulder.

Aware of all this, Drew's eyes didn't leave Emily's. By force of will, he held her gaze, daring her to look away and concede that he was right. Bright stains of color stood out in her white face, and her lower lip trembled as she fought to control her fury.

Emily cringed at his words. She was honest enough to recognize that there was a great deal of truth in what he said, but he was wrong about one thing. It wasn't George Parks that she sought to avoid anymore. It was Drew Rutledge. She was afraid of what she felt in his arms, of the weakness in her character that made her want him, even when he humiliated and insulted her. And she wouldn't let him know. Not now, and not ever.

She stared back at him resolutely, striving for the most quelling tone she could muster.

"I am afraid of very little, Mr. Rutledge, although why my fears are any of your concern, I have no idea. Isn't it odd how angry you always are with me? Don't I recall you telling me quite philosophically that anger was not necessarily the most expedient means of dealing with conflicts? I suggest you heed your own advice."

It was Drew's turn to face the truth in her words. He told himself that he didn't understand why she infuriated him so, but inside he knew it was because he wanted her so badly, and she didn't appear to be interested in him. Oh, she responded to him physically, all right, but he wanted more than that. He'd foolishly expected more from her, deluding himself with ridiculous notions simply because she had eyes that touched his dreams. She'd judged him and his adopted people as everyone else had, not even giving him a chance to get to know her.

Emily's voice continued, thick with sarcasm. "I suppose, however, that that is rather a lot to ask of a man of your ilk."

She clapped her mouth shut. She hadn't meant to say anything that would reveal her knowledge of his shadier dealings.

As she knew he would, he pounced on the statement. Both Sam and Black Wolf looked at her curiously.

"What do you mean, a man of my ilk?" he exploded thunderously. "You don't know anything about me! I could say the same thing to you! After all, what type of woman goes about kissing strange men the way you do?"

All eyes turned to Emily in surprise.

"I do not go around kissing strange men!" she shouted back indignantly. "You kissed me, if you will recall!" She stamped her foot in frustration. Everyone was staring at them with open mouths, except Sam, who looked as if he were choking.

"You kissed me back," he drawled accusingly.

"I did not!" Emily sputtered hotly.

"Yes, you did. The second time," he corrected, a smug grin spreading across his face.

There was nothing more to say. Emily was shocked. Her brother and sister-in-law were trying hard not to laugh, and the Indians had apparently understood quite a lot and were openly guffawing. Only Zach was not amused. Really, the whole thing was ridiculous, but it wasn't funny.

Rutledge was an absolute fiend! He'd compromised her reputation in public and embarrassed her in front of her family. Even if he had no care for what people thought of him, and clearly he didn't, the things he'd said to her were inexcusable. After this demonstration, Emily knew more than ever that Drew Rutledge would never give her anything but grief. She watched him stalk back to his hitching post and lean against it, savoring his triumph.

Emily caught Black Wolf's attention.

"I think I will be going," she said with great effort, trying to salvage what pride she could. "Would you please tell Chief Red Cloud that I would be honored to accept his invitation at the first possible opportunity. I will look forward to meeting him again." She looked at the chief as Black Wolf relayed her message.

"The chief says he is glad to have met you, Emily Parker. He has enjoyed seeing Íśte Śkan Niyapi lose his temper. Now he says he knows the man is truly human."

Drew looked at his brother in exasperation but was ignored.

"Red Cloud cautions you not to judge him hastily, though, for he has much to think about lately. We will look for you in the autumn, woman with eyes like the earth in spring and hair like the summer sun. Red Cloud bids you goodbye."

Emily wondered why he would expect her in the autumn. She didn't know if she would even still be in Dakota then. And she swore to herself that she'd burn in hell before she'd reconsider her opinion of Drew Rutledge.

"Goodbye, Maĥpiya Luta and Śunkmanitu Sapa," she said formally.

Then she turned and walked quickly up the street with Zach.

During the ride home, Zach was distant, but Emily barely noticed him. Her thoughts were occupied with the day's upsetting events. Emily was relieved when they finally reached the ranch and rode silently into the corral. She felt compelled to apologize to Zach.

"Zach, thank you for being so patient and for going along when I wanted to meet Red Cloud. You were right in the first place. It didn't turn out so well after all. I'm terribly sorry.' She sounded quite miserable.

Zach looked at her a long moment. His brown eyes still held a trace of anger, and she was afraid he wouldn't accept her apology.

"It's all right," he finally said, his eyes softening. "I'm sorry your day wasn't perfect. I know how much you were looking forward to it."

Emily couldn't help thinking how kind he was. She had put him through a public spectacle, and here he was expressing concern that her day had been ruined.

"Yes, well," she replied, "it wasn't all a fiasco. The dancing was marvelous."

"And we had a pleasant morning and an enjoyable lunch," he added.

She'd forgotten. She guiltily hoped that he didn't realize it.

"That's right," she said, mustering what felt like a pathetic smile.

"Emily, are you all right?" Zach asked with concern. "You look a little pale."

"Actually, I am rather tired. I think I'll go in and lie down for a while. I think Frank is around somewhere. He can take care of my horse." Her voice was flat. She turned toward the house.

"Emily, wait." Zach hesitated. "I need to ask . . ." He paused, as if hoping she might divine what he wanted to say.

She turned back to face him. When she said nothing, he continued.

"I think you know that I have a lot of admiration for you. It might save us both some trouble—that is, if you have some sort of understanding with Rutledge, or anybody else, I would understand."

Emily was not surprised he asked, but she was uncomfortable. To admit that there was no bond between Drew and herself was a virtual admission of licentious behavior on her part. To lie would be to compound her sins. She felt trapped, but she had to be honest.

"There's nothing between us," she said quietly. "And there's no one else. What's more, if I ever see Drew Rutledge again it will be too soon!"

Zach appeared pleased with her answer. A warm smile lit his dark face.

"Then you mean there's hope for me yet?" he asked in a gently teasing manner.

Emily was startled, not sure what to say. It seemed that she had run into an awful lot of interested men for a girl who had left home to get away from them long enough to figure out exactly what she wanted from life. She managed a little smile as she answered.

"Zach, right now I don't know that I want to pursue *any* relationships beyond friendship. I'm trying to sort a few things out, and I'm not ready yet for more than that." Zach didn't respond. "I hope you understand," she said imploringly.

His eyes were patient and kind, a fleeting twinkle flickering through them.

"Just as long as there's no one else, I can wait," he promised her, his smile making her feel better. "So, for now, what do you say? Friends?" He offered her his hand.

She accepted it.

"Friends," she agreed with a smile that finally reached her eyes. "Goodbye, Zach," she called as he mounted his horse. "And thanks. For understanding."

With a wave, he rode off.

Sam yawned as he stepped out of his trousers. Maggie turned from the window, where she had been listening to the crickets and thinking, her white nightgown billowing as she moved.

"That was quite some show this afternoon," Sam observed.

"Mmm," Maggie agreed absently. "The children had a wonderful time," she responded automatically.

"I meant my little sister and Rutledge," Sam said, throwing back the quilt.

Maggie looked at him, nodding. "Oh. Yes, of course. That's just what I was thinking about. You know, I really don't have the faintest idea why they dislike each other so."

"I think Black Wolf may have been on the right track when he made that joke about them arguing because they like each other so much," Sam speculated. "It sure tickled those Indians to see Drew so hot under the collar. I have to admit, I had a laugh or two myself there. Did you see Emily's face when Rutledge said she kissed him back?'' He grinned at the memory. "And I just bet she did." He chuckled.

"I think something is really bothering Emily, and this whole ordeal upset her more than we thought. She didn't say a word when I went up to see if she needed anything,'' Maggie reproved gently. "I wish I knew what was eating at her.''

"I think Drew came pretty close when he said she's afraid of something. She got as pale as a ghost. But, if I know my sister, we'll have to wait until she's ready to tell us what it is. Growing up with three nosy brothers taught her to guard her secrets if she didn't want them broadcast to the neighborhood. She's not much good at hiding her feelings, but she'd take the reasons for them to the grave.'' He sat down on the bed. "Are you coming to bed, Mags?''

"Yes," she answered, moving toward the turned-down bed. "Maybe we should hold off on trying to get Drew over here for a while. We don't seem to be having very good luck, and I don't want to upset Emily anymore.''

Sam sighed. "I think you're right. I'd sure like to see them decide they like each other, but we don't seem to be real efficient matchmakers. It's a good thing we have other things to fall back on.''

"Isn't that the truth!" Maggie laughed softly as she climbed into bed.

Chapter 8

During the next few days, Emily threw herself into any project that presented itself and created several new ones. She helped Mary with the washing and ironing, something she normally hated. She mended clothing and helped Sarah sew together fabric scraps for a doll quilt. She made new pillow covers for the parlor sofa from an old pair of curtains that Maggie had replaced. In addition, every day she worked in the garden and helped prepare the family's meals, and in the evenings she read aloud to Josh and Sarah and told them stories from her and Sam's childhood in New York state. Emily wanted no spare moments when her thoughts might stray to the infuriating Drew Rutledge.

Zach stopped by several times, ostensibly to discuss lumber orders with Sam, but more often than not, he spent most of his time chatting with Emily as she sewed, weeded, or baked. He never stayed longer than an hour, and his conversation was always cheerful and amusing. He said nothing about the day in Deadwood, nor, to Emily's relief, did he ever mention the discussion they had had about his intentions. He was the perfect gentleman. Emily perceived that Sam was not entirely thrilled with Zach's frequent visits, but he said nothing about it. She couldn't think why that should be so, but she didn't let it trouble her.

Maggie worried about her, Emily knew. Twice Maggie had tactfully broached the subject of Drew Rutledge, but Emily had managed to avoid talking about him. The first time, Kenny had burst in with a badly cut hand that needed attention, and the second, Daniel had conveniently created yet another of the messes for which he was famous. Finally, Maggie had given up, attempting instead to keep her sister-in-law from working too hard. She had found herself with far more leisure time than usual due to Emily's frenetic activity. If she hadn't been so concerned about Emily, she might have enjoyed the respite.

It was the nights that were most difficult for Emily. The August weather was hot and dry, and the sultry night air made sleeping uncomfortable. The pleasant evening breezes that normally brought relief disappeared, and Emily lay atop her bed, staring into the darkness, willing herself to sleep. Her body was tired, but her mind would not let her rest. She spent long hours thinking about what it was she really wanted for her future.

She loved teaching, but it wasn't enough. Emily longed for a sense of purpose. She often considered Red Cloud's invitation to come talk to him on the reservation about schools. She tried to think of how schools could be adapted to the Indians' needs, so that their children could learn enough about the white man's world to survive in it without abandoning their traditions and ways. It would have been wonderful to be able to visit the camps and to learn what they needed so she could help. She imagined herself teaching in a new schoolhouse, built especially for an experimental school that she and the Indians would design. In her dream, dark-haired, dark-eyed Indian children would scamper happily, eager to study English and to learn about the new country they had become a part of, as well as about their native culture. She imagined a great sense of accomplishment and pride, but even that was not enough.

It was then that the memory of Drew Rutledge, crouched between Josh and Sarah, gentle, reassuring, his strong arms cradling them, flashed through her mind, and Emily would thrash her pillows and toss wildly on the bed. The image conjured up a longing for children of her own, a house, a loving husband. But Drew Rutledge would never be the man to give her that, she knew with certainty. Despairingly, she wondered if she would ever find another man who aroused the passion in her that he did, then decided it would be better if she did not. It was too dangerous. As with Drew, there would be no guarantee that someone else would be suitable. No, it was better to find someone with whom she could build a secure, stable family life. She thought of Zach and punched her pillow again. She liked him, but she felt the same way about him that she had about George Parks. She couldn't imagine spending the rest of her life with him, and her dilemma remained; she wanted security *and* passion.

Sometimes, when she was far from sleep, she would slip out of the house and walk barefoot across the lawn, looking up at the bright Dakota stars. She loved the night sky here, so soft, so close around her. Emily felt a comforting presence in the inky depths, and she usually slept when she returned to her room.

About a week after the Indian dancing, Sam sat at the breakfast table watching his sister pick listlessly at her food. Despite the attractive golden cast her skin had acquired from working outside in the sun, there were dark shadows under her eyes. Sam knew she hadn't been sleeping well. He and Maggie had heard her moving around in her room late into the night, and more than once he'd heard the kitchen door swing softly shut as she came or went in the early morning hours. He was worried about her.

"You feeling all right, Emily? You've hardly eaten a thing," he observed.

Emily looked up, a little surprised. "I feel fine. It's too hot to eat, that's all."

"Seems it's been too hot to sleep much, lately, too," he replied knowingly.

Emily didn't say anything. She looked down at the cold food on her plate.

Maggie interrupted gently. "Are you sure nothing's wrong, Emily?"

She felt badly for worrying her family.

"Really, there's nothing the matter," she repeated, glancing between Sam and Maggie. "I've just been thinking about a lot of things. I've been wondering if I should try to find a teaching position when school starts," she announced.

"That's an idea," Sam agreed without enthusiasm. "Although you know you don't have to work unless you want to. You know we'd be glad to keep you busy around here for as long as you like," he teased.

Emily smiled.

"Thanks, Sam. I was just thinking that I was wasting all my training and experience, that was all. You know I love it here."

As she said it, Emily realized that she really did love the ranch and being with her brother and his family. The time she spent with them was full of meaning and joy. Suddenly she felt better than she had for days. She'd been concentrating so much on trying to figure out her future that she was neglecting the present. She resolved to change her outlook. Sam noticed a difference in her expression.

"I'm glad to hear that. And, if you want me to ask around about teaching positions, I'd be happy to," he offered. "Today, however, I think you ladies should take off and do something daring." Sam noted with satisfaction that he had caught both Emily's and his wife's attention. "Is Mary coming today?"

"Yes," Maggie said quickly. "What do you have in mind, Samuel Parker?" she demanded, her eyes dancing.

"I thought a nice hot day like this might be just the time to go for a ride up the canyon to the falls. I have to get on into Sturgis, but if Mary will be here to watch the children, I think you two will be safe enough without me. What do you say?"

"It sounds delightful!" Maggie exclaimed enthusiastically. "Emily?"

It did indeed sound delightful. It would be just the thing to help her raise her spirits.

"It does sound like fun," she agreed. "I love riding, and it would be cooler, wouldn't it? Why didn't you tell me before that there was a waterfall nearby?" she asked, her interest growing by the second.

Because, Sam thought, it's on Rutledge's property, and he doesn't generally like people on his land, and you jump like a fox caught in the chicken house whenever I mention his name.

"It isn't a very big waterfall, and at this time of year there won't be much water in the creek, but it's a pretty ride. You'll enjoy it," Maggie promised.

"Well, now that that's decided," Sam said as he pushed back his chair and rose, "I've got a building going up that needs my attention. You ladies have a good ride." He kissed Maggie on the cheek and strolled out the door.

The two women immediately began planning their trip. They wanted to leave shortly after Mary arrived, so they put together a picnic of ham sandwiches on thick slices of homemade bread, pickles, fresh carrots and tomatoes from the garden, and leftover pieces of spice cake from supper the night before. They located a couple of canteens in the cellar and filled them from the pump, then went to dress.

"What are you going to wear, Emily?" Maggie asked. "Do you have any trousers?"

Emily stopped short. She had thought she would wear her riding habit, but now realized that it was far too hot for the wool gabardine.

"Trousers?" Emily asked doubtfully. "You ride in pants?"

Maggie laughed wickedly. "You keep forgetting you aren't back East, Emily. It's really much more comfortable and practical. Follow me, and we'll see what we can find for you."

She led Emily into her bedroom, where she opened one of her bureau drawers and drew out a pair of well-worn jeans. "These are my old pair. Try them on. I think they'll fit."

Emily looked at the pants, wondering what her mother would say if she ever heard that her daughter was going riding, unescorted, dressed in trousers. She grinned.

"Now, about a shirt. You need something loose, but heavy enough to protect your arms from branches and insects. Sam's are too big. Wait, I know. I'll be right back. Go ahead and try those on," Maggie urged.

She disappeared through the kitchen. Emily heard the screened porch door slam shut. She could hear the children's voices floating in from the yard. She looked again at the faded blue denims in her hand. Why not, she thought, as she began removing her skirt and petticoats.

Maggie returned triumphantly a few minutes later bearing a dark green cotton twill shirt, a fringed buckskin jacket, and a dark brown hat. She caught sight of Emily staring at her reflection in the long mirror that stood in one corner. She had on the jeans and her camisole.

"Do they fit?" Maggie queried.

Emily laughed. "I guess so. Do they look all right?"

Maggie surveyed her critically. "I think you'll be more comfortable with a belt. Your waist is smaller than mine is. Just wait 'til you have three children, and you'll know what I mean! Put these on while I find a belt," she ordered, thrusting the clothes into Emily's arms. She turned and began digging through another drawer.

"Where'd you get these?" Emily asked.

"I took them out of Kenny's dresser. He won't mind if you borrow them for the day. I know it's hot, but up in the canyon, you may still need the jacket. Besides, it will give you a real pioneer air. Just like Calamity Jane," she added wickedly. "Here's the belt I want!" She turned back to Emily.

When she had put on the belt, Maggie pinned Emily's hair up on top of her head in a knot, then shoved the hat down over her ears. She stood back to admire the effect.

"Your mother wouldn't recognize you," Maggie stated with a delighted grin. "You could be mistaken for Kenny from a distance. Why don't you go get your boots on while I get ready?" she suggested.

Emily ran upstairs to get her riding boots. She was having a grand time. The clothes made her feel daring and reckless. All I need, she thought, is a six-shooter strapped to my leg, and I'd look just like some wild desperado. She could have kissed Sam for suggesting the ride.

When Emily came back downstairs, Maggie was gone. She heard her talking to someone outside. A moment later, she came into the kitchen, her face crestfallen.

"What's the matter?" Emily asked with alarm.

"That was one of the Guthrie boys. It seems Hannah

sprained her ankle yesterday afternoon and needs Mary to help at home. Oh, dear,'' she moaned. ''I was so looking forward to our ride.''

The disappointment was obvious in Emily's face. ''Oh, well,'' she said with a wan smile. ''We can go another day.''

''Yes, I suppose we can,'' Maggie agreed. ''But here you are all ready to go. It's such a shame.''

''I'll just go change back into my own clothes,'' Emily said dispiritedly, turning toward the door.

''Wait, Emily.'' Maggie had an idea. ''I can't go, but if you don't mind going alone, there's no reason why you shouldn't. I can draw you a map. It would still be a nice ride.'' Her voice sounded hopeful.

''I don't know, Maggie,'' Emily replied with a frown. ''I would enjoy the ride, but is it safe to go alone?''

''I should think it would be as safe as going with me,'' Maggie reasoned. ''You can shoot can't you?''

Emily nodded. Sam had taught her to shoot when she was not much older than Josh was now.

''If you're worried, take one of the rifles. I doubt you'll need it, but maybe you could get us a rabbit or two for supper.''

Emily thought for a minute. She really did want to go. Maggie's right, she decided, I'll take the rifle, just in case, but I'll be perfectly fine. ''It might be fun to do some hunting,'' she admitted.

''Then you'll go?'' Maggie asked. ''I'd feel better if you did.''

Emily smiled. ''Yes, I think I will.''

An hour later, Emily was riding along a pretty creek that ran down the bottom of a narrow canyon. Trees and bushes grew thickly along the banks, and dark pines rose straight and tall on the rocky slopes on either side. At intervals the creek bottom widened, and waist-high grasses waved their heads in the faint breeze. Grasshoppers filled the warm air with the sound of their buzzing, and the stream tumbled noisily through its uneven bed. The sky was a deep, clear blue, and the sun shone brightly in the cloudless dome. In the shade of the trees it was deliciously cool. Emily breathed deeply, enjoying the solitude and tranquillity.

The waterfall lay about five or six miles west of the Parkers' in the hills. Maggie had assured Emily that it was unlikely she would meet anyone. When she had asked why, Maggie had mumbled something about it not being in a mining district, although what that had to do with anything, Emily wasn't sure. True to Maggie's prediction, she didn't meet a soul. The only living creatures she saw were a couple of deer and the many birds that called and twittered in the trees around her. The ride was peaceful, and Emily relaxed as she had not for many days.

After a leisurely couple of hours, Emily stopped to look at her map. She thought she should be nearing the falls soon. Maggie had told her to watch for a distinctive granite outcropping that looked like a giant anthill. This was now in sight, on the hill above the canyon on the left. The falls should be only a half mile away now, around a sharp curve in the stream.

After several minutes, Emily rounded the bend and looked about her with pleasure. The creek flowed through a wide meadow lined with tall pines and spruces. At the far end of it, perhaps two hundred yards away, she could see the short falls, glinting in the sunlight. The water fell from a ledge of rock about fifteen feet in height, into a deep pool. There was a stand of very old, very tall Ponderosa pines that went down to the edge of the pool on the left side and wild cress showed bright green in the water where the stream continued past the pool. It was idyllic.

Far above, in the noon sky, Emily heard a shrill cry. Looking up, she watched a small speck drop rapidly toward her. She recognized the broad wingspan and graceful flight as that of an eagle. The mare pricked up her ears and stood listening, then whinnied softly, almost as if in greeting. Looking around her, Emily felt a deep presence in the meadow of something greater than herself. She let it wash over her, enjoying the magic. At length, she urged the horse forward to the falls. Suddenly, Emily was overcome by a sense of being at home, as if she were welcome, as if she were expected here. Contentment welled up from within her.

The eagle's eerie call filled the glade a second time. Riding up the left bank of the stream, Emily crossed the meadow and entered the pine grove, where a thick layer of fallen needles muffled the mare's footfalls and the sharp scent of resin mingled with that of the damp earth. The air was cool beneath the trees. The eagle cried once again, this time very close above the treetops. Emily heard powerful wings beat, then the creak of a high bough as the bird settled himself on some unseen lofty perch. Emily could no longer see or hear it, but she felt the presence she had detected earlier more strongly than ever.

At the edge of the grove, Emily dismounted and led the mare to the pool to drink. She knelt on the bank and dipped her handkerchief into the clear water, wrung it out, and rubbed it over her neck and face. It was deliciously cool. She removed her hat, accidentally dislodging a few of the pins that held her hair. She pulled out the remaining pins and stuck them in her pocket, allowing her long, golden tresses to fall freely past her shoulders. Then she rose to explore the falls.

Looping the mare's reins around a low branch, Emily stepped out into the sunlight, skirted the pool, and came to the rock wall over which fell a shimmering curtain of water. Looking up, she saw a magnificent, towering pine rising from the bank above. From the very uppermost branches, the eagle was watching her. She was startled. Staring back at the regal bird, Emily felt a queerly familiar sensation that she couldn't place. She wasn't frightened, nor even uncomfortable, but she was uncertain. At the same time, a wild excitement fired her spirit and she again noticed the curious sense of belonging that she felt. Gazing up at the unmoving bird of prey, she felt a sudden rush of freedom and joy, of being a part of the beautiful mountains around her, the grass-covered earth beneath her feet, the cool spray of water drifting on the light breeze, the deep piney smell of the clear air and the endless, azure depths of the sky. She laughed out loud, a rich, full sound that carried the hopeful promise of happiness throughout the meadow. The eagle tilted his head at her curiously.

Caught up in the exuberant enjoyment of the enchanting world around her, Emily clambered on the rocks around the falls and stuck her hands into the tumbling waters. She splashed and threw little rocks into the pool, watching the ripples lap toward the edge. She removed her boots and stockings, rolled the jeans up to her knees, and waded in the shallow creek as it spilled out of the pool. Finally, she sat down near the mare in the shade of the tall pines and ate her lunch. She found she was ravenous for the first time in days, and she ate almost everything that Maggie had sent. As she ate, she saw that the eagle still stood in his tree looking down at her. Normally, she would have been unnerved; today, she accepted his presence without a second thought.

Emily yawned. She was drowsy and decided to take a short nap before heading home. She spread her blanket half in the shade and half out so that she could feel the warm sun and still have her eyes shaded. Telling herself that she would only doze for a few minutes, she drifted off, content and happy.

They marched very slowly, facing first the west, then the north, the east, and finally the south, a parade of riders on horseback led by a buffalo. On the buffalo's head rode the eagle, his eyes flashing like the sky. A song of lamentation filled the air, and there were tears and much distress. They stopped and all faced west again. Then the drumbeat changed, and painted dancers began to spin in the firelight. Drums pounded and rattles punctuated the wild leaps and gestures. They were as many whirlwinds, chasing, hunting, flying through the night. In the center stood the buffalo, the eagle perched upon its horns. There was laughter and happiness all around. The people were celebrating as they had not done for many years. Their song lifted into the night air.

Then, in the midst of the dancing, the sky began to rumble, and the stars were blotted out. Fear gripped the people, and they fled.

Emily's eyes flew open. Her heart was pounding and she was breathing rapidly. A distant murmur of thunder reached her ears. Oh, dear, she thought, what time is it? How long have I slept? The sky overhead was full of huge, puffy clouds, racing along in a high wind. On the earth below, the air was still. Emily sat up quickly.

The eagle lifted off his perch and glided to the ground. He landed right in front of her, not ten feet away. Her dream was forgotten as she gazed in wonder at the bird. He was larger than she had thought, but she was not alarmed. She noticed several spots of white peppering his dark plumage. Then she looked into his eyes. Her heart stopped. The eagle's eyes were a deep, dark blue, glinting with moving flashes of white light. They were eyes Emily knew. She stared, stupefied.

Then, in a great rush of noise, the bird spread his powerful wings and rose into the air. Catching a wind current, he glided westward, ever higher into the clouds.

Emily shook her head in amazement. It had to be a bizarre coincidence, she told herself. This place was affecting her strangely, or perhaps she had simply not had enough sleep lately. Whatever the problem, Emily was experiencing things she had never imagined possible, queer, gut-wrenching emotions and soaring exhilarations, and this elusive sense of connection with something she could neither name nor understand. Unable to relate her feelings to anything in her previous experiences, she tried to dismiss them.

As her heartbeat and breathing returned to normal, she noted that the sun was lower than it should have been. She must have slept for several hours. It was now late afternoon, and the scuttling clouds overhead carried the threat of thunderstorms. She rose from her blanket and stepped into the clearing where she could see the sky better. Sure enough, an ominous bank of clouds was rising in the west, throwing out a wide anvil that would become a thundercloud. There was no telling when and if the storm would reach her, but Emily hurriedly collected her gear and returned to the mare. Hastily stuffing her hair under her hat, she took out her map to check it one last time. She mounted, took a last look around the meadow, and started for home.

She rode for an hour, urging the mare to as quick a pace as was possible through the rocky underbrush. There was no real trail. This hadn't mattered as she had leisurely climbed toward the falls that morning, but now it was a hindrance. Sam and Maggie would be worried about her. The sun had already sunk behind the hills, and it would be too dark to see before she reached the ranch if she did not hurry. At the rate she was going, however, she wasn't sure she would make it. She could become hopelessly lost in the dark, and she knew there were all sorts of dangers: coyotes, wolves, bears, even mountain lions in the hills. Emily forced herself to still her rising panic, knowing that she needed to keep her wits about her if she were to get home safely.

An idea occurred to her. The creek twisted and turned around the hills, making several wide bends. Perhaps if she went straight over the hills and cut out the meanders, she would make better time. The trees didn't look too close together, and the sloping hills were not steep. The mare should have little more trouble than in the narrow valley. Before her, the creek turned sharply to the south. Emily guided her bay through a shallow part of the stream to reach the north bank. She hesitated briefly, taking note of the angle of the lowering rays of the sun before plunging into the forest.

At first, the going was smooth enough, and Emily felt her spirits rise as the creek wound further and further to her right. The hill was not high, and she made good progress. Soon she was riding along the crest of the broad ridge.

Descending the east side of the hill, Emily found herself on the edge of a steep gulch that she didn't dare take the mare down. She turned to the right, hoping to make an easy return to the canyon. Riding parallel to the gulch, she came to a sharp granite precipice. Far below her, the creek gurgled. Emily wondered grimly what she should do. She could either go back the way she had come or turn north and hope to get around the gulch that way. She leaned forward to pat the mare's neck.

"Which way should we go, girl?" she asked softly.

A shrill cry echoed overhead. Emily turned her gaze skyward. An eagle soared above, headed north. A shiver ran down her spine as she followed it.

A threatening rumble of thunder sounded from the dark clouds at Emily's back. There should have been another hour of daylight, but the sun had dropped behind the towering stormcloud in the west, and the dim light was filled with deep shadows. A chill breeze prompted Emily to don Kenny's buckskin jacket, and she pushed her hat low on her brow to protect her face from the branches and leaves that lashed at her as she rode. She was heading east, but she was north of the canyon she had followed that morning. How far, she had no idea. Casting a worried glance over her shoulder at the approaching storm, she urged the patient mare through the trees.

The pines thinned somewhat, and Emily noticed that the breeze had stopped. The atmosphere was tense with the coming storm. Lightning flashed in the western sky, still some distance away, and the booming voice of the thunder growled threateningly over the hills. Then a different sound reached her ears. She pulled up on the mare's reins to listen.

Voices echoed through the pine forest, then a heavy thud. Emily slid off her horse and cautiously followed the sounds until she was standing perhaps twenty yards from the edge of the trees. Peering out between the dark trunks, shielded from view by a thicket of wild plums, Emily saw four men unloading two wagons. With surprise, she recognized the men as Indians, members of Red Cloud's tribe. They had been among the dancers she had seen the week before. What were they doing here?

Watching the men, she saw that they were unloading heavy boxes from the wagons. They were transferring the freight into a cave that opened into the mountainside where it met the open meadow. The opening was wide enough for the men to load the boxes onto a small sledge that they then dragged into the cave. They looked as though they had just begun work and were in a hurry to finish before the storm broke. While she watched, a third wagon arrived, escorted by two more Indians. These men stopped further down the field and walked up to a tangle of wild blackberry canes. One of them stepped behind it and pushed. The screen of greenery moved aside to reveal a second cave. Why, Emily thought in astonishment, the area must be riddled with hidden caves! What were these Indians hiding in them?

At that instant, a flash of lightning illuminated the scene and Emily caught a glimpse of lettering on the side of a large crate. Her eyes widened in understanding as she made out the words, SEVENTH CAVALRY, U.S. ARMY, stenciled on the wood. Her blood ran chill as the thunder boomed ever closer.

Red Cloud's warriors were unloading stolen army goods! Her mind flew quickly back to the conversation she had overheard between Sam and Maggie. Were the Indians involved in stealing guns as Colonel Reynolds suspected, or were they stealing supplies for those who refused to live on the reservations? It was worse than she'd thought if the goods smuggled to the renegade Indians had been stolen from the army.

She gasped, realizing that Drew Rutledge had to be the instigating force behind this treason. A wave of cold anguish settled over her. This must be Rutledge's land. She remembered Maggie saying his place lay west of the Parkers', in the hills. She had probably spent the last few hours wandering around his property. No wonder she hadn't seen anyone! Few people would have risked raising his anger by trespassing. And now she knew why he was so unsociable. He was hiding a deadly secret in these caves.

Emily realized the danger she was in. She looked around to see if there was any way to escape without being seen. She didn't want to stay hidden in the woods with a thunderstorm nearly upon her, but neither did she want to risk being captured by the Indians or Drew Rutledge. She shuddered when she thought what might happen to her if they caught her. Looking around, she saw a gully that headed east, toward home. If she were quiet, she might be able to slip away. The thunder would cover some of the noise she would make, but the lightning could unexpectedly reveal her should she venture into the open. Indecision gnawed at her. Then, as the wind picked up fiercely with the advancing edge of the thundercloud now overhead and the first drops of rain beginning to fall sporadically, Emily saw one of the Indians shout and point toward the woods, directly at her hiding place.

She froze. Had they seen her? The seconds ticked by as though they were eons. Emily realized with relief that she hadn't been discovered. The Indian must have seen something else, but she no longer felt safe in the woods so close to such treacherous activity. Slowly, cautiously, she led the mare toward the gully.

When she reached its mouth, she stopped to inspect it. She discovered that it was only a short ravine that led to another open meadow about a hundred yards beyond where she stood. Emily couldn't see very far into the meadow, but there didn't appear to be anyone there. Cautiously, she led her horse along the bushes that filled the gully bottom, keeping low. She hoped the failing light and the wind would hide her movements from any watching eyes. She was thankful that her light brown jacket blended well into the growth of small trees and bushes that choked the shallow ravine.

It took five minutes to reach the upper end, but it seemed like as many hours. Emily breathed a sigh of relief as she paused to survey the scene before her. The pine trees marched down to the right side of the wide meadow, and a swift creek wound out of the hills on the left. It was probably the same creek that flowed through the Parker ranch, since few creeks carried so much water this time of year. Emily decided to ride just inside the pines, along the base of the hill, following the creek downstream until it led her home.

The raindrops were falling more frequently, and the dark stormcloud flashed lightning overhead. The mare pawed nervously at the ground when a loud crack of thunder quickly followed the bright stab. Knowing she would be caught in the imminent downpour, Emily swung rapidly into the saddle and turned the nervous horse toward the trees. She hoped they would have some protection from the rain there.

As they stepped into the short space of open ground that separated them from the sheltering forest, Emily heard a shrill whistle, not unlike the eagle's cry. She wondered what it was, frowning, and urged the mare forward.

Suddenly, Emily heard hooves pounding behind her. She looked back in alarm to see a buckskin-clad rider on a buckskin horse racing toward her along a track cut into the side of the gully. She hadn't seen it for the high grass. The whistle must have been a signal. Drew Rutledge was bearing down on her at a furious pace.

A burst of energy surged through Emily's blood. She instantly turned her mare, kicking her into a wild gallop. The already frightened animal bolted forward as a thunderclap ricocheted through the valley. Emily hung on with her knees pressed tightly to the horse's sides, unsure of her ability to control her mount. Instinctively, Emily felt her only chance was to make for the open pastures along the creek. She prayed that her horse had the speed to outrun Rutledge's and would not throw her, but she knew the bay was tired from being ridden all day and wasn't at her best. Hoping against hope, Emily bent low over the mare's head. She didn't look back.

Lightning blazed in the sky, and thunder crashed. The rain began to fall in earnest, quickly soaking both riders. Emily was halfway down the meadow when a bolt of lightning streaked white hot, hitting a lone cottonwood not twenty yards across the creek. A deafening crack of thunder accompanied it, and the tree exploded in a shower of sparks and flames. The mare reared in panic, and try as she might, Emily couldn't hold on. She slid from the saddle, landing hard on the ground.

She rolled away from the horse's kicking hooves, her arms protectively over her head. The mare tore wild-eyed down the pasture, lost to her. Glancing up, she saw that Drew was almost upon her.

The buckskin's nostrils flared as they pounded toward the figure huddled on the soaked ground. Pulling back on the reins, Drew leaped from the horse, landing mere yards from Emily. She could see the lightning that flashed around them reflected by the rage in his steely eyes. Rain whipped at his face, but he advanced, unmindful of it. Emily scrambled to her feet and ran as she had never run in her life.

"Stop! You goddamn little sneak!" He raced after her. "If I have to stop you, boy, you'll regret it!"

Emily's lungs burned as she ran through the rain. It was nearly dark. She prayed she wouldn't stumble or slip. Tossing a glance backward, she saw that he was gaining on her. She willed herself to go faster. She had to!

He hit her from behind, his full weight slamming her to the ground. She lay unmoving, the breath knocked out of her. Her hat went flying, and long, blond hair spilled onto the sodden earth. Drew's hard fingers clamped brutally onto her wrists, and his body trapped hers beneath his own. As the air rushed back into her lungs, her eyes opened. Through the streaming rain, she beheld a look of startled fury in his glinting eyes. His mouth was open as if he had been about to speak and had forgotten what he was going to say.

Emily twisted her hands and tried to wriggle out from under him. In response, he jerked her arms up and pinned them between their bodies, still painfully gripping her wrists. She tried to kick at him, but he shifted his weight so that it was impossible for her to move. She glared at him fiercely. She wouldn't show her fear, nor would she admit that she had seen anything. He continued to regard her with a mixture of surprise and wild anger.

Emily couldn't endure Drew's furious gaze. It looked to her for all the world as if he intended to kill her there with the storm raging about them. Both of them were wet to the bone, and Emily began to be uncomfortably aware of the heat of his skin emanating through their cold, wet clothing. His body was hard against hers, calling to mind the passionate kiss they had shared at Fort Meade, sending alarming shivers over her chilled skin. She had to get away from him. His silent fury was intolerable. Her growing physical awareness of him was worse.

"Cat got your tongue?" she spat angrily to break the tension. "Let me up, this instant, you brute!"

His blue eyes narrowed. "What the hell are you doing poking your prissy little nose around my property?" he demanded, making no move to release her.

"I'm not here intentionally, I can assure you," she returned venomously.

A rock gouged sharply into her back. She tried to move away from it, but he wouldn't let her, pressing even closer to her. She could feel the muscles of his chest hard against her fists. The backs of his hands pressed intimately into her soft breasts.

"Why are you here, then?" he insisted roughly. "Tell me!" He gave her a shake that rattled her teeth.

Emily was becoming frightened now. She decided quickly that it would be imprudent to fence with him.

"I got lost on my way home from a waterfall," she told him, still uncomfortably aware that his face was but inches from her own. Rain dripped off his chin onto her neck. She turned her head to avoid his penetrating gaze.

"Look at me," he ordered tersely.

Reluctantly, Emily turned her eyes back to his.

"How could you possibly have gotten lost? Any idiot could follow that canyon!" A clap of thunder punctuated his angry words.

"I didn't follow the canyon, and I'm not an idiot!" she practically screamed at him. "Must we continue this interview in the middle of a thunderstorm?" she demanded.

To Emily's surprise, Drew looked up at the pouring rain as if he hadn't noticed it before. Abruptly, he rolled off her, hauling her to her feet with him. Before she could protest, he scooped her into his arms and whistled to his horse. As he strode through the rain to meet the animal, Emily sputtered incoherently. He thrust her roughly onto the buckskin's back and jumped up behind her.

"Where are you taking me?" she asked in alarm as his strong arms came around her.

"Shut up!" he commanded. His weight pressed her painfully into the saddle horn.

"You're hurting me!" she retorted, jabbing her elbow

into his stomach to give herself room. "You probably broke half my ribs jumping on me like that!"

He jerked her closer against him. "Just sit still and shut up!" he ordered again.

Emily drew breath to protest his rough treatment, but he squeezed her hard in warning. Instead she threw him a withering look as he urged the horse into a bone-jarring trot.

Chapter 9

It was nearly dark, and the rain was falling in sheets. In the light of the flashing storm, Emily saw that they were riding back up the valley. They rounded a small outcropping of rock and made for a wooden cabin tucked up against the trees. The horse slowed and headed for a large shed to the left of it.

In the shed, Drew dismounted and unceremoniously dragged Emily off the buckskin. He pushed her into a corner, towering over her.

"If you so much as move an inch, I promise you'll be very sorry," he ground out between clenched teeth.

"What are you going to do?" she shot back. "Scalp me?"

Their eyes locked for a moment in mutual challenge before Drew turned his attention to his horse. She watched him remove the bridle and give the horse a rapid rubdown. She looked around her. There were a couple of stalls, a hay mow, and a trough visible. The building was not enclosed, and, to her left, she could see a fenced corral. Huddled at one end, their heads turned away from the rain, was a small herd of horses. How could he leave those poor animals outside in such a storm? She whipped back to glare accusingly at Drew. His back was to her, but he answered her unspoken criticism.

"They're Indian ponies. They're used to the weather. You'd do better to worry about how you're going to explain what you're doing here than how I care for my livestock." His voice was hard.

Emily shivered as much with anger as with the cold. Despite the hot resentment coursing through her, goosebumps prickled her flesh and she ached all over. She probably had several bruises from her fall and from being tackled by Drew. Thinking about how late it was and how worried Sam and Maggie must be only compounded her frustration. She closed her eyes and took a deep breath, trying to gain control over her emotions. She wasn't going to give Drew the satisfaction of reducing her to either a tirade or tears.

His horse taken care of, Drew reached out and encircled Emily's wrist in a painful grip. She wrenched away from him, but he didn't let go.

"I've about had it with you yanking me around!" she exclaimed.

"Can't you tell when it's wiser to just shut up?"

"Not when you're bullying me like this! Who do you think you are? Ow!"

He dragged her roughly along behind him as he ran toward the cabin. She stumbled and slipped along behind him, hating him more with each passing second. When they reached the porch, he opened the heavy wooden door and pushed her into a cold, dark room.

Almost instantly, a match flared and the soft glow from a kerosene lamp lit the room. Drew's face looked hard, all angles and planes in the lamplight, his wet hair plastered to his head, his eyes snapping angrily, but he was indisputably handsome. Emily cursed herself for thinking so and pulled her arms close to her body, shivering.

Drew reached a hand toward her cheek, but she shied away. He grasped her chin in his hand, then slid the backs of his fingers down her neck. He felt her rapid pulse as his fingers skimmed her throat, but he also felt the chill in her white skin before she batted his hand away.

"Don't touch me," she ordered.

In response, he pushed her further into the room.

"I said stop it!" She jumped away from him. He advanced toward her, and she retreated until he'd herded her across the room to stand in front of a stone fireplace.

"Don't move," he warned her, kneeling to arrange wood from a large box for a fire.

Within a minute, bright flames were licking at the twigs and logs, sending a red glow into the room and promising a welcome warmth. Drew rose and pushed Emily close to the fireplace.

"Don't drip on the fire," he snarled at her.

"If you touch me or push me or poke me again I'm going to scream," she threatened.

"Scream away," he drawled, deliberately placing his hand in the middle of her back and pushing her closer to the fire. When she screamed, he smiled with mean satisfaction before moving away from her.

The fire felt wonderful, but Emily couldn't afford to relax. She turned her back to it and watched Drew as he went to a large chest at the foot of a big oak bedstead and lifted the top. He rummaged around, removing several pieces of clothing. He turned to a wardrobe and took out several towels and a comb. The expression on his face remained one of controlled fury as he stalked back over to her and threw the items down on the trestle table that occupied the center of the large room.

"You'd better get out of those clothes and dry off or you'll catch pneumonia," he told her gruffly. "You can wear these," he said, pointing to the pile on the table. "Here." He threw her a towel.

Emily caught it, then stood with it in her hands. She looked around for a screen.

"Are you going to stand there dripping on my floor all night?" Drew demanded sharply.

Emily found her voice at last.

"I'm certainly not going to undress in front of you!" she exclaimed indignantly.

"Excuse me, Miss Parker, for not having a dressing room available for your convenience," he said sarcastically. "Maybe the next time you decide to drop in on someone uninvited, you'll remember this embarrassing experience and think better of it."

"You insulting bastard!" Emily exploded at him. "I am not going to disrobe in front of you. You'll have to find your amusements elsewhere!'' She spun to face the fire.

"What makes you think you have anything that would 'amuse' me?'' he asked coldly.

Emily straightened her shoulders and turned slowly to face him again.

"My impression was that you had more than a passing interest in my physical charms, Mr. Rutledge,'' she taunted before she could stop herself.

"Perhaps you naively assumed that I reciprocated your feelings of desire toward me,'' he pointed out smoothly.

Emily stared at him in stunned silence for a moment before her pride prodded her to respond.

"You presume a great deal. Perhaps you have mistaken passionate dislike for passion of another sort. Your reputedly finely trained legal mind might lead you to conclude that it's highly unlikely that I would desire a man who has subjected me to public humiliation and physical abuse.'' Her voice shook with controlled emotion.

"Since when have either women or passion followed a logical course?''

"I hadn't thought it possible, but I think I've come to dislike you quite a lot more than I did after our last encounter.''

He smiled unpleasantly and walked away from her to the end of the room where the bed and his clothing were. Stripping off his sodden shirt and wet moccasins, he said, "If you don't want me to do it for you, you'd better have your clothes changed by the time I'm finished. You've got some explaining to do, and I don't aim to wait all night to hear it.''

Emily watched Drew's back as he toweled his torso dry before the open wardrobe. He turned his head over his shoulder and raised an eyebrow at her.

"I mean it,'' he said crisply. "I didn't start out this day with a whole lot of patience, and what I had is long gone.'' He unbuckled his belt and flipped open the buttons on his denim pants, his eyes never leaving Emily's. The waistband sagged away from his waist in the back. "Look all

you want, sweetheart, but if you don't want me to return
the privilege, you'd better see to your own attire.''

She watched in fascination as he turned his head and
shucked off his pants. She'd never seen a grown man naked, even from the back, and the sight transfixed her. Furious as she was, there was no denying that he had a
magnificent body. She felt heat flood across her cheeks yet
again and belatedly responded to his threat.

"You may enjoy exhibiting yourself in public but I
don't, and you will not . . .'' He pulled on a dry pair of
trousers. She whirled away from him and started fumbling
with the wet buttons of her shirt.

"I'll do what I damn well please. You don't give me
orders in my own house!'' He reached for a shirt and
shrugged into it.

One of Emily's buttons wasn't cooperating. She cast a
look over her shoulder and saw that he was nearly dressed.
"You will not undress me, do you hear? You have no
right to treat me this way!'' She jerked at the button and
it came off with a pop, landing in the fire. "Damn!'' she
swore, slipping out of the shirt. Without removing her
damp camisole, she reached back to grab the shirt he'd
dropped on the table. Instead, her hand contacted solidly
with Drew's stomach.

He didn't so much as flinch. "If you expect people to
respect your rights, then you'd better learn to respect
theirs. You're the one who was trespassing today, and''—
he paused to grab Emily from behind—"you could have
been badly hurt wandering around in the hills alone.'' He
pinned her arms and undid her belt and the top button of
her pants. She bent forward to deter him, but he pulled
her up easily, hooking her elbows behind her back in one
of his. "And there are reasons why I don't like people
hanging around my place.'' He grunted when she caught
him in the chest with a sharp elbow, but he continued to
work the buttons. "And when you make somebody as angry as you've made me you can expect to suffer the consequences.'' He tugged the wet denim over her hips,
dragging her drawers along with the pants. He paused to
yank off her boots and stockings.

"Stop it!" Emily screamed, pressing her legs together in an attempt to keep her undergarment and some shred of her modesty. "For God's sake, what kind of a lout are you? You make yourself angry. I think you like being angry because it gives you an excuse to act like a savage!"

"Wrong choice of words, sweetheart," he growled, removing her pants and drawers with a final tug and tossing them onto a chair. "I don't need an excuse to act like a savage when I practically am one, do I?" He spun her around to face him.

His eyes were hard and cold as she met his gaze. "I didn't mean savage Indians, you idiot. I meant barbarian." Her only consolation in the tight embrace he held her in was that he couldn't see her nakedness. Then she felt his hand settle onto her bare hip. "Get your hands off me!"

He moved his hand up her back and scrunched up her camisole. When she tried to push away from him, he used the space between their bodies to slip his other hand against her midriff and push the damp cotton up over her breasts. In a trice, he had it over her head and had thrown it on the chair behind her.

It was too much for Emily. She was standing naked in Drew's arms, angry beyond expression, mortified as she had never been in her life, and faced with a dilemma. She could stand still where he couldn't really see her, or she could try to break away from him, guaranteeing that he'd get an eyeful. When his hands started roaming over her back and hips, she added another element to the equation. He could feel her if she stayed in his arms, and she could feel him. His arms held her tightly, and he'd wedged her bare feet between his own, pressing her legs together at her knees to keep her from struggling. She felt him along the whole length of her body, the smooth denim of his pants against her naked thighs, and the soft flannel of his shirt against her bared breasts. She raised her eyes to his in mute appeal.

Something more than anger blazed in his eyes when they dropped to her parted lips. He started to dip toward her, then pulled back. "You're quite a handful, aren't

you?'' he asked, his voice suddenly thick. ''And we both
lied about not wanting each other. Right now I don't know
whether it'd be more satisfying to shake the stuffing out
of you or to kiss it out.''

''Don't kiss me, Drew. I don't want this,'' she said,
shaking her head and looking away.

He stood silently, his hands caressing her back for a
long minute. Then he tangled one hand in her damp hair
and tugged on it so that she was forced to look him in the
eye.

''I don't want it like this, either, Emily. I've never made
love to a woman in anger and I don't intend to start now.
When we make love, you'll want it as much as I do.''

''You are insufferably arrogant,'' she enunciated carefully.

''Yeah, I am, and you're a prissy little pain in the butt.
I don't even know why you get under my skin, but I'm
going to pass on the lovemaking just now. Unfortunately
for you, I might not be able to pass up the temptation to
administer a well-deserved wallop,'' he said tautly,
smacking her backside sharply.

She tensed, swatting at his hands behind her back.
''Don't even think it,'' she answered in a controlled voice.
''I'm guilty only of getting lost in all those twisting canyons and dark hills, and I deserve nothing of the sort. I
don't understand why you're treating me this way. What
have I done to earn this kind of humiliation?''

Drew seemed to gain control of his temper at last. He
reached behind him, grabbing a skirt off the table. ''I'll
tell you once you're decent.''

''I am not indecent!'' Emily exclaimed. ''I'm just n—''

''Naked,'' he finished for her. He tipped back his head
and flicked a bold look down at her breasts where they
rested against his chest. She pressed into him so that only
the tops of them were revealed to his insolent gaze.

''No, I'd have to say you've got me there.'' He looked
back up into her green-brown eyes. ''You're a damn sight
above decent, at that.''

Her response was muffled by the skirt he thrust over her
head. By the time she had her arms through it and was

holding it above her breasts, he had the shirt in hand. With a swift tug he pulled the skirt to her waist and dropped the shirt into her hands. She whirled away from him and had it on in a second. The clothes were warm and dry, made of light-colored leather as soft as cotton and beautifully decorated with colorful beadwork, and she'd never been so appreciative of clothing in her life. She figured Drew had seen her breasts but she was so relieved to be out of his embrace that she hardly cared anymore. She'd be lucky if she got away from him with a shred of dignity left.

While Drew tended the fire, she collected her wet clothes and draped them on the backs of the wooden chairs that surrounded the table, moving them so that they could catch the drying heat of the fire. The clothes steamed as the fire roared up, filling the room with warmth. The sooner her clothes were dry, the sooner she'd be on her way. She wasn't going to spend one minute that she didn't have to alone with Drew Rutledge.

Outside, the lightning and thunder continued and rain hammered at the roof and windows. Watching him move about the room, lighting more lamps and swabbing at the puddles they'd dripped with the wet towels, she thought he didn't look so angry now, but she knew that his temper could be set off by the slightest remark. In the red-gold light of the fire and lamps, pushing a towel across the floor with his bare foot, he didn't look especially threatening. No more dangerous than a cannon cooling between rounds, she reflected.

He collected the towels and dumped them into a bucket by the sink in the kitchen area that occupied one end of the cabin. Then he turned to Emily, gesturing to one of two dark red arm chairs that were arranged near the fireplace.

"Sit down," he said grimly.

Emily sat reluctantly, drawing her bare feet up under her skirt. He dragged the other chair close to her so that only a few inches separated them. He sat down and calmly scrutinized her face. She held his blue gaze unwaveringly.

His voice was cold and unemotional when he spoke.

"I want to know everything you've done today. If you

withhold anything, or lie, you put your life, your family's lives, and a lot of other people's at risk. I don't think you want to do that," he told her.

His stoic expression was more frightening than his anger had been.

"Are you threatening me again?" Her back stiffened against the upholstered chair. "What are you going to do? Kill Sam and Maggie and the children? Are you serious?"

Seeing the flash of anger in her eyes, he held up his hand in warning before she could continue.

"I don't want a tirade now. I want the truth. You can tell me willingly, or I can force you to tell me," he threatened calmly.

Emily's pupils widened. "You really are a barbarian, aren't you? Attila the Hun could have used men like you."

"Emily, this isn't the time for jokes. This is important. The future of the Lakota people and everyone who lives in the Black Hills is at stake. Now just tell me what you did today."

Her eyes narrowed. "It seems to me that what you did today is more at issue. That's the real problem here, isn't it?"

"Don't question me, Emily. Tell me what you did," he ordered softly. "Now."

She took a deep breath and decided to get it over with.

"Maggie and I planned to visit the falls. Sam suggested it," she began, and she told him everything that had happened. She didn't mention the eagle, because it hardly seemed relevant, and she had forgotten the dream she had. She told him how she got lost in the hills, and how the storm came up, and how she'd heard some strange noises. Then she stopped. It was difficult to go on, even though they both knew what she had seen.

"Then what?" Drew prompted gently. "You have to tell me, Emily."

She closed her eyes for a second, then looked him squarely in the eye.

"Then I saw your Indian friends unloading your stolen guns and supplies!" She looked at him challengingly.

He gazed back blankly. He'd been right; she'd seen the

men unloading the wagons into the caves, and he was relieved she'd admitted it. But what was this nonsense about stolen guns? Why was she glaring at him as if he were a mean old rattler poised to bite a small child?

Then it hit him. She must have overheard something about the guns that had been bound for Fort Meade. She thought he was involved with the stolen shipment. She thought he was a thief. And probably a murderer. He struggled with his temper for several moments, then forced himself to relax and breathe evenly.

"What makes you think they were unloading stolen guns?" he finally asked.

"I saw the crates," she said as if it were obvious, "with the words Seventh Cavalry, U.S. Army, clearly printed on the sides."

"Ah." Drew paused. "Did you see inside the crates?"

"No, of course I didn't. Do you think I walked right up to your henchmen and asked to inspect their cargo? I'm not that bold, Mr. Rutledge!" she stated emphatically.

"Have you ever seen guns crated up?"

"No." What did that have to do with anything?

"How can you be so sure there were guns in the crates?"

"What else would it be? What are you getting at? I don't see what good it will do you to deny taking the guns after I've already seen them."

Emily searched his face for any clue to his thoughts. There was none.

"You didn't see any guns. You saw crates. You're awfully good at jumping to conclusions based on scant facts." Drew was faintly derisive, but calmer.

"What else would have been in stolen army crates?" she asked, beginning to see some flaws in her reasoning. She wasn't ready to let him off the hook, though.

"How do you know the crates were stolen?" Drew asked her.

"Because . . . because they said Seventh Cavalry on them, and whatever you and your Sioux friends may be, you're certainly not the U.S. Army."

"No we're not, but you don't suppose it's possible that

you're mistaken in your conclusions, do you?'' Drew suggested. He regarded her intently.

Emily fidgeted nervously. She turned to stare at the fire, thinking as she watched the flames leap and dance. Part of her wanted to believe that he had nothing to do with stealing anything from the army, yet the evidence indicated he might have. Sam himself had said that Drew ran a fine line with the law, and she really didn't know how trustworthy he was. Could she take him at his word? Was it possible that there was another reasonable explanation?

"I'll allow I *might* be mistaken. What was in the crates?'' she asked, her voice unsteady. "And I'll know if you're lying.''

Drew looked into her dark eyes and knew that if he told her, he'd be putting her in a certain amount of danger. Yet if he didn't tell her, all his work could be destroyed before it was finished, because he was sure she wouldn't keep quiet if she thought he was stealing from the army. More people would suffer, the people that had adopted him and treated him as one of their own, the people who were his family now. And Emily would hate him.

"What's in the crates?'' she repeated.

He answered her simply.

"Blankets. Grain. Clothing. Supplies for the winter. All legally purchased. All packed in legally purchased army surplus crating.''

Emily looked at him in astonishment.

"Purchased by whom?'' she finally asked suspiciously.

He sighed and sat back in his chair.

"By my father mostly, and a few other people from back East who sympathize with the Indians and who protest the theft of Indian land and the thoughtless slaughter of the game.''

"These supplies are for the Indians at the agencies?''

"They're for Indians, all right, but not the ones on the reservations. I've been helping the people who've refused to report to the agencies. People who are having a hard time feeding their children and old people.'' He frowned. "Do you understand what that means?''

"I think so,'' she said in a subdued voice. "I overheard

Sam saying he thought you might be doing something that wasn't quite on the right side of the law.''

"What I'm doing is very much illegal, Emily. There's no doubt about it,'' he said seriously. "And it's dangerous.''

"How illegal is it to feed and clothe starving people?'' she asked quietly.

Drew rose and went to the fire where he stood gazing into the flames. "It's a treasonous offense for an American citizen to arm and supply enemies of the United States, no matter how destitute they are.'' He swung around abruptly and stared at her, daring her to challenge him.

Emily sensed the suppressed anger in him, and knew for once that he wasn't angry with her. She sat back in her chair and waited for him to go on.

"The Indians who aren't on the reservations are considered hostiles by the federal government. Since most of the game has been killed off or driven into the high mountains, the Indians almost never have enough to eat. There aren't any hides for clothes and tipis. Even on the reservations, times are hard. The government takes their guns and their horses so they can't fight, but they can't hunt, either. Many of the agents are incompetent, and others are corrupt. They give the Indians a fraction of what the treaties promise and then the rations consist of rotting meat, rancid flour, and whiskey to make Indians oblivious to what they've lost.

"But to give aid to the hostiles is a crime. And I don't feel like I have a choice. What I do doesn't help much, but it's saved some, and I have to continue. Since the fort was placed so nearby, it's become a risky line of work. And now you know enough about it that you could be in trouble, too. It's a crime to conceal a felony, Emily.'' He sighed and his shoulders sagged. "Do you understand now why I've been so angry with you? There's a lot at stake here.''

She looked away from him. She hadn't known what he had at risk when she'd stumbled onto his land, and she didn't know what to think. Never had she had to consider a course of action that put her at odds with the law. Never before had she had to weigh the consequences of acting according to her conscience so carefully.

"What are you going to do, Emily, now that you have to face the responsibility of knowing my secrets?" He walked toward her, then crouched in front of her, a hand on each armrest, his gaze unwavering. "What are you going to do?"

She leaned back into the chair, but held his eyes. "I won't say anything. To anyone. Not even Sam and Maggie," she said quietly. "I hope you'll trust me."

"Why should I trust you? We hardly know each other. Why would you do this for me?" The intensity in his expression intimidated Emily. "You've had your suspicions about me for longer than tonight. Why the sudden change?"

She looked away into the dark corners beyond his shoulder, avoiding his eyes. "I didn't understand. When Sam said he thought you were doing something illegal I assumed it must be something wrong. What you're doing doesn't seem wrong and I don't want to do anything that will harm innocent people."

"The government doesn't think they're innocent," he pressed.

"I won't say anything to anyone, not even Sam and Maggie. Please try to trust me."

His blue eyes caught the light and blazed with silver streaks. "I don't have a lot of choice, so I hope you mean that." He paused for a long time. "I've been angry for another reason, too, Emily. You could easily have been killed today. If you'd made it fifty yards farther from where I caught you, Yellow Thunder would have shot you. I don't know how you slipped past the other lookouts to get that close, but you took a mighty big risk. Have you got any idea how I would have felt trying to explain to Sam that one of my men shot his sister, thinking she was a spying boy?" He shook his head. "You scared me, Emily. You may be a pain in the backside, but I don't like the idea of you getting hurt. It makes me mad that you almost were, and it makes me madder that you might be in danger for what you know now. It made me so mad I wanted to hurt you myself, and I'm not proud of that. And I'm . . . I'm sorry if I hurt you." His eyes blazed again in the lamplight.

Suddenly Emily remembered the eagle at the falls. She caught her breath and stared at Drew.

"What's wrong?" he asked, frowning.

"I just remembered something I saw today. By the waterfall. It was nothing, I suppose, but . . ." She hesitated. "Do eagles have blue eyes? I thought it was odd, but . . ."

There was a knock on the door. Neither of them moved, but the intensity in Drew's expression startled Emily.

"You saw the eagle? At the falls?" he whispered.

She nodded as the knocking on the door grew insistent. Neither of them moved until a voice called loudly over the noise of the storm.

Drew finally rose and went to the door.

It was one of the Indians, and he stepped in out of the rain and spoke quietly to Drew for several minutes. Emily adjusted her clothes, turning wet sides to the fire. Her underthings were nearly dry and she thought her shirt would be dry before too long.

After the Indian left, she turned to find Drew looking thoughtfully into the fire. The thunder and lightning had receded, but rain still fell steadily, drumming on the cabin roof.

"My clothes will dry enough to wear in an hour or so," she said aloud. Drew seemed to take no notice of her. "Will you be able to lend me a horse? Sam and Maggie must be worried sick by now. In another hour or two they'll probably think I've been drowned or struck by lightning."

Drew looked up instantly.

"You aren't going anywhere tonight," he announced with finality.

"What? Of course I am! I certainly can't stay here!" she exclaimed.

"I don't see why not."

"Well, it wouldn't be proper," she said, a blush creeping into her cheeks.

"After seeing each other naked, you're worried about

what's proper?" he asked with an amused grin. "I'm sorry Sam and Maggie will be worried, but there's nothing I can do about that. This storm has dumped a lot of water in a short time, and the creeks are flooding. You'd never make it home if you left, so don't bother arguing. Let's see if there's anything to eat here," he finished, dismissing her objection. He started rummaging in a cupboard.

Emily chafed at his dictatorial tone as she glanced around the cabin, trying to avoid looking at the big double bed at one end. Things had a tendency to get out of hand all too easily with Drew Rutledge around. She had to get home.

"I don't think it's such a good idea for me to stay here," she protested.

"It's a little late to worry about that," Drew pointed out, chuckling in amusement. "I can't think when I've heard a more gracious acceptance of my offer to lend a lady my bed."

Emily's eyes widened with shock.

"I didn't accept any such offer, and if I have to stay here I'll just sleep in one of these chairs by the fire," she said nervously.

"Relax. I don't have to share the bed with you. I won't stay, if that'll make you more comfortable," he offered more generously than she knew. "I usually sleep in the camp when the wagons are in, and I have to go down there to check on something anyway."

Emily experienced a sudden attack of frontier panic. What if lightning struck the cabin? What if a wild animal came prowling out of the hills? Her imagination couldn't begin to describe what might occur if the rest of the day was anything to go by.

"You mean you're going to leave me alone here?" she said with alarm. "How far away would you be?"

"Only about half a mile."

"Half a mile! What if something happens?" she cried. "I wouldn't know what to do!"

Drew threw her an exasperated glance. He'd expected her to gratefully accept his offer.

"I doubt seriously if anything will happen."

She looked at him balefully, trying to determine the lesser of two evils.

"Do you want me to stay?"

Emily felt torn as she had the night he'd asked her to dance with him in the darkness. She was inviting disaster if she said yes, but she was afraid. Too much had happened that day, and she didn't want to be left alone, regardless of the alternative. Looking into his blue eyes that were alive with moving, shifting lights, she slowly nodded her head.

"Yes," she said so softly he barely heard her. "Stay." A little louder she repeated, "I'll sleep in the chair."

An hour later Drew lay propped on one elbow on top of his wide bed, long legs stretched out before him, pretending to read. Instead, he was watching the woman who sat dozing in one of his armchairs before the fire. Her bright hair fanned out against the maroon upholstery reflecting the red glow from the flames. Her head was thrown back, revealing the long column of her throat and the classic line of her jaw. One leg was tucked up beneath her, the other bare foot resting on the floor. Below the hem of the ivory-colored skirt, a shapely calf was visible. As she fell deeper into sleep, the nervous tension eased from her muscles, and she looked alluring and inviting. She shifted, and the skirt hiked higher on her leg, above her knee. Drew's eyes darkened and he sucked in a sharp breath. He rose, knowing he had to talk to Yellow Thunder. He welcomed the opportunity; if he stayed, he didn't think he could resist the temptation Emily presented much longer. As it was, all he could think about was the way she'd felt when he'd held her naked in his arms.

He blew out the lamps, grabbed an oilcloth poncho, and made for the door. As an afterthought, he picked up a blanket and walked to the sleeping woman. Gently, he draped it around her. He placed a hand on the soft golden hair that spread across the armrest. With a muffled oath, he withdrew and quietly slipped outside into the rain.

The interview with Yellow Thunder was disturbing. Recent messages had come from Canada that some of the bands there had received generous promises from unknown parties in exchange for leading an uprising to reclaim the Black Hills. Secret messengers were beginning to visit the reservation communities, trying to gain support for the rebellion. Unfortunately, there was no trace of the leaders behind the foolhardy scheme. At Pine Ridge and Rosebud, the chiefs and tribal councils were concerned. They knew that renewed warfare would only give the army a much-wanted excuse to completely eradicate the Sioux tribes. The chiefs feared the army might be involved, or possibly some of the corrupt agents at the agencies along the Missouri River, and they wanted Drew to use his contacts to see if he could find out what was going on. Drew had a queer feeling about this plot, a marked sense of foreboding. It could mean the end of the Lakota people if it were successful, and the thought chilled him. In the morning, he would ride for the Cheyenne River Agency.

As he left the Indian camp, Yellow Thunder had pulled him aside away from the others.

"I don't want to alarm you needlessly, *kola*," he had said, "but there's a rumor that a reward has been set for your hair. We don't know who's behind it, or if it's related to the rebellion plot, but you should be careful. Men will come looking for you with the promise of gold to spur them. Take care, my friend."

Returning the buckskin to the shed, Drew's thoughts turned to Emily. He cursed the luck that brought her into his life at this time, for he was pretty certain now that she was the woman from his vision. He had feelings for her that he'd never known before, feelings that he wanted to explore further, but it was impossible. He couldn't offer her the security and the safety that she needed to trust him. He could sense that she was powerfully drawn to him, and he knew that her feelings frightened her, probably more than he did himself. Only in the sanctified bonds of marriage would she be free to relax and give the love he so desired, and he couldn't bind her to him knowing that he might be killed.

Worse, Emily herself was now in danger should anyone discover what she knew. Whoever was behind the rebellion plot was ruthless, and he doubted that the man would hesitate to use a woman if it would serve his ends. The best thing he could do would be to leave her alone, avoiding her completely. Maybe after this mess was settled, there might be a chance for them. Until then, and assuming he could keep the authorities off his back a little longer over the supply operation, there was no point in torturing himself by seeing her and not feeling free to pursue her affections. It was an agonizing decision, but he didn't feel he had any real choice in the matter. Drew leaned in weary resignation against the wooden planks, staring unseeing into the rainy night.

Suddenly, a woman's scream rent the darkness. Drew looked up in terror and raced toward the cabin.

Chapter 10

Once again, she saw the eagle and the buffalo lead the horseback procession, praying to the four quarters, praying for mercy, praying with tears, pleading for pity. Once again, the music started and brightly costumed dancers reeled in the red glow of flames. The song of celebration rose into the night. Joy filled her heart as she beheld the ecstatic abandon of the people.

Then the stars were blotted out again and the earth trembled. From nowhere, a dark rider appeared on a rearing red horse. He rode into the circle, scattering the people before him, destroying all in his path. The buffalo and the eagle stood still at the center of the ring. The rider advanced upon them menacingly. He turned his head, laughing cruelly and heartlessly, and she saw that his face was a mask. The painted mask smiled benignly, but the laughter sent dread creeping down her spine. He turned again to the eagle and the buffalo. She saw the blue glint of the eagle's eye as the bird spread his mighty wings and rose. Something flashed cold in the firelight, and she watched in horror as the rider drew back his bow and sent a golden arrow straight into the eagle's breast.

No! she screamed, No! You can't kill him! But it was to no avail. The eagle threw back his head and cried piercingly, his death song shattering the night. He began to fall. She couldn't bear to look a moment longer. Turning into the darkness, she fled, grief tearing at her very soul.

* * *

As Drew reached the porch, the door was flung wide and Emily hurtled straight into his arms. He almost fell, she hit him so hard. She was screaming in terror, tears coursing down her cheeks.

"He shot the eagle!" she cried in agony. "The eagle that was at the falls! No! It can't be! All the people ran away, and he shot the eagle!" she wailed. "I couldn't help! How could he do it? He was so beautiful," she sobbed incoherently, pounding on Drew's chest. "Let me go! I have to get away!" She struggled violently, but was held firm.

Drew was thunderstruck. The eagle at the falls! She *had* seen it! Excitement pumped through his veins.

"Emily!" he shouted. "Stop it! You're hysterical!" He grabbed at her flailing hands before she could scratch his face.

"Let me go!" she screamed again in terror. "He'll come after me! Let me go!"

Drew pulled her roughly into his arms, crushing her to him to still her thrashing. He shook her but she continued to sob and fight him, screaming to be released.

"Emily! Stop! I have to know what you dreamed. Wake up!" He shook her again. Still she cried and fought, her eyes wild with fright.

His hand came up to the back of her head. Sliding his fingers into her silky hair, he jerked her head back and forced her to look up into his eyes.

"Stop it! Wake up!" he commanded, his face mere inches above hers.

Gazing into his blue eyes, Emily thought she again beheld the eagle. A keening wail rose from her throat, torn from the depths of her soul.

Drew instantly bent his head, covering her mouth with his own. The screaming stopped abruptly as he ground his lips against hers. He could feel her chest heaving against the tight circle of his arms. One last surge of energy gave her the strength to desperately push away from him. She almost succeeded in breaking his grip, but he held her firmly, his lips locked to hers. Finally, her muscles went lax, and she sagged weakly against him. He maintained the embrace, making sure she was awake. Then he slowly lifted his head, still holding her tightly.

Emily looked about in confusion. She didn't know where she was or what time it was. Her heart hammered wildly, and she felt a terrible anguish.

"Emily?" Drew asked gently.

"What happened?" She gasped softly, making no move to free herself.

"You had a nightmare," he told her carefully. "Something about an eagle. Do you remember what happened?" He watched her eyes intently.

A tear spilled down her cheek as she closed her eyes against the frightful memory. "Yes," she whispered. "There was an eagle, and a rider shot him with a golden arrow. He was so beautiful! It was horrible to watch, and it wasn't just a dream! It seemed real."

Suddenly her eyes flew open, locking on Drew's scintillating blue gaze. For a moment, looking into his face, she saw the eagle. The vivid images in her mind jumbled with reality, and she saw Drew instead of the eagle standing before the masked rider, bow poised to shoot. The thought of him fallen with a bright arrow in his chest brought forth yet another cry of agony. Then she realized it wasn't real. Her relief that he was alive, holding her securely, knew no limits. How short life seemed, how tenuous, in that moment. Before he could ask the questions that burned in his mind, she flung her arms around his neck and pressed as closely to him as she could.

"Hold me!" she begged. "Don't leave me alone! Hold me tightly!" She buried her face against his neck, clinging to him.

Drew's questions dissolved in the whirling cascade of sensation her embrace aroused. It was too much for him. His resolve to distance himself from her evaporated. His arms tightened possessively around her, and he smoothed her fine hair with his hand.

"Shhh," he whispered softly, wiping the tears from her cheeks. "I'm here now. No one can hurt you."

As he rocked her in his arms, he knew that was a lie. He could hurt her. Deeply. Try as he might, he couldn't stem the turbulent wash of conflicting emotions that warred within him. Even as he told her he would keep her safe, fierce desire welled up in him, and he acknowledged that his feelings for her at that moment were far from simply protective. He struggled to regain composure, to put her away from him, but he couldn't. The feel of her softly yielding body, the fresh rain scent in her hair, and the first stirrings of fragile trust between them fired his blood. Since he had first held her in his arms that hot, dusty afternoon in Deadwood, he'd thought often of what it would be like to have her come to him, eager for his touch. And now she was so close. He hated himself for his weakness, but with her pliant body pressed against his, he knew he couldn't deny his need. He stopped moving and gazed down at her, his eyes dark with suppressed desire.

Emily sensed a change in him and looked up. For long seconds, his wild, unearthly blue eyes held hers. Fear clambered in her mind when she recognized the intense hunger he sought to control, but it was mixed with a deep curiosity and longing that she couldn't dismiss. Her heart beating rapidly, Emily felt an answering tremor of response shudder through her, but she hesitated.

"Drew?" she whispered. "I don't . . ."

"Shhh," he murmured. "Don't say anything."

"But . . ." she paused. The tiny circles his thumbs were tracing on the back of her neck entranced her. He was pressing his hips against her as well. Shivers of alarm joined the array of rich sensations dancing through her body.

"Drew, I don't want to . . . you know. It's not right." She tried to move away from him, but he held her close with a strong hand in the small of her back.

"I want you, Emily, like I've never wanted any woman." He folded his arms around her, crushing her against his chest. "And I know you want me, too."

"I'm not sure I even like you," she countered. But when his fingers skimmed down her back and he pulled her hips toward him, bolts of delicious excitement shot through her.

"You want me anyway," he whispered against her ear.

"But it's not right."

"Is it so wrong?" he asked, tipping her head back against his arm. He dropped a series of tiny kisses along her jawline, ending below her ear, and heard her release a shuddering breath. "Does it feel wrong when I do that? How do you feel inside?" He ran a finger down her backbone and pushed her hips against his again. "Feel how much I want you, Emily. Feel the fire between us."

"Oh!" she gasped, squirming in his arms, trying to put some distance between them. But Drew swiftly silenced her protest with a kiss and lifted her into his arms. Carrying her through the open door into the firelit room, he shrugged off his poncho and kicked the door closed. He strode with her in his arms to the bed, where he laid her gently on the quilt, her head resting on his pillow. Her luminous green-brown eyes shone in the dim light. Emily sat up. "Drew, what are you doing?" she asked, feeling a bit dazed.

As he lay down beside her, he pressed her back against the pillows. "Relax, sweetheart," he drawled softly. Then, cupping her cheeks in his hands, he kissed her deeply with all the desire he'd been holding in check since he'd first met her. When the bold thrusts of his tongue elicited a groan from her, he felt a surge of satisfaction and heightened desire. His hand slid to her breast, cupping the firm fullness there, his warm fingers teasing her nipple into a hard bud. Emily moaned softly, knowing she couldn't stop him, knowing she didn't want to stop him. His hands moved to her waist and pushed the soft leather upward, lifting her. Quickly he pulled her shirt over her head, and his hands captured her soft, rose-crested breasts. Pressing her back against the pillows, he caressed her and kissed her, revelling in her beauty.

Overwhelmed by delicious sensations she'd never before experienced, Emily slid her hands inside Drew's shirt, feeling the corded bands of his hard chest muscles beneath her palms. He was so firm, so hard, so different from anything she had ever known. When he bent his head to her breast, she gasped as he took one nipple into his mouth. She started to push him away, but somehow she ended up holding his head to her, wondering at the new sensation. His mouth moved to her other breast, leaving a searing line across her pale flesh where his tongue caressed her.

As he kissed her breasts, Drew's hands slid across the satiny skin at her waist, then encircled her, loosening the ties that held her skirt. He was eager to see and touch all of her. Emily felt a moment's panic as he pushed the ivory leather low on her hips. She tensed, and he withdrew his hands. Instead, he removed his own shirt, inviting her hands to trail irresistibly through the light brown hair on his chest, then drop to his flat, hard belly. He took her again in his arms, and Emily gasped. Every place he touched burned as if with fever, and the ache deep inside her grew more intense. When Drew's hands pushed at her skirt again, she grabbed his wrists and brought them up to cup her face.

"Let me see you, Emily," he whispered against her mouth.

"I've never . . . I mean, no one's ever . . ."

One of his hands traced down her arm to come to rest at her waist. "I know, sweetheart, it's okay. You're beautiful, and I want to see you. I want to touch you." He kissed her deeply. "Touch *me*, Emily."

He guided her hands to his back while they kissed and worked her skirt down over her hips slowly, exploring her stomach and hips while she kneaded and caressed his back. At length, she let him lift her and slide the skirt down her legs, though she raised one knee protectively, turning slightly to her side.

Drew caught his breath at her beauty as she lay naked before him, her pale limbs glowing pink in the firelight.

"Relax, Emily," he said, easing her knee down. "I won't hurt you."

He caressed her smooth thighs and the soft skin of her stomach, his hands moving ever closer to the golden triangle between her legs. His lips pressed against her throat, and he felt her tremble in his arms. His lips returned to hers, and as his mouth again tasted the moist sweetness there, his fingers slid into the soft folds between her legs. She moaned softly but didn't stop him. For endless minutes, his fingers inflamed her desire, bringing her to the brink of passionate release, her hips arching to meet his hand.

His hands and mouth left her heated flesh, but only for a moment, as he rose to strip his pants away. Emily's eyes widened at the sight of the firm length of him. His skin, bronzed by the firelight, stretched over the hard muscles of his flanks and strong thighs. As he turned, white scars gleamed on his broad back, over his shoulder blades. Otherwise, he was perfect. He stood before her, a warrior from a different age, dark and confident, his power strong, leashed by an iron will. Her eyes met his, and the raw desire that lit them caused her heart to tumble madly.

He came back to her and lay down beside her, allowing her to get used to the feel of his bare flesh against hers. She lay stiffly for a moment, but the gentle sweep of his hand along her arm and the soft kisses he pressed to her forehead soon melted her resistance. Tentatively, she ran her hand across Drew's chest, sliding to his waist and around to rest it low on his back, where she stroked her fingers lightly back and forth. Their lips met again in a reassuring kiss that quickly escalated into a more demanding passion.

Drew thrilled to her touch. One of his hands slipped down across the velvet skin of her stomach, then lower, and again his sure fingers found the valley between her thighs.

Tantalizing ripples of sensation followed his every touch. Emily caught her breath as his daring, invasive fingers slid into her. She moved against him, her hands clutching his strong shoulders, her thigh brushing the smooth length of him. He kissed her mouth, her throat, and her breasts as his fingers drove her again to a peak of sensation and tension. She clung to him, racing her fingers up and down his arms and back, and raking through his hair as the intensity of feeling grew. When at last she arched against him and he felt the soft pulsing deep within her, a small cry escaped her throat.

"I've never felt like this," she whispered between deep breaths.

He smiled down at her. "It's good, isn't it? It's so good between us."

"Mmm," she murmured, rubbing against him unconsciously.

Drew could deny himself no longer. He shifted so that he lay atop her and kissed her hungrily. As his tongue delved, exploring her mouth, his hand gently urged her thighs apart. Parting her knees with one of his own, he lowered himself slowly, resting himself against her silken, warm flesh. Emily writhed convulsively beneath him, aching for more of his touch. Drew pressed into her carefully. He met the barrier of her maidenhead, then, with a quick thrust, buried himself deep within her, reveling in the hot sweetness that held him.

Emily gasped at the sharp pain, but it eased quickly, replaced by exquisite ecstasy as he moved skillfully inside her. Never had she felt the sense of rightness and completion she knew in that moment. Slowly, she began to move her hips to match his rhythm. Delicious new sensations coursed through her as she followed his lead, building to yet another pinnacle of unfamiliar but irresistible tension.

All reason was replaced by urgent desire as they lost themselves to the world defined by their mutual embrace. They moved together as one, each meeting the other with unrestrained passion until their fulfillment came, exploding between them in incandescent joy. For an instant they were as one bright star, flaming in the uncertain darkness.

They lay for long minutes, their limbs entwined, the fire dying slowly in the hearth. Drew's cheek rested against Emily's, his arm thrown possessively across her. His eyes closed sleepily and a gentle smile curved his lips.

"*Isté maka niyapi, mitawin,*" he whispered tenderly against her ear. He slipped into a light sleep, his heart full.

Emily lay wide awake, her eyes staring sightlessly at the ceiling. Joyous contentment seeped slowly out of her. As her mind began to work clearly, shame and despair caught at her with cold fingers, even as she lay inside the warm circle of Drew's arms. She flinched at the memory of her wantonness. The worst of it was that she had allowed him to make love to her. No, not allowed, if she were honest. She had given herself, seeking his kisses and everything he had to offer. She knew that had she fought him harder, he wouldn't have pressed her. She'd been so foolish. She bit her lip and shuddered in an effort to control the tears that threatened to overcome her.

Her movement roused him. He smiled against her neck and stretched, drawing her closer to him. When he felt her stiffen, he looked up in concern. One glance at her pale face, eyes squeezed tight against her tears, caused remorse to flood through him. He had succumbed to the moment's passion, telling himself that it was what she wanted too, but inside, he'd known that he'd seduced her. She'd been frightened and vulnerable, and he shouldn't have made love to her. Then his conversation with Yellow Thunder came back to him, and Emily's ravings about her dream. Thoughts tumbled in confusing chaos through his mind. The only thing that seemed clear was that he had infinitely complicated matters by making love to her, but, curiously, despite his sorrow over her hurt, there was a joy in him that he'd never felt before.

Emily made a feeble attempt to pull away from him. She was cold, so very cold. Strangely, she didn't really wish to leave his embrace. Guilt washed over her again.

Drew's voice sounded soft, against her temple now. "Emily," he began, not sure what to say. "I didn't mean—" He broke off, his attention focused on the soft feel of her hair against his cheek. "I didn't mean for this to happen," he said finally. "I know you're upset, but I don't want you to blame yourself." He held her comfortingly, drawing the quilt over them. "I should have stopped. I don't know what else to say."

His words chilled her. She might have been able to bear it if he'd told her he loved her, that he would be there for her for the rest of her life. Instead, he regretted that he'd made love to her. The tears began to run from her closed eyes, trickling into the hair at her temples.

He felt the wetness against her lips, still pressed to her forehead. He groaned, and the anguish that Emily heard in his voice increased her misery. She had given herself wholly unto him, foolishly granting him one of the greatest gifts she would ever give a man, and he was sorry. He didn't want her.

"God, Emily, don't cry," he begged, lifting his head. "Did I hurt you that much? Talk to me. Rail at me if you must. But don't torment me with silent tears." There was grief in his voice. He grimly thought that he couldn't have found a better way to turn her from him had he searched for eternity. Perhaps it was for the best, but he couldn't bear to hurt her so.

"Look at me," he said gently. "Emily, don't do this to me."

Her eyes opened. She'd been about to retort viciously that it was he who was tormenting her, but the unexpected pain in his eyes stopped her. Could he really be so concerned? Uncertainty overwhelmed her.

"I'm sorry," she whispered through choked tears. "I don't understand what happened. I should never . . ." She looked away miserably, unable to speak.

Drew gathered her to him, smiling at her innocence.

"No, sweetheart, I'm the one who shouldn't have. You simply responded to me, beautifully, passionately, giving me a taste of heaven. You're perfect, and I don't deserve you," he said quietly, knowing that in the morning he would ride away from her without an explanation and with no idea of when he would be back. He cradled her in his arms, stroking the long, golden hair that spilled down her back. He couldn't tell her.

Emily heard no regret in his voice now. She was confused. If he meant what he'd just said, then why was he sorry? But he hadn't said that he cared for her, only that he had desired her, and she'd pleased him. She tried to pull away.

"I think I should go back to the chair," she said dejectedly.

"No," Drew told her firmly, not understanding her reactions at all. "I want to sleep with you in my arms tonight. After what just happened, there's no reason not to. Are you sure you don't want to talk about how you feel? I might understand more than you'd think," he offered on a gentler note.

"I don't really want to talk," she replied without energy. He said nothing, but his expression was kind, with a hint of fire still kindling his starry blue eyes. He looked, she thought with surprise, almost loving.

"Drew, do you care? About me?" Emily asked hesitantly, dreading his answer.

He looked long into her green-brown eyes, noting the calm strength mirrored there, along with the twinge of despair that wouldn't let him lie, even though he knew it would hurt her less in the long run if he did.

"Yeah, Emily. I care," he said as he lowered his head, kissing the tear streaks along her temples, then her eyelids, her nose, the fine line of her jaw, and finally her mouth, tenderly caressing her lips with light movements. "I care a lot."

He cared. He hadn't said that he loved her, but he cared. She felt better. Suddenly, she couldn't keep her eyelids open another minute, and she drifted off to sleep held close in Drew's arms.

The sun had just peeked through the lingering clouds on the eastern horizon when Drew and Emily set off the next morning. Emily rode a pinto Indian pony, next to Drew on his buckskin. He guided her up a trail along the hills to avoid the rain-swollen creek that ran through the valley. They descended once they were past the narrow gorge where the stream ran between steep rock walls that barely accommodated a track at normal water levels. Soon they were riding side by side toward the Parker ranch.

Neither of them spoke much, and Emily tried to concentrate on the morning's beauty. Everywhere she looked, droplets of water hung from leaves, shining like prisms where the sunlight caught them. It was enchanting.

"Emily, what happened when you were at the falls yesterday?" Drew's voice startled her in the silence.

"I told you last night," she said flatly.

"You didn't tell me everything." He paused, waiting for her to speak. When she didn't, he continued. "Sometimes the most important things may seem unimportant or foolish,'' he coaxed.

Emily eyed him warily. "You won't think I'm being ridiculous? You won't laugh?''

"No,'' he promised.

Reluctantly, Emily told him about the eagle in the pine tree at the falls, how it had watched her all day, then landed in front of her, and later how she'd seen it again flying north. Drew said nothing, but she thought she saw a faint smile hovering about his lips.

"You told me you wouldn't laugh!'' she accused.

"I'm not laughing,'' he told her. A strange excitement seemed to burn in his strange eyes. "Go on. Tell me about your dream.''

As she spoke, he nodded his head, as if they were speaking about some everyday occurrence, something familiar. When she got to the part where the rider entered the circle, he stopped his horse, reaching out a hand to catch her arm, stopping her also. His eyes bored into hers with unnerving intensity.

"Go very slowly now. Try to remember everything that happened, no matter how insignificant it may seem.''

Emily described the rider and how the people scattered before him, leaving the buffalo and the eagle in the center of the circle to face him. She told about the smiling mask he wore.

"*Iteha Kiton!* The Mask Wearer.'' Drew spat the unfamiliar words with hatred. Emily was startled. "Go on,'' he ordered.

She finished her story, then sat silently for a moment, watching the wild lights flash in Drew's eyes.

"Your eyes,'' she told him, "are just like the eagle's.''

He nodded, looking at her steadily.

"Do you know that there was an eagle hovering just above the edge of the woods yesterday, right before the storm?'' he asked pensively. "Cut Finger saw it and pointed at it, then it flew off.''

Emily remembered the Indian pointing straight at her. But it hadn't been at her, it had been above her. Her dark eyes clouded, and she frowned.

"I don't understand any of this," she said in bewilderment.

"I daresay it's a bit odd by your usual standards," Drew said with a slight smile.

"It's downright bizarre, by any standards! What do you mean, 'usual' standards? I certainly haven't changed my standards any!" she retorted briskly.

The lazy smile she was becoming familiar with quirked his mouth. "Haven't you?" he drawled insinuatingly.

Emily's head dropped. She averted her gaze, belatedly acknowledging that her standards did appear to have altered radically, and not for the better, in the short weeks that she had been in the Dakota Territory.

Drew was instantly sorry for teasing her. "I'm not criticizing you, Emily. I'm merely pointing out that this is a different place, with different ways. It's not the East. There are things out here that you don't know much about, things that most settlers aren't even aware of—magical things, mystical things. Powerful things that are part of the land and the sky. You're aware of them for some reason, and it's understandably confusing. I've lived with this land and its people since I was a boy, and I still don't know why things happen the way they do. There are mysteries beyond knowing in these hills."

"What does it all mean?" she asked plaintively.

"I'm not completely sure," he answered cautiously, unwilling to tell her anything that might increase the risk to her.

"But you have some idea. Please tell me. Tell me I'm not losing my mind," Emily pleaded.

Drew knit his brows and looked up into the sky, his hands resting on his thighs, fingers drumming. Finally, he looked back to her, as if he had made a decision. When he spoke, his voice was serious.

"You were right, those weren't ordinary dreams. And the eagle is . . . Well, I'm not sure how to describe him so that you'll understand, but he's a messenger. The Oglala believe he's the messenger of Śkan, part of Wakantanka, the Great Mystery, or God as the Lakota understand Him. I've seen the eagle before by the falls. He always sits high in the pine where you saw him. I've seen him other places, too. The first time was in my first vision, when I was fourteen years old.'' He didn't tell her that he had stood beside the eagle watching wide, smiling eyes, the color of dark green needles against the dark pine bark, of the rich prairie earth in spring, covered with rich grass. Impossibly deep brown and dark forest green. Emily's eyes.

''I know this dream you had, because I've had it too, in the last year, but I've never seen it end. You've seen farther than I have. Maybe that's why the eagle sent you to me. It's important for me to understand something, and I don't see it clearly yet. What you've seen and told me may help me understand more fully what I have to do.'' His voice was grave.

Emily shook her head incredulously. ''How can this be?'' she whispered in amazement. She felt as though her whole world were being turned upside down. Nothing seemed to make sense.

''There are always mysteries for those with the eyes to see them, Emily, for those who dream.''

''What do you have to do? How can a dream tell you what to do? I feel as if I'm being drawn into some medieval fairy tale!'' she exclaimed in frustration.

''I wish I had time to explain it all more fully. For now, accept my word that I have an important task to accomplish, one that may help the Lakota, and that what you've experienced is related to that somehow. It's dangerous, though, and I can't tell you too much without putting your life at risk. Try to understand that the Lakota don't live in the same world that you've been living in until now. It's different out here. Maybe it's more like the past. Try to understand that these things are a little bit beyond us, and we can't control them, though we can use them. Knowledge can come through dreams and visions, knowledge of ourselves and of the world, and if we're brave, we don't turn away from this knowledge, even when it's unsettling. I can't explain to you how or why it happens.'' His eyes pierced hers with intimidating intensity. ''I don't want you to tell anyone else about what you saw and dreamed. If you have more dreams, tell me. If you can't find me, get word to Black Wolf. You can trust him. Don't say anything to anyone else about this." There was a grave warning in his words. Emily listened in absolute astonishment.

"Surely this isn't necessary, but if you insist . . ." she replied hesitantly.

"I insist. The consequences could be tragic if you don't do as I ask." His voice was coldly matter-of-fact.

"All right. I won't say anything," she finally conceded, unable to fathom why her crazy dreams should elicit such a strong reaction.

"Good. We need to go on now," he said, relaxing somewhat and gathering his reins. "I have a lot to do." He moved off down the trail.

Emily followed in silence, Drew's confounding words echoing again and again in her head as she tried to make sense out of them. Dear God, she prayed, what had she stumbled into? Visions, dreams, and messengers from the gods belonged to a different era, a time long past. This was the nineteenth century, for heaven's sake! She was a college-educated, God-fearing woman! She didn't believe in mystical revelations and hocus-pocus magician's tricks. And yet, here was an educated man of her own race telling her he took these things seriously! That he had shared the same experiences. That they had had the same dream! Emily felt dizzy and disoriented.

Staring at Drew's broad back as they rounded a bend in the creek and came in view of Sam and Maggie's white farmhouse, Emily decided that she had been right in thinking that she would never have a moment's peace with this man. Even so, he drew her as a flame draws a moth. She craved his company, thrilled at the sound of his deep voice, and melted under his touch, but he was too different, too unpredictable, too wild for a prim schoolteacher from New York state. He belonged in the untamed Dakota wilderness. She told herself that she did not, even as her heart lightened at the sound of the clear, joyful call of a meadowlark. She knew that she couldn't continue to see him when there could be no future for them. He would only drag her further into this chaotic realm of unbridled passions and unnerving mysteries.

They rode up to the house, where Drew dismounted and lifted Emily out of her saddle. His hands lingered at her waist, and before she realized what he meant to do, he bent his head and kissed her deeply, folding her into his arms. Her arms moved instinctively around his neck, and she returned his ardor, despite her intention not to. She heard the kitchen door slam, and Sam and Maggie call her name excitedly. She immediately sought to break his embrace, but he held her firmly.

"Remember," he said softly against her ear. "Tell no one. I care too much to see you hurt."

The look in his eyes left her no doubt that he did.

Chapter 11

The next days passed slowly for Emily as she tried to put what had happened with Drew Rutledge into perspective. She worked with Maggie and spent a great deal of time with her niece and nephews. Zach continued to visit the ranch regularly, and his invariably cheerful and newsy conversation helped Emily set aside her preoccupation during the rides they took together and the hours they spent chatting with her family. No diversion kept Drew from her thoughts for long, however. She finally decided it would be better not to think of him at all, because it sent her into a spiral of doubts and questions about his intentions and her own good judgment, for which she had few satisfying answers.

Her resolve to stop thinking about Drew disintegrated rapidly when he didn't appear after a week. She found herself pondering the strange things he'd told her at odd moments, wondering if they were really true. Away from his unsettling presence, able to think clearly, Emily began to doubt that he'd been completely honest with her. He'd openly admitted being engaged in illegal activity, and even if it was humanitarian in nature, it made Emily nervous. If he could justify one sort of crime, he might throw other scruples to the wind as well. It was possible that the stories he'd told her about visions and dreams were made up to frighten her into staying away from his place, although when she recalled the mixture of concern and desire she'd seen in his eyes after he'd made love to her and when he'd left her the next morning, she wasn't even sure of her doubts. The only thing that was certain was that the farther away in time Emily got from her visit to the falls, the more ludicrous it seemed that she could have had prophetic dreams. She more than half convinced herself that she'd simply imagined everything that had happened.

With shame, however, she acknowledged that she hadn't imagined what had taken place between herself and Drew Rutledge. To make matters worse, she found she missed him and began to worry as the second week passed and he made no appearance at the Parkers'. She clung to his words reassuring her that he cared for her as a salve to her wounded pride.

By the end of the second week, however, it occurred to Emily that she was being naive to have taken him at his word. With a sickening jolt, she contemplated the possibility that he'd lied about his feelings for her. Could he have told her that he cared merely to make meager amends for having used her? If he'd really cared, he should have come to her and honorably stated his intentions. That he hadn't was a blow, even though Emily had decided she could never commit herself to such an unorthodox man. She knew that he'd never mentioned marriage, or even any further contact, other than to tell him if she had any more dreams. Even then, he'd told her to find Black Wolf if she couldn't find him. Had he already decided not to see her again? The thought made her furious, and it hurt deeply, yet it had the hollow ring of truth to her ears. He must have lied to her, she decided. Otherwise, he would have surely come to her by now, or at least sent word. Despite her initial intent to reject him, Emily was sorely wounded that the man had used her and abandoned her in such a callous fashion. Worse, she felt a fool for ever having taken him at his word. Gradually, the shame receded, and a cold anger replaced it. If she ever saw Drew Rutledge again, he would rue the day.

The first Saturday in September, the Colonel and Caroline Reynolds came to the Parkers' in the afternoon for an end-of-summer picnic. The whole family went along, riding into the hills south and west of the house to a favorite glade near a small spring. Maggie and Emily packed a big meal in wicker baskets, and Caroline brought a chocolate cake and horehound sticks for the children. The whole party chattered gaily as they wound their way into the hills. It was hot, and it seemed to Emily as if summer would never end.

"Oh, but it will, and any time now we could get the first freeze," Caroline assured her. "If we're lucky, the cold weather will hold off for at least another month or so. Even after the first cold spell, it can get warm again and we can have beautiful Indian summer well into November."

"I hope it stays like this for a while," Emily said, tilting her head back to feel the sun's warmth on her face. "It's such a lovely day. There's not a cloud in the sky."

"You sound like you're becoming attached to this uncivilized land, Emily," Caroline teased with a smile. "Have you decided to stay through the winter? That's the real test to see if you can make it out here or not."

"So I've heard," Emily mused. "I looked into trying to find a teaching post, but the only ones available were too far from the ranch. I didn't want to leave Sam and Maggie," she explained. "I'm having such a good time with the children that it just didn't seem quite right to move twenty miles away or more. I was thinking I might stay until the end of October. Probably I will go back then."

"You don't sound very happy about that," Caroline observed, stooping to pick a late-blooming brown-eyed Susan.

"I really do like it here," Emily admitted. "I'm just not certain I want to stay forever."

Caroline looked at her. "Why not?"

Emily had no answer. She couldn't tell anyone that it was because Drew Rutledge would always be here and she couldn't bear to be near him. Every time she thought of him now it pricked her conscience, and guilt washed over her at the memory of her immoral behavior.

"I'm not sure I can explain it," she answered with a sad smile. "I simply don't think it would be . . ." She paused, unable to explain. "It's a feeling, I guess," she finished vaguely.

Caroline looked at her appraisingly, but said nothing. They continued to walk through the peaceful hills in silence.

When they reached the glade, the children ran off to explore the spring and surrounding woods, escorted by Kenny. The three women set out the lunch, and Sam and Matt Reynolds took out their tobacco pouches and walked through the glade, smoking and talking. Eddie produced a fishing pole and dropped it into the pool that formed near where the spring bubbled up from the ground. He pushed his hat down over his eyes and was soon snoring lightly. Maggie, Caroline and Emily talked happily, sharing local gossip and comparing notes on Jack Langrishe's latest theatrical production. After an hour, they rounded up the children and men, and everyone sat on a big red blanket in the grass, enjoying the picnic. When lunch was finished, the children convinced the adults to participate in a horse race, so they marked out a course through the meadow and argued over who would ride which horse. Josh and Eddie ended up riding together against Sam and Sarah. Kenny rode alone, as did Caroline and Emily. There were not enough mounts for everyone, so Colonel Reynolds and Maggie, holding a wiggling Daniel, declined graciously. They stood at either side of the finish line to judge the winner. It was close, but Josh and Eddie edged out Kenny by a head, much to Josh's delight.

When the racing was finished, the adults all retreated to the shade under the trees. There they sat down on the blanket and talked idly. The children trailed along behind Eddie and Kenny, hoping to get in some fishing. Josh ran over to ask Sam a question after a few minutes.

"Can I take the saddle off Shaker to practice bareback riding, Pa?" he asked, reaching into one of the food baskets for a cookie.

Sam didn't look up but remained lying with his eyes closed, chewing on a grass stem. "No, you may not. You know you can only do that in the corral with me right there."

"Well, can I practice riding hanging on the side of the saddle like the Indians do?" he tried again hopefully. Emily had to repress a grin at Josh's determination to ride like an Indian.

"Not unless you want to break your neck and have us go off and leave you for dead," his father replied, eyes still closed.

"Aw, Pa!" the boy wailed. "How am I ever going to learn to ride as good as the Indians if you won't let me practice?"

"That's enough, Josh," Sam warned him patiently. Josh grabbed a handful of cookies and rose resignedly to his feet. He trudged off toward the horses, his head hanging.

"Stay off those horses," Sam called after him, never opening his eyes.

Josh looked back in disbelief at his recumbent father, then stalked off in the opposite direction. Everyone chuckled.

"That reminds me," the colonel said, "Caroline and I are going down to Pine Ridge this week for a quick trip."

Instantly, Emily and Maggie turned to look at him in surprise. "How exciting! Any particular reason?" Maggie asked curiously.

"I want to check in with McGillycuddy to see how he's coming along, ask his opinion about a few things that I'd rather not trust to messengers," Colonel Reynolds answered.

Emily wondered if he were referring to the stolen guns and the Indians' reputed involvement. Then she recalled Red Cloud's invitation to her. Excitedly, she wondered if she might be able to go along, though she wouldn't dream of inviting herself. But if there were some way for her to accompany them, that would show Drew Rutledge, she thought with satisfaction.

"Caroline, why are you going?" Emily asked.

"I thought it would be interesting to see the Indians. Besides, it will be a little adventure. We're traveling alone, with only a guide," she confided, her blue eyes sparkling.

"Is that safe?" Maggie asked with concern. "There are a lot of outlaws on the roads."

"Our guide is reliable, and we'll be well armed, of course," Matt said casually. "I'm afraid Caroline gets a bit bored with the routine at the post, and I couldn't talk her out of this excursion. She's quite set on it." The tall man smiled merrily at his pretty wife.

"I don't get bored," she corrected. "I simply could not resist the temptation of not having to share my husband with a couple of hundred soldiers for a few days," she teased, tossing her blond curls.

Everyone laughed. Emily thought how lucky Caroline and Matt were to have found each other, as were Sam and Maggie. She hoped that someday she would know the same happiness.

"Got room for one extra on your little jaunt?" Sam asked the colonel. He was sitting now, his back to the trunk of a broad ash tree. "About a month ago, when Red Cloud and his band came to Deadwood, we met some of the Indians. Black Wolf, the old medicine man's son, invited Emily to visit them and talk about education with any of the chiefs who would listen. Might be something McGillycuddy would approve of. I can't think of any other opportunity Emily will have to get out to the reservation."

"Really, Sam," Emily said with some embarrassment as he voiced her thoughts. "You shouldn't invite me along on other people's business."

Caroline clapped her hands at Sam's words. "Oh, it would be delightful to have Emily come! What do you think, Matt?" she asked, looking hopefully at her husband.

"I think it's an excellent idea. It would give me a good cover, at least. I can claim to be escorting my wife and her friend on a tour of the hills and the agency. Having two women along ought to stop any suspicions about this trip." The colonel chuckled thoughtfully. "And I daresay McGillycuddy would indeed be pleased at the prospect of a teacher talking to the Indians. I understand they argue quite a bit about the schools at the agency. Seems old Red Cloud thoroughly disapproves of them," he added with an odd little smile.

"Will you come?" Caroline asked Emily. "It would be awfully exciting. We'll have a grand time!"

"You're sure I won't be in the way?" Emily asked cautiously, tempering her excitement.

"Not a bit," the colonel assured her.

"I would be miserable now if you didn't come," Caroline insisted.

She needed no more convincing.

"In that case, I'd love to," Emily responded warmly. "When do we leave?"

The following Monday morning at dawn, Sam rode with Emily to the point where she was to meet the colonel and Caroline and their guide. At the Colonel's insistence, she was dressed in pants and carrying a rifle. The horse was carefully packed with the provisions needed for the ride to Pine Ridge. They would be riding fast, although they were going through the hills, ostensibly on a sightseeing tour, should anyone ask. The cloak of secrecy about the colonel's true purpose of this trip intrigued Emily, and she had questioned Sam to find out what he knew. If he knew anything, however, he wasn't telling, and Emily was left to speculate. She felt certain that it had to do with the stolen guns.

About a mile north of the Parker ranch, Emily spied the Reynoldses waiting for them in the shelter of a high bank. There was the suggestion of a chill in the light breeze, but the day promised to hold fair and warm. The grass was beaded with heavy dew, and birds sang to greet the sun as it peeped its head above the eastern horizon. It was a perfect day to travel, and Emily felt her spirits soar.

"Hello!" she called.

They exchanged greetings and chuckled over the women's appearance. Emily had on Kenny's green shirt and buckskin jacket and the brown, wide-brimmed hat she had worn before. Caroline was wearing dark brown twill trousers with a tan shirt and a similar jacket. The colonel was not in uniform, but he was riding his huge bay stallion, and his upright military bearing was unmistakable.

"No one would believe that these two ragamuffins here

are among the prettiest ladies in the territory," Matt Reynolds told Sam humorously. "I only hope that Caroline doesn't become too fond of her new style. My men would be scandalized, and should my commanding officer see her, I might well be demoted for permitting my wife to run amok."

"Darling, you're being ridiculous," Caroline protested. "You yourself said this would be safer, and it will permit us to ride much faster. And don't you worry about me not going back to dresses. After all, I have that beautiful new blue satin that would go utterly to waste if I did!"

Sam addressed his sister before taking his leave. "However you're dressed, I want you to promise me you'll take care, Emily, and not do anything dangerous. Listen to the colonel and his guide, and remember to bring a little something back for Josh." Her nephew had been sick that he was not allowed to accompany Emily on the trip. "I'm going to head back now. Take care, all of you!" he said, pulling his horse around and galloping off.

"Where is our guide?" Emily asked when Sam had gone. "I thought he'd be here before the rest of us. Are you sure this man knows what he's doing?"

"He's the best there is," Colonel Reynolds told her. "Mind you, he can be a bit rough, but I've worked with him in the past, and I wouldn't let you and Caroline come if it were anyone else. I believe you already know him, Emily."

"What's his name, colonel?" she inquired, puzzling to think who might be the man in question.

"Here he comes!" Caroline called, pointing to an approaching rider on a big, dark brown gelding.

Emily turned in the direction Caroline indicated. Her heart leapt into her throat as she recognized the man who would be their guide for the next week. It was Drew Rutledge, tanned and fit, his curling brown hair bleached light at the temples by the sun, dressed in regular clothing instead of Indian gear. He was even wearing boots instead of moccasins. On his big horse, he looked every bit the white settler. Emily was struck dumb. One part of her rejoiced to see him alive and well, while another part wanted to run after Sam.

"Morning," Drew said, smiling as he came abreast of them. "It looks like a fine day. Are you ready to move out?"

Emily sat stiffly in her saddle, unsure of how to respond. He was so at ease and relaxed, and his eyes were warm when he caught her gaze. How dare he act as if nothing had happened between them? And what on earth was he doing escorting the Fort Meade commander on a trip when he was engaged in illegal activities that put the man's troops in danger? Drew noted the cold reception he got from her.

"Is something wrong, Emily?" he asked politely.

Acutely aware of the colonel and Caroline watching her, she forced a smile and shook her head.

"Everything is fine, Mr. Rutledge," she replied formally. Emily noticed his jaw set at her formality. "I was simply surprised to see you. I had neglected to find out the name of our guide until this moment, and it never occurred to me that it might be you."

"Having second thoughts?" he queried smoothly, knowing that she was.

"Whyever should I?" she replied, looking him straight in the eye. "I've been very much looking forward to this trip. I wouldn't miss it for the world," she added bravely, wishing the guide could have been anyone but him.

How could she tolerate his presence for a full week? She willed herself to be calm and to master her temper because she knew she couldn't back away from the trip. After the spiteful taunts he'd hurled at her in Deadwood, she wouldn't give him the satisfaction of being right. Moreover, she truly wanted to go.

"Well, then," the colonel's voice interrupted. "Shall we be off? Lead the way, Rutledge."

Drew took the small party through the winding canyons into the hills. He told them that his plan was to proceed through the center of the hills south toward Hill City the first day. From there they would continue through the southern hills and camp the second night near a hot spring that the colonel had expressed interest in. The third day, they would ride to Pine Ridge Agency. Drew kept mainly to old Indian trails and avoided mining camps and lone prospectors. Several times, Emily heard men's voices ringing through the forest, but she never saw anyone. She wondered why it was so important that they not be seen. It hardly made sense to her.

Emily found that she had little time for worrying about Drew and that it wasn't difficult to avoid talking to him. He set a good pace that took all her attention to maintain on the sometimes rocky trails. During their periodic stops to rest the horses and eat, Emily stuck close to Caroline so she wouldn't have to be alone with him. She listened attentively to his instructions, knowing that it would be foolish to disregard them, but she said little in reply.

During the afternoon, they stopped for a few minutes by a lovely stream. As the horses drank deeply, Caroline sat on the bank next to Emily. Drew and the colonel were immersed in a discussion over Drew's maps.

"You've been awfully quiet, Emily," Caroline observed, sounding concerned. "Is anything the matter?"

"Have I? Nothing's wrong. I've just been enjoying the solitude and the mountains."

"You were surprised to see Drew this morning, weren't you?" Caroline persisted. "Does your being so quiet have anything to do with him?" she suggested slyly, a small smile tugging at the corners of her mouth.

"Good heavens, no!" Emily said vehemently. Caroline smiled at her adamant response.

"Ah ha!" the colonel's wife exclaimed triumphantly. "You like him, don't you? Sam said he thought you might."

Emily looked down at the ground to hide the blush that was rapidly spreading across her cheeks. "That's not quite it, Caroline," she explained, thinking that whatever it was she felt for Drew, she wouldn't describe it as liking him. "We don't get along very well. And why does everyone seem to be discussing my affections? I'm going to have to tell my big brother to keep his thoughts to himself."

Caroline laughed at her. "Single women don't tend to stay that way for long in Dakota, Emily. Surely you've noticed there are about six men for every girl. When someone as attractive as you happens into a community, there's a lot of speculation about how long it will take her to get married, and which man will be the lucky one." Emily stared at her in astonishment. "Most folks regard Zach Stevens as the odds-on favorite with you, but Sam quietly let it drop that he thinks otherwise. Stevens has done a real good job of keeping other would-be suitors away, but he wouldn't dare say anything to Drew. Personally, I think Drew is a much better catch."

"Caroline, you can't be serious!" Emily's voice rose with indignation. "This is ridiculous!"

"Isn't it?" Caroline laughed merrily. Emily couldn't entirely suppress a smile herself. "You simply have to laugh about it, though. At least you aren't being courted by the officers at the post. When Matt and I were courting, they actually took bets on how long it would take him to ask me to marry him."

"No!" Emily couldn't believe it.

"Yes, they did. When I found out, I was mortified, but gradually it got so it didn't bother me anymore. There isn't always much that's entertaining out here," Caroline pointed out. "It doesn't really do any harm."

"I suppose not," Emily agreed. "But it is a trifle irregular."

"Most things out here are."

"That certainly seems to be true."

"So why don't you and Drew get along?" Caroline said, returning to her original line of inquiry.

Emily thought for a moment. "I'm not sure why," she finally said. "We just don't."

"There must be some reason. Everyone knows he can be terribly aloof and intimidating, although he seemed quite warm this morning when he saw you. Then that wall of his slid into place again. Has something happened between you?" Caroline asked with sudden insight.

Emily hugged her knees to her chest and looked at her

feet. She shouldn't have allowed herself to talk about Drew.

"No," she lied. "I don't understand him very well. He confuses me."

"That's not surprising," Caroline said comfortingly. "You never know when he's coming or going, and he's almost as foreign as the Sioux themselves most of the time."

Emily felt some relief at Caroline's understanding.

"Yes, he is," she agreed. "You know I hadn't seen him for almost a month? He never said a word about where he was or what he was doing. I don't think I mean very much to him, Caroline, and I don't think I have room in my life for someone who isn't reliable and honest." The words spilled out before she could stop them, her voice hurt and a little angry.

"So you do care about him," Caroline said softly, putting her arm around Emily's shoulders.

"I guess I do," Emily admitted miserably. "But it would never work. We're too different." All the despair she had felt in the last weeks welled up, and tears pricked at her eyes. She stoically blinked them back.

"You never know about that," Caroline told her archly, lifting one eyebrow.

"Are you ladies ready to ride?" the colonel called to them, ending their conversation.

They rose to their feet and walked to their horses. Emily avoided looking at Drew. Caroline noticed the penetrating look he shot at her, and couldn't help thinking that he seemed to care about Emily, as well. She hoped that in the week ahead they might make some headway toward resolving whatever it was that was keeping them apart. If she were wagering, she would still have put her money on Drew as the best bet for Emily's future.

That evening Drew stopped to camp in a secluded valley near Hill City. They were approaching the highest part of the hills, and he didn't wish to get into the difficult terrain with darkness coming on. The night was warm, so he didn't build a shelter. They would sleep in the open air under the stars.

Emily had managed to avoid being alone with him all day, but after supper Caroline and the colonel wandered off for a few minutes alone together. Rather than stay with Drew at the campfire, Emily rose and walked over to her horse.

Drew watched her go. He knew she was avoiding him, and he didn't blame her. He'd made love to her, then disappeared for almost a month without a word to her. He'd known that she would think the worst, but he felt it was a better protection for her than anything else he could have done. The information he'd gathered on his travels to the Cheyenne River and Standing Rock agencies had confirmed his suspicions that the plot to incite the hostile Indians in Canada and the threats to his life were related. The same person was behind both, but he'd been unable to uncover any leads to who that person was. All he'd been able to determine was that whoever it was, he was clever and very cautious. So far there had been no slip-ups that revealed the man's name, or even his appearance. It was not at all the right time to involve Emily in his life, yet he seemed unable to stay away from her.

When the colonel had asked if he minded if she came, Drew had almost refused. The trip had been organized so that the colonel could consult with the Pine Ridge agent, V. T. McGillycuddy, about the threat of an uprising among the Canadian hostiles and its possible effects among the reservation Indians. Reynolds hadn't wanted to make the visit official because there were those among his commanding officers, and several in his own command, who strongly felt that any excuse to eradicate the Sioux should be encouraged. They had decided that a sightseeing trip with his wife taken on a week's leave would provide the necessary cover for the trip. Drew was concerned that Emily might accidentally overhear a conversation or see something that would increase her danger, and he hated the thought that his activities might put her at needless risk. At the same time, because of the dreams she'd had, he felt that she was already involved at some level beyond his control. And he longed to be with her, to listen to her musical laughter and very proper speech, to hold her in his arms again in passion. In the end, he'd agreed that she could come to Pine Ridge, knowing that her presence would test his resolve, but powerless to deny himself her company. Now he found the cold hurt in her eyes painful, and her every refusal to meet his gaze stung bitterly.

He decided to give her five minutes before he went to look for her. When she didn't return, he rose to follow. He found her leaning against her horse, murmuring softly to the animal. Silently, he approached her. When he was barely a foot from her, he stopped and called her name quietly.

She turned instantly. "Must you sneak up on me like that?" she snapped in annoyance.

She looked at his broad shape looming above her in the darkness. He was so close, she had but to put out her hand to touch him.

"I'm sorry. I didn't mean to frighten you. You were gone for several minutes. I was only making sure you were all right." He moved even closer.

"Thank you, but I can get along fine without you," she told him coldly.

"Can you?" he asked, his voice deep and resonant.

Emily turned back to her mare, brushing his shoulder as she did so. The righteous anger she had felt for weeks flooded through her, and she sought to control it. There was a touch on her cheek that she instinctively shied from. When Drew's hand sought her face again, she turned back to him, ready to vent her feelings.

As soon as she turned, he slid his arms around her and pulled her away from the horse, lifting her as he moved. He backed her up against a tree and quickly lowered his mouth to cover hers, one hand holding her head still.

She clamped her mouth shut and kicked him in the shin as hard as she could. He didn't even flinch.

"Mmm." He groaned. "I missed you. I missed kissing you."

"Let me go," she stated firmly. "I don't want you to kiss me. I don't want you to touch me."

"I think we already had this discussion and decided it was silly," he reminded her.

"That was quite a while ago," she replied, unable to mask the hurt in her voice. "And as I recall, it wasn't much of a discussion. And what happened was a big mistake."

He stepped away from her, but when she started to walk away, he caught the sleeve of her jacket and pulled her back. "Wait, Emily. I had work to do. You knew that."

"You said you had work to do, not that you were going to vanish for nearly a month. You didn't tell me on purpose. Why? Where have you been? What have you been doing?" she asked.

"Did you miss me?" Drew couldn't resist the jibe.

"Hardly," Emily continued cuttingly, dismissing the idea as if it were preposterous. "I was merely surprised. I thought you had things to attend to with your little supply operation. It doesn't seem the sort of thing that one would up and abandon midcourse, but, then, I'm sure no one has ever accused you of taking a normal course of action."

"No, they haven't," he agreed. "Sometimes things beyond our control force us into actions we might not otherwise take, Emily."

Something in his tone gave her the distinct impression that he was not referring only to his smuggling operation.

"I must say, I was surprised to see you this morning. Does the colonel know about your efforts on behalf of the renegade Indians?" she asked, trying to raise his ire.

"If he does, he's never said anything to me about it," Drew countered lightly. "And I'll thank you not to bring it up and force him into the awkward position of having to do something about it."

"Are you threatening me again, Mr. Rutledge?" Emily inquired calmly, her anger sizzling just below the surface.

"I'm protecting your damn foolish hide, Miss Parker. If you wish to construe that as a threat, then by all means, go right ahead."

"I hardly see how keeping your secrets protects me. You seem quite bent on 'protecting' me, as you call it. I wonder why?" she asked disparagingly. "I think I've had quite an enlightening dose of your so-called protection, and I don't really care to have another.''

She saw immediately that she had hit home. Drew let out a long breath.

''Touché,'' he granted quietly.

They stood in silence for several minutes.

Drew finally spoke. ''I need to talk to you,'' he began seriously. ''I wouldn't have had things as they've been, but sometimes we don't have the luxury of choosing the course of our lives. Do you understand what I'm telling you?''

Emily wasn't sure she did. ''You're telling me you're sorry we made love,'' she said, looking at the ground.

Drew reached out for her hands. He took them gently in his own.

''I probably should be, Emily, but I'm not sorry for that. I think you know that.'' He paused. ''I'm sorry I hurt you. I'm sorry I can't offer you the life you want and deserve.''

Emily felt tears well in her eyes. He cared for her, it seemed, but not enough. He didn't really want her, not for longer than a night here and there. Desperately, she reminded herself that he wasn't what she really wanted, either, but she knew that wasn't completely true. In that moment, she acknowledged with bittersweet honesty that she could easily fall in love with Drew. And that it would cost her dearly if she did. Too dearly.

''Then there's nothing more to say, is there?'' she said softly.

''There's a great deal left to say,'' he corrected. ''Now just isn't the time. Have you had any more dreams?'' he asked, changing the subject abruptly.

Emily only wanted to go to her bedroll and sleep. Perhaps then she would forget the dull ache that was growing inside her.

''No, nothing,'' she replied absently. ''I'm going to sleep now. It's been a long day for me.'' She pulled her hands out of his and walked to the campfire.

Drew followed close behind her.

''Be sure to tell me if you do,'' he told her.

"Yes, of course," she answered flatly.

The unhappy look in her eyes caused him to swear volubly under his breath. He hated the circumstances that forced him to choose between wooing Emily and driving her away from him to keep her safe. He knew what was best for her, but he doubted his strength to do it. With supreme self control, he walked away from her and threw himself wearily onto his bedroll on the opposite side of the fire.

Chapter 12

The next day was beautiful again, and the scenery captured Emily's heart. In the east, Harney Peak rose high above them and the sharp rock spires of the Needles broke the skyline. Drew steered them west of the high peaks through broad valleys toward Custer City. Emily had decided the night before, as she'd dropped into an exhausted slumber, that she would try her best to treat Drew as she would if he were no more to her than the guide he posed as. She couldn't realistically continue to avoid him under the circumstances, but she could maintain her dignity. Unexpectedly, she found herself enjoying the rugged scenery and listening avidly to the Indian stories Drew told them during their stops. Drew didn't attempt to speak with her alone, but several times she looked up to find his eyes fixed on her, his expression intense. She was sure Caroline and Matt noticed him staring, and it embarrassed her.

The southern hills were broad and full of high, wide mountain meadows. The tall grasses waved golden in the bright sun as they proceeded toward a hot spring that had long been used by the Indians. By late afternoon, they had almost reached the edge of the hills again, a last rounded hill rising dark and tall before them. Drew led them out of the meadow and back into the cover of the pines as the sun sank toward the western horizon. They made their camp in the shelter of a grove of ash and cottonwood trees along a small creek. A short distance away, the hot spring gurgled forth from the earth, then flowed toward the Fall

River, an unusual stream that ran with slightly warm water down to the Cheyenne River.

Emily and Caroline bathed in the spring while Drew and Colonel Reynolds saw to the horses and started a fire. It was deliciously warm and relaxing after two days in the saddle. Emily was surprised to find that a sort of bathtub had been carved out of the rock that lined the spring. She wondered how it had gotten there. After what seemed like only a few minutes, they heard Colonel Reynolds calling for them to hurry and get dressed as he wanted his turn in the reviving water. Reluctantly, they rose, dried themselves, and put on their clothes. As soon as the women returned to camp, Drew and the colonel headed for the warm spring. They returned about fifteen minutes later, laughing together, water dripping from their wet hair. Emily's heart caught at the sight of Drew walking barechested to where his saddlebag hung from a branch. She watched the muscles in his back flex beneath his brown skin as he removed a clean shirt and donned it. Again she noticed the scars over his shoulder blades.

Drew turned back to the fire and saw Emily look away quickly. Her high cheekbones and slender neck held a grace that he had never seen equaled, and even the jeans and boy's shirt she wore now did little to disguise the soft curves of her figure. He was reminded of the first time he had seen her standing on the porch at the stage agent's office in Deadwood. Had that really been only two months ago? Every time he saw her, he wanted her more. He looked away to hide the desire that flashed in his eyes.

Caroline's lilting voice interrupted his thoughts. "Drew, how did you get those unusual scars on your back? I've never seen anything quite like that."

He stepped closer to the fire and seated himself on a rock. "I got them in a sundance when I first returned from back East," he explained briefly.

Emily and Caroline gasped. The colonel whistled softly under his breath.

"You danced a sundance?" Caroline asked in awe. Everyone had heard of the Plains Indian religious ritual in which the dancers were pierced through the breast and had rawhide ropes inserted beneath the skin. These ropes were attached to a center pole, and the dancer's objective was to pull himself free of the ropes by breaking through the flesh. He danced in the hot summer sun and sometimes the skin would not break for hours. It was a gruelling test of will and strength.

"I never heard of a white man participating in a sun dance," Matt Reynolds commented, shaking his head.

"I thought you would get scars on your chest," Caroline said, a little confused.

"I danced dragging buffalo skulls, not tied to the pole," Drew explained as though it were nothing out of the ordinary. "The skulls are attached to the back by rawhide ropes and the dancer dances until the weight of the skulls tears through the flesh, freeing him."

"It must have been quite an ordeal," the colonel commented. "I can't say as I understand why you'd do such a thing."

Drew smiled patiently. "I was young. It was something I had to do when I came back and saw the straits the Sioux were in. I felt responsible for what had happened to them at the hands of our government, although no one ever held the government's policies against me personally. I left right after the war, and when I came back things had changed so much. There were so few buffalo, other game was fast disappearing, and the land was unable to support the people any longer. The sundance was my way of reaffirming my commitment to the tribe and seeking guidance on how best to help."

"Most times you seem more Indian than white, Rutledge," Colonel Reynolds observed.

"Most times I am," Drew agreed easily.

"Why aren't you wearing your Indian clothes?" Emily asked, speaking at last.

His blue eyes reflected the warmth of the firelight when he looked at her. "Because it's safer to be dressed as a white man. I don't want to draw any fire just because of the way I'm dressed. It would put the rest of you at risk unnecessarily." He didn't tell her that with the high reward that had been privately offered for his scalp, every opportunist and bounty hunter in the hills was looking for a white man who dressed as a Sioux.

"People would shoot at an Indian from a distance without any idea whether he meant harm or not?" Emily asked incredulously.

"Some folks would, some wouldn't," Colonel Reynolds answered. He stood and stretched. "I'm getting pretty hungry. What do you say we rustle up some supper?"

The suggestion was promptly acted upon, and soon everyone was busily eating, their appetites stimulated by the long day in the fresh mountain air. Emily noticed that both Drew and the colonel kept their rifles within reach at all times. As the foursome sat around the fire after supper, sipping coffee from tin cups, Emily suddenly realized how heavily armed their small party was. She and Caroline both carried rifles in their scabbards as they rode, and Drew had instructed them to sleep with the rifles within easy reach. In addition to rifles, both men also carried a pair of six-shooters with extra shells in their gunbelts. And Drew had his knife hidden in his boot. Emily had seen it when he cleaned the fish they had eaten for lunch that noon.

"Are you expecting any trouble?" she asked, eyeing the rifles propped against the tree trunks beside the men.

"I don't expect it, but I don't intend to be caught unawares," Drew told her as he poured himself another cup of coffee from the pot hanging over the fire. He leaned back against a rock and eased his long legs out in front of him. "You never know what might happen."

"But I thought we were safe from Indian attacks with you," Emily said.

"You are, unless some renegade Crows are able to figure out who I am and remember a particularly lucrative horse-stealing raid that took place about seven years ago." He chuckled wickedly as Emily's eyebrows shot up.

"You steal horses?" she exclaimed, forgetting her original question. The man just went from bad to worse. He was hopeless!

"Indians do these things," he told her with mock resignation. "How else is a young warrior supposed to get enough horses to get a wife? They don't grow on trees."

"You mean the Sioux buy their wives? With stolen horses?" Emily was appalled. "How utterly barbaric," she said disdainfully.

"No, it isn't," Drew argued equably. "The horses are like a bride price, a longstanding European tradition."

"One that is thankfully no longer observed, and which did not rely on stolen property," she pointed out. "Who decides how many horses a woman is worth, anyway?" she asked, her interest piqued in spite of the vulgarity of the topic.

"Her father, or her brothers if her father is dead. If there are many suitors, or if the girl is especially pretty and industrious, they can get a higher price."

"So a woman's father sells her to the man with the most horses. How lovely for her," Emily said sarcastically.

"It works pretty well for the most part," Drew informed her, still calmly sipping coffee. Caroline was leaning against her husband, interestedly listening to this exchange. "Most fathers consult their daughters before they make a decision, however."

"I'm glad to hear it," Emily replied briskly, "and I am certainly glad I was not born an Indian."

"If you had been, you'd have been married at least ten years ago and you'd probably have two or three children by now. You might even have to share your husband with a younger second wife." Drew smiled into his cup as he drained it.

"I would do no such thing!" Emily cried indignantly. "That is downright immoral!" Her dark eyes flashed as she spoke. Caroline smiled, and her husband chuckled in amusement.

"Morality is a matter that varies according to custom. If it makes you feel any better, a woman could probably have two husbands if she wanted to and all parties involved agreed. It isn't real common, but that makes things fair, wouldn't you say?" Drew asked her, pretending seriousness. "How would you like two husbands, Emily?" he teased, enjoying the dark flush that stained her cheeks.

"I wouldn't like any husbands, thank you very much!" Suddenly, she realized that he was baiting her. Her eyes narrowed. "Although now I can see better why you like living with the Sioux so much, if they'll let you have two wives."

"Or more," Drew added, swirling the grounds in the bottom of his cup, "depending on what you can afford and if you can convince the other wives to live in peace with the new ones. Some chiefs have four or five."

Suppressing her horrified reaction to this revelation, Emily abruptly remembered the clothes he had given her to wear the night she had spent at his cabin. They were an Indian woman's clothes. She asked him a question she was not entirely sure she wanted to hear the answer to.

"Do you have an Indian wife? Or wives?" Her tone was studiedly even.

Drew grinned at her. "Not yet. Why? You interested in signing on?" Emily sputtered her denial, but he continued, ignoring her. "I guess I might be able to get Sam to accept maybe five or six ponies for you. If you were a few years younger, I couldn't afford you. He'd know he could hold out for at least eight."

"You are incorrigible!" Emily fairly shouted at him, faintly shocked though she told herself that by now she should know better than to be shocked by anything he said or did. Remembering that they had an audience, she struggled to control her outburst. Impishly, she decided to turn the tables on him.

"Some women merely improve with age, Mr. Rutledge. Sam would demand at least ten ponies for me, and probably a few pounds of good tobacco," she told him tartly with a flip of her head. "I'm out of your league, sir," she added haughtily.

Drew looked up in surprise, and Caroline and the colonel both erupted in gales of laughter. Drew's face creased into a merry grin, and soon even Emily was laughing. As the laughter died away, Caroline began asking Drew about Indian legends and tales and about his name.

"Tell us your Sioux name, Drew. I've heard it refers to your eyes," Caroline prompted.

"Yeah, it does. When I was a boy, my father and I first met Long Feather down along the Platte River, and he gave me the name because he'd never seen eyes the color of mine. He hadn't seen too many white folks and didn't realize how many of us have blue eyes," Drew explained. "My Lakota name is Iśte Śkan Niyapi. Iśte means eyes, while *śkan* can mean blue, though it also refers to Takuśkanśkan. Takuśkanśkan is the sky and gives the power of movement to all things, and it refers to the way my eyes flash when I get excited or angry." He looked at Emily and grinned.

She blushed but remained silent.

"Niyapi means 'they live it' or 'they breathe it.' So all together, my name means something like 'eyes that are alive with the sky'. A little more poetic than Andrew, isn't it?" He chuckled.

"I think it suits you. Your eyes are rather distinctive, now that you mention it," Caroline commented. "Now tell us some more stories."

Soon they were listening raptly as he told them about Śkan, Wi, Maka, Inyan and the creation of the Lakota world. He explained the different aspects of *Wakantanka,* the Great Mystery, and how the first four—Sky, Sun, Earth, and Stone—had made the rest of the cosmos. If Emily was not overly thrilled with Sioux marital customs, she loved the stories Drew told. She closed her eyes and imagined a world to go with the words he spoke. All too soon, he stopped, saying that they still had a day's ride ahead tomorrow and should get some sleep.

Colonel Reynolds rose and offered his hand to his wife. "I think I could use another dip in that spring, Caroline," he said warmly. "Care to join me?"

"Matt!" she exclaimed, blushing. "We're not alone," she reminded him.

"No, but we will be if you come with me," her husband told her, his eyes twinkling.

Drew chuckled as the colonel led his wife away through the trees. Emily watched them leave with a wistful smile. It was wonderful to see people as in love as the Reynoldses were after several years of marriage. She wondered if she would ever have the same kind of warm, secure, yet passionate marriage. Her gaze strayed absently to watch Drew as he sorted through a saddlebag. For a brief moment, she allowed herself to imagine what it would be like to be married to him, to walk so confidently and openly by his side, to lie safe in his arms night after night.

She sighed. It was only a daydream. The reality of who they were made a future between them impossible. Still, he was so handsome, so strong, and at times he could be caring and gentle. His insights often touched her, and his sense of humor made her laugh, even at herself. Then he could turn around and shut himself off, cold and hard, unyielding in the expression of his iron will, willing to flout convention and the law to accomplish his ends. He seemed deliberately to push her away whenever she let her guard down and responded to him. Emily wondered why, of all the men in the world, she had to be attracted to this most impossible one.

Arranging her bedroll, Emily lay back with her arms under her head. Above her, she could see a thousand sparkling stars winking at her through the leafy branches. She remembered the stories Drew had told about Śkan, the Sky. She drifted off to sleep with the image of deep blue eyes glinting with little lights like stars, dancing across her closed eyelids. Iśte Śkan Niyapi, she thought. Eyes that are alive with the sky.

Some hours later, Emily awoke. All around her, it was dark and still, and the cool air smelled of damp earth and pine. The stars above her pulsed with light and color against the fathomless sky. She lay listening to the night sounds, expecting to fall right back to sleep. When she didn't, her thoughts began to wander. After long minutes passed and she was no closer to sleep, she sat up, peering about her in the darkness. The Reynoldses were asleep on her right. She thought she saw Drew's bedroll in the shadows across the faintly glowing coals of the fire. She was wide awake now, unable to sleep. She remembered the deliciously warm waters of the hot spring. Perhaps a swim would relax her enough so that she could get some rest.

Quietly, so as not to rouse anyone, she found her boots and slipped them on, then rose and worked her way carefully toward the spring, testing each footfall so that she would not step on noisy leaves and branches. It took several minutes to reach the pool, but finally she emerged through the trees and stood beside it.

Curls of steam wafted upward into the cool night air, barely visible in the starlight, as Emily shed her clothes, leaving them folded in a pile on a sturdy branch. It was extremely dark. There was no moon, only the stars and their reflections in the calm water. The bushes that overhung the far side of the spring were nothing more than a black outline against the spangled sky. Emily stood for a moment beside the water, exhilarated by the heady sense of freedom she felt surrounded by the concealing night. She stretched her saddle-sore limbs luxuriously, then slid into the steaming pool.

She felt the tenseness seeping out of her muscles at once. She hadn't realized how sore she was until the warmth of the water began to relax her. Walking further in, until the water reached nearly to her chin, Emily rolled her head back and closed her eyes, reveling in the pleasant sensations that prickled along her skin from the heat.

A small sound like a fish jumping and a swirl in the water at her back caused her to open her eyes instantly and turn her head in alarm. She started to scream, but a large hand clapped over her mouth in a firm grip that allowed only a muffled protest to escape her throat. An arm snaked around her bare waist, and Emily was pulled back against a man's hard, naked body. Panic quickened her pulse, and she tried vainly to struggle out of the viselike hold.

A voice sounded softly in her ear. "Shhh, Emily. It's only me," Drew whispered. "Stop fighting me. I'm not going to hurt you."

Relief surged through Emily, only to be immediately followed by an intensely uncomfortable awareness of Drew's bare flesh pressed against her own below the water. She went rigid, trying to hold herself as far from him as his intimate embrace allowed.

"You'll be quiet?" he queried softly.

She nodded. Did he honestly think she was going to wake Caroline and the colonel so they could find her in this compromising position?

Drew took a step backward and released her waist, his fingers trailing slowly across the smooth skin of her stomach. Emily felt her body quiver at his touch. Then the hand at her mouth relaxed its hard grip, but didn't move away. A bold finger traced the outline of her lips, probing the moist fullness of her lower lip when her mouth opened in surprise.

"Not again, Drew. Don't you ever give up?" she whispered against his finger.

"No, never. Not with you," he whispered above her ear.

"Let me go."

Slowly, tortuously, his fingers withdrew, caressing her cheek and the line of her jaw, sliding down the graceful curve of her neck to rest on her shoulder, just below the water. Emily fought to overcome a powerful, coursing languor that left her quiescent, unwilling to move away from his mesmerizing touch, despite her determination to do just that. She struggled to control her body's wanton response.

"What are you doing here?" she finally managed raggedly. His fingers were moving in delicious little circles along her shoulders and the back of her neck.

"I could ask you the same thing." Drew's voice sounded low and deep. He slid his thumbs across her shoulder blades as his fingers continued their caress.

"I woke up," Emily spoke through a haze. His stroking fingers seduced her, robbing her of her will to step away from him. Warmth invaded her from all sides and from within. "I couldn't get back to sleep. I thought the water would . . ." She paused. ". . . relax me." Her voice was but a whisper.

"I couldn't sleep, either," Drew told her, running his hands over the upper portion of her arms, slowly, languorously, delighting in the feel of her satiny skin in the heated water.

"Why not?" Emily asked, her eyes closed. She told herself she would pull away. In just another minute. His hands felt so good. Just a minute more.

"Because I want you so much," he whispered so softly that she almost didn't hear.

"So you insist whenever I conveniently land in your path. But what about when you left without a word to me? I can't believe you want me so badly after that," she protested. "It would have only taken a sentence, Drew. You can't make love to me when it suits you and then disappear whenever you feel like it. I don't want you like that, and you can't want me very much if that's enough for you."

His hands returned to her back, tracing lines and circles from her shoulders to her waist, increasing her desire and his own torment.

"I'll want you for a thousand years, Emily. I can't bear to be so near to you and not have you in my arms. Every time I look at you, I want to kiss you and carry you away to a place where no one will find us."

"I don't understand," she whispered, losing her thoughts in the wash of tingling sensations that flooded over her. "How can you say that? Do you expect me to believe you?"

"I can't explain it now. Maybe someday you'll understand." He sounded resigned. His hands continued their gentle explorations along her spine.

Physical passion, Emily thought distractedly. That's all he feels for me. Pull away now. But his fingers slid through the warm water along her skin, slipping beneath her arms to cup her full breasts, buoyant in the mineral pool. Shivers lapped over her in pleasant waves, and she didn't move.

"Emily, do you want me as I want you?"

There was a trace of desperate uncertainty in his low voice. He found her nipples, kneading them between his fingers, massaging her soft breasts in slow circles. He stepped closer, and his muscled thighs brushed her own. His taut belly pressed against her back. Against her hip, she felt his hard shaft.

She couldn't answer him. Yes, she wanted him, but she

wanted more than lovemaking. Her only reply was an un-certain murmur as she tried to pull away.

With a groan, Drew wrapped his arms around her and stopped her. He pressed fiery kisses to her neck, then turned and lifted her face to him.

The stars glinted in her eyes, and without meaning to, she raised her arms to twine around his neck. As their lips met, Emily felt her scruples fall away. She savored every moment of his burning kiss and possessive touch. She opened her mouth to him, inviting his tongue to invade and plunder the sweet softness there. She pressed herself to him, her hands running over the damp skin of his broad back and shoulders.

Drew caught his breath at the fervor of her response to him, in such contrast to her words. Her tongue tested the edges of his teeth, then boldly probed deeper, exciting his senses to new heights. If he couldn't give her the security of his name and home, he would give her his love this night, his passion, and his soul. He would give her ec-stasy. He would give all he could.

He drew her back with him toward the bank, where he lifted her easily onto the thick grass. He raised himself from the steaming pool and joined her there. Reaching into the pile of his clothes, he found the blanket he had brought to dry himself with and spread it on the grassy bank. Bend-ing on one knee, he stretched out his arm to Emily, offer-ing her his hand.

Her fingers closed firmly on his. There was a certain joy in surrendering to their mutual passion, and if there was to be nothing else, she would embrace the pleasure of the moment. She smiled sadly, searching the darkness for any hint of his own expression. She thought he smiled also, though in the starlight, it was impossible to tell.

Drew pulled her gently into his arms and removed the pins that held her long braid high on her head. Slowly, he unwound the strands of silky hair until it fell about them both in a billowing cloud. He tilted her head back to re-ceive his kiss. She could have run away, she knew, but she didn't. Instead, she pressed herself against his chest, feeling her damp skin slide sensuously against his. Their lips met again, this time less frantically.

Drew lazily flicked his tongue across Emily's mouth, teasing, testing the corners of her lips. He marveled at how perfect her soft skin felt beneath his roving hands, and at how small she felt as she sat across his lap within the warm circle of his arms. One hand stroked her shoulder tenderly, then dropped to close over her breast. Emily tipped her head back as Drew's mouth inched down her neck and chest. His lips moved across her breast, suddenly capturing the rosy peak, his tongue flickering against it like a lick of fire. He turned his attention to her other breast and slid his arms around her, lifting her from his lap. He laid her beneath him on the blanket, his mouth still pressed to her breast, supporting himself on his elbows. Emily's hands ran over the hard muscles of his upper arms, holding him to her as she delighted in the ripples of enjoyment that his tongue excited.

Drew shifted so that he knelt, his knees on either side of Emily. His hands came up to caress her breasts as his head moved lower, across the sensitive plain of her stomach, and then lower still. He brought one hand down to rest between her legs, his fingers gently sliding into the moist flesh there. He placed one knee between her legs and spread them open, revealing her most private place to him. His strong fingers touched her with surprising sensitivity, drawing a small cry from her lips. Then, before Emily knew what he was about, his fingers dipped inside her, and his head dropped to rest between her thighs. Her surprise was soon lost in the wild arousal wrought by Drew's flaming tongue. Her fingers curled into his wet hair as her passion rose, and she rocked her hips against him, inviting more of his searing touch. Almost too soon, a molten wave of sensation erupted through her, shaking her so that she gasped for breath.

Drew raised his head, working his way back toward Emily's mouth, pressing heated kisses to her heaving belly and breasts. When his lips again touched hers, he felt her smile. She laughed softly in delighted wonder, and he

clasped her to him tightly, an echoing chuckle in his throat
as he shared her joy.

Sliding one hand down her arm, Drew took Emily's
delicate hand in his and carried it to his groin. Her slim
fingers stopped motionless for a minute as she felt him
pulsing in response to her touch. Then, cautiously, she
began to explore the smooth length of him, running her
fingers up and down his long shaft, tentatively at first, then
with increasing confidence. Drew's hands slipped upward
along her back, pulling her close against him, and he held
his breath against the excitement her touch evoked. He
loved the feel of her hand moving lightly between their
bodies, fanning the flames of his passion as he had hers.

The urgency of his need increased, and Drew caught
Emily's mouth once more in an insistent kiss. His hands
found her breasts, kneading their sensitive tips as he once
again parted her legs. This time, she guided him to her,
arching up to meet him as he entered her.

A familiar sense of completeness assailed Emily, a sense
of being home, of rightness, and she was surprised to find
tears of release and happiness trickling from the corners
of her eyes. She gloried in his possession, giving herself
to him freely with unchecked abandon. Clutching at his
powerful shoulders, she moved to match Drew's rhythm
as he took her.

His heart swelled in fierce rejoicing even as his desire
drove him on. Each thrust brought them closer to the brink
of ecstasy, until finally, together, they met in one last surge
of mindless passion, their fulfillment shuddering through
them in pulsing waves. When at last they lay quiet, their
breathing even once again, their lips met in a sweet and
gentle kiss that bespoke the unacknowledged love between
them.

After they had lain together silently, gazing at the stars
for what seemed like hours as time hung suspended in the
black night around them, Emily gently disentangled herself from Drew's protective limbs and made to rise. He
caught her hand, pulling her back.

"Emily," he whispered, "I—"

She pressed a finger to his lips.

"Shhh. No words tonight," she whispered softly, and he understood. Words would only bring back reality and pain.

He kissed her finger, then released her hand. She dressed quietly, then slipped back through the trees to their camp. Drew lay for a long time staring at the sky, smiling at the memory of their ardor, trying to figure a way to get beyond the sword that was hanging over him, keeping him from being with her. Only time could provide the key. He hoped that she would wait.

The next day, the party left the hills traveling southeast across the high rolling grasslands, cut by rugged buttes and gullies, toward Pine Ridge Agency, close to the Nebraska border. Drew seemed to know the open country as well as he knew the hills. They rode quickly, hoping to make the agency by late afternoon.

Emily carefully avoided being alone with Drew that morning, though she took pains not to be obvious about it. Neither did they speak. Emily didn't know what she could possibly say, and she had no wish to hear that he wasn't interested in a more lasting relationship. She tried to act as if nothing had happened, to avoid drawing the Reynoldses attention to them. If she'd shamelessly chosen to let Drew make love to her, she certainly didn't care to advertise the fact.

About an hour after breaking camp, Drew led them up a near treeless ridge on the very edge of the hills. The sun was climbing higher into the eastern sky and the tall grass rustled softly in the breeze. As their horses neared a shallow depression, the air suddenly exploded with the rapid beat of many wings as a small covey of pheasants flushed from the brush. The colonel reached immediately for his rifle, but Drew stopped him.

"I wouldn't, Matt. The stage road from Sidney is just over this ridge. There's been a lot of trouble along it lately. Until we know what's ahead, I'd rather not let anyone know we're here," he cautioned.

The colonel nodded approvingly. "I didn't realize we were that close to the road," he said looking about.

"That's because I brought us around and about a bit so as to approach from this direction where we can't be seen unless we want to be," Drew explained. "There's a turn down below that has been increasingly used as an ambush site. Since a lot of settlers and teamsters use the road as well, there's always a chance we could run into someone."

"Which I'd prefer not to do," Colonel Reynolds affirmed.

As they neared the top of the ridge, Drew instructed Caroline and Emily to dismount and lead their horses toward a thicket of scraggly bushes. Emily's feet had just hit the earth when the crisp report of a rifle cracked through the air. Before she had time to look up, a rapid volley followed, echoing in the clear morning sky, and the blood-chilling sounds of war cries and mayhem rose from beyond the crest of the hill.

Chapter 13

Before the echo from the first shot had faded, Drew had grabbed his rifle, leaped off his horse, and breasted the hill, dropping behind the shelter of a rocky outcropping. The colonel followed on his heels, motioning for Emily and Caroline to stay where they were. They paid no attention and scrambled up the slope behind him. Looking down into the valley, Emily beheld the spectacle of a small wagon train besieged by a band of wildly painted, screaming Indians. They were riding in a circle around the ox-drawn wagons, forcing the train to a halt.

"My God!" Colonel Reynolds exclaimed, lifting his rifle to the top of the rocks and sighting down the barrel.

"Don't shoot," Drew ordered tersely, nodding at the women. "Don't draw their fire up here. Something's wrong with those Indians," he said, a deep frown creasing his forehead.

"Do you recognize them?" the colonel asked quickly, shielding his eyes against the sun with his hand.

"No," Drew replied. "The clothes are Sioux, the horses are Indian ponies, but their paint and their war cries are strange. And they don't ride like any Indians I ever saw."

Emily gasped as she comprehended the implications of Drew's remarks. The colonel spoke her thoughts.

"You don't think they're Indians," he stated, nodding as if this made sense. "We need to get down there and stop them."

Drew turned to Emily and Caroline. "I want you to stay here and don't move. That's an order. We'll let you know when it's safe to come down. Understand?'' he said urgently, the lights flashing in his eyes.

Emily nodded as his eyes bored deep into hers. Then he looked back to the colonel. Below, the freighters had stopped and were surrounded by the reeling riders.

''Come on. There's a gully we can ride down and surprise them over there,'' Drew said to the colonel with a jerk of his head. ''We'd better hurry.''

The men mounted quickly and were out of sight in seconds. Emily looked at Caroline, then at the disturbing scene below. The teamsters had somehow managed to get their wagons into a circle and they now stood inside it, cautiously watching the attackers. The shooting had subsided to intermittent fire, and it didn't look as though anyone had been hurt yet.

''I'm getting my rifle,'' Emily told Caroline, scooting down the hill toward her horse. Caroline followed, and the two of them secured their horses' reins, removed their rifles from the scabbards, and crept back up to the outcropping. Emily rested the barrel on a rock and tried to quell her rising nausea.

Just then, she caught a flicker of movement in the valley to her right. Her heart pounded as she watched Drew and Colonel Reynolds lead their horses cautiously into the cover of some trees in the valley bottom. She and Caroline exchanged worried glances. Caroline smiled bravely.

''They can take care of themselves,'' she said, assuring herself as much as Emily.

''I know,'' Emily mumbled. ''It's only that . . . '' She could not finish as she contemplated what it would be like to live in the world should something happen to Drew. She told herself that she was prepared to live without him, but she wasn't certain she could face his death. Even thinking about it brought a lump to her throat.

''They'll be all right,'' Caroline promised.

The two women watched as Drew and Matt edged closer to the cornered wagons. It was hard to see them through the trees. The Indian impostors were riding around the teamsters, tightening the circle, dodging pistol shots and making a tremendous racket. It was unlikely that they would hear Drew and Colonel Reynolds until it was too late.

In a sudden movement, with the most unearthly yell Emily had ever heard, the two men broke from the trees at a gallop, firing their breech-loading rifles at the attackers' horses. Instantly, two of the eight ponies stumbled to the ground, throwing their riders. The other Indians turned their attention from the teamsters, looking about in bewilderment, trying to determine where the rapid fire was coming from. Another pony dropped, and its rider ran madly about, searching for cover. In another second, he fell dead with a bullet in his throat. The attackers began to return Drew and Colonel Reynolds's fire in earnest. Drew hung off the side of his saddle, using his horse's body as a shield from the whizzing bullets, shooting with deadly accuracy from across or below the animal's neck.

The teamsters also began to fire upon the attacking Indians with renewed vigor when they realized that they had help. With bullets coming from two directions, the Indian circle disintegrated. One man fell with a bullet in his leg. Then he crumpled as if struck again, this time mortally. Another horse screamed in panic as a piece of lead tore into its stomach. Only four of the Indians remained mounted when they began to retreat up the valley. A shot from one of the teamster's rifles stopped another of the men who was on foot. Emily watched in horror as the impact of the bullet slammed him to the ground. The last man on foot chased after his retreating comrades, yelling frantically. One of them turned back and pulled the unseated man into the saddle behind him. Then they raced off in pursuit of their friends, leaving the field of battle.

As suddenly as it had begun, the attack was over. Drew and Colonel Reynolds dismounted and walked to the wagons to speak with the men who were emerging from their makeshift stockade. Emily and Caroline remained hidden at the top of the hill, watching and waiting for a signal to go below. Gradually, the tension eased out of Emily's muscles, leaving her feeling weak and a little faint. She had never seen men killed before, and she was quite certain she never cared to again.

Emily watched as Drew and the colonel conferred with the attacked men, none of whom seemed injured. Then Drew walked toward one of the dead men. He turned the man over and called the colonel to his side. They examined the corpse, carried it to the wagons, then moved on to the next one. Emily saw the men shaking their heads as they turned the second man over and carried his body to lay beside the other. Finally, they approached the last body, lying in a bent heap, bright bloodstains clearly visible even from a distance.

A scream rose in Emily's throat as she saw the motionless man roll suddenly and bring up his pistol, aimed straight at Drew's chest. There was a single ringing shot. Helpless terror blazed through Emily, and she collapsed against Caroline, her scream becoming a sob. The attacker fell a last time to the ground already wet with his blood. Drew stood above him, his revolver smoking in his hand. The colonel stooped and removed the weapon from the dead man's grip. Then they carried him over to where the teamsters were already digging a grave to bury the three men.

Emily clung to Caroline for a few moments, unable to believe her eyes at first. Then silent tears began to flow, and she couldn't stop them. She wept for her grief over all that was wrong between them, and for relief that he hadn't been killed.

"I told you they'd be all right," Caroline told Emily soothingly.

She wrapped her arm around Emily's shoulder, handed her a handkerchief, and thanked God that neither her husband nor Drew had been hurt. She was used to seeing Matt in dangerous situations, knowing that he would leave her possibly never to return someday, and inside she, too, shuddered at the close call they had witnessed. At least she had known the joy of living with her husband in love, and if anything ever happened to him, she would have that to hold on to. She hoped that Emily and Drew would find that same joy.

* * *

Only after the dead were buried and the pack train on its way again did Drew signal to Emily and Caroline to descend the hill. As soon as they reached the valley floor, Drew hustled them along, saying that he would tell them what they had learned after they were a safe distance away from the stage road. Once they'd reached the seemingly trackless, empty plains again, he slowed their pace. The four of them rode abreast.

"Drew was right," Colonel Reynolds began. "Those men weren't Indians. They were as white as any of us are."

"I don't understand why they would go to so much trouble to dress up like that," Emily said pensively. "Most outlaws wear a simple scarf over their faces, if anything. It doesn't make much sense."

"It does if they were trying to stir up anti-Indian sentiment and provide evidence of depredations against whites," Drew pointed out in a tired voice. "I can't think of a better means of getting the army involved in campaigns against the Sioux. I'll bet the last person those scoundrels expected to run into was the Fort Meade commander." He smiled with grim satisfaction. "We put a pretty big hole in their plans today."

"Do you have any idea who's behind this?" Emily asked with concern.

"No, not yet," the colonel answered carefully. "We didn't recognize any of the men in the attack party. They could be from outside the territory. I doubt if that particular bunch will be any trouble for a while. They'll be counting on those teamsters to spread the story of being attacked by Sioux, and licking their wounds."

"Did they know who you were?" Caroline asked her husband.

"I don't think they did, though they may have figured out who Drew was from the way he rode. Hanging from the side of a horse while shooting isn't a normal cavalry trick," the colonel said with some concern. "We didn't tell the teamsters who we were, either. Just made up a couple of names. They saw for themselves that those men weren't Indians, though."

"Why don't you want anyone to know who you are?" Emily asked.

The colonel started to speak, but Drew cut him off. "Because we don't want to draw unnecessary attention to this trip, and we want to keep you and Caroline as safe as possible." He looked straight ahead as he spoke.

Emily was once again aware that there were secrets here that she wasn't privy to. As they rode on, she wracked her brain, trying to figure out what they weren't telling her and what the true relationship was between the army commander and Drew, a self-confessed illegal supplier to hostile Indians. They seemed to enjoy a high level of mutual trust and esteem. There was no unease or suspicion between them at all. Sam was the only other man she knew who had a similar relationship with Drew. Everyone else disliked or feared him. How was it that the two men she most liked and respected, her brother and the colonel, got along so well with Drew? It wasn't like them to trust such an unpredictable, and, at times, unscrupulous man. Again she wondered, as she had in the past, if they knew something that she didn't.

She remembered the story she had overheard Sam telling Maggie about the stolen weapons and how the teamster had insisted that he had been attacked by a band of Indians led by a white man in Indian garb. Today's incident was clearly related. Someone was trying to frame him, along with the Sioux, for the attacks.

"What were those wagons hauling?" she asked the colonel innocently, hoping Drew wouldn't hear. She knew by now that he would tell her as little as possible, that he would even lie to keep her from knowing the truth. "They must have had some valuable cargo to invite such an attack," she speculated.

"It was a load of household goods for some homesteaders near Custer City. It doesn't take much to provoke attacks like this in country that's virtually unpatrolled. Especially if the main purpose is to generate fear of Indians rather than to garner booty."

It made sense, but Emily suspected he was lying. She would bet that the wagons had been carrying at least a good supply of ammunition, and possibly some guns. She could tell by the firm set of the colonel's jaw that she would get no information from him. She'd have to wait to confirm her suspicions.

The one thing that still puzzled her was why Drew felt such an overwhelming compulsion to protect her at all times, when he'd as much as said that the only feelings he had for her were motivated by lust. She supposed it was possible that that emotion could be very strong indeed, but it struck her as odd. After all, he could find any number of women willing to satisfy his carnal desires. Why did he think he was protecting her by not telling her what was going on? Last night, he certainly hadn't been any too concerned about protecting her. It seemed to Emily that for all he talked of looking out for her, he himself was the biggest threat to her peace of mind.

The rest of the ride into Pine Ridge was uneventful. As they neared the agency, the little settlement where the government annuities were distributed and the reservation's affairs administered, they passed several small camps. Most of these consisted of tipis made of hides or canvas, but there were also quite a number of small, one-room square cabins strung out along the creek valleys. The colonel and Caroline would be expected to stay at the agent's house, but Emily would stay in the camp across the creek with the Indians. Drew explained that he always stayed at Long Feather's wife's tipi. Emily would stay at Black Wolf's wife's tipi.

Drew entertained them with stories about the troubles between Red Cloud and Agent Valentine McGillycuddy. He advised Emily to be on her best behavior with the acerbic agent, for he was a stickler for formalities and protocol.

"Red Cloud hates him, and the feeling is entirely mutual," Drew told them. "McGillycuddy is only in his thirties, and he looks young, besides which he can be a real martinet. Red Cloud considers him a baby, and it's an insult to him to defer to such a young man. McGillycuddy is not your typical Dakotan, either, who will tell you to use his first name on meeting you. He insists on the respect he feels is due him, and he's recruited a force of Indian police to enforce his many rules and regulations. Chief among those is that all visitors to the reservation must report immediately to his office, so that's where we'll head first. He's not going to be too thrilled at your staying in the Indian camp, Emily, but I'll take care of it. Don't let him get your back up.''

As he finished speaking, two Indians dressed in blue uniforms approached on horseback. Drew exchanged greetings with them in Lakota and explained who the others were and their purposes for being there. Since they were expected, there was no difficulty. The policemen turned to escort the foursome into the agency, smiling and chatting amiably with Drew. One of them pointed at Emily and asked him a question. Drew shook his head and made a lengthy reply. The man looked appraisingly at Emily. Drew's eyes narrowed a fraction as he made a further comment.

''What did he ask you?'' Emily inquired.

Drew looked at her a moment before answering.

''He wanted to know if you were my woman,'' he said with a little smile.

Emily shifted uncomfortably in her saddle. ''What did you tell him?'' she asked, aware of Caroline and her husband's amusement.

''The truth, of course,'' Drew shot back casually, leaving Emily with the quandary of whether to ask what that was in front of their companions.

''Ah,'' she said, dying to know what he had said but unable to ask for clarification. ''Well, how noble of you,'' she finally finished.

Drew chuckled at her dilemma. ''I told him you aren't my woman and that you're here to visit my brother and his family. Satisfied?'' He grinned at her from beneath the brim of his hat.

''Yes, of course,'' Emily replied evenly. ''That's the truth, isn't it?'' She smiled sweetly, trying to hide her disappointment with his answer.

* * *

Pine Ridge was aptly named, a long ridge dotted with pine trees rising above the little agency community. As it was late in the afternoon, Drew deposited the Reynoldses with Agent McGillycuddy and introduced Emily, anxious to get settled at the Indian camp and to see his family. He hadn't gotten to see them as often as he would have liked over the past summer.

As Drew had predicted, the agent was not especially taken with the plan for Emily to stay at the Indian camp. Drew skillfully used the man's antipathy for Red Cloud, however, and portrayed her visit as a monumental affront to the old chief. Emily knew Red Cloud would be delighted to hear that his plan had gone off without a hitch. Apparently, McGillycuddy thought better of Black Wolf that he did any of the other Indians in Red Cloud's camp. When Drew told him that Emily was visiting at his request, and staying at his tipi, with the express purpose of discussing the education of Indian children, the agent finally relented and granted his permission.

"This should stick in that old blatherskite's craw," McGillycuddy had said of Red Cloud. "A teacher, of all people, staying in his camp. Maybe I'll come up and watch the fireworks." The agent had chuckled through his lavish moustache.

"I'm sure everything will be fine," Emily had insisted.

"Hmph!" had been the agent's only reply.

When they reached the cluster of buff-colored tipis, they were immediately surrounded by a large group of children. Drew appeared to be quite a favorite. As he dismounted, he was swamped by little boys who hung all around him. He laughed and joked with them, then dug into one of his saddlebags and produced a bag of lemon drops. The children went mad for them, and Emily laughed heartily at their antics as some of the bolder among them tried to finagle more than their share. Emily also dismounted, removing her saddlebags, and Black Wolf gave their horses into the care of one of the older boys. He led them into the center of the village, the children tagging along.

Black Wolf showed Emily to a tipi decorated with colorful buffalo and wolves painted on it. He called out, and a pretty woman only a few years older than Emily, with dark, braided hair and lustrous black eyes, emerged from the opening. She was dressed in a blue wool dress and leather moccasins decorated with quillwork in many bright colors. She was clearly pregnant, and the proud gleam in Black Wolf's eyes told Emily that this was his wife. He introduced her as Wambli Luta Win, which he explained meant Red Eagle Woman. She smiled at Emily in welcome. Black Wolf explained that she didn't speak too much English, but she was honored to have Emily as a guest in her tipi. Emily thanked her, liking the Indian woman immediately.

Then Black Wolf called to the group of children around Drew, and a little boy and girl separated themselves from the throng. The boy was perhaps eight or nine, and the girl about five years old. Black Wolf introduced his son as Sees Far at Night and his daughter as Little Star, and they smiled shyly at Emily. Their father dismissed them, and they ran gaily back to join their companions.

Red Eagle Woman held the tipi flap aside and motioned for Emily to enter. Inside, Emily found that it was not as smoky as she had thought it would be; the smoke from the fire rose straight to the opening at the top of the structure. Soft furs and skins were scattered around the floor, and the family's possessions hung suspended from the lodge poles in leather bags. Numerous painted leather boxes and parfleches were neatly stacked behind willow backrests that served for seats and beds. In addition, a number of household items, such as cups and bowls, rested on a pair of trunks covered with dark red woolen trade cloth. Emily was surprised at how comfortable the lodge was. She spread her arms, indicating everything around her, and smiled and nodded to Red Eagle Woman.

"You have a pleasant tipi," she said, doubtful that her hostess would understand.

"Thank you," the other woman replied shyly, surprising Emily.

"You understand English?" Emily asked.

"More than Black Wolf thinks." Red Eagle Woman

laughed quietly. "I listen often to him when he talks to mišíc'e in your language. Ište Škan Niyapi's father also taught me some English when I was a girl. I know more than my husband thinks," she repeated, smiling widely.

After Emily had washed and changed into a clean dress, it was almost dark, and Red Eagle Woman was setting out the evening meal. Drew came to the tipi to eat along with Black Wolf and Shining Cloud, Long Feather's pretty niece.

The meal was hurried because a social dance was planned for that evening. Emily discovered that a group of four or five Hunkpapa young men had come that day, looking for suitable young women to court. The Hunkpapas were one of the Lakota tribes who ranged mostly to the north of the Oglala country. Many of the hostiles who had fled to Canada under Sitting Bull and Gall were Hunkpapas. These young men had heard from one of their cousins, whose wife was an Oglala, that many girls of marriageable age lived at Pine Ridge. Emily was told that it was not unusual for the Sioux to seek their mates from other bands, and in fact, it seemed to be encouraged. The party of several young warriors, however, had caused quite a stir. Red Eagle Woman told Emily that young men almost always went by themselves to court a woman.

The dancing took place in a circle at the center of the camp. Many of the girls were dressed in beautifully quilled and beaded dresses, and the Hunkpapa men were dressed impressively as well. Their faces were painted, and they wore feathers and other symbols that indicated their deeds in the hunt and in battle. Emily noticed that one of these young men stood out particularly, and many of the Oglala girls eyes him with approval. He was as tall as Drew and Black Wolf, though not as broad, having a more wiry build. He looked as though he might be in his mid-twenties, and he wore badges indicating great prowess as a hunter and warrior. His face was handsome, and he had very striking, large, dark brown eyes that held an intriguing hint of sadness blended with a marked sensuality. It was clearly a potent combination, for he was never at a loss for a dancing partner. Emily learned that his name was Iron Thunder.

Emily enjoyed the dancing tremendously. Shining Cloud had pulled her into the line of dancers, and she had quickly learned the steps and rhythms. It was completely different from the dancing that the warriors had demonstrated in Deadwood, but it was exciting to be participating in something she had never dreamed she would be a part of. Even Drew danced, which surprised Emily. He was normally so detached, more of an observer than anything else. He seemed much more relaxed here, less guarded and mysterious. It struck her forcibly that the colonel had been right in his observation that Drew was more Indian than not most of the time.

During the course of the evening, Emily became aware that every time she happened to notice Iron Thunder, he was looking at her. He didn't approach, nor did he try to speak with her, but his gaze became a trifle unnerving. She put it down to the fact that she was white. While the camp was used to Drew, and to living close to the whites at the agency, these wild Hunkpapas from farther north probably hadn't had much peaceable contact with white people. She tried not to let it bother her. After all, she had been accepted here with far more civility than any of the Indians had received in the local white towns. She tried not to worry about Iron Thunder and turned her attention to enjoying the evening.

The next afternoon, Emily was to meet with Red Cloud. Black Wolf would translate for her, as Drew had some business to attend to and was riding to one of the other camps. Before he left that morning, he came to Red Eagle Woman's tipi to see how Emily was faring. Hearing her name, Emily rose from examining the beadwork that Shining Cloud was stitching, and found Drew and Black Wolf standing outside the lodge. She greeted them. Drew told her his plans, then asked if she needed anything.

"No, I'm fine," she told him. "I can't remember having such a wonderful time. I'm learning so many things!"

Her bright smile brought one in response from Drew, and his eyes held approval.

"Good." He nodded pleasantly. "I'll be off then," he said, turning away.

Before he had gone two steps, Iron Thunder emerged from around the side of a nearby tipi and called to him. Drew stopped and greeted the younger man in Lakota. Iron Thunder's eyes were on Emily as he spoke quietly to Drew. Drew's back was to her, but she saw him straighten, and when he glanced at her, there was surprise in his eyes. Beside her, Black Wolf chuckled under his breath.

"What did he say?" she asked Black Wolf immediately. "Why are they talking about me?" She was afraid Iron Thunder didn't like her, and that he might cause trouble. "Iron Thunder doesn't like me, does he?" she ventured doubtfully.

Black Wolf shook his head and smiled. "He asked my brother if you are his woman. He heard that you came into camp together, but also that you slept in different lodges, so he's curious."

Drew seemed to recover his tongue and he answered briefly. Black Wolf's lips formed a disapproving line at whatever he said.

"Why is he asking that? What did Drew say?" Emily wanted to know.

"My brother says you're not his woman, but that he's responsible for you while you're here," Black Wolf said, still looking annoyed.

Iron Thunder began a lengthy speech, and Black Wolf waved Emily to hold her questions until he was finished. He translated in a low voice.

"He tells *misun* that he and his companions are here to seek women. He tells Drew that he is a great hunter and warrior and that he can provide a good life for a wife. He says he'd like to court you and he has offered *misun* eight horses for you."

Emily was flabbergasted. She stood openmouthed, watching Drew calmly listening to this man offering to buy her!

Drew placed his hands low on his hips and regarded the

Hunkpapa evenly. He spoke, gesturing toward Emily with his chin.

"What's he saying?" Emily hissed at Black Wolf impatiently.

"He's explaining that you wouldn't make a good wife because you've been raised by the whites and you know nothing of how to live like a Lakota. He says you wouldn't be a good worker, that the man's mother and sisters would have to teach you everything, and that you don't even have a tipi and household goods to bring to him. He says you can't even make a pair of moccasins. Also, he's not sure you would want to live with the Lakota."

Everything Drew said was true, and she certainly would never consent to be the wife of a man she didn't know at all, sold for a few ponies, but for some reason it irritated Emily to hear Drew say so. She glared at his handsome profile resentfully, aware that her reaction was ridiculous.

Iron Thunder appeared to consider this very seriously. He folded his arms across his chest and nodded for several minutes in silence, glancing surreptitiously at Emily all the while. At length, he spoke. Black Wolf translated when Emily pulled insistently on his sleeve.

"Iron Thunder is persistent. He says he can perhaps offer ten horses, and he thanks my brother for being honest about your shortcomings, but he's very taken with you. He'd like to talk with you. He thinks you're pretty enough to make up for not being a good worker, and perhaps he can trade for a tipi and goods at the agency. He asks my brother to consider his offer seriously," Black Wolf finished. "It's an extravagant offer. Few have even one horse anymore."

Emily was taken aback, though also a little flattered. She watched Drew intently, wondering what he would say in response. She noted that he no longer appeared relaxed. When he looked in exasperation at Black Wolf, as if in silent appeal for aid, there was a tight set to his jaw that Emily was more than familiar with. She tensed, waiting for some sort of outburst.

Instead, Drew took a deep breath, his wide shoulders

expanding beneath his leather shirt. When he spoke, his tone was forceful, but quiet.

"My brother says that you are your own woman and that you will make your own decisions, but that he is responsible to your brother for your well-being. He doesn't wish Iron Thunder, nor anyone else, to court you. He will not accept any ponies, not even one hundred, and you are a white woman and thus not looking for a husband among the Lakota. He suggests that Iron Thunder consider Pretty Beaver, Yellow Thunder's sister. She would make a much better wife for him," Black Wolf told her.

Iron Thunder wasn't pleased with Drew's response. He regarded the white man with a scowl spreading across his features. He made a terse comment, then stalked off, throwing a backward glance at Emily.

"Do you think that was wise?" Black Wolf asked Drew in English.

Drew shot him a look full of ire. "I don't want to hear it," he snapped as he, too, stalked off in search of his horse.

Emily looked after the two men in amazement.

Chapter 14

Drew had had a long day. He had ridden up to Wounded Knee Creek and back, a distance of several miles, after hearing that a small party recently returned from Canada was staying there. He'd hoped to uncover a lead to the identity of the man behind the rebellion plot, but had learned nothing new. Drew was frustrated and tired, and his face showed it as he slid off his horse, throwing the reins to one of the boys tending the village's small herd. Black Wolf met him at the edge of the camp.

"Any luck today?" he asked, guessing the answer already from Drew's resigned expression.

"Not a damn thing. Whoever's behind this, he's as slick as anybody I've ever seen. He doesn't leave any tracks anywhere," Drew said angrily, slapping his gloves against his thigh. "I don't know where to look next. I'm afraid I'm going to have to force his hand somehow."

Black Wolf shook his head thoughtfully. "You told me that Miss Parker had a dream that might help. It was the same one you've had?"

"Yeah, but she didn't see much farther than I did. I'm not sure what she saw meant. Tonight I plan to consult your father about it," Drew told him.

"Why don't you have her tell him?" Black Wolf suggested.

"I don't want to get her involved, and I don't want her to start putting all the pieces together. That kind of knowledge can only increase the danger she's in." His tone was final.

"She's the woman from your vision," Black Wolf stated.

"Yeah," Drew sighed in agreement. "She is."

"She's already involved. She'll begin to understand even if you don't tell her. She's no fool, and she cares for you. You should tell her everything," Black Wolf advised.

"How can I?" Drew asked in an agonized voice. "She could be killed. I could easily be killed, and where would that leave her? In the middle of a problem that has nothing to do with her, without help. What am I supposed to do?"

"What does your heart tell you, brother?"

Drew was silent.

Black Wolf continued. "You lied to Iron Thunder when you told him she wasn't your woman, *misun*. I can see it in your eyes when you look at her. Everyone can. You're a fool to drive her away from you. You want to take her as your woman, and you need her help. Wakantanka has sent her to you."

Drew looked at the sun as it set in a fiery ball behind the bluffs in the west, and shook his head wearily.

"The timing isn't right yet," he said softly, a trace of sadness touching his features. He looked back to Black Wolf. "Let's go see what there is for supper."

"All right. We won't talk about it anymore tonight. Come to my wife's lodge, *misun*," Black Wolf said quietly, understanding the pain Drew suffered.

They walked in silence through the camp to Red Eagle Woman's tipi. Outside it, seated on the ground, Iron Thunder was playing a light melody on a large wooden flute. Drew spun to face his brother.

"What the hell is this?" he bellowed. "How long has he been there?"

Black Wolf stared at the Hunkpapa with annoyance. "I don't know. I'll find out," he said tightly, advancing to the lodge. He stopped at the opening and faced Drew. "This is your own fault," he announced tersely before he entered.

Outside, Drew glared at the younger man who sat wrapped in a blanket, calmly playing little tunes on his flute. Drew hadn't anticipated Iron Thunder's tenacity in pursuing Emily, yet there was little he could do to stop the display. Traditionally, when a Lakota man wanted to court a woman, he waited around her lodge, hoping she would stand inside his blanket with him for a few minutes of private conversation. If he really wanted to make an impression, he might get one of the old, duck-shaped flutes and try to coax some love music out of it. Drew hadn't even seen a flute in years, though as a boy he'd learned to play one. With a tremendous effort, he remained silent until Black Wolf and Red Eagle Woman came out of the lodge.

"He's been here about an hour," Black Wolf informed Drew. "When Emily heard the music, she immediately looked out to see what it was before Red Eagle Woman could stop her and explain what was happening. She asked to see the flute and listened while he played a song. Then she stood with him in his blanket for a while. Iron Thunder was most pleased."

"Damn!" Drew cursed vehemently. "I told him not to court her! What kind of idiot is he? He has to know this is futile!"

Black Wolf looked at Drew with patient resignation. "He's bewitched, *misun*. I'd think you might have more sympathy, given the circumstances."

Drew scowled furiously at his adopted brother. "There's a difference, and you know it," he ground out between clenched teeth.

"I do, but he doesn't. Since you told him Emily isn't your woman, he's not going to understand why you don't want others to court her. He's too taken to recognize that the fact that she's white makes it most unlikely his suit would be accepted. You know what he might try, if you continue to reject his offers for her," Black Wolf pointed out ominously.

"I know," Drew snapped irritably.

It was possible that Iron Thunder would try to abduct Emily, especially if she had shown any interest in him, as it appeared she had when she stood inside his blanket. Under Lakota customs, it was permissible to steal a woman if her guardians wouldn't release her to be married, and if the woman was agreeable. Emily's friendly behavior might easily have led Iron Thunder to believe she would accept him.

Red Eagle Woman spoke softly in Lakota. "There are a couple of things you could do," she suggested. Drew gave her his full attention. "You could wait. You'll be leaving in two days. He might not act so quickly."

"But he might follow you," her husband added. "It would be risky."

"Or you could send Emily to stay with Mc-Gillycuddy," she continued.

"Red Cloud would be gravely insulted," Black Wolf pointed out. "He'd never forgive you." Drew looked at him with chagrin.

"Or you could claim her as your woman," Red Eagle Woman finished.

Drew allowed her last suggestion to sink in. "I can't do that," he finally said flatly. He looked away.

"It would solve the problem," his brother said evenly, the ghost of a smile on his lips.

"But it would create a lot of others," Drew stated firmly.

"Don't you want her?" Red Eagle Woman asked coaxingly in Lakota. "You obviously care very much for her."

"That isn't the point!" Drew exclaimed in exasperation. "I can't claim Emily. It wouldn't be right. Besides, she wouldn't have me. I've tried to make her think I'm not exactly good husband material."

"You are being difficult, *miśic'e*. If you had told Iron Thunder this morning that she was your woman, there would have been none of this problem. He wouldn't have known any better, and Emily wouldn't have known. Now you are willing to let her be carried off onto the plains by this love-crazed Hunkpapa! I wonder what her brother would think if he heard about this!" Red Eagle Woman chastised him.

"I have an idea that might work," Black Wolf interrupted. "It's a compromise of sorts. We should have thought of it before. What about an engagement?" he asked hopefully.

Both Drew and Red Eagle Woman considered the idea. "Do you think Iron Thunder would accept it as binding?" the woman asked doubtfully.

"He seems an honorable man. If Emily accepts Drew, he'll abide by her decision. There's a chance he might not, but he'd risk his standing in his tribe if he attempted to take her after she was promised to another man. He's a proud man. I don't think he'll risk his social position readily," Black Wolf argued convincingly.

Drew appeared to be weighing the merits of the idea seriously. "What about Emily?" he asked. "She won't go along with this. She'll refuse to believe that the situation is as serious as it is, and I'm pretty sure she'll refuse to become engaged to me."

"I wouldn't be so sure of that, *misic'e*," Red Eagle Woman told him. "There is a solution, however, that would resolve the problem," she added with a little smile.

"What's that, *mitawin?*" Black Wolf asked, anticipating his wife's machinations.

"We won't tell her what's going on. I can make up something to get her to do the things she needs to. She won't know what any of it means, since only the two of you will be involved. When the announcement is made in the camp, she won't understand it, and I'll simply tell her we are having a celebration in honor of her visit."

Drew looked from his brother to his wife and back again. He was defeated, and he knew it. They were right that he had to do something, and this seemed like the best option. He pursed his lips and closed his eyes. When he opened them, he had an unobstructed view of Iron Thunder playing his cursed love flute.

"All right," he agreed grimly. "I'll do it."

Black Wolf led Drew off to Long Feather's tipi and explained to his parents what they were going to do. Long Feather, a holy man, insisted that Drew join him in the sweat lodge before dressing for the evening. The sweat bath was prepared, he told his sons. Drew looked at him in surprise.

"I just know things, sometimes, *cinkś.*" The old man laughed. "This is a good thing you're doing. Everything will work out fine. You'll see."

Drew felt somewhat comforted by his *hunka* father's words and prepared himself for the ritual.

In the lodge, the hot rocks glowing faintly red in the darkness, Drew accepted the pipe offered by Long Feather. He raised it to the four winds, to the sky and the earth, and to the Spotted Eagle. Then he inhaled deeply and uttered the ritual response. As the sweat poured from his body in the intense heat, cleansing him, he felt his mind cleansed as well. His thoughts became clear. He wanted to marry Emily. This night he would go through with the engagement sincerely, even if she didn't understand what he said. He would hold it as a promise that would guide him to the end of the mystery that continued to thwart him and that threatened his adopted people, the Lakota Sioux. Suddenly, it came to him with certainty that he could triumph over his hidden adversary. He would have a future with Emily. He would make it happen, with the help of Wakantanka. He relaxed in the blasting heat, a slight smile playing upon his lips.

Red Eagle Woman fed her family, then sent the children to play at her aunt's lodge. She told Shining Cloud what had to be done, and the girl slipped away to get the things they needed from her clothing chest. In a few minutes, she had returned with an armful of dresses and embroidered leggings.

"Emily," Red Eagle Woman began, "how would you like to dress up like a real Oglala woman?" she suggested temptingly. "I would like to see what you would look like. What do you think?"

Emily was soon laughing and trying on the clothes that Shining Cloud had brought. When she put on a soft, long-sleeved dress of the finest elk skin, embroidered with white and blue quills in geometric patterns and trimmed with long fringes and elk's teeth, Red Eagle Woman and Shin-

ing Cloud nodded their heads in approval. They chose a
pair of knee-high leggings, also made from the same soft,
creamy leather, and a pair of lavishly decorated moccasins. Then they arranged Emily's hair in twin braids that
fell down her back, tying the ends with dark green ribbons
that Shining Cloud said Drew had brought her one time.
When Emily protested, the women laughed and brushed
her objections aside. They tied a beaded leather headband
across her forehead, and then, finally, they hung a beaded
ornament from the back of her hair. They stood back from
Emily and made her turn in a circle so they could examine
their handiwork.

"You look beautiful!" Shining Cloud exclaimed.

"My brother-in-law will be pleased," Red Eagle
Woman added softly in Lakota.

Emily smiled with pleasure at the borrowed finery. "I
wish I had a mirror. Now what?" she asked, suspecting
there was a reason behind this change of clothing.

"I think Drew would want to see you," Red Eagle
Woman said with a smile. "I don't think he has ever seen
a white woman dressed this way."

Emily remembered the night she had worn the Indian
blouse and skirt, but she had had no ornaments in her hair
or beaded headband then. "No, I don't suppose he has."

"He will probably come sometime this evening. Maybe
White Tree Woman has a mirror at her lodge. Drew can
take you there to look," Shining Cloud told her.

"Yes, perhaps," Emily said. "Why don't we go for a
little walk around the village? Then I could show off a
little for other people as well. I'll bet almost no one has
seen a white woman dressed like an Indian." The idea
tickled her. If she thought her mother would have had a
fit seeing her dressed in trousers, it was nothing compared
to the reaction she would get in this outfit!

A noise outside the tipi caused Emily to look toward
the entrance flap. For the second time that day, she heard
the reedy voice of an Oglala flute playing a simple melody. Red Eagle Woman had not explained the significance
of the serenade to Emily, but she had figured out that Iron
Thunder's earlier performance was linked in some way to

his interest in her. Her eyes widened in surprise. Had the
Hunkpapa returned already? This flute sounded a little different, and the tune was played with more skill.

"Who's that?" Emily asked Shining Cloud. "It doesn't
sound like Iron Thunder. Unless he took a lesson during
supper." She giggled.

The Indian women laughed. "Why don't you look out
and see?" Red Eagle Woman suggested, her eyes twinkling. Shining Cloud nodded encouragingly.

Emily moved to the lodge opening, lifted one corner
aside, and peered out into the darkness. About thirty feet
away from the tipi, she saw the shape of a tall man. He
was wrapped in a voluminous dark robe, and he held the
flute to his mouth. The pleasant melody drifted across
the air to her, but she couldn't see the man's face or dis-
cern his shape very clearly beneath the robe.

"I can't tell who it is," Emily whispered back to Red
Eagle Woman. "He's all wrapped up in a big robe. Come
look."

The other women crept to the opening and looked out.
As they did so, the man began to pace backward and forward before the tipi, gradually inching closer. Emily
watched, but she still couldn't make out the man's features. Something about him was familiar, but she couldn't
place him. He was elaborately dressed, his face was
painted brightly, and many eagle feathers attached to a
headband hung on either side of his face. The paint reflected the moonlight, and the feathers swung with his
movements.

"Who is it?" Emily asked in a whisper.

"Why don't you go see?" Red Eagle Woman suggested. "I can't tell."

"Should I?" Emily queried doubtfully.

"Yes, it will be fine. Go ahead." The older woman
gave her a little push through the opening.

Emily emerged from the tipi and stood uncomfortably
for a moment. There was no one else about, just the man
who was now only about fifteen feet from her, still pacing.
Suddenly aware of the Sioux clothing she was wearing,

Emily was overcome with shyness and tried to retreat back into the lodge. Red Eagle Woman was in the opening.

"Go on, Emily. Go a little closer. See who it is," she cajoled, her hands turning Emily's shoulders back to face the man.

"He won't bite you." Shining Cloud giggled.

"You're sure?" Emily asked again, doubtfully.

"We want to know who it is! Go ahead!" Shining Cloud urged.

Emily stepped resolutely forward, straining her eyes to see who the man was. He was closer, but the sliver of moon had disappeared behind a cloud so she still couldn't see his features beneath the paint and the robe. As she moved away from the tipi, he stopped and put the flute away. They stood facing each other for a moment in silence.

Drew was impressed with how well Red Eagle Woman and Shining Cloud had maneuvered Emily at the tipi opening. Anyone watching would think she knew exactly what to do. She showed just the right amount of reluctance, then stepped forward confidently, her head high. Now it was up to him to get her to walk willingly into his arms. If he failed, their efforts would have been in vain, for while no one was looking directly at them out of respect for their privacy, many eyes were watching them. Iron Thunder would know precisely what transpired.

Slowly, with an unconscious grace that Emily recognized as belonging to only one man she knew, Drew threw one side of the robe back over his shoulder and stepped forward. She saw that he was indeed dressed in a warrior's finest garb, wearing a finely decorated leather shirt covered with a bone breastplate and quilled leggings and moccasins. The painted red and yellow and white stripes on his face made him look untamed and foreign, exciting and dangerous. His hair curled softly around his face. Emily could not think how she had not recognized him immediately, for none of the Oglalas had hair like his. She felt suddenly foolish, embarrassed by their strange dress, and by standing alone with him.

Drew held out his hand to her, and Emily took an involuntary step backward. Drew felt a moment's panic. She had to come to him. He spoke gently, reassuringly.

"Emily, you look beautiful. Come closer so I can see you better in the moonlight."

The husky timbre of his voice made Emily's stomach flutter. He was so handsome! She wanted to look at him, and she wanted him to look at her, to admire the Indian dress, to tell her again that she was beautiful. What harm could it do? she asked herself. This would only happen once, in all her life, standing under the stars, dressed like an Indian maiden. They were surrounded by people. Nothing could happen. It was harmless.

She smiled at his compliment and walked the few steps toward him. Placing her hand in his outstretched palm, she looked up at Drew. He was smiling deeply.

The most critical part was past. Now he had to keep her with him long enough to tell her the tale of Okaga, the South Wind and Wohpe, the Falling Star, but he knew she would stay once he began the story. He had chosen it because he was sure it would enchant Emily.

"I see Red Eagle Woman and Shining Cloud have been busy with you," he finally said, his eyes roaming over her approvingly.

"It looks as if someone was busy with you as well. I didn't recognize you. At first I thought you were Iron Thunder when I heard your flute."

"These are my own clothes. White Tree Woman keeps them for me." The mention of Iron Thunder made Drew impatient to get on with his tale.

"That's the biggest buffalo robe I've ever seen," Emily commented nervously.

"It comes in handy in the winter," he told her, releasing her hand. "It's big enough for two." He lifted the edges of the huge robe and reached out to envelop Emily in its folds, resting his arms along her shoulders, his hands lightly clasped behind her head. The robe encircled them both.

Emily began to squirm uncomfortably. Drew held her away from him, but she could feel his warmth inside the robe.

"Yes, well, in the winter, I'll make sure I have a buffalo robe," she said with a mixture of annoyance and embarrassment. She tried to back away, but his arms held her firmly.

"Don't run away just yet, Emily. I remembered a story that I thought you might like to hear. It's about the South Wind and the Falling Star. Would you like me to tell it to you?"

"Yes, I'd love to hear it, but right here? Right now?" she asked uneasily, bringing her hands up to Drew's forearms to try to dislodge them from her shoulders. She felt the hard bulk of his muscles under her fingers. Almost unconsciously, she ran her hands up to his elbows, then along his strong biceps. She remembered how his skin had felt when it was damp from the waters of the hot spring. She remembered other things, as well.

"Now, yes. Do you have other plans?" Drew pulled her a little closer.

"I guess not," Emily admitted, her hands now caressing the breadth of his shoulders beneath the heavy robe.

"Then come with me," he said, drawing her back into the crook of his right arm, keeping the robe around them. He steered her through the camp toward the ridge that rose behind the camp.

"What about Red Eagle Woman and Shining Cloud?" Emily said, suddenly remembering that they wanted to know who was outside the tipi.

"They saw me. They know you'll be with me. Come on."

Emily was relieved to get away from the village. She was self-conscious in Shining Cloud's beautiful dress, afraid she would say or do something to offend her hosts. She and Drew walked rapidly up the ridge, which was not too steep. At the top, Drew led her to a point east of the camp that looked out across the southern sky. They had come perhaps a mile from the village, walking in silence. To the south, they could see the few lights at the agency buildings glowing in the darkness.

In the west, the waxing crescent moon was setting. All around them, the black dome of the sky pressed close, and a warm breeze wafted out of the south, gently fanning their faces and bringing a faint scent of pine. The stars glittered brightly, some red, some yellow, some blue, and some a pure, clean white. They stood side by side, gazing at the incomparable Dakota night. There was a sense of anticipation, as of magic about to be unveiled, in the late summer air.

Then, as they watched, a bright streak flared in the canopy of stars, cutting across the Pleaides toward the west, traveling half the arc of the sky. Emily had never seen such a brilliant falling star. She caught her breath in wonder.

Drew was startled for a moment. Then he laughed, a full, rich sound that spoke of heartfelt joy. A sense of rightness surged through him, as it had in the sweat lodge. He wanted to shout before the heavens. He pulled Emily into his arms, flung the robe around them, and lifted her, spinning in a circle.

Emily had no idea why Drew reacted thus to the meteor, but she thrilled at the sound of his happiness and abandon. She had never seen him this way. She smiled, wondering at the different sides to him, one minute dark and brooding, the next mysterious, then furiously angry, then calm and detached, now rejoicing as if in discovery of some wonderful, fantastic secret. She wondered if he would share the cause of his joy with her. She leaned close against him when he put her down, her palms flat against his chest, underneath the breastplate. She felt the vibrations of his laughter against her as she smiled up at him. The smile he gave her in return bespoke a full heart and a soaring spirit. But he was silent.

"Weren't you going to tell me a story about a falling star?" she finally reminded him quietly.

"I am, indeed," Drew replied warmly, hugging her to him. "Just look out at the stars and I will tell you about Tate and his sons, the Four Winds. Tate was a god, the messenger of Śkan, and he fell in love with a beautiful woman, Ite. She was the most beautiful woman in all the world. Ite bore four sons at one time, and they became the

Four Winds. Later, she bore a fifth son, little Yumni," he began.

Emily settled comfortably into his supporting arms and rested her cheek on his chest, looking beyond his shoulder at the star studded sky. Drew told her how Ite had used her beauty to make the moon look foolish, and how she and her family had been banished to the earth to live alone. He told of Ite's punishment, whereby she was given a second face, horrible and ugly, and came to be called Anog Ite, meaning double face. None could bear to look at her ugly face, so she wandered alone. Tate and his sons had to live by themselves with no woman to cook or sew for them, but they were happy. Then one day, Tate saw a shining object fall to earth. Pretty soon, a woman came to his lodge, and Tate knew she was Wohpe, the daughter of Śkan. He accepted her as his daughter and invited her to live with him and his sons. Little Yumni liked her immediately and they became friends.

When the sons met Wohpe, the North Wind, the West Wind and the East Wind were suspicious of her and would not accept her. Only Okaga, the South Wind, treated Wohpe with respect and friendliness. Drew told Emily at length about the doings of the four older brothers when they found Wohpe at their father's lodge. He told how the North Wind wanted to take her as his wife, but Wohpe would not accept him because he was selfish and cruel. He told how Okaga brought Wohpe presents, but said nothing to her, nor she to him. He omitted the part about Okaga staying up late at night playing songs on his flute, but he told of the growing, unspoken love between the South Wind and the Falling Star.

Then he told of the journey the Four Winds made around the edge of the world to establish the fourth time, the year, and about their adventures along the way. Wohpe and Okaga thought of each other every day. Finally, the brothers returned home. They had been gone for a year, and Wohpe prepared a great feast to welcome them back.

"As the Four Winds returned to their father's camp, Tate and Yumni and Wohpe all came forward to greet them. Okaga came last, as he had established his direction, the

south, last. When he met Woḣpe, he took her in his arms
and kissed her. She stayed with him and accepted him as
her husband.'' He did not tell Emily that Okaga had
wrapped his robe around Woḣpe when he greeted her. She
would understand too much if he did. ''So that is the story
of the South Wind and Falling Star.''

''What a lovely, romantic story.'' Emily sighed contentedly. It had taken at least an hour to tell the tale, and
the moon had set. It was very dark. ''Thank you for telling
me.''

Inside, Emily dreamt what it would be like to be Woḣpe
and to finally welcome home her handsome lover after
such a long separation. She thought of all the barriers that
kept her apart from Drew. Even as she stood so peacefully
in his arms, she knew that they had no future together. He
had made that clear. She was now content to take the moments like this when he didn't push her away. She could
pretend, if only briefly, that all was right and well between
them and that Drew wanted her as she wanted him, completely, not only for a night. She would pretend that they
were Woḣpe and Okaga, with all eternity together. She
looked up at his face, dim in the starlight.

Drew took her face between his hands and spoke softly
in Lakota. Emily thought she heard the names Woḣpe and
Okaga. Then all was lost in the gentle sweetness of his
kiss, as light as the southern breeze that lifted the hair that
curled beneath her twining fingers. She felt in him none
of the fiery passion that had driven him before; instead
there was an elusive promise in the tender movements of
his lips that brought Emily close to tears. If she hadn't
known better, she might have thought he loved her in that
moment. Then he withdrew his mouth from hers and held
her very close, swaying slightly, back and forth. They
stood that way for long minutes, each bound in the spell
of the starlit night and their own souls' deepest yearnings.

Chapter 15

Emily awoke the next morning in a fine mood. She was to meet again with Red Cloud and some of the tribal elders for an hour or so that morning, then the rest of the day was hers to do with as she wished. She planned to trade some of the coffee, sugar, and tobacco she had brought for small gifts for her brother and his family. She was also hoping to get a chance to explore a bit in the vicinity. Red Eagle Woman told her there was to be a feast that evening, given by White Tree Woman in honor of Emily's visit. Had Emily known it was to celebrate her betrothal to White Tree Woman's adopted son, Drew, she would have been aghast.

After donning her gray dress, Emily stepped outside the lodge. The morning was bright and clear, but a nip in the air foretold autumn close at hand. Emily decided to take a walk through the village before breakfast. She had gone only a short distance when she heard Drew's voice speaking in Lakota. He was talking to another man whose voice sounded familiar. It was Iron Thunder. Emily crept closer to the voices, not wanting to be seen by the men. She wished fervently that she understood the language. Finally, she peered around the edge of a lodge and saw them standing with their backs to her in front of Long Feather's tipi. In astonishment, she saw that both men were smiling amiably as they talked. What a change from yesterday's exchange between them! Drew said something that raised a chuckle from Iron Thunder, then the men shook hands and the Hunkpapa walked away.

Emily approached Drew, her hands on her hips, looking after Iron Thunder. "What was that all about?" she asked suspiciously.

"Good morning to you, too, Emily," Drew replied with a grin that caused her insides to melt. "Did you sleep well?"

"Yes, of course I did."

"I had some of the most interesting dreams, myself," he interrupted suggestively. "I wondered if you did, too?"

Emily blushed. He stepped close to her and took one of her hands between his own. She looked away, unsure what to make of his behavior.

She cleared her throat. "I was surprised to see you talking so peaceably with Iron Thunder," she tried again, ignoring the increase in her pulse.

"Afraid I might accept his offer of ten ponies for you? You were right about how much you were worth."

"No!" she denied hotly, although the thought had occurred to her. "I was only curious. After all, you weren't exactly cordial to him yesterday."

"You're so persistent at times, Emily. All right, I'll put your curious mind at ease. He was asking my opinion of one or two of the young women he's considering courting. Are you happy now?"

"I thought he wanted to court me," Emily stated, allowing herself to sound more disappointed than she felt. She was rewarded by a flashing look from Drew.

"He changed his mind," he informed her curtly.

"Oh."

"Are you disappointed?"

"Well, it was rather flattering."

"You wouldn't have thought so if he'd have kidnapped you and carried you back to his people across the plains."

"Actually, it sounds very romantic."

Drew's eyes shot daggers at her. "Do you want me to accept his offer for you? I'm sure he'd still have you if he thought you were willing. I can take care of everything," he said in a neutral voice. He released her hand and made as if to follow Iron Thunder.

"No!" Emily panicked, her bluff called. The alarm in

her green-brown eyes caused Drew to quirk his lips in a satisfied smile. Instantly, she knew he'd gotten the better of her.

"I don't advise that you try little games like that with me, Emily. I take people at their word for the most part, so say only what you really mean." He was aware as soon as he spoke of the irony of his telling her to be honest with him. "Look," he said, changing the subject abruptly, "I thought I'd translate for you and Red Cloud this morning, then I wondered if you'd like to go for a ride to visit one of the other nearby camps this afternoon," he offered. "There are some old friends I want to talk to there, and I think you might enjoy seeing more of the country."

"That would be lovely, thank you," Emily responded graciously, her annoyance over his teasing evaporating. Her spirits rose as she contemplated spending the day with him, though she tried to still her enthusiasm, telling herself that she was living for a dream that had no chance of becoming reality.

The discussion with Red Cloud went well, though Emily doubted that she'd said anything the old man hadn't heard before. She'd been impressed with his intelligence and his understanding of the position his people were in with respect to the army and the government. He was fighting to preserve his nation as best he could in a difficult situation, and he viewed education as one of the weapons in the white man's arsenal against the Sioux. Emily felt that by learning more about white people, and especially by learning English, the Lakota would stand a better chance of defending themselves in the white man's world. Red Cloud and some of the others feared that schools wouldn't do this, but that they would steal the children away from Lakota ways. They came to no agreements, but she hadn't expected to, and she felt she had learned much. She counted it a great privilege to speak with the old chief. When they were finished, he dismissed her and detained Drew for a few minutes. Emily waited outside the lodge for him.

"What did he say?" she asked as soon as Drew emerged from the open flap.

"All you ever do is ask questions!" Drew chided her. "Can't a man have any privacy with you around?"

"Not a bit. Now tell me, what did he say," she repeated with a smile.

"He told me that he approves of you. For a *wašicu*, you're all right, in rough translation," Drew chuckled, not relaying Red Cloud's blessing on their betrothal.

"Why did he tell you that?" Emily pondered aloud.

"You'll have to ask him," Drew told her, knowing that without his or Black Wolf's help, she couldn't ask anyone anything. "Go change into those pants and meet me at Long Feather's tipi when you're ready to go," he called to her as he walked off through the camp.

Black Wolf's cousin and her husband lived at the camp they were visiting, and Drew deposited Emily with her before going to find the men he was looking for. He'd learned from Iron Thunder that a small band of Canadian refugees had recently joined this camp after becoming alarmed by offers to sponsor a rebellion against the U.S. Army. It was rumored, however, that one of the young men, named Dark Faces, had come unwillingly. His father was very old, and near death, and had begged his son to accompany him on this last journey to make sure that his mother and sisters arrived safely. When the old man died, Iron Thunder expected that the younger man would return to Canada. Dark Faces was anxious to win honor and fame in battle, and he hated the whites. Drew thought it possible that such a man might have more information about the men behind the plot. He doubted the Dark Faces would talk to him, but he might have carelessly said things that could prove useful. It was the best lead Drew had had yet.

He shouldn't have brought Emily with him, but White Tree Woman had insisted that he take Emily to meet her niece. Since Long Feather's wife had been as his own mother for more than twenty years, he hadn't had the heart to refuse her. He reflected that he'd been wise to avoid entanglements with women for the most part in his life.

They always seemed to be able to talk him into things he knew were foolish. Now he would simply have to trust that Emily wouldn't realize what he was doing.

Riding home in the afternoon, with the sun's westering rays slanting across the dry landscape, Drew was preoccupied and said little. Emily wondered what the real purpose for this visit had been, as he had disappeared almost as soon as they arrived. She assumed it had something to do with his secret activities, since there had been people in camp who had recently returned from Canada. Emily had had a pleasant afternoon, and she respected Drew's silence now. After an hour's ride, they stopped along the creek to water their horses. Drew walked to the crest of a nearby hill and stood gazing westward. Emily followed him and stood at his side, her eyes gazing after his.

"Are you looking for something?" she finally asked, breaking the silence.

"Hmm?" He looked at her as if aware of her for the first time. "Oh, no. I was just thinking."

"About what?"

"Never mind. I want to get back to camp. We don't want to be late for our feast . . . I mean, your feast tonight. Let's go." He wanted to talk to Black Wolf and Long Feather about what he had learned. He turned and started down the hill.

Emily sighed in exasperation, staring after him for a minute. She wished she knew what was on his mind. She hated being kept in the dark. Drew realized she wasn't with him and looked back at her.

"Aren't you coming?" he said impatiently.

She started after him as he marched back down to the creek, not waiting for her. Really, she thought in annoyance, he can be the most difficult man!

By the time Emily reached her horse, Drew was already astride his mount, gazing distractedly at a thicket of buffalo berry bushes. Emily gathered her reins from the branch where they were looped. As she was lifting a foot to the stirrup, she heard her name called. It was not Drew who spoke.

Turning her head in surprise, Emily saw a rider approach from the south. She gasped out loud, her heart pounding. Her eyes flew to Drew in panic, but he merely looked at her curiously. She focused on his brilliantly blue eyes, and she remembered the eagle she had seen at the falls. She glanced back at the rider astride a huge horse, its flanks glinting red in the afternoon sun.

The man smiled in recognition. He waved, and suddenly the panic left her as quickly as it had come. She recognized the rider as Zach Stevens.

"Zach! Whatever are you doing here?" Emily was astonished to see him.

"Emily! Thank God!" he exclaimed as he halted his sorrel and dismounted. "I've been looking for you for days! Are you all right? I came as soon as I heard you'd come out here alone! I can't believe you took such a risk! I've been terribly worried about you."

"I hardly know what to say," Emily began in confusion. She couldn't believe that Zach had come all this way just to make sure she was all right. It was a complete surprise, and she wasn't at all certain she was pleased. She looked to Drew for help, but he returned her regard blankly.

"Emily," Zach continued urgently, "you haven't been in Dakota Territory very long. You aren't aware of all the dangers to a woman in these parts. You've taken an incredible risk coming out here. I would feel duty bound to pursue any woman attempting to travel without a full and proper escort in these lands," Zach went on piously, implying that Drew was not adequate protection for a lady. "Now that I've found you, I hope you'll allow me to take you back to the agency where you can find some suitable accommodation. Shall we go, Emily?"

It cost Drew dearly to refrain from leaping out of the saddle and strangling Stevens on the spot. Something held him back though, some spark of intuition. He decided to trust Emily's reactions to the unexpected situation. When she appealed to him silently for help, he kept his gaze fixed on the other man.

"No, Zach. Mr. Rutledge is my guide, and I'm a guest

at Red Cloud's camp. I'm perfectly safe, and I'll not insult my hosts by deserting their hospitality," she told him firmly, but as pleasantly as she could. "I appreciate your concern for me, but I'm in good hands. I really can't believe you came all this way just for me." She didn't tell him that she didn't appreciate his efforts at all.

"You can't seriously propose to remain at the Indian camp?" Zach asked in a shocked voice.

"That is my intention," Emily informed him, striving to keep her anger out of her voice. "Please accept my wishes."

Zach walked rapidly to her side and placed his hand on her elbow. "Emily, you're being unreasonable. This is no place for a lady!" His face flushed a deep hue as his anger got the best of him.

She jerked her arm from his grasp. "Zach, I came with my brother's full knowledge. It's hardly your place to set limits on where I may or may not go. I'm flattered that you seem to care so much about my well-being, but, really, it's not your concern. Was it necessary to come all this way?"

"I didn't ride all the way down here to have you refuse my help!"

Emily exhaled loudly, unable to reason with him. Drew was no help at all, looking as if nothing unusual were happening.

"Zachary, I am not going with you. I am as safe with the Oglala as I would be with anyone, whether or not you choose to believe it. Now, I repeat, I am *not* going with you. That's final." Her voice shook, and it took every ounce of willpower not to scream in his face.

"Well, then, I fear I have made a fool of myself." He wiped his brow with his handkerchief, and his tone was still angry. "I apologize most sincerely, Emily. As you know, my feelings for you run rather deep, and I'm afraid I overreacted to the news of your journey into Indian lands. Please forgive me if I've caused you any embarrassment."

Emily didn't know what to say. She *was* embarrassed by this display which indicated that Zach's feelings were much more serious than she had admitted to herself. The man had traveled for three days on horseback to find her! Nevertheless, she wasn't going to allow his unwanted attentions to disrupt her visit.

"It's quite all right, Zach," she said stiffly. "Please think no more about it. Do you want to accompany us back to Red Cloud's village?"

"No, I don't believe so, thank you. I have a business associate who lives just across the Nebraska line. I'll stay with him. If you'll excuse me, I'll be off now," he said brusquely. He wheeled the sorrel stallion around, and its coat gleamed red in the golden rays of the westering sun. Then he galloped off southward, the way he had come.

"Thanks for all your help." Emily flung the words accusingly at Drew as she swung into her saddle.

"You managed fine without me," he pointed out evenly. "It didn't look to me like you needed any help. Thanks for not saying anything about the Reynoldses being here."

She looked at him thoughtfully for a moment, letting the tension drain from her. "No, I don't suppose I did need your help, but I would have appreciated it. I can't believe he came all the way out here chasing me. It seems rather odd, don't you think? He told me last week he'd be on a business trip this week. Why on earth would he forego that to chase me down? And how in the world did he find us out here?" she asked, shaking her head.

"It would seem the man is smitten with you," Drew said sarcastically. "And as to finding you, he could have stopped at the camp and asked."

"I doubt it. He wouldn't willingly ride into an Indian camp," Emily countered logically. "For all his good qualities, Zach is not overly fond of Indians."

"Men in love do strange things, Emily," Drew said as he urged his horse forward.

As they rode back to camp, Drew watched the trail carefully. At one point, he stopped the horses for water, although Emily didn't think there was any need to rest. He disappeared for a few minutes across the shallow creek. When he returned, he was whistling under his breath. His mood seemed to have lightened somewhat, though he still wasn't inclined to talk.

As they neared the camp, Drew turned to Emily abruptly. "Do you remember when you saw Stevens ride up to us?" he asked conversationally.

Emily nodded.

"Was it my imagination, or were you frightened for a minute?"

"I wouldn't say frightened. I didn't recognize him at first," she recalled. "No, that's not quite right, because he seemed familiar, but not like Zach. That doesn't make much sense, I'm afraid."

"You looked at me then. What did you see?"

"I saw you, of course. Well, actually, I noticed your eyes. I thought about the eagle I saw at the waterfall."

Drew nodded as if this made sense, but he didn't say anything more. The village came into sight as they rounded a bend.

"Would you mind talking to Long Feather about that eagle you saw?" he asked almost hesitantly as they approached the camp. It wasn't really proper for Emily and Long Feather to speak together, since everyone in the camp thought she would be Drew's wife, but the older man might be able to learn something from Emily that Drew had missed.

"No, of course not. If you think I should. Didn't you tell me he's a powerful holy man?"

"He is," Drew told her, nodding. "He's a very wise man."

They had reached the edge of the village, where they dismounted and turned their animals over to the boys who would care for them. Together, they walked to Red Eagle Woman's lodge.

"Ask Shining Cloud if you can wear that dress again tonight. Oh, and here," he said, digging into his saddle-bag. "I meant to give this to you earlier. I got it from Black Wolf's cousin." He produced a beautiful necklace made of white shells and blue beads. It would be perfect with the white and blue quillwork on the dress.

"It's lovely!" Emily said, fingering the pretty beads.

They were a deep blue, darker than the sky, but still only blue, not gray or green. They were almost exactly the color of Drew's eyes. She smiled at him warmly. "Thank you. I'll wear them tonight."

Without warning, he pulled her into his arms and kissed her hard, his tongue quickly thrusting into her mouth when she gasped in surprise. Just as abruptly, he released her and turned, walking rapidly away.

Emily smiled happily at the necklace in her hand, wondering what on earth had gotten into him today.

Drew located his adopted brother and father in the lodge of the warrior society to which they belonged. They jokingly told him that they'd had to get out of the way of White Tree Woman's preparations for the feast. Black Wolf noticed Drew's excitement as he dropped to the floor beside him. He spoke softly, and in English, so there would be less chance of being overheard.

"You finally have some information," Black Wolf stated, nodding his head.

"Iron Thunder was right about the young man there, Dark Faces. Apparently, he's one of the main contacts for whoever's behind this. He wasn't in camp today, which was just as well. I talked to the men there we can trust, and I've been able to piece together some information from comments Dark Faces made to the others. Someone brought some whiskey into camp about a week ago, right after the new people arrived, and Dark Faces had more than his share. He got up in front of his father's lodge and started preaching about how he and his friends were going to push the army back across the Missouri."

Long Feather made a disapproving noise and shook his head. Drew continued.

"The men there got the impression that the man behind the plot works out of the northern hills. He uses at least one soldier as a messenger, or he may be a soldier himself because he has easy access to army-issue weapons and ammunition. That points to someone at Fort Meade. Dark Faces referred to someone he called Leaky Eyes. I don't know if this is the leader or a messenger. Anyway, it appears that Leaky Eyes offered some of Gall's people all the guns they could use, plus plenty of ammunition and free and clear title to all the Powder River country and the Black Hills in exchange for driving the army back to the forts along the Missouri.''

"I can't believe those gullible fools listened to such an offer! And from a soldier! It has treachery written all over it,'' Black Wolf spat contemptuously.

"You know how desperate they are up there. If we're poor down here, you should have seen what I saw up there last spring. Some of those men will listen to anything that offers hope, even an impossible hope,'' Drew reminded him sadly.

"A rebellion would never succeed. We'd all be slaughtered in our camps before it even got started. It'd hurt the whites around here, too. What would anyone gain in such a war?''

"Most likely a lot of money. There's an awful lot of folks that are out here after an easy fortune. My guess would be that some merchant's cooked up this plan to bleed the army, the retreating settlers, and the poor Indians, lining his own pockets in the process. It wouldn't matter to most of the whites if the Indians ended up massacred, but whoever we're dealing with apparently doesn't mind seeing hundreds of white settlers killed, either.''

The three of them discussed the problem until other men wandered into the lodge and began to tease Drew about his upcoming marriage. He fielded their comments good-naturedly, making himself the butt of more than a few ribald jokes. Finally, he and Black Wolf rose to prepare for the evening ahead. On the way out the door, Drew caught Black Wolf's arm.

"Ask Walks in the Rain and Cut Finger to come see me. There's someone I want to keep real good track of for a few days.'' He didn't explain further.

Emily had a grand time at the feast. She wore Shining Cloud's dress and the necklace that Drew gave her, and to her surprise, Drew remained at her side throughout the evening. He was attentive and charming, smiling and re-

laxed, and Emily thought that if she had not already succumbed to his powerful presence, she would have had no
choice after the evening. Drew conversed animatedly with
many people, and soon the comments and queries flew so
quickly among the guests that Emily rarely received a
translation. She found that she didn't really mind. It was
enough to watch Drew, admiring his handsome profile
when she looked up at him, leaning against his solid frame,
feeling his warmth and strength. Several times his arm
stole possessively around her waist, and she found herself
accepting his attentions happily.

Long Feather and White Tree Woman gave away many
gifts of robes, blankets, beaded clothing, and even a couple of ponies. Emily watched all this in fascination. When
she asked Drew about it, he explained briefly that Lakota
customs dictated that the givers of a feast present gifts to
their guests to demonstrate their generosity, a great virtue
among the Oglala people. It seemed terribly lavish to Emily, and she felt rather guilty at having precipitated what
amounted to a very expensive undertaking. Noting the
concern in her face, Drew assured her that Long Feather
and White Tree Woman counted the feast and the gift giving as a great honor, and that she shouldn't worry about
it. Then he was drawn into yet another conversation that
Emily couldn't understand and said no more about it.

The next morning, Shining Cloud took Emily to see
Long Feather. Drew was nowhere to be seen. He hadn't
told her his plans for the day, and no one mentioned where
he'd gone. Emily felt her familiar annoyance with his
abrupt comings and goings, but the pleasant mood from
the previous night lingered, so she let it pass. Long
Feather, it appeared, didn't speak English terribly well,
but he understood a great deal. Thus Emily related to him
her experiences at the waterfall and the dream that she had
had twice. She was disappointed when the old holy man,
or *wicaśa wakan*, as Drew had taught her, said little in
response. He merely looked very satisfied and made a
comment in Lakota to Shining Cloud, who smiled briefly.
Then he sat silently for several minutes, gazing intently at
Emily. His penetrating expression reminded her of Drew,

though his eyes were so dark they were almost black. Finally, he spoke to her.

"My son is right to ask you to tell me these things. I must think about them," he said. "Daughter, you are a good woman, and Wakantanka will use you to help my people. I am glad about this. You mustn't be afraid, and you will be given the strength to do what you must."

Emily's eyes widened at these words.

"What will I have to do?" she asked apprehensively.

"You'll know when the time comes," Long Feather replied cryptically. He rose to his feet easily, his body old but still agile and strong. He reached to take Emily's hands in his when she stood with him. His expression changed suddenly, indicating that he would say no more. Mischief now glinted in his dark eyes.

"You like my son?" he asked her, a merry grin twisting his thin lips.

Emily blushed at the unexpected question. "Well, uh, he's certainly different from anyone I've ever met before," she finally said.

Long Feather smiled knowingly. "I think you like him," he told her, nodding. "He's a good man. Sometimes he acts stupidly, but that's probably because he was born to the white man's world. Don't worry too much about it."

Emily was baffled by these comments. She had no reply. Fortunately, the old man didn't seem to expect one. After thanking her for coming, Long Feather dismissed the women. Emily asked Shining Cloud what her uncle had meant by his last words.

"Nobody ever knows what a *wicaśa wakan* means," she answered glibly. Then she took Emily to trade for the gifts for her family, and Emily had no further chance to pursue the matter before she and Drew left the Indian camp amid a flurry of well-wishing relatives.

Chapter 16

❝**M**a! Pa! Aunt Emily! Come out here, quick! You got to see this!❞

Joshua's voice pierced the quiet Sunday afternoon. The kitchen door slammed, and in seconds the excited boy burst into the parlor where Emily was reading the latest issue of *Godey's Lady's Book*. "Indians are coming!" he announced dramatically. Then he disappeared out the front door.

Sam and Maggie looked at each other with raised eyebrows. Emily put down her periodical and looked at them questioningly.

"I, for one, am curious," Sam said mildly. He offered his wife his arm. "Shall we go see?"

"Absolutely," Maggie agreed, heading for the door. Emily rose and followed silently, wondering what on earth was going on.

From the front porch, Emily saw two Indians on horseback leading a pretty brown and white spotted pony and a second horse loaded with several packs. As the Indians approached, she recognized them as members of Red Cloud's camp. She thought they were cousins of Black Wolf. Josh and Sarah were hopping about excitedly. Maggie scooped up a madly careering Daniel and held the wriggling toddler on her hip as they walked to the gate to meet the visitors.

The older of the two Indians greeted Sam with a raised hand. *"Hau,"* he said solemnly before launching into a short speech in Lakota. Emily thought she heard a familiar

240

name, Ište Śkan Niyapi, and she stiffened. They had returned over a week ago from the reservation and Emily had not seen or heard from Drew since he had left her at Sam's. As each day passed, her chagrin deepened, as much with herself as with him. She knew better than to expect him to change, she really did, but she couldn't help being profoundly disappointed and angry that he didn't.

To Emily's utter amazement, her brother answered the Indian in his own language. She stared at him as he spoke haltingly in slow syllables. How had Sam learned Lakota? Every time she turned around, it seemed there was another surprise in store for her! The Indians dismounted, and Sam led them toward the barn where they could stable their horses. Joshua and Sarah marched alongside importantly, gazing with undisguised fascination at the Oglala men.

Sam called back to Maggie over his shoulder. "We'll be having company for supper, Mags."

Emily, standing at the gate beside her sister-in-law, looked after the departing figures. "When did Sam learn Lakota?" she asked.

"Drew began teaching him when we first got out here to the hills," Maggie informed her. "He really only speaks a little of it."

"Why didn't he tell me?"

"I don't know. It probably never came up. He doesn't think he does very well, and he's self-conscious about it."

"Why do you suppose those men came here? Shouldn't they have gone to Drew's place?" Emily queried.

"It is unusual. Maybe Drew's away again. Whatever their reason, I'm sure Sam will tell us when he gets back. In the meantime, I'd better go add some extra vegetables to the stew. Want to help?"

"Of course," Emily replied, following Maggie into the house, her lips pursed as she tried to figure what could have brought the Oglalas to the Parker ranch.

That evening, the children finally asleep after the day's exciting events, Sam and Maggie retired to their bedroom.

Sam sat on the bed as Maggie lit the lamp on her dresser. She turned to face him, her eyes sparkling.

"All right, Sam Parker, I want to know exactly what this visit was all about. You may have fooled your sister with that story about Drew sending a pony for the children, but I know there's more to it than that. He has plenty of horses here if he wanted to give them one. Why did those men bring a horse to us all the way from Pine Ridge?"

Sam's mouth quirked into a merry grin, and his dark eyes danced in the yellow light. "It was a present from Long Feather and his wife to me. And there wasn't just the pony. All the stuff that was tied on the other horse is down in the barn as well. There are robes, moccasins, some shirts, and some jewelry. I hid it in the tack room."

Maggie tilted her head in confusion. "Why did Long Feather send you all these things?"

"They're wedding presents."

"I don't understand," Maggie said, shaking her head.

Sam chuckled softly. "I'm not sure I do, either, but it seems that my little sister got engaged to be married while she was at Pine Ridge."

"What?" Maggie exclaimed. "But she didn't say anything about this to us! Who did she get engaged to? Oh, my goodness!"

"Who do you think? Drew, of course," Sam said with a wry smile. "The odd thing is, that as near as I can tell, she doesn't know about it."

"Honestly, Sam, that's absurd. How could a woman not know if she is engaged to someone?"

"She doesn't speak any Lakota, and she's not familiar with their customs," Sam pointed out. He lifted his foot and began tugging at his boot. "I think he went through the whole rigmarole without telling her what was going on."

Maggie moved to the bed and caught his heel in her hand, slipping the boot off. She frowned slightly. "Why would Drew do something like this? It doesn't make any sense!"

"If I understood right," Sam answered, lifting his other

foot for his wife's help, "it had something to do with a visitor from another tribe courting Emily. The young man was quite determined, so Drew used this as a ruse to deter him. And, apparently, the whole camp is very pleased about it. They're understandably sorry that Drew didn't choose a Lakota wife, but his family had begun to fear that he'd never marry. Long Feather is most supportive of the arrangement and is acting as if it were legitimate. I don't know what to make of it."

"This is the strangest engagement I've ever heard of," Maggie said as she placed Sam's boots at the end of the bed. "Clearly, Drew's Indian family is taking it seriously, but Emily doesn't even know about it. I wish Drew were around. I'd like to ask him a thing or two. Should we say anything to Emily?"

"I don't think so. I'm going to leave that up to Drew. By the way, I thought you might like to know that I gave a couple of steers, that new roan, and several of the blankets in the linen chest to our guests. I figured I might as well go along with things for now. You never know," Sam added with a sigh as he raised his shirt over his head. "With any luck, Emily and Drew just may straighten things out and get married after all. It would be a shame to insult her future in-laws." He grinned.

"I hope you're right, Sam," Maggie said slowly as she undid the buttons of her dress and stepped out of it. "I don't want Emily to be hurt, and I know she isn't going to like it when she finds out about this engagement. If Drew isn't careful, he's going to drive her away from him. She hasn't said anything, but I know she's upset that he disappeared again without a word."

"He must have his reasons for what he's doing, Mags," Sam said carefully. "I may not agree with him, but he's always shown the best judgment in the past. Things will work out. It looks as if we're not the only ones playing matchmaker, though, doesn't it?" he finished with a chuckle.

"I just don't want to be around when she finds out about this," Maggie said grimly, turning to face her mirror as she brushed out her long hair.

"Neither do I," Sam agreed.

* * *

As soon as Emily had returned, Zach once again became a frequent visitor at the Parkers'. He apologized profusely and quite charmingly for any embarrassment he had caused Emily, blaming his excesses on his growing feelings and respect for her. He maintained a completely gentlemanly demeanor, and Emily found it difficult to remain annoyed with him. She told him openly that she didn't share his affections, but she didn't discourage his visits because he helped take her mind off Drew.

And her mind was frequently on Drew. She'd used the Reynoldses' presence as a buffer between them on the trip home, not knowing what to expect as they returned home. With the grueling pace Drew had pushed them to, she'd been so exhausted at the end of each day's ride that she'd dropped immediately into her bedroll and the oblivion of sleep. Drew had seemed preoccupied once again and made no attempts to be alone with her. While she'd been relieved about this for the most part, a niggling voice inside her admitted that she was also disappointed. She longed for a return to the easy camaraderie they'd shared for a few brief days, and for the tender kisses of those few nights, but she knew Drew too well now to expect it would happen. He wasn't any closer to letting her into his life than he had been before.

The afternoon after the Indian visitors left, Zach found Emily searching for the last of the wild plums along the creek bank some distance from the house. She had on a red and white striped dress that stood out clearly among the leaves, and there were two pails beside her, one of them half full of red fruit. She didn't see Zach until he was right behind her. A branch moved, causing her to whirl around. Recognizing Zach, she greeted him cheerfully, but as she disentangled herself from the thick growth, she saw that his mouth was set in a grim line.

"Is something wrong, Zach?" she asked with concern.

He didn't respond immediately, but there was hurt and annoyance in his brown eyes. "I just heard some news that I found difficult to believe," he finally said in a tight voice.

"Well, what is it? Does it concern anyone I know?" Emily was confused by Zach's attitude. He seemed displeased with her, and she hadn't the faintest idea why.

"It concerns you." He paused as if he thought she should say something.

"What did you hear?" Emily asked.

Zach eyed her doubtfully. "Are you sure there's nothing that happened on your trip to Pine Ridge that you should have told me about?"

There were many things that she hadn't told him about, things that she didn't intend to tell anyone, but there was nothing that he should have known.

"Zach, this would be much easier if you'd simply tell me what you heard. I have no idea what you're talking about."

Zach looked vaguely bewildered for a fraction of a second, but his eyes remained wary and hostile. "All right," he said, taking a deep breath, "I heard that you and Rutledge became engaged to be married while you were at the Indian camp."

Emily didn't think she could have heard right. Her expression remained blank for a moment, then the words slowly took on meaning.

"What?" she gasped, her mouth dropping open in amazement. "Wherever did you hear such a ridiculous rumor?"

Zach watched her reaction carefully, missing nothing. Her surprise seemed genuine. He relaxed infinitesimally.

"I heard it from one of the men who works at the mill. He used to be a trapper before the gold rush, and he knows the Sioux pretty well. He even speaks a little of their lingo. He met a couple of Red Cloud's braves riding up here yesterday with a load of presents and a pony for Sam. They said they were wedding gifts from Rutledge's Indian friends, seeing as he'd just declared his intention to marry the blond woman he brought to camp."

"That's ridiculous!" she protested. "The pony was a present for the children from Drew, and I certainly think I would know if I'd gotten engaged! Your man must not speak Lakota as well as he thinks he does, for he misunderstood horribly.''

Even as she denied it, though, Emily acknowledged that it could be true. She began to put odd pieces together. That business with Drew all dressed up outside the tipi, playing the flute, took on new meaning. Iron Thunder had played the flute for her as well, and he had clearly stated his desire to take her as his wife. She remembered Drew speaking about *their* feast, and quickly covering his mistake. Then there was the way he'd stayed so attentively at her side that night, no doubt carefully monitoring any translations she might have heard, keeping her in the dark. Many things made a great deal of sense in light of this new information. Obviously, he'd tried to keep this mock engagement—for she could see it as nothing else—a secret from her. The question was, why had he done it at all? Hadn't he said they had no future together, that he could offer nothing? A deeply buried hope surged briefly in her breast. Perhaps he'd changed his mind and not known how to tell her. Perhaps there was a future for them after all.

Then, in a flash of comprehension, she realized that Drew must have become engaged to her to stop Iron Thunder from pursuing her. Her hopes shriveled. Of course, why hadn't she seen it immediately? He'd felt responsible for her, and it had been an effective ruse. Iron Thunder had instantly ended his suit.

Anger and shame at having been made a fool built to a tension point. How dare he use her this way? Who had given him the right to meddle in her life, to play with her emotions, to make her decisions for her? Her shame at having played perfectly into Drew's cunning little scheme caused a bright flush to mount from her collar to her forehead. She'd been so willing, so open, and she had allowed herself to revel in his attentions, thinking he was sincere! How could she have been such a dolt?

Zach watched the lightning flicker of conflicting emotions cross Emily's face. He said nothing in reply, waiting for her to speak, but he was furious.

She turned away from him and stared unseeing into

the plum bushes, her shoulders rising and falling rapidly as she took deep breaths, trying to control her temper. Zach had done nothing wrong. She wouldn't vent her rage on him.

When Emily said nothing, Zach finally spoke. "If you don't believe me, ask Sam. I'm sure he'll tell you the truth."

Emily had her doubts about that. Her brother hadn't seen fit to tell her yet, so why would he now? Anger coursed through her once again, this time directed at Sam. What did he think he was accomplishing by lying to her? Fighting her urge simply to flee into the hills and be alone, Emily turned back to face Zach.

"No, I believe you, Zach. It's rather a shock, however, to find that one has gotten engaged somehow and not even been aware of it," she said with a sarcastic edge to her voice. "I'm afraid that this must be some perverse joke on Drew's part, as he didn't see fit to inform me what he was doing. You see, a visiting Indian at the camp took a fancy to me, and I expect that this was Drew's way of trying to keep me from being carried off by him. Whatever the people at Red Cloud's camp think, we are *not* engaged, and we will most definitely not be getting married at any time, ever," she said adamantly.

Zach watched Emily pensively. "Emily, I'm sorry if I've upset you. It seems that's all I do."

"It's hardly your fault. I'm not upset with you," Emily replied.

"I can't say that I'm not relieved," Zach ventured. "Emily, I know I asked you before, but are you sure there's nothing between you and Rutledge? I'd understand if there is, but you have to be honest with me." His tone was firm.

"There's nothing to understand. There's nothing in this world or the next that would ever tempt me to marry that cad!" she responded hotly. "If I ever see him again, I . . . I . . . I don't know what I'll do!" She spun way from Zach again as tears stung the backs of her eyes. Suddenly, her shoulders slumped and she felt powerless to control her feelings any longer. Tears spilled down her cheeks, and when Zach touched her shoulder, she turned into his arms, burying her face against his chest.

"Shhh, Emily, go ahead and cry," he whispered against her soft hair. "It'll be all right, I promise you. He won't keep hurting you."

He let her cry. When she'd finished, he tipped her chin up.

"Emily, look at me."

Her large green-brown eyes, translucent with a last tear or two, rose to meet his unwavering regard.

"If you ever need help with anything, anything at all, I want you to come to me. Will you do that?"

She nodded.

Emily waited until the children were in bed that evening before confronting her brother with the news Zach had brought her. She asked him to walk down to the barn with her, as she wasn't sure she'd be able to control her temper or her tongue, and she didn't want to disturb the entire household. When she revealed her knowledge of the Indians' visit as designed to exchange wedding presents, Sam was immediately contrite.

"Emily, I figured you didn't know what was going on, and I didn't want to upset you needlessly," he explained.

"Needlessly? It's my life! Why can't anyone leave the details of my life up to me? I'm not some imbecile who is incapable of making her own decisions! At home it was always Charles and Henry and Mother, and then George, telling me what I should and shouldn't do, what would be good for me and what wouldn't, what to think, what to wear, what to say, whom to marry and when! I thought I was getting away from that! But between you and that damn Drew Rutledge, and even his adopted Indian relatives, I have just about as much say as I did at home! Can't you let me decide what I want to do about things that affect me? At least give me the choice!" Her voice positively shook with righteous indignation.

To her surprise, Sam agreed with her. "You're right. I should have told you. As for Drew, I wish you'd wait and let him explain his reasons to you. Emily, I know you care about him. Won't you give him a chance to set things to rights?"

"I will not," she stated firmly. "And I don't care about Drew Rutledge, other than being sick to death of him. Besides, I have no idea when or if I'll ever see him again, and if I have my druthers, I won't see him at all. The man is overbearing and impossible. He comes and goes as he pleases and lives only unto his own laws, as near as I can tell. I don't want his interference in my life any longer. He's done quite enough damage as it is." Far more than Sam knew, she thought unhappily.

"If it'll make you feel any better," Sam told her, realizing that there was little he could do, since most of Emily's anger was directed at Drew, "I promise that I'll be on guard against making any assumptions about what you want, or any decisions that affect your life. And I'll graciously accept a kick in the pants if you catch me overstepping the boundaries."

Emily couldn't remain angry with Sam. He was genuinely sorry, and the whole situation was Drew's fault, anyway.

"Thank you, Sam," she said, smiling just a little. "You know, you're really not as bad as Charles and Henry. They never apologized. Not even once."

"We all just want you to be happy, Emily."

"I know. But I want to find my own happiness."

"Just as long as you don't think so much about it that you miss it," Sam told her softly.

She wondered what he meant.

As September passed, the last vestiges of true summer were swept away with the first cold nights and the appearance of frost early one morning. The garden had only a few hardy root vegetables and winter squash left, and the potatoes were dug on a cold morning with a gray, overcast sky threatening a cold rain. The root cellar and the shelves in the basement were full to overflowing, the excess stacked on the floor alongside them. The leaves on the trees along the creek began to turn yellow, and then flutter to the ground in the autumn breeze. The days were warm and lazy, despite the cool nights. The only event of any import was Frank's announcement one night at supper, astonishing everyone, that he would be marrying the widow Cornelia Epps, from Spearfish. The wedding would take place the following Tuesday afternoon at three o'clock, and Frank would be moving to her place and looking after his own ranch from now on.

Emily began to seriously consider returning to Elmira before the winter. Try as she might, she couldn't dismiss Drew from her mind. The best way to get over him and the pain he'd caused her would be to put as much distance between them as she could. She supposed he was out distributing his supplies to the Indians before the winter, and she wondered, if she left, would she ever see him again? The thought was agony. When she was honest with herself, she knew the pretend engagement had not changed her feelings for him. She longed to know where he was, what he was doing, and if by chance he ever thought of her. She found herself reliving the tender moments they had had the evening he had come to her tipi playing his flute, remembering the reverberations of his deep voice against her cheek as he spoke of Okaga and Wohpe. And she relived their moments of passion at the hot spring, longing for his fiery kisses and the magical touch of his fingers on her bare skin. She was no longer shocked that she wanted him so. Nonetheless, she knew she would never seek his company. He was unreliable, and she doubted she'd ever be able to trust him. Drew Rutledge couldn't figure in her dreams, even if his memory refused to be banished.

When Emily mentioned to Sam and Maggie that she thought it best if she returned home before the winter made traveling difficult, they were disappointed. True to his word, however, Sam tried hard not to influence his sister's decision unduly. As much as Emily knew she should make firm plans for her departure, she didn't. There was still plenty of time. It was only the beginning of October, and the hills were stunning as the trees turned yellow and red against the azure skies of autumn. It was too beautiful to leave just yet. She set herself a goal of tackling the details of returning by the end of the month. She only hoped that Drew did not reappear during that time. She didn't think she could bear to see him again after learning of the false engagement.

Emily was sitting on a blanket on the lawn, Daniel in her lap, Sarah cuddled up next to her as she read to them from one of the picture books she had brought with her from New York. The sun was warm at midmorning. Maggie was cutting Josh's hair as he tried to sit still in a straight chair on the back porch.

"Aw, Ma, why do you have to cut it?" he wailed. Emily smiled as she continued reading. "I'll never be able to grow my hair long enough to braid it. I'm never going to look like an Indian."

"There's a very good reason for that, young man," his mother teased him.

"What's that?" he asked dispiritedly.

"You aren't an Indian."

"Drew isn't an Indian, and he looks like one. Remember when he had braids? I wish he hadn't cut his hair."

"Drew is a grown-up, and when you're a grown-up, you can grow your hair as long as you want to. You can even dye it blue. But for now, please sit still. If you keep wiggling so much, you're going to lose an ear."

"Aw, Ma," the boy repeated in exasperation.

Emily felt a little prickle along her neck when Drew's name was mentioned. She sat a little straighter and took a deep breath.

"Are you all right, Aunt Emily?" Sarah asked, sensing the change.

"Yes, honey, I'm fine. I just had a little crick in my neck. Now, where were we?"

"Papa!" the little girl cried suddenly, leaping to her feet as she saw her father ride up to the gate. "Why is he home already?" she asked Emily.

"I don't know. Let's find out," Emily replied, closing the book and rising with Daniel in her arms.

"Horsy!" he squealed at the sight of Sam's stallion.

"That's right," Emily said automatically, wondering

what had brought Sam back from town so soon. He had said at breakfast that he wouldn't be home until quite late that evening.

Maggie hadn't seen Sam yet, because her back was to the gate. As Emily met her brother, she saw that he had removed a piece of paper from his breast pocket. His face was grim.

"Sam, what's happened? What's wrong?" she asked in alarm.

"Sarah, go tell your mother that I want to see Josh over here right now. It's important. You come back with him." The child ran back to the house, her hair streaming out behind her. Sam looked at Emily and sighed. Fear rose in her breast.

"Emily, can you take the children out for an hour or so? Maggie and I are going to need some time alone. When I got into town this morning, there was a wire just in for us from Maggie's sister, Helen. Their parents were killed yesterday in a wagon accident." His voice shook as he spoke. He had been close to Maggie's parents.

"Oh, Sam." Emily gasped. "I'm so sorry. Of course I'll take the children."

"Thanks. I'll tell them about it when you get back."

Josh and Sarah reached them, and Sam explained that they were to take a walk with Emily while he talked to their mother alone. Cheerfully, they accepted the idea, not realizing that anything was wrong. Emily led them toward the barn, stopping to pick late prairie asters and capture the few remaining grasshoppers that jumped among the grass stems along the way. Her thoughts were with her brother, and especially with Maggie. Her sister-in-law came from a tightly knit family, and the news of her parents' untimely death was sure to be a severe blow.

When Emily judged that sufficient time had passed, she guided the children back to the house. Sam met them on the front porch and ushered the children into the parlor. He drew Emily aside in the hall before following them.

"Maggie's lying down. She's terribly upset, but she's doing better than I thought she would. Would you go check and see if there's anything she needs?" he whispered.

Emily nodded and walked through the dining room into the kitchen. She filled the kettle with water and set it on the stove, then knocked softly on the bedroom door. She pushed it open tentatively.

"Maggie?" she called softly.

"Come in, Emily," Maggie answered, her voice thick with grief. She was sitting in the rocker in front of the window, one palm pressed flat against the windowpane. Her eyes were swollen with tears, and she clutched a handkerchief in her left hand. As Emily entered, she looked up.

"Oh, Maggie," Emily said, nearly in tears herself at the thought of the grief her sister-in-law must be suffering, "I'm so sorry. I wish there was something I could say or do." She crossed the room and knelt beside Maggie, putting her arm around her shoulders.

"Thank you," Maggie said quietly. "There is something you can do, Emily. I know you were planning to go back to Elmira soon, but I wondered if you would stay a little longer." She paused.

"Of course I will," Emily agreed immediately.

"You see, in the wire Helen said they need Sam and me to come home to help settle everything. I'm so much older than my brothers and sisters. Helen is the next oldest, and she's only twenty. Jamie only turned twelve last month." Her voice broke at the thought of her brother growing up without her parent's love and care. "They really do need us. It would be a tremendous comfort to me if you'd stay with the children while we're away. We should be back before the weather turns," she finished, a tear sliding from the corner of her eye.

"I'll stay as long as it takes, Maggie. Don't even think about it a second time," Emily assured her.

"Thank you, Emily. There's a stage bound for Sidney this afternoon. I want to leave right away. As it is, we'll probably miss the funeral. Can you keep the children occupied while I pack a few things?"

Emily nodded. "May I get you a cup of tea or anything?" she asked.

"Maybe a glass of water. Are you sure you don't mind staying, Emily?" Maggie's eyes reflected her concern.

"I don't mind a bit. I doubt if I could love my own children more than I love Josh and Sarah and Daniel. It will be a joy to stay. I'm only sorry that it took such a tragedy to make it necessary," Emily consoled.

Maggie rose and went to her wardrobe. "Well, I'd better pack. I'll have time to mourn on the road."

"Maggie, are you certain you're up to such a long journey? This is a terrible shock."

"Yes. I have to go. My family needs me. I'll get through it." She sighed.

Emily went back into the kitchen and returned with a glass of water, then went in search of her brother. She found him comforting Josh and Sarah, an arm around each of them, explaining that he and Maggie would be going away for a while. She entered the parlor and sat down on the sofa beside them.

"Who's going to take care of us?" Sarah asked uncertainly.

"I am," Emily answered before Sam could reply. "And we'll have such a grand time that before you know it, your mama and papa will be back again," she promised with a reassuring smile.

"Thank you, Emily," Sam said over the children's heads, relief evident in his dark eyes, so like his sister's.

"Now, why don't the three of you come help me prepare lunch? Your papa has a lot to do before he leaves," Emily said as she rose and took Sarah's hand in her own. "Who'd like to help me make sandwiches?"

The children followed her dutifully into the kitchen but remained somewhat subdued as they fixed their meal. Even the normally energetic Daniel seemed to perceive the somber mood and played quietly in a corner with some blocks. Sam disappeared, and Maggie finished packing. She sat with the children at lunch but only picked at her own food.

Sam returned as they were finishing and sent the children outside while he explained the arrangements he had made to Emily.

"I don't want to leave you here alone, and since Frank

left, I'll arrange for a man to come out and stay with you," he told his sister.

"Is that necessary?" Emily asked. "Eddie will be here, and Kenny. I'm sure we'll be safe enough."

"Kenny's just a boy, and I've asked Eddie to take over running the business while we're gone. I think he can handle it, but just to make sure, I want him to stay in town where he'll be closer to the work. And I don't think you and Kenny and Josh can handle caring for the livestock yourselves. Besides, I'd feel a lot better with someone I can trust to protect you and the children should anything happen."

Sam's arguments made absolute sense. Without a man on the place, they would be easy prey for outlaws and ruffians. While she would have argued with him had it been her alone, knowing that she could take perfectly good care of things, she understood Sam and Maggie's need for assurance that the children would have every possible protection.

"Who will you ask to come?" Emily asked.

"I'm not sure. I don't know who I can find on such short notice, but I'll get someone reliable. I'll send a note with him so you'll know without doubt who I've hired."

"Do you have to leave this afternoon? If you took a day longer, it would be easier to tie down these details," Emily pointed out.

"I know, Emmy, and I'm sorry if it's unsettling, but the Sidney stage leaves today, and it's the fastest. If we wait even a day, it will add several days to our trip. For Maggie's sake, I want to get to Illinois as quickly as possible," he explained. "Damn, there are times I wish the railroads reached the Hills!" he said forcefully, slamming his hand against the table.

"Everything will be fine, Sam. You'll get there quickly, I'm sure. We'll all miss you, but I'll do my best to see that the children are well taken care of," Emily promised him.

"You'll be all right, Emily. It won't be that difficult," Sam said, his eyes suddenly apologetic. She marveled at his concern for her in the midst of this crisis.

"It won't be difficult at all, and I shall be perfectly fine," Emily said positively. "You should be worrying about yourself and Maggie now, not me. Is there anything else you need to tell me about before you leave?"

Sam looked at her a long moment, as if making a decision. Then he shook his head. "No, that's it. Let's find Maggie and the children. We need to hurry if we're going to make that stage."

Chapter 17

L ate that afternoon, as the sun's rays slanted across the hills, throwing long shadows out before them, a rider approached the Parker house. He rode a buckskin horse, and his saddlebags bulged with gear. Sliding from the saddle, he looped the reins around the gatepost, then extracted an envelope from one of the bags. He pushed the gate aside and strode confidently to the back porch, where the door to the kitchen stood open.

A small form flew out the kitchen door toward the man. "Drew!" Joshua exclaimed with delight. "What are you doing here? Ma and Pa had to go to Illinois because my grandparents got killed. Where've you been? I missed you!"

The boy flung himself at the tall man, clad once again in Indian buckskin. Drew dropped to one knee to receive Josh's hug. Then he held him at arm's length and grinned. "You look like you've grown a bit since I last saw you," he observed.

"Half an inch," Josh told him proudly, throwing his shoulders back. "Pretty soon I'll be as tall as you!"

Drew laughed. The warm, relaxed sound of his deep voice floated across to the kitchen. As he got to his feet, he glanced toward the house. Emily appeared in the doorway, one hand braced against the support. For a split second, her face bore an expression of welcome. Then her features settled into an angry scowl, and her lips parted in an audible gasp. Drew's laughter died instantly.

"Josh, you run along in and keep an eye on your brother. I have to talk to your aunt for a minute alone."

"You won't leave without talking to me, will you?" the boy asked, clearly disappointed. "There've already been too many of these private grown-up talks today," he complained.

"Go on," Drew urged, giving him a nudge toward the house. "We'll have lots of time to talk over the next few weeks. I promise."

Josh crossed the grass, mounted the porch step, and ducked around Emily.

She didn't know what to do. She'd rehearsed this moment when she would confront Drew countless times, inventing all sorts of clever remarks designed to reduce him to contrite misery. Now, her mind was blank except for the thought that she'd been a fool to think she could ever make this strong, self-assured man quail before her wrath. He didn't approach the house but simply stood in the middle of the yard, waiting. Almost against her will, Emily stepped onto the porch, then glided across the lawn. She stopped about four feet in front of him.

Drew watched her come, her chin held high, her back straight. A flush tinted her cheeks, and her long hair cascaded loosely around her shoulders, glinting almost red in the last rays of sunlight. She looked like an angry goddess, bent on destruction. At the same time, there was a tenuous vulnerability in her dark eyes. When Sam told him earlier that day that she'd found out about the Indian engagement, he'd known she wouldn't be glad to see him, but nothing had prepared him for the remorse he felt and the anger that things couldn't have been different between them.

"Emily," he said neutrally, nodding in greeting.

"What are you doing here?" she asked in a tight voice. She refused even to think about the most likely reason. Sam wouldn't do that to her.

Without a word, Drew handed her the envelope he had brought.

Emily took it, staring for a long moment. She knew what the letter would say. She recognized her brother's bold script. Slowly, she turned the missive over in her hands. Finally she opened it and read the note.

Dear Emily,

I know that you are not going to be pleased, but I have asked Drew to stay with you and the children while we are away. He is extremely busy now, but he agreed to do it anyway, despite the inconvenience it poses him. I trust you two will be able to work out an acceptable solution to your problems since you are both intelligent, mature adults. As you know, Maggie is most concerned about leaving the children, and Drew's presence will go far in reassuring her that all will be well until our return.

I told Drew to use Maggie's and my bedroom. That way he will always be at hand should you need him.

Please try to understand that I am doing this for Maggie and the children's sake. I am sorry that you will be upset, but I am certain that you will manage and make the best of the situation, as you always do.

With love and apologies,
Sam

Emily stared at the words for long seconds, letting their full impact hit her. Drew was back again, standing nonchalantly before her, ready to walk into the house and stay. For how long? A month? Longer? She didn't think she could bear it. Every morning, he would be at breakfast, every evening at supper; every night, he would be mere footsteps away, and he would be in her mind every conscious moment. Even now, she was unnervingly aware of him, of the masterful strength he exuded, of his lazy, sensual mouth, and of his deep blue gaze. He could not stay. She couldn't endure him here, day after day.

Drew watched her blanch as she read the note. It struck him like a blow to realize how distasteful his presence would be to her. Everything was in a mess. He should never have allowed Sam to talk him into this. He had so much work to do before winter, and he would be able to accomplish little while he stayed at the Parkers'. In addition, he was probably putting them all in danger, but when

Sam had pleaded with him to stay, assuring him that it would be for no more than a month, and that it would reassure Maggie tremendously in her time of grief, he'd relented and agreed to come.

Now, gazing at Emily so unhappy before him, he admitted to himself that he'd come primarily because he hadn't been able to resist the thought of being so close to her for a period of time. He'd naively hoped that they might be able to work things out, given enough time. He found that he thought of little besides her. On the trail, in the camps he visited, at night on the plains, she was always with him. The sound of her lilting voice, the scent of her soft hair, the feel of her satiny skin against his own and her lush curves beneath him were ever but a hair's breadth away from his conscious mind. And now he'd foolishly risked the security of his supply operation and her safety by giving in to his weakness and coming here.

"Look, I know you aren't going to like this very much, but I made a promise to your brother that I intend to keep. He told me that you heard about the engagement business. I'm sorry you found out, but I did it to protect you from Iron Thunder, not to hurt you." His voice was brusque, his words slicing into Emily's heart, dashing forever her faint hopes that he might have been the tiniest bit sincere. "If we look on this as a job to be done, we should be able to get through it until Sam and Maggie get back. Just think of me as you would any other hired man, and you should be able to tolerate me."

Emily didn't understand the cold anger in his tone, and her temper rose in response to his easy dismissal of all that had passed between them. Hired man, indeed! If that was what he wanted, that was what he would get, the arrogant bastard!

"Fine, if that's what you want. Sam's note says you're to use his room, although I see no reason why a hired man," she said emphasizing the words, "shouldn't sleep in the bunkhouse. Be that as it may, I don't believe anyone has checked on the horses today, and there are probably some cows that need milking and some other stock that need to be fed. After you stow your things, you can take care of it. Supper is at six o'clock.'' She stalked back into the house, slamming the door hard behind her.

Drew stared after her, not sure whether he was angry or amused by her display.

The children were delighted that Drew was to be staying with them. Josh begged to be allowed to stay home from school the following Monday to trail after Drew and help him with the chores, hoping for a lesson or two in how to ride bareback. Emily wouldn't hear of it and sent him off on his pony to the little schoolhouse in Sturgis. She worried about sending him alone, but Drew insisted the boy would be fine. Emily did keep Sarah at home, and she worked with her in the mornings for an hour or so, teaching her her letters and working on her reading, writing, and sums. Daniel was always underfoot, demanding constant attention. Mary Guthrie continued to come to help several days a week, and Emily found she welcomed the girl's company. It helped keep her mind off Drew.

It quickly became apparent that he was not simply a hired man, and there was no way to treat him as such. For the first few days, Emily coldly informed him of every chore she could think of that would take him away from the house and said little else to him. He politely answered and went about the work quietly and efficiently, not attempting to speak much with Emily. He spoke warmly and frequently with the children, though, teasing them, telling them stories about his adventures and about the Indians, playing with them, and helping Josh with his homework if needed. He had an amazing knack for keeping Daniel occupied and quiet that Emily secretly marveled at. While her anger with him didn't abate, she found it increasingly difficult to maintain a safe distance between them.

One evening during supper, Sarah turned her blue eyes to Emily and innocently asked her why she didn't like Drew.

Emily didn't know what to say. ''What makes you think I don't like him?'' she finally returned with a forced smile.

''You almost never talk to him, and when you do you only say, 'The horses need fresh water' or 'There's a leak in the chicken house roof,' and things like that. You don't laugh and have fun like you do with Mary or Kenny, or like you did when Mama and Papa were here." An idea occurred to the little girl. "Do you miss Mama and Papa a lot? I do." Her expression was troubled.

Emily grasped the proffered excuse, stoutly refusing to look at Drew. "Yes, honey, I do miss them. That's all it is. Please don't worry about it, and try to cheer up," she encouraged gently. "Your mama and papa will be back soon enough."

That night after the dishes were all cleaned up and put away, Emily looked around for the children. The house was silent. She passed through the dining room and stopped in the hall outside the parlor. She could hear Drew's deep voice almost chanting in a slow rhythm. Moving into the open doorway, she looked into the room, lit with the yellow light of the oil lamps. Drew was sprawled on the sofa, Daniel balanced on one thigh facing him, sitting absolutely still and staring at the big man as though transfixed. Sarah was nestled in the crook of his right arm, Josh in his left. He was telling them a story about Inktomi, the trickster who went around playing tricks on the Lakota gods and men. His face mirrored the emotions of the characters in his tale, and he looked back and forth at the three children, constantly asking what they thought happened next, teasing them, making them think he was going to stop the story each time he reached a climactic point. Emily leaned against the door frame and allowed herself a little smile. He was so handsome, so gentle, so kind. And yet he had treated her so carelessly, using her with no apparent regrets. He would make such a good father, and such a terrible husband.

Saturday night was bath night for the children. Emily herself washed daily from her basin, but she looked forward to a long soak in the tub late on Saturday nights after the children had finally been put to bed. She supposed she should offer Drew a bath as well, but she was feeling churlish toward him, so she didn't. In the afternoon, she pumped water into the hot water heater that Sam had installed in the little washroom that opened off the kitchen, next to the pantry, and built a fire under it. The best thing about the water heater was that it allowed each bather to have fresh hot water. It was a chore, however, to tend the fire and pump the water into the heater.

Sarah was first, followed by Josh and Daniel. Emily left the boys alone to help Sarah locate a missing nightgown, which they eventually found misplaced in one of Daniel's drawers. When Sarah was dressed for bed, Emily left her tucked in for the night, her hair tied up in rags, looking at a picture book. She headed back downstairs to the washroom.

Glancing at the watch pinned to her shirtwaist, Emily realized that she'd left the boys alone for over fifteen minutes. Drew had gone out after supper, saying only that he'd be in the barn if she needed him. She really shouldn't have left her nephews unattended for so long.

As she reached the bottom of the steps in the front hall, Emily heard the boys laughing raucously. Pushing open the dining room door, she heard water slapping noisily. Her step quickened, and she ran across the kitchen to the washroom door. Water seeped out below it. She opened the door and stepped into the room just as Josh swung a squealing Daniel through the air, dropping him with a huge splash into the tub. Water flew up, splashing all over the walls, and drenching Emily as she stood gasping at the spectacle. The boys looked at her in startled surprise, their grins turning immediately to expressions of guilty trepidation.

Emily was more startled than her nephews were. The whole front of her skirt and shirtwaist was soaked.

"What on earth is going on here?" she demanded sternly.

"We were just playing," Josh ventured tremulously.

"Look at this mess you've made!" Emily exclaimed, gesturing about her. "There's water all over the kitchen floor as well."

"I'm sorry," Josh said in a small voice. "I'll clean it up, honest I will," he promised.

A tingle along her spine told Emily that Drew had just moved into the doorway behind her. She glanced back at him and saw his mouth turn up in a quick grin, which he quickly suppressed when he caught her set expression. His eyes traveled insolently down to where the wet material of her shirtwaist clung to her breasts, outlining their fullness. She turned abruptly back to her nephews, walking into the room. She picked up a towel that wasn't too wet and reached for Daniel. He raised his arms and let her lift him out of the tepid water.

"It's time for you two to get out and get to bed," she told them calmly. "I'll clean up this time, Josh. Please promise me you won't do this again. One of you could have gotten hurt, and I would have been absolutely sick. How would your parents have felt?"

"Not very good, I guess," Josh mumbled. "I won't do it again, Aunt Emily."

"Thank you. Now, if you can find a dry towel, you'd better get out of that water before you freeze to death." She smiled at him, letting him know he was forgiven. She was rewarded with a shy smile in return.

With Daniel in her arms, his chubby limbs pink from the bath, Emily turned to the door. Drew was still there, watching her closely, an oddly tender light in his eyes.

"Excuse me," she said.

He stepped aside, but as he did, his hand brushed her waist, whether or not on purpose, she wasn't sure.

When the boys were finally dry, dressed in their nightclothes and tucked into bed, Emily returned to the kitchen to clean up the mess they'd made. She was tired, and she decided not to change her clothes, since she'd probably get all wet again. She'd planned to take her own bath after the boys, but it was now so late, and she was so sleepy, that she thought perhaps she would wait until tomorrow.

When she reached the kitchen, she discovered that the floor was completely dry. She opened the washroom door and found it was also dry and set to rights. The fire was burning steadily in the heater, and fresh towels had been laid out on the chair next to the tub. The wet towels and rug were hung neatly on the wooden drying rack, and the floor was clean. Emily looked around in surprise. Drew must have cleaned everything up.

His broad form loomed suddenly in the doorway. He walked in past her and turned on the taps and began filling the tub. Then he leaned against the side of it, his arms folded in front of his chest, and looked at her, his expression inscrutable.

"Thank you for cleaning up," Emily said, avoiding his eyes. "You didn't have to."

"I know," he said easily.

She waited for him to say something more, but he merely watched her.

"Yes, well, I guess I'll go upstairs so you can have your bath," she said, stepping toward the door.

Drew reached out, his warm fingers closing over her arm. He pulled her to stand in front of him, slipping his hands behind her waist.

She tried to pull away, but his grip tightened, and he stood, bringing her closer. She could feel the hard warmth of his forearms pressing lightly along the sides of her breasts through the wet cotton of her blouse. Again she backed away, this time successfully ducking away from him and moving quickly toward the door.

Drew came after her, pushing the door shut so fast that the hem of her skirt caught in it.

"Now look what you've done!" she exclaimed, tugging at the material. Her hand went to the doorknob but his was already there. She snatched her hand back the instant she touched him.

"Christ, Emily, do you have to act like I've got hydrophobia?" He caged her in the corner between his arms.

"Do you always have to touch me? Couldn't you try just talking to me for a change?"

"Would you listen?"

She didn't answer.

"I didn't think so. Besides, I like to touch you. I can't seem to help myself," he said with a wry smile.

"Then learn some discipline."

She tried to open the door, but he held it closed and leaned nearer until his chest almost touched hers. She put her hand up and pushed hard, but he didn't budge.

"Don't touch me," he taunted.

She dropped her head and stared at her hand on his chest, feeling his steady heartbeat. She started to move it away, but he pressed into her so that her hand was caught between them.

"We can talk if you want," he offered. His breath fanned her cheek when he spoke.

"I don't want to talk now. I can't talk to you when you're on top of me like this."

"Would you rather I was on top of you another way?" She shoved at him with both hands.

"You are insolent, presumptuous, insensitive, bad-tempered, arrogant, and disgustingly single-minded. You are deceptive, disrespectful—"

Drew cut her off by wrapping his arms around her and hauling her up against him, his mouth covering hers. One of his hands cupped the back of her head, keeping her from turning away from him. His lips moved confidently across hers as he began licking and sucking at her bottom lip. He groaned deep in his throat when he felt her mouth open to him. He immediately slipped his tongue past her lips.

"Hey!" he bellowed, rearing back suddenly. "You bit me!"

"You asked for it!" She reached around quickly to open the door and free her skirt.

He knocked it closed again and grabbed her wrist.

"Jesus, Emily!" he swore, "What the hell is wrong with you? Why shouldn't I kiss you? Have you got any idea what you do to me?"

"I have a pretty good idea, and that's why you shouldn't kiss me. It wouldn't stop there, would it?"

"Probably not," he admitted. "We could try it and see." He pulled her back into his arms.

"Just stop, won't you? Can't you understand that I don't want this?" She turned her head away from him.

"Why not just enjoy it? Forget about everything else and let me make love to you," he said against her ear.

Emily went still.

"I can't forget. I can't forget the hurt, or the embarrassment, or the shame." Her voice wavered with emotion.

"I'm sorry. I told you that." His hands moved across her back. "I can't forget, either, you know. I can't forget the passion or the joy we've given each other. At least let me give you pleasure."

He caught her chin and brought his mouth against hers. He felt her strain away from him, but he held her firmly and kept kissing her, gently and tenderly. Gradually, she became softer in his arms, and after many minutes, he lifted his head and looked at her.

Drew watched the slow light of desire kindle in her greenwood eyes before she looked down. He held her lightly, his hands clasped behind her waist. When he felt her tremble, he kissed her again, with more pressure. He coaxed her lips apart with his own and enticed her tongue to duel with his. The kiss deepened, and he felt his reaction heavy and low in his belly, then taut and full in his groin.

Abruptly, he withdrew his hands and stepped away from her. "By the way, it's not my bath," he said, a ragged edge to his voice. "It's yours. Take your time." With that, he left the washroom, pulling the door closed behind him.

Emily stood staring at the wooden door. Then she shook her head and began to undress, hardly able to believe that he'd left her. As she settled into the blissfully warm and soothing water, a single tear trickled out of the corner of her eye.

The weather remained pleasant, gradually growing cooler as the month progressed. Drew began to look worriedly at the sky, and, more than once, Emily noticed him turning his face into the wind, testing it. About the end of his second week with them, a permanent frown settled onto his features, and Emily had no idea what caused it. He was not short or irritable with her or the children, but something was bothering him. Several times, he made brief trips over to his place, and Emily assumed that he was supervising the distribution of goods to the Indians. Then he began to take Sam's wagon and bring it back fully loaded with wood, coal oil, and hay. He took Emily into town and insisted that she purchase a large supply of canned food and candles, some new lamps, and other supplies. Within a few days, the Parker house was well stocked with every commodity that Emily imagined they would ever need. The coal bin was full, wood was stacked several feet deep around the outside of the kitchen, and the cellar looked like a dry goods store. More supplies were stored in the barn.

One afternoon, Emily found Drew and Kenny driving tall stakes in a row stretching from the kitchen door all the way to the barn. She asked what they were doing.

"These are snow stakes," Kenny informed her.

"What are they for?" she asked, not understanding.

"In a blizzard, you can get disoriented real easy. You have to string a rope along between the stakes so you can grab hold and follow it to the barn to care for the livestock. Then you don't wander off and freeze ten feet away from the house," the teenager explained.

"Surely the snow doesn't get that bad!" Emily exclaimed in alarm.

"Not always," Drew answered, "but this year it will." There was certainty in his voice.

"How do you know?" Emily challenged him suspiciously.

"I watch the earth and the animals, the wind and the sky. It's a feeling as much as anything." He didn't look up from his work. Emily watched his muscles ripple under his shirt as he lifted the sledgehammer and brought it down on the stake he had positioned.

"Then you might be wrong," she concluded.

Drew cast her a serious look. "I hope I am. A lot of people are going to suffer otherwise."

Emily knew that he was thinking about the off-reservation Sioux. Suddenly, she felt terribly guilty. Drew should have been spending the past few weeks getting as much food and clothing to them as possible, but, instead, he'd been preparing this one little household of his neighbors for a hard winter. She knew it wasn't her fault, and she'd almost ceaselessly wished that he hadn't agreed to stay with them, but she felt badly anyway. Drew noticed the concern and sudden understanding in her eyes. Because Kenny was there, neither of them said anything, but each knew what the other thought.

"It can't be helped," he finally said sadly. "We do what we can."

That night at supper, as Emily was moving around the big oak table cutting wedges of apple pie for everyone, Sarah asked Drew a question out of the blue.

"Do you have a wife?"

Emily felt her muscles tense, but she went on cutting Kenny's pie without looking up. She heard the smile in Drew's reply.

"No," he answered slowly. "Why do you ask?"

"Josh was telling me about Miss Caldwell, his teacher. She's getting married next month. Even Frank got married and left us. Does everybody get married?" Sarah asked.

"No. I'm not married."

"Why not?" she asked candidly.

Emily continued moving around the table, not looking up.

"I've been too busy," Drew told Sarah easily. "I travel too much to have a wife."

"Couldn't a wife go with you?" Sarah wanted to know.

"Sometimes she could, but sometimes I go to dangerous places. It wouldn't be right to take a woman with me. Besides, if I had children, they'd never see me."

"Like we almost never see you," Sarah observed.

"That's right," Drew agreed. "That wouldn't be fair." Sarah nodded in understanding.

"Will you ever get married?" Josh broke in. "I think it'd be more fun to travel."

Drew grinned at the boy. "Sometimes traveling gets old, Josh. Lately, I've been thinking I might like to get married."

His gaze rested on Emily, who stared at the pie she was cutting as if it held all the fascination of a sultan's treasure chest.

"Who would you like to marry?" Sarah asked innocently, stabbing her fork into a thick slice of apple and sliding it out from between the crusts. She twirled it on her fork.

"Don't play with your food, Sarah," Emily scolded.

Drew was silent for a moment. He continued to watch Emily's graceful form as she moved to Josh's side. Her pale hair caught the light from the lamps on the sideboard and the wall, gleaming like gold against her navy-blue dress. The full curves of her figure seemed to beckon to him, inviting his touch. His groin tightened, and he had to force himself to look away from her. Josh saved him from having to answer.

"You could marry Aunt Emily, Drew," the boy suggested cheerily. "She doesn't have a husband. Everyone in the family thinks it's time she got married."

"Joshua!" Emily reprimanded him, color flooding into her cheeks. "That's quite enough of that kind of talk!"

Drew smiled broadly, and Kenny snickered into his napkin.

"That's a perfect idea!" Sarah exclaimed with obvious excitement. "Then you'd be our uncle! We could come and see you all the time!"

"And I heard Pa say that Emily likes you a lot more than Mr. Stevens," Josh added quickly. "He said he'd like nothing better than to see you get married, that you two were made for each other. So why don't you marry Aunt Emily, Drew?"

Emily looked up finally, her face aflame. "Joshua, you will stop this nonsense at once," she commanded. "It's rude to bring up such . . . personal topics. Do you want some pie?" she said abruptly to Drew, hoping no more would be said. She didn't like the lazy grin that spread across his face, or the light in his blue eyes.

"Please." He nodded. She hastily dumped a large piece onto his plate and tried to scuttle away. His fingers closed around her wrist, halting her retreat.

"Now, just a minute, Emily," he drawled, pulling her to his side. He scooted his chair back a ways from the table and turned slightly toward her. "I think Josh and

Sarah may have something here. I'm getting older, you're getting older''—he paused to watch her lips purse into an angry line at his teasing—"and I *am* thinking about getting married.''

"Well, I'm not!" she snapped at him. She tried to wrench her wrist away and was instead pulled inexorably closer. His arm came up behind her and pushed her down onto one thigh. The other thigh immediately closed to trap her skirt between his legs. She still held the pie server in one hand and the apple pie in the other and was unable to stop him from wrapping his arms around her waist. The children and Kenny looked on with interest, barely containing their amusement.

"That's not true, Aunt Emily," Sarah insisted, giggling. "You told me that someday you wanted to get married. I remember."

Emily tossed her niece an exasperated look. She was far more attuned than she wanted to be to the solid feel of Drew's legs pressing firmly against hers and to the steady rhythm of his chest rising and falling under her arm.

"What do you say, Emily?" Drew said with his most winning smile.

Her heart flipped over.

"Will you marry me?"

Their eyes locked and held. There was an urgency in his tone that belied the teasing nature of the exchange. She gazed into his eyes for a long moment, trying to decide if there was the slimmest chance that he might be serious. The white lights danced in those blue depths, their intensity disturbing. Emily was confused. Damn him, if there hadn't been the false Indian engagement fiasco, if she didn't know so many things, she might have thought that he was really asking. But she knew too much.

Putting the pie and the server on the table, she placed her hands on his and removed them from her waist.

"Don't be ridiculous," she said quietly.

She pushed his leg aside and rose. Then she walked through the swinging door to the kitchen and out into the October night.

Emily didn't return to the house for several hours. She

followed the creek into the broad valley that ringed the hills, thinking all the while about the scene that Sarah had so innocently brought about at supper. The more she thought about it, the angrier she became. She'd known Drew could be insensitive, but to tease her the way he had that evening was nothing short of despicable. He had to know how she felt about him, but he'd said there could be nothing more between them than physical passion, and he knew her well enough to know that she couldn't allow herself to settle for that alone. Did he enjoy tormenting her? He was heartless, and he seemed to have no care at all for her except when she was in his arms responding to his caresses.

Emily walked for a long time. When she finally returned to the house, she made purposefully for the kitchen door, determined to tell Drew Rutledge exactly what he could do with his nasty little jokes at her expense. The light still burned in the window, and she saw Drew's shadow cross the window. None of the children seemed to be about, and all the other lights were out. They were probably in bed. So much the better, she thought, placing her hand on the door handle. She wouldn't have to worry about watching what she said in front of them. She pushed open the heavy door and stepped into the kitchen.

Chapter 18

Drew was sitting at the pine trestle table, leaning back in a straight chair, his legs stretched out before him, braced on the lower supports of the table. He took a last swallow of coffee from a heavy mug and set it down on the table with a solid thud. He watched impassively as Emily opened the door, stopping abruptly when she saw him. There was an angry, defiant light in her eyes as she walked primly to the opposite side of the table and faced him.

"I want to talk to you," she announced aggressively.

Before she could continue, Drew dropped all four feet of his chair to the floor with a thump and rose. He walked to the sink and began rinsing his cup as if she weren't even there.

"I said I wanted to talk to you," she repeated, her voice rising with her temper.

"Maybe I don't want to talk to you," Drew said over the swish of running water.

"Fine. Then listen," she snapped, "because I've had about all I can take from you and everyone else, and I won't tolerate your careless inconsideration of my feelings any longer."

He turned to face her.

"I'm inconsiderate of your feelings? You haven't seen fit to speak two civil words to me since I got here unless someone else was around, and then you've made it painfully obvious that you wouldn't if you felt you had a

273

choice. You have the gall to claim that *I've* been inconsiderate to *you?*"

Drew's eyes flashed with the anger that Emily had seen often enough before, but she didn't heed it now.

"You know damn well I never wanted to see you again!" she said, controlling the urge to scream at him. "After everything you've put me through, from the very first time I saw you, what's happened that should make me want to sit down and spend a Sunday afternoon chatting with you on the porch?"

"Plenty, and you know it," he growled, his gaze insinuating.

"I didn't ask you to come here, but since Sam did I've tried to make the best of it. You're making it impossible," Emily continued accusingly, ignoring his comment. "How could you tease me the way you did at supper? How dare you mock me in front of my family that way?"

"Is that what this tirade is all about?" Drew moved so that the table no longer stood between them.

"That's part of it, but there's more. I'm sick to death of everyone telling me what to do, and worse, deciding what I should do, or what should be done for me, and you're the worst offender. Who gave you the right to interfere in my life? Who gave you permission to make decisions for me, for God's sake?"

"Somebody needed to do it," he ground out between clenched teeth.

"That's a laugh! Whatever gave you that ludicrous idea?" Emily asked indignantly.

"That's right, I forgot. You could have handled everything yourself that first day in Deadwood," Drew sneered. "And you were doing a wonderful job of handling Iron Thunder. What was I supposed to do? Let you hang yourself?"

"Yes, well, you really waited to see what I could do before you jumped in, the great hero rescuing the damsel in distress," she retorted sarcastically. "That's exactly what I mean. Right from the beginning, you decided that you knew what was right for me better than I did. You drop into my life for a day or two here and there, totally disrupting everything, then you disappear without a word, expecting to walk back in and pick up where you left off meddling in my affairs. You seduced me, then told me you didn't want me, and you've continued to play with my emotions as if I were no more than an amusement to you. And you have everyone else singing your praises to me night and day, telling me to give you a chance, to wait until you explain why you're being such a cad, telling me to be patient and then fall into your arms when and if you finally decide you want me! Even Josh and Sarah, for heaven's sake! Why doesn't anyone ever ask me what *I* want? Is that really so much to ask?'' There was a pleading note in her voice despite the fury glinting in her eyes.

Drew didn't answer immediately. He stepped closer to Emily so that she had to tilt her head to maintain his gaze. She moved backward to put more distance between them and caught her heel on a chair leg, stumbling.

He caught her elbows instantly, preventing her from falling. As she shrank from him, the white lights in his blue eyes blazed, and he jerked her roughly into his arms. She struggled to break free of his embrace, but couldn't. With each movement of her twisting torso and legs, she felt yet another part of her touching the hard muscles of his chest and thighs.

"What do you want?" he asked, giving her a little shake.

"I want you to leave me alone," she said firmly.

"I don't believe that. Tell me the truth. What do you want?"

The urgent intensity in his deep voice made Emily look up at him. Her fingers closed convulsively on the soft material of his cotton shirt, then pushed against him.

"I want to live my own life without a lot of interference from you!" She pushed harder, but his hands closed over hers in a tight grip.

"Quit trying to get away. We're going to have this conversation now, and you're going to be honest with me. You're always mad about something, and now's the time to get it out."

He waited for her to speak. Instead, she tried to wriggle away from him.

"For God's sake, Emily, if you know what you want, then tell me!"

She stopped tugging at her hands but remained tense.

"I don't want you. I know that." Her voice was cold.

"Huh-uh. You do want me. We both know that." He drew her toward him.

The color in her cheeks deepened. "All right, I do! But only in the physical sense. I can't help that. It's just animal lust."

He smiled grimly. "That's quite an admission coming from you, but it's still not the truth. Not the whole of it. You want a lot more than that from me."

Emily finally looked away from his eyes, focusing on his shoulder. "I don't expect anything from you."

"Yeah, you do. That's why you're always so quick to fly off the handle with me. And why you're afraid to admit what you really feel for me." His hands tightened on hers.

"I won't get what I want from you," she said tautly, "so just leave me alone."

"You want a husband, don't you?"

She didn't answer.

"And you want kids of your own. And a nice house in a nice town or a ranch. I know what you want, Emily."

"Then why do you keep after me so? Can't you let it go?"

He shook his head. "You want all those things, but you want me, too. You want it all."

Her cheeks burned with shame, and she refused to look at him.

"No other man's ever made you feel what I make you feel, have they?"

She wouldn't dignify that with a response.

"Have they, Emily? Nobody else makes you burn inside. Nobody else's touch makes you wild and hot like mine does. No other man's kiss have ever made you wet with wanting and—"

"Shut up!" she finally cried. "No, damn you! But it won't work between us. I need more stability and more of your time than you're willing to give me. I need more than the fire we set inside each other. I don't want to keep fighting you, Drew, but don't you understand?'' she pleaded.

He jerked her against him.

"Then stop fighting me. I need you and I want you. Let the fire be enough.''

Emily felt Drew's chest expand against her and his hand slide to her neck, pulling her head back. Then his mouth claimed hers in a fervid assault that carried away all the pent-up frustration and pain of the past weeks in a flood of frenzied release.

She strained against him to no avail.

"Stop fighting me,'' he commanded against her mouth, "Stop fighting yourself.''

And gradually, as he continued to kiss her, pressing for a response with his lips and hands, her resistance faltered. Ironically, there was a comfort in his embrace that she craved. His kiss was fierce, but his hands were warm and supporting as they moved across her back.

"Oh, God,'' she breathed. She let her arms curl around his waist, then settled her hands across his hips. "Heaven help me, but I can only take so much . . . ''

"Let me kiss you, sweetheart. Let me love you tonight,'' Drew whispered. He cupped her hips in his hands and seductively pressed her tight against his hips, rocking so that his swollen flesh touched her intimately.

Her lips parted in a soundless cry of arousal.

Desire overcame reason, and at last she gave herself over to it. When he kissed her, she welcomed his tongue into her mouth, delighting in the ravishing splendor of their shared need. She felt his teeth nip at her lower lip, then along her jaw and down her neck to her shoulder before she pulled his head back to her mouth and finally plunged her tongue into his mouth, dueling with his in frantic abandon. Set free from the restraint of the past weeks, she found she couldn't get her fill of him fast enough. Her hands tugged impatiently at the buttons on his shirt so that she could feel his warm skin beneath her palms. As they slipped from their holes and gave her access to him, she pulled the shirttails from his trousers and slid her hands along his sides to his back, where her fingers devoured the feel of his firm flesh, no longer denied to her.

Emily was so engrossed in the feel of Drew's body that she was surprised to realize that he had undone all the buttons on her bodice. She shifted her arms so that he could push her dress off her shoulders, exposing the lacy camisole below. The peaks of her breasts stood taut against the fine white material. Their kiss continued, deep and driven by furious passion, and as Emily stroked Drew's bare stomach, dragging her nails lightly across his bronzed skin, his fingers found her swollen nipples, kneading them so that mindless tingles of sensation raced through her veins. She arched her back, pressing her breasts into his hands, and his mouth dropped to her throat, his tongue darting along her collarbone, dipping into the hollows there, testing her fine skin lightly with his teeth. His kisses traveled lower, and he brushed his cheek against the fine lace on her camisole, his lips barely touching the peaks of her breasts as they strained at the cotton cloth. As Emily gasped at the shivers that coursed through her, he placed his hands below her breasts, and, raising one taut nipple, he lowered his mouth to it. A soft moan escaped her throat as the moist warmth penetrated the thin material and his tongue teased her, pulling and flicking at the hard nub, driving her desire to the brink.

When she thought she could stand the exquisite torment no longer, Drew shifted his attentions to her other breast. Emily felt weak, able only to cling to his powerful shoulders. She managed to push his shirt down his arms, baring his torso. Her hands ranged across his back, her fingers touching the smooth skin of the scars he had received in the sun dance. As the glorious flames of pleasure at her breasts became almost too much to bear, Emily raised Drew's head and invited him to kiss her lips once again. He shrugged out of his shirt, letting it fall to the floor, and wrapped his bare arms around her back. His mouth fastened firmly to hers, he lifted her off her feet and crossed the short distance that separated them from the bedroom door. Emily held him tightly to her, pressing her breasts into his chest, her fingers winding into the curling locks that lay against his neck.

As he was swinging the bedroom door shut, the scrape of a chair on the wooden kitchen floor caused him to stop in mid-stride. Emily instantly pulled away from him and looked back into the kitchen, her eyes wide with panic, her hand hastily grabbing at her dress in an effort to cover herself. Drew turned with her still in his arms, and she twisted her head to see who was there.

Daniel was climbing the chair rungs to lever himself up onto the flat seat of the chair he had pushed away from the table. He spun for a second on his stomach, then used the table to pull himself into a sitting position. Then he looked up at Emily and Drew, who stood in the bedroom doorway, both breathing heavily. He gave them a cherubic smile.

"Dwink o' wato," he chirped, gazing at them expectantly.

Emily felt Drew's chest start to shake against her. Glancing at his face, barely an inch away from hers, she saw him laughing. She didn't think anything was funny.

"Put me down!" she hissed, and he instantly lowered her feet to the floor. She turned her back to her nephew and hurriedly pulled her dress back up over her shoulders. As she buttoned it, she couldn't help noticing the wet spots on her camisole over her breasts. Oh, God, she thought, what have I done? What would Sam and Maggie say? Bright stains of color appeared in her cheeks as she turned to face Daniel.

Drew had already given the child a tin cup of water, which he thirstily drank. When he was finished, he carefully placed the cup on the table and raised his arms to Drew, who easily lifted him and nestled him against his bare chest.

"Go sleep," Daniel told them. He yawned and dropped his head onto Drew's shoulder, still watching Emily. She shook her head at him and smiled wanly. What if it had been Josh or Sarah who had walked in on them making love? This could never happen again.

Drew pushed the dining room door open and walked through into the hall, then up the stairs. Emily followed a short distance behind. If she remained in the kitchen, she had no doubts about what would happen when Drew returned. It would be better to go upstairs where he would do nothing that might awaken the children.

The boys' bedroom was the first door on the left at the top of the stairway. Drew walked through the open door with Daniel, and Emily continued past them to her own room, ducking inside quickly and closing the door behind her. She walked across the soft carpet to the window and looked out at the darkness. A minute later, she heard the doorknob turn behind her as Drew entered. A match flared, and he lit the lamp on her dressing table, then came to stand behind her. His hand settled lightly onto her shoulder, his fingers idly toying with the strands of her hair.

"You shouldn't be in here," Emily said at length. There was no conviction in her voice.

"Then come back downstairs with me," Drew countered, his touch light, yet full of promise.

"No. It wouldn't be right."

"Why not, Emily? Isn't it what you want? Isn't it what we both want?"

"No! I tried to tell you, but you won't listen . . ." She searched for the words to express what she felt. "This isn't right, Drew, and you know it. I have a responsibility to Sam and Maggie to take proper care of the children, and sleeping with you just isn't right. You have a responsibility, too. It would be the worst possible example. Don't ever put me in this position again."

Drew was silent. His fingers twined in her silky hair, pulling gently at the locks.

"They need never know," he finally suggested, knowing that she was right but reluctant to give up.

"How long do you think it would take them to catch us? What if that had been Josh or Sarah tonight? And even if they didn't know, it would be betraying Sam and Maggie's trust," she insisted. "Do you have so little regard for them?"

"You make everything sound so sordid and disgusting.

Do you really feel so horrible when I touch you? When I kiss you? Does it feel so wrong, so sinful when I take you in my arms and touch your skin, your breasts . . . ?"

"Stop it!" Emily commanded, admitting to herself that it didn't feel wrong at all. Nothing in her life had ever felt more right, and yet it wasn't. She couldn't change that.

"I think your brother knew this was a possibility when he asked me to stay here, Emily," Drew pointed out. "In fact, it's probably the reason he asked me, and not someone else. You heard what Josh said at dinner."

Emily knew Sam well enough to realize that Drew was most likely right, but she wouldn't say so. It was yet another example of someone meddling in her life.

"Marriage is one thing, Drew. Sam wants to see me married, but I don't recall either of us seriously suggesting that we get married tonight," she said sarcastically.

"I seem to remember proposing," he said softly, in his familiar teasing tone. Emily's back straightened.

"Don't tease me. I already asked you not to once this evening."

He released her hair and stepped away from her.

"I'm sorry," he apologized with a sigh. "You're right, of course."

These were not the words Emily had hoped to hear. A lump formed in her throat.

"After all," she said aloud, more to herself than to him, "you'll be gone in two weeks, and then where would I be? Other people could get hurt. My reputation would be in ruins. Sam and Maggie would be disappointed with me. I might get pregnant. It would be utterly foolish."

"I'm not worried about anyone but you, Emily, and taking responsible care of this place and the children. And I'd never leave you alone with a child, no matter what you think of me. There are ways to avoid that. I'll accept that you're right only for the children's sake, not for any of your other reasons. It wouldn't be foolishness to make love to you every night as I want to, but absolute joy, for both of us. Don't lie to yourself about that."

Then, as if to impress upon her the truth of his words, Drew pulled her around and into his arms again, kissing her hard and deeply. She finally tore herself away from him. He stopped in the doorway before closing the door behind him. His look was knowing.

"Sweet dreams," he said as he walked down the hall.

The next days were horrible for Emily. The tension that existed between her and Drew had only been aggravated by the brief taste of release that they'd had, and while he said that he accepted that it wasn't right for them to make love under the circumstances, it seemed to Emily that he took every chance he could to brush against her, touch her hand, or place his hands on her arms or back. A few times, he even went so far as to drop a light kiss on her cheek or forehead if they were inadvertently alone. No matter how strongly she protested his actions, he wouldn't stop.

Fortunately, he spent most of the days working outside or going back and forth between his place and the Parkers'. Emily learned that Black Wolf had brought his family with him and was staying at Drew's cabin. When she had expressed a desire to visit with Red Eagle Woman, Drew refused to allow it.

Toward the end of the third week in October, Emily had begun to count the days until Sam and Maggie would return home. They'd written to say that things were proceeding as smoothly as could be expected and that they planned to leave for home shortly after the first of November. She looked forward to their arrival because it would put an end to the terrible strain of living in the same house with Drew, but she also dreaded it because she knew he would leave again, and then she would go back to Elmira and never see him again. The thought was so painful that she chose not to dwell on it.

One morning, as Emily was walking back to the house from the chicken coop with a basket full of fresh eggs, she noticed that the wind had turned unusually cold. She had left the house without a sweater, and now she regretted it. At the gate, a great gust of wind blew the wooden gate out of her hand, slamming it against the picket fence that encircled the yard. Turning to secure it, Emily saw a forbidding, leaden sky in the north. She wondered if it would storm. Shivering, she walked rapidly to the house.

Just minutes after she entered the warm kitchen, the door slammed again and Drew burst into the room.

"There's a big storm brewing," he told her shortly. "We could have a bad blizzard before this afternoon, so I'm going to get Josh at school and I'm sending Kenny to his folk's place in Sturgis. I want you to keep an eye on Daniel and Sarah and don't let them wander off. Bring in as much wood as you can before I get back, and don't leave anything out in the yard," he said tersely, picking up a hat and shoving it down low over his forehead. "I'll be back as soon as I can."

Emily worked quickly to bring in all the children's toys that were scattered about the yard and then began carrying in armloads of wood until the wood box next to the stove was full and there was a big pile in the storeroom off the pantry. Her arms were sore, but she brought some coal oil up from the cellar. She had no idea how much of anything they would need. How long could a blizzard last? She kept Daniel and Sarah at the kitchen table drawing so she could keep track of their whereabouts easily.

When Drew returned with Josh, they stopped in at the house briefly before heading for the barn to make sure the animals had plenty of food and water. On their way to the barn, they strung long lengths of sturdy rope along the snow poles. Drew had brought most of the cattle in from the far pastures two days previously, and now he drove them into the corral where they would be partially sheltered from the north wind that was already blowing hard and cold. There weren't that many of them, perhaps twenty, and in a short time, Drew had them settled where he wanted them for the duration of the coming storm.

In the early afternoon, the snow began to fall in earnest. The wind continued to howl, filling the air with a swirling white cloud that made it impossible to see more than a few feet with any clarity. Icy arctic blasts found their way into every crack and crevice around the doors and windows, and the temperature inside the house dipped. Emily bundled the children up in extra sweaters, and she brought their mittens and gloves in from the hall, and woolen blankets from the upstairs bedrooms. Then she stoked the fire in the stove and lit two lamps, placing them on the table so the children could see to read or draw. There was a pile of their toys in one corner where Daniel sat on the floor stacking the colorful blocks that Sam had made for him. At last, Drew returned from the barn and closed the shutters on the north side of the house, casting the kitchen into an even darker gloom. Finally, he stepped back into the kitchen, the wild wind blowing a cloud of snow through the door with him, and they were all safely ensconced in the sheltering walls of the big room.

Drew removed his snowy outer clothing in the washroom, then joined Emily beside the big, cast-iron stove. He helped himself to a steaming cup of coffee.

"How long will this last?" Emily asked him, looking out the windows on either side of the door at the madly whirling eddies of snow and wind.

"Hard to say. Maybe an hour, maybe a day, maybe two or three. The problem isn't so much the snow as the wind. A strong wind can play with a little bit of snow for a long time, although this storm is dropping a lot real fast. It'll be impossible to tell how much until the wind dies." His eyes drifted to the window, and he shook his head slightly. "This is early for a storm this bad."

Emily knew he was thinking of the Indians out on the plains, sheltering in river bottoms and hollows on the prairies, or perhaps caught out away from their camps, unprepared for such a storm so early in the season.

"Will the snow melt quickly when it's over?" she asked hopefully. "It's only October. We could still have an Indian summer."

"I hope so," Drew answered, his mouth set in a grim line.

"Is there anything you can do?" she almost whispered. Her face reflected her deep concern.

He shook his head. "No. Not now, anyway. Perhaps after the storm, there will be. It's cold in here," he observed. "I think I'm going to have to stop the cracks around that swinging door. They're letting in a strong draft. Do you have everything down from upstairs that you and the kids will need for a couple of days?''

"I brought down some winter clothes and blankets, but that's all,'' she answered doubtfully.

"Well, I want you to collect nightclothes and whatever you'll need for a couple of days for all of you. The upstairs isn't heated, and this is an awfully cold storm. By evening, there'll be ice on the inside of the windows, and by morning there may be a good thick coating on the walls as well. The drafts from the dining room are sucking all the warmth out of this room, so I want to close it off. We'll all sleep down here until the storm is over and it warms up some,'' Drew announced authoritatively.

"Where will we sleep?'' Emily asked, a panicky feeling rising in her breast.

"In Ma and Pa's room,'' Josh interrupted. "That's what we always do when it gets real cold. Pa brings down Daniel's crib and Sarah and I sleep in the trundle.''

Emily considered this information dubiously, looking warily at Drew, who was smiling faintly as he watched her emotions play across her expressive face. She supposed it was reasonable, but she didn't know where she would sleep.

"I could sleep in the parlor on the sofa,'' she finally said. "There's a fireplace there.''

"No good,'' Drew told her casually. "I'm going to block the dining room door so you won't be able to get to the parlor. Besides, we need to conserve as much fuel as possible. This could be a long winter, and you'll need to keep warm in March as much as you do now. We'll use the stove and the fireplace in the bedroom, that's all.''

"I would appreciate it if you would refrain from simply assuming all the decision making,'' Emily told him tightly. "I believe I've mentioned this irritating tendency on your part before. I'd like to know where I'm supposed to sleep with this arrangement.''

Drew grinned at her lazily, raising an eyebrow mockingly. "Are you afraid something might happen with three children in the same bedroom with us?'' he said so quietly that the children couldn't possibly have heard him. "That's a most intriguing prospect."

Emily blushed deeply. He was so infuriating, she could hardly bear it at times!

"You can sleep in the trundle with Sarah, and I'll sleep with Drew," Josh answered her question without looking up from the picture he was drawing. Drew smiled wickedly at her.

"My plan, exactly," he said. "Does it meet with your approval, Emily?" His tone was sweetly innocent.

"Do I have a choice?" she responded in the same sugary tone.

"Not really," Drew replied pleasantly.

Emily flounced out of the kitchen through the swinging dining room door, sending a chill blast of air into the room. She stomped up the stairs and gathered the things she and the children would need, fuming all the while at what a dictator Drew Rutledge was.

After supper, Drew built up the fire in the bedroom fireplace while Emily straightened the kitchen. The children followed Drew into the bedroom, and he soon had them playing a Lakota game called moccasins that involved hiding a button under one of four shoes and betting buttons from Maggie's sewing box on the outcome. Emily thought the game was awfully close to gambling, but her disapproval was ignored, and she soon found herself drawn into the game.

When Sarah lost her last button, Drew announced that the game was over.

"Looks like it's bedtime," he said. His eye caught Emily's.

"It's too early," Josh complained. "I'm not tired yet."

"Neither am I," Emily added quickly. She watched the creases in Drew's cheeks deepen as he fought a smile. "Would you like me to read a story? How about a chapter from Oliver Optic?"

"Great!" Josh exclaimed. "Let's hear *Plane and Plank*. Did you bring it down?"

"I certainly did," Emily responded, picking up the book.

Josh and Sarah immediately crawled up onto the bed and settled themselves among the pillows, leaning against the headboard. They made a space between them. "Come on," Sarah invited, patting the bed beside her.

Drew swung Daniel up from the floor and plopped down next to her. He shot Emily a taunting grin. "We're waiting," he prompted.

"Hurry up, Aunt Emily," Josh echoed. "Sit here by me."

"I don't know about this," she muttered, reluctantly crawling up between Josh and Sarah.

Drew reached over and took the book from her, his hands brushing the length of hers. When she was seated, he handed it back to her but didn't let go until she looked up at him. The warmth in his eyes made her breath catch.

"All right," she said, her voice husky. She cleared her throat. "Where did we leave off the last time?"

"Here," Josh said, opening the book for her.

"Can I sit in your lap?" Sarah asked, climbing in before Emily could answer. Drew immediately moved closer, dropping his arm down to rest on Emily's shoulders.

She looked up at him, brows raised disapprovingly.

"It's cold," he explained with an innocent shrug. He shifted closer to her so that their sides touched.

"Come on, Josh," Drew said. "Snuggle in close." Then he reached for one of the quilts piled on the bed and shook it out, spreading it over them, snuggling closer himself.

"Body heat," he whispered in Emily's ear. "Got to take advantage of it."

Emily shook her head at him, unsure she could breathe regularly, much less read *The Mishaps of a Mechanic*. Her body was definitely warming up and a little too fast, at that.

"Read," Sarah insisted as Josh put the book in Emily's hands.

The children were soon absorbed in the convoluted plot of robberies and lost relatives. About halfway through the chapter, Drew began to play with the skin behind Emily's left ear, dancing his fingers up and down her neck, tracing the outline of her ear, and tugging wisps of hair loose from the knot at the back of her head. More than once, her voice seemed to catch on a sharply indrawn breath. He smiled with satisfaction, and she felt his contentment in the warmth that radiated between them.

She read on automatically, her thoughts drifting with the gentle sensations caused by Drew's wandering fingers. The moment captured the essence of what she wanted: a family, safe and close, shared with a man she could love passionately. But she couldn't forget that it was an illusion. The desire she felt was real, but the family was her brother's, and the man didn't want a future with her. Sadly, she couldn't imagine Drew settling down and being content with a family of his own. He would be happy for a time, then need to go back to his adventures.

Near the end of the chapter, Emily felt Sarah's head fall back against her breast as she drifted between sleep and waking. Daniel was blinking like an owl, periodically rubbing his cheek on Drew's chest or Emily's arm. When Josh yawned for the third time, Drew reached over and closed the book, his left hand still fondling Emily's neck. She fell silent.

"Bedtime," he said softly.

She nodded.

Josh tumbled off the bed and stretched. "Want me to pull out the trundle?" he offered.

Drew looked at Emily and mouthed a single word. *No.*

"Please, Josh," she answered. "Drew can help you."

She scooted Sarah off her lap and pushed back the quilt. Drew handed Daniel to her as he silently rose, his eyes never leaving hers.

Within fifteen minutes, the trundle was made up and the children dressed in their nightclothes and tucked into bed. Emily escaped into the kitchen while Drew built the fire up and turned down the lamps.

An hour later, she had set out dough for sweet rolls in the morning, scrubbed the already clean table and countertops, and rearranged the spice shelf twice. She hadn't heard a sound from the bedroom. Finally, she crept back to the door and pushed it open silently.

Drew looked up at her from the floor where he lay reading the Oliver Optic book by the firelight. A quick smile lit his face.

"I wanted to see how it ended," he explained, closing the book and rising.

"You should have kept on a light."

"The kids are asleep. I didn't want to disturb them."

"Oh." She paused. "I thought you'd be asleep by now, too."

"No such luck, sweetheart. You ready to turn in?"

She nodded and began searching self-consciously for her nightgown in the piles of clothes she'd brought down. Then she felt Drew's hand on her shoulder.

"Looking for this?" She blushed as he handed her a white flannel gown. "I should have figured you slept in something prim and proper like this. More's the pity." His hands spread across her shoulders, and he pulled her back against him. They could see their dim reflections in the mirror over the dresser. Their eyes met.

"Remember?" he whispered.

She bowed her head, and he knew she did.

"I've wondered ever since why I didn't do this," he said, his fingers gliding to the buttons on her shirtwaist, flicking them open.

"Drew!" she hissed, clutching his hands. "The children!"

"I know. So you're safe. Relatively." He shook off her hands. "Let me."

He continued opening buttons until her blouse gaped open down the front, then pulled her shirt free of the waistband of her skirt. Taking the nightgown from her, he eased her shirt down her arms and dropped it onto the dresser.

Emily arched her head back when she felt his arms wrap around her waist and his head drop to nuzzle her shoulder. Then she disentangled his arms and moved away.

"No, Drew." She retrieved her nightgown and held it up in front of her.

Drew began undoing the buttons of his own shirt, his eyes on hers. He worked slowly, spreading the material apart as he went, revealing his chest inch by inch. Emily's eyes followed his hands, and her lower lip dropped a fraction of an inch.

"Your words say no, but everything else about you says yes," he whispered. He dropped his shirt beside hers on the dresser.

"Are you willing to settle down? Are you willing to give me all of what I want and not just the passion?" she asked sadly.

"If I could, I would."

She crossed her arms across her chest and backed into the dresser.

Frustration built inside him. He wanted to explain it all to her, but there was too much at stake. For a brief moment, he thought to hell with it, he'd tell her anyway. Then he looked down and saw Daniel asleep in his crib and realized that he'd be a fool to tie her to him until he was free.

"Then I stand by what I said. No." Her gaze lingered on his chest.

He unbuttoned his pants under her watchful eye. "Your eyes are saying yes, Emily."

He advanced toward her, but she turned away from him. She felt his hands at her waistband, and, in a moment, her skirt had fallen to her feet. She stiffened, but didn't struggle because she didn't want to wake the children. His hands loosened her chemise from her petticoats and drew it quickly over her head. She gasped as he took up her nightgown and dropped it over her head, guiding her arms through the sleeves. As the fabric draped down over her body, Drew slid his hands up to cup her breasts beneath it. He held her close to him, feeling her nipples harden against his palms.

She felt him hard and stiff beneath her hip as he leaned into her. A low groan of pleasure escaped his parted lips. "God, what you do to me!" he whispered, closing his eyes. One of his hands skimmed down her torso and settled to cup her feminine flesh in his palm.

"Don't," she said with quiet intensity. But she rolled her hips reflexively, straining into his touch and not away from it. He brushed his hand back and forth lightly until she shuddered with need.

He raised his eyes, meeting hers in the mirror.

Josh shifted in his sleep, murmuring. Drew moved his hands once more in a brief caress, then backed away.

"Someday soon, sweetheart," he promised. "Someday very soon."

Late that night, a noise awakened Emily. Disoriented, she was aware that she wasn't in her own room. Sarah's warm, sleeping form was curled up next to her, and the air in the room was very cold. She remembered the blizzard as her ears picked up the wind still beating at the sturdy walls of the house, and she remembered that she was sleeping on the trundle in Sam and Maggie's room.

Suddenly, the fire blazed, and Emily raised her head. Drew was crouched before the fire, naked, stirring the coals to life. The red and yellow flames illuminated the hard planes of his chest and the strong column of his neck. His thighs were muscular, hiding his manhood from her view. The sight of him caused her breath to stop and her stomach to contract.

The sound of wood snapping and crackling was loud in the quiet room; the only other sound was the children's even breathing. Dropping her head back onto her pillow, Emily was both grateful for and frustrated by their presence. Her heart was pounding as she closed her eyes, willing herself to sleep again. The bed moved slightly as Drew climbed back under the blankets and quilts above her. She could hear him breathing, deep and slow, but she knew he wasn't asleep. They lay thus for a long time, each aware of the other, neither able to sleep, separated by only a few feet and two small children—a most effective barrier.

The blizzard lasted three days. When the wind finally stopped, there were drifts twenty feet high in some places. The storm had left perhaps two and a half feet of snow, had it all been evenly distributed, but the wind had piled high drifts against buildings and in gullies and swept the ground nearly clean in some exposed areas. The cold remained, and the snow showed no signs of melting quickly. Emily could tell from the tense expression on Drew's face that he wasn't pleased with the weather. After making sure that everything was in order at the Parkers', he told Emily that he was going to his place to check on things, and he disappeared on snowshoes into the hills.

Emily was relieved to see him go for a while. Being cooped up with him at such close quarters for so long was wearing on her nerves. She hated to think what would have gone on had the children not been present every minute of each day and night.

Drew didn't really need to visit his cabin. He knew that Black Wolf would be fine and that nothing could possibly have happened during such a severe storm, but he, too, needed a break from the ever increasing physical tension that existed between him and Emily. He was getting dangerously close to opening the dining room door and packing the children off to sleep in their freezing bedrooms so that they could finally be together. The situation was impossible. He scowled at the bright sun, wishing it would send them enough heat to melt the blasted snow rapidly. It was a bad sign that it was still so frigid. Weather like this shouldn't come until at least December, even January. What would he do if Sam and Maggie couldn't get back from Illinois?

In some respects, it wouldn't really matter, because he wouldn't be able to resume his work until the weather improved, but there was the growing problem of what to do about Emily. Clearly, they couldn't spend the entire winter shut up together without sleeping together, and while he knew he could convince Emily that the children would survive such scandalous behavior, he knew he shouldn't. Black Wolf might have some suggestions, and, of course, the snow would probably melt in a day or two. Drew told himself that he was worrying unnecessarily.

Chapter 19

The snow did not melt in a few days. The weather continued cold and crisp, and one night an additional four inches fell on top of the first storm's wintry offering. Despite the fire that Drew kept burning all night in the fireplace, the pitcher on the washstand had a crust of ice on the water every morning. Drew told Emily that since the blizzard the temperature hadn't climbed over five degrees above zero. Most of the time, it hovered between zero and thirty below, the wind making it seem much colder at times. He couldn't remember such a cold spell so early. Sam and Maggie would be delayed in returning if there wasn't a break soon, and even the children had grown tired of the extreme cold that made outings brief and uncomfortable. They were all becoming irritable after a week of the cold.

Finally one morning, the air was not quite as crisp and dry as it had been. The mercury in the thermometer on the porch finally cleared the twenty-five degree mark about noon, and with great relief, Emily bundled the children up and they all went for a long walk. It was amazing how different the ranch looked in its white mantle, and they had to be careful where they walked to avoid the deeper drifts. They visited the barn and the chicken coop, and then returned to the house for steaming cups of cocoa. While it didn't warm enough to melt any snow, Emily felt better than she had for days.

That afternoon, Drew opened the dining room door again, and everyone slept that night in his own room, except Sarah, who slept with Emily. It was still cold, but it was bearable underneath the warm layers of quilts and blankets. There was indeed a thick coating of ice on the walls, and the windows were frozen shut, but Emily slept much more easily than she had in the warmer room downstairs where she was constantly aware of every breath that Drew took.

The next evening, Emily had just finished putting away the last of the supper dishes when there was a loud pounding on the kitchen door. She was alone. Drew was upstairs with the children. She wondered who would be out in this weather as she placed the dish towel in her hand on the table and walked toward the door.

Opening it somewhat uncertainly, Emily threw it wide when she saw Black Wolf standing there, his face panic stricken, Red Eagle Woman in his arms. Her face was contorted with pain and she clutched at her belly, swollen with child.

"Oh, my goodness! What's happened?" Emily exclaimed, ushering them into the brightly lit kitchen. Behind the man and his wife, she saw their two children sitting on a pony near the steps.

Before Black Wolf could answer, Drew came through the swinging door, followed by Josh, Sarah, and Daniel. He sized up the scene immediately. Black Wolf said something in Lakota, and Drew nodded. He took Red Eagle Woman in his own arms and backed through the door with her. Black Wolf followed on his heels. As he went, Drew called to Emily.

"Bring in the kids, Emily. Josh, you and Black Wolf's son stable their horses at the barn. And, Emily, put some water to boil on the stove and get me some clean sheets," he ordered as he disappeared.

Emily stepped outside and lifted Little Star off the pony's back. The little girl looked frightened. Josh was at his aunt's side, looking with excitement at the Indian boy still astride the horse. Emily looked between the boys uncertainly.

Josh met her gaze confidently. "I can explain," he assured his aunt. "Drew taught me some Lakota words, and I can use sign language. We'll take care of the horses."

He immediately launched into an elaborate pantomime for Sees Far at Night, and soon the two boys were leading the horses toward the barn.

In the house, Little Star allowed her curiosity to overcome her fear when she met Sarah, and soon the girls were playing with Sarah's dolls in a corner in the kitchen. Emily filled a large wash boiler and the kettle with water and put them on the stove. Then she went upstairs to find out what was happening. She assumed Red Eagle Woman was in labor, but Black Wolf's agitation led her to believe that something was amiss.

She met Drew coming out of her own bedroom. His expression was grave as he headed for the stairs.

"What's wrong?" Emily asked, following after him.

"The baby's coming too soon," he said, not bothering to look back. "It wasn't due for another month." He rapidly descended the stairs and walked through the hall and dining room into the kitchen.

"Can I do anything to help?" Emily asked, almost running in her efforts to keep up with Drew. She didn't know much about babies at all, much less about delivering premature ones. She followed him into the downstairs bedroom. "Should I go for a doctor?"

"There isn't time, even if the roads were in good shape, which they're not. We'll have to do what we can here," he answered, rummaging in a box that held some of his things. He took up the bag that contained herbs and medicines, then strode back into the kitchen. The kettle was just boiling. He opened a cupboard and removed a large teapot, into which he crumbled a large handful of bark.

"What's that?" Emily asked.

"Willow bark. It helps pain."

"Isn't there something I can do?" Emily asked for the second time.

"Yeah, there's a lot you can do," Drew said, pouring the boiling water into the teapot. "I'm going to fill the hot water heater, just to make sure we have enough hot water. You can take this tea upstairs and get Red Eagle Woman to drink it. It'll be a comfort to her to have a woman present. Normally Oglala men don't have anything to do with birthing, but we don't have any choice tonight. Until the baby's ready to come, you'll need to keep an eye on the children, too. Do you think you can get them into bed early? Put the boys in one room and the girls in another. And where's Daniel? We'll also need some clean sheets and blankets and something warm and soft to wrap the baby in.'' He shoved the teapot into her hands and went into the washroom.

Emily stood speechless for a second, wondering where to start. Then she found a tray and a cup and hurried upstairs. She sat on the bed next to Red Eagle Woman and coaxed her to drink the tea. The Indian woman did seem relieved to see her, and Emily got a cloth and the wash basin from her dresser and bathed the woman's face. She held her hand when the spasms of pain wracked her body as Black Wolf paced nervously back and forth, chanting under his breath. When Drew came back into the room, she left for a few minutes to see to the children. Josh and Sees Far at Night had returned from the barn, and Emily found Daniel sitting on the sofa in the parlor, tearing apart a periodical that had been left within his reach. She scooped him up and took him upstairs where she undressed him and put him in his crib with a pile of toys to keep him occupied. After she'd settled the girls in Sarah's room and the older boys in with Daniel, she checked back in on Red Eagle Woman.

Emily spent that evening running back and forth between her bedroom and the kitchen, fetching things that Drew asked for, and stopping to check on the children whenever she remembered. Black Wolf prayed constantly for the safety of both his wife and his child, unbraiding his hair and crying piteously. Emily found his behavior unnerving, but Drew told her not to worry about it, he needed her help with Red Eagle Woman. Finally, just after midnight, the baby was born, a second son. He was tiny, but well-formed and strong, considering his early birth, and it appeared that he would live. Red Eagle Woman and Black Wolf were thrilled, and they fussed over the new baby while Emily gathered the soiled bed-clothes and took them downstairs. Drew also came down and had a quick bath, then disappeared. Later, when Emily made a last check on Red Eagle Woman, she found mother and son both asleep, the baby wrapped warmly in Daniel's old blankets and cuddled in his mother's arms. On her way back downstairs, she noticed that Black Wolf had gone to sleep on the parlor sofa. The children were all long asleep, and Emily realized that she too was exhausted as she cleaned up a last few things in the kitchen. She would be grateful to fall into bed.

Then it struck her. There was no place for her to sleep. Every bed in the house was occupied, and the parlor sofa as well. Emily sank into a chair, resting her head wearily on her hand. She supposed she could sleep in the kitchen. If she pulled a chair around in front of the rocker, she could stretch her legs out a bit, and if she put more wood on the fire, she should be warm enough. She decided to have a bath first since the water was hot. If she had to be uncomfortable, at least she would be clean.

Fifteen minutes later, Emily stood in the kitchen in her chemise and petticoats, arranging the chairs as close to the stove as she could get them. When she was satisfied, she turned out the lamp and sat down gratefully, expecting to fall asleep quickly. It had been an extraordinary evening, and her muscles ached from all the activity. She closed her eyes and settled into the rocker.

It took only a few minutes for Emily to realize that sleep wasn't going to come easily. First she couldn't find a comfortable position for her head. Then she was cold. She fidgeted and shifted, this way and that. Finally she got up to look for a blanket. Searching the kitchen and wash-room, she found nothing she could use. All the linens were wet or dirty. She knew the upstairs bedrooms were cold enough that she hesitated to take any blankets away from anyone sleeping there. At length her gaze rested on the door to Sam and Maggie's room. The blanket chest was there, along with several pillows on the bed. Did she dare go in there and take what she needed? If Drew were awake, he might not let her return to her bed of chairs in the kitchen. Yet if she stayed where she was, she wouldn't get any sleep at all, and the morrow promised to be busy with so many extra people and a new baby in the house. Creeping close to the door, Emily pressed her ear to it. After hearing nothing for almost five minutes, she cautiously turned the knob and pushed the door open an inch.

The fire had burned low, but it still threw an eerie red light into the bedroom. Emily saw Drew's form asleep on the bed to her left. He was lying on his stomach, one arm thrown wide across the center of the bed. When he didn't stir, she eased the door open further and slipped in. Soundlessly, she walked on bare feet over to the chest that stood at the foot of the big bed and crouched before it. She raised the lid, praying that it wouldn't squeak, and withdrew the quilt that was on top. Wrapping it over her left forearm, Emily lowered the lid and stood up. She watched Drew for any sign of movement, debating whether to test her luck and take a pillow from the bed. He seemed to be sound asleep.

Moving carefully, lest she make any noise or cast a shadow over his eyes, Emily edged around the right side of the bed toward the headboard. With relief, she saw that one of the pillows had been pushed aside so that it was right on the edge of the mattress. When she was within reach of it, she stopped for a moment and looked at Drew. The bedcovers were wrapped around his waist, and his bare torso tempted her with memories of their passionate night at his cabin, when she had first seen him naked in the firelight. God, but he was beautiful! His proportions were perfect, from the firm, tapered waist to the broad width of his muscular shoulders. His arms were big, and his large, competent hands were well shaped, his long fingers resting now on top of the quilt.

It was all Emily could do not to crawl under the covers alongside him. She'd wanted him for so long now without any satisfaction. What had he said? The children would never know. Yes, she argued with herself, but she would know, and she knew it would be wrong. His words came back to her again. Did she feel sinful in his arms? No, despite his refusal to make a commitment to her, she didn't. In the space of seconds, Emily fought an internal battle. In the end, her promise to her brother to take good care of his children held her back as much as her own resolve to avoid any further involvement.

Breathing a sigh of relief at the moral victory she had won, Emily shifted the quilt to her right arm and reached with her left for the edge of the pillow that was closer to her. She inched it carefully toward her. Then Drew's arm moved suddenly, and his strong fingers closed tightly around her wrist. She pulled back abruptly, but he didn't let go. He heaved himself up so that he was leaning on his left arm, and he pulled her close to the bed.

He hadn't been asleep at all, she realized. His eyes were wide awake as they blazed in the dim light. The quilt fell from her grasp as he pulled her closer, dragging her across the mattress into the inviting circle of his arms.

"I was afraid I was going to have to come after you," he whispered against her ear, his mouth nibbling gently at the lobe.

"Drew . . ." she tried to protest.

"Shhh. Don't fight it, Emily. I don't think either of us can wait any longer." His voice was urgent. "Besides, where were you planning to sleep?" There was a pleasantly humorous note in his voice that thrilled Emily to the core of her being. His fingers ran up her backbone to the nape of her neck.

"In the kitchen," she answered breathlessly.

"I want you to sleep here with me tonight, Emily." He paused, his breath warm on her temple. "Do you want to?"

"Yes," she breathed, unable to lie. "And no."

"You're the stubbornest woman in the territory," he groaned, burying his face in her neck.

"Think of the children!" She clutched his shoulders and arched her neck, shivering at his touch.

"Not tonight, sweetheart." He touched his lips lightly to hers and spoke against her mouth. "The time for reckoning has come. I'm not going to wait any longer." The pressure of his mouth increased, and he slid his hands inside her chemise. He gave a shuddering sigh.

"Stay with me and touch me. Release this tension in me and let me pleasure you." He took her hand and brought it to the back of his neck, thrusting her fingers into his hair, leaning back into her touch.

"How can you make me feel this way?" she whispered, bringing her other hand up to his head, fanning the hair away from his temple. "You know I don't . . ."

"I know," he said, rubbing his cheek against her palm. "I know there are problems. But we need each other, Emily. We have so much to give each other." He dropped a hand to her waist, then moved it lower until he was pressing against her, feeling her heat and moisture through her petticoat. She groaned and tried to push his hand away.

When he rubbed lightly, she stopped pushing. His fingers seduced her until her hips moved with his hand.

"Stay with me tonight," he repeated.

"Mmm," she purred. "Maybe."

"You won't get much sleep," he cautioned, his voice deep and sensuous. He pulled away from her to look into her eyes. His groin tightened when he saw her smile, a beguiling mixture of shyness and anticipation.

"Kiss me, Ińte Śkan Niyapi," she demanded softly, offering her lips to him.

With a groan, Drew complied. His mouth covered hers in an insistent, fiery assault that brought an immediate, hungry response from Emily. As their tongues clashed, plundering each other's mouths in turn, their hands eagerly roamed each other's bodies, urgent yet gentle in their caresses. Drew tugged at the hem of Emily's chemise, and she shifted so that he could draw it up over her head. Her bare breasts brushed tantalizingly against his hard chest, the crisp hair tickling her nipples, teasing them into arousal. His hot hands covered her naked back, stroking the silken cascade of her hair and her sensitive skin, and he pressed his weight against her, pushing her back onto the mattress so that he could slide her petticoats down over her hips. He threw the garments to the floor and clasped her to him, only the blankets tangled around his waist separating them. Impatiently, murmuring against his dominating mouth, Emily pulled at the impeding cloth, aching to mold herself so tightly to him that not even a breath could come between them. All her scruples evaporated in the heat of his touch.

Drew lifted her off the bed with his left arm along her back as he whipped the bedcovers down to their feet with his right hand. Emily caught her breath at his raw, leonine beauty as the firelight played across his handsome face, his powerful chest, and his tight, smooth stomach. She admired his long, hard legs and the straight length of his erect manhood as it rested on his belly. Her fingers reached out to touch him, and he watched her, glorying in her obvious pleasure and the smoldering desire in her dark eyes. Her fingertips trailed along his firm jaw, lightly dancing down the column of his neck, outlining the hollows of his collarbone. She laid her palms flat against his chest, feeling the hair curl beneath her hands, and the steady beat of his heart. She left one hand on his breast and slid the other lower, rasping her nails lightly along his smooth skin. She dipped a finger into his navel and rested her hand for a moment on his stomach. When her questing fingers moved lower yet, she felt his stomach tighten involuntarily, and his heartbeat increased its pace beneath her still palm. Emily smiled and looked deep into his lapis-blue eyes, her hand sliding to his hip, then down his outer thigh, all the way to his knee, where her fingers traced lazy circles. Then, slowly, a bare inch at a time, her fingers began moving back up the inside of his thigh. Drew's heart thudded under her hand on his chest, and she leaned forward to press her lips to his neck, flicking him with her hot, wet tongue. As her fingers moved up his thigh, her mouth moved up his neck, then to his jaw, to his chin, and almost to his lips. Drew forced himself to wait in silent, exquisite agony until finally, in a rapturous release of tension, he felt her slender fingers close over his throbbing shaft as her lips met his and her tongue slid into his possessive mouth. A shudder of sheer ecstasy rippled through him, and he gathered Emily into his arms, crushing her to him. He groaned against her, lifting his mouth from hers to nibble greedily along her cheek to her ear.

"Witch," he murmured in her ear, smiling. "Whoever taught you such tricks?"

"You did," she whispered throatily, arching her neck against the tantalizing sensations his tongue created. "Who else?" she teased provocatively.

"Only me, Emily. Only me for the rest of your life, *mitawin*," he whispered fiercely.

"Only you," she repeated, thrilling at his words, not thinking beyond the moment.

Her fingers continued to explore the silken length of his manhood as he pulled back her hair and kissed her neck, then her shoulders, finally moving his lips across the flat of her chest to the mounds of her breasts. His fingers followed, wreaking havoc with her senses as he increased her unfolding passion with every movement. In her excitement, her hands gripped his arms, and she arched her neck to grant him full access to the sensitive, hardened tips of her breasts. When his mouth closed over one straining peak, she grasped his head to her, her fingers tangling in the thick waves of his brown hair, delighting in the sound and feel of his mouth.

His right hand trailed along her body, from the small of her back, across her smooth hips, and down to the back of her knee. He urged her leg upward to rest between his thighs, her thigh against his hard and pulsing erection, as he sought to control his raging desire. He pressed his loins against her satin flesh, his mouth still at her breast. Keeping Emily's thigh against him, Drew slipped one hand between her legs, his fingers instantly sliding into the warm, moist folds of flesh there, feeling how much she wanted him as she trembled at his intimate exploration.

Suddenly their passion flared red hot, and he pushed Emily onto her back, unable to wait a moment longer for the ultimate release of his untamed desire. She willingly parted her legs for him and welcomed the thrust that seated him deep within her. He rested against her briefly, his head swimming with the tight, moist, velvet heat enfolding him, hers with the warm, filling sense of completeness that she felt only in this most intimate of embraces. Only with him.

Emily wrapped her arms around his neck, hugging him to her as she felt him start to move rhythmically inside her, his strength drawing her with him, until they moved in wild tandem, straining madly, reaching for the inevitable, long awaited, shattering climax of their mutual excitement and pleasure. In almost no time, they soared into the mind-exploding sensations that rocked their bodies with spasms of uncontrolled release and joy.

They lay together, their limbs entwined, for long minutes as their breathing and heartbeats returned to normal. The warmth of Drew's body covering hers filled Emily with an indescribably sweet sensation, a wistful longing that the moment of close, mutual fulfillment could last forever. He shifted his weight so that she could breathe easily, and she clung to his shoulders, lightly caressing his back and playing with the thick hair that lay along his neck, unwilling to break the spell that held them in its precarious bond.

Drew began to feel the chill in the air as the first intense heat of their passion faded, and he gently, reluctantly raised himself and bent his head to kiss her lingeringly. Then he rose to leave the bed.

"No!" Emily whispered, her voice stricken. She looked away immediately, afraid of how much she had revealed in that fleeting, unguarded plea.

Drew leaned back toward her, dusting feather kisses on her shoulders, then all the way down her left arm to her fingertips.

"I'm only going to put some wood on the fire," he assured her. Then a slow smile spread across his handsome face, causing the fires so recently quenched in Emily's blood to roar to life again. "Then I have a few more tricks to teach you," he promised.

Emily smiled in answer, watching him lovingly as he built the fire up into leaping flames that danced madly, casting a flickering play of light and shadow throughout the room. She sat up in the middle of the large bed, her golden hair falling like a shimmering cloak around her shoulders, half covering her breasts, reflecting the gold and red flames.

Drew rose and stared at her a heart-stopping moment, hardly able to believe that she was there with him, so willing, so enticing. He didn't even give a second's thought to the morrow or his plans and concerns. For months he'd been obsessed with imagining what he would do when he next had Emily in his bed, in his arms, wondering if it would ever happen. Now, with her sitting naked before him, her eyes filled with love and desire, he didn't intend to waste a second of their time together. He wanted to show her how he felt, to demonstrate the love that circumstances didn't allow him to declare.

He approached the bed slowly, his face in shadow, but Emily could see the hunger that lit his eyes, along with something more. Was it tenderness? No, it was too fierce, too possessive, and yet there was an unmistakable gentleness about him. Their eyes held, the love they felt and did not speak of, communicating itself just as surely through their gaze as if they had spoken. Emily's heart nearly burst within her, and she felt a sob irrationally rising in her throat. As Drew reached the bed, she rose to her knees, pressing into his arms, and her cry was muffled against his neck.

Gradually, the hypnotic effect of his mouth gently moving across her skin subdued the tremors that wracked her slender body. They eased once again to the mattress, and Emily murmured sleepily as Drew tickled her neck with his tongue. He raised his head to look at her face, dim in the firelight, her eyes closed.

"You aren't going to fall asleep on me, are you?" he asked with a teasing smile, rubbing his nose against hers.

"Aren't you tired?" she said in a low, husky voice that sent thrills of renewed desire coursing through his blood.

"I don't think I'm going to be tired for a long time yet," he answered, his fingers massaging the small of her back and slipping lower over her hips. "And I can think of lots of things to keep you wide awake." He dipped his head to her breast, flicking at one nipple with the tip of his tongue. At the same time, one hand slid between her legs, unerringly finding the place that pleased her most.

Emily's eyes opened with a start. He raised his head

and met her gaze with a knowing grin, his own need glowing in his eyes. His hand moved sinuously, and she felt his fingers slide into her, stroking in and out in a delicious rhythm as his thumb massaged the swelling nub of flesh, sending wild surges of excitement through her. She gasped at the sensations his erotic caress aroused, and his mouth closed over hers, sliding his tongue against hers, pulling and sucking, in concert with his dexterous fingers.

Through the mind-numbing lassitude that enveloped her, Emily's fingers found his once again rigid shaft pressed warmly against her thigh. Her hand curled around it, and Drew's hips thrust forward, causing her hand to slide down the silken length of him. He groaned into her mouth as she repeated the motion. Suddenly, he rolled with her so that she lay atop him, settling her warm, feminine folds over him. His fingers slid out of her, and he nudged himself against her moist, waiting heat. His hand covered hers as he guided his entry into her. A satisfied gasp broke from her lips as he thrust upward, wondering again at the perfect way he filled her.

Drew reached for her rosy-tipped breasts, his fingers closing over their hardened peaks, twisting just enough to cause Emily to throw her head back as the shooting licks of pleasure traveled along her inflamed skin to deep within her. He started to thrust beneath her, in a slow, controlled rhythm that drove her mad. She fell slightly forward over his chest, her hands braced upon his shoulders, and found she could better match his movements. Their tempo increased as she brazenly rocked her hips, feeling his hard length sliding in and out of her in this new way. His hands moved constantly along her thighs and buttocks, sometimes across her breasts, adding exquisitely to her burgeoning climax. A small cry escaped her as the waves of pleasure suddenly burst with intense release, shaking her body with quivering tremors. She collapsed onto Drew's chest, and he continued to move slowly within her, feeling the spasms of her ecstasy, lengthening her pleasure. Their lips met once again in abandon, Drew now seeking his own release.

Supporting her back, he rolled again so that Emily lay

once more beneath him. She kissed him passionately, testing his lips with her tongue, nibbling at his lower lip as he had done to her, boldly exploring the hot depths of his mouth. She wrapped her legs around him, feeling him slide more deeply into her, arching to meet his every thrust. Their muscles tensed and their breathing labored as they strove together, the firelight throwing their wild shadows into stark relief against the pale walls. At last Drew's fingers tightened convulsively around her shoulders, and he sagged down onto Emily, his passion erupting like fire within her, taking her with him again into the mindless rapture that seared their spirits, as well as their bodies, with purest ecstasy.

In the quiet minutes that followed their spent passion, Drew suddenly laughed. Emily snuggled against him contentedly, thrilling at the unspoken love she felt in him. He whispered against her hair in Lakota; sweet words, she knew, words of love. And she acknowledged at last that she loved him as well, and that she was tired of fighting her own conflicting desires. Her last thought as she drifted into slumber was that everything would work out somehow. Their love was simply too great, too consuming to be denied, and she would work now to overcome the obstacles between them, no matter how impossible they might seem. As Drew pulled the bedclothes around them, she smiled and then slept, held possessively in his arms, her head pillowed on his shoulder, his heart beating strong beneath her cheek.

The winter sunlight poured through the window, brightly lighting the bedroom. Emily squinted against the light and noticed at the same time that she was naked beneath the sheet and blankets. The memory of the night's passion brought a warm smile to her lips, and she stretched her arms wide. No solid male warmth met her hands, and she realized she was alone. Sitting up, she blinked at the window, wondering why the light looked so peculiar. All in a rush, she remembered that she had a houseful of extra people, including a newborn baby, and it was late morning, if not nearly noon. The fire was burning brightly in the hearth, a sign that Drew had recently been in the room.

She panicked. How could they have slept so late? The children! Who had taken care of them? A dozen thoughts raced through her head as she threw back the covers and leaped from the bed. She washed quickly in the cold water on the washstand, then found her undergarments in a heap by the night table and hastily stepped into them. Then she opened Maggie's wardrobe and found a dark green skirt and a white cotton blouse to wear since she could hardly go prancing up to her own room in her underwear. After combing her hair and tying it back loosely with a piece of blue ribbon she found on the dressing table, Emily went to the door. She paused with her hand on the knob, breathing deeply as she tried to envision explaining her presence in Drew's room. She felt the color mount in her cheeks, and she pushed the door open before she could think any more about it.

Her head high, Emily stepped into the kitchen. To her surprise and relief, it was empty. The house was quiet. Wondering where everyone could be, she padded in her bare feet to the washroom to get her shoes and stockings. Then she sat at the table to put them on and went upstairs to check on Red Eagle Woman and the baby.

Emily found the Indian woman up and dressed, sitting in a chair in front of the window with her baby at her breast. There was a tray with water, food, and a pot of some type of herb tea that made the room smell like summer sitting on the dressing table beside her. Emily was startled to see Red Eagle Woman out of bed.

"Good morning," she said, smiling. "How are you feeling? How's the baby?"

The other woman motioned for her to come over to where they sat.

"I am well," Red Eagle Woman answered, "and my new son is well. Isn't he small?" Emily nodded, looking at the tiny child in amazement. "He is strong, though. He will be just fine," she added proudly, smoothing the dark hair that stuck up on the baby's forehead.

"Should you be up?" Emily asked doubtfully. "And

wouldn't you be more comfortable downstairs where it's warmer?''

"No, no. I am having a wonderful rest. My husband and *miśic'e* have taken the children out, and I am happy here doing nothing. It is too warm in the kitchen for the baby. He might get sick," Red Eagle Woman told her. Emily was surprised, but she didn't argue. She supposed the other woman knew what she was doing, seeing as she had already had two babies.

"Is there anything I can get you?" Emily asked hopefully. "I didn't mean to sleep so late. I really should have been in earlier to make sure you were all right," she apologized.

"I have everything I need. My brother-in-law and my husband have done a very good job, although I will not tell anyone at home. It would cause a great scandal if the camp knew that two such great warriors could take such good care of a new baby and his mother." Red Eagle Woman laughed gaily. *"Miśic'e* said you needed to sleep this morning. He is a good man, no?" she asked, slanting a knowing glance at Emily, who blushed instantly.

"Sometimes he's a very good man," she said cautiously. Her doubts about him flooded back in a rush, and she questioned the wisdom of believing he loved her.

Red Eagle Woman looked at her carefully, then smiled and turned back to the infant in her arms. "I think it is time for us to sleep a little."

Emily helped them into bed, noticing that Red Eagle Woman seemed a bit uncomfortable in the big oak bed. It was a far cry from the tipi that Emily had visited at Pine Ridge.

Downstairs again, Emily went about preparing dinner for the men and children, for it was already eleven thirty. An hour later, everything was ready, but there was no sign of anyone. Emily stepped out onto the porch, wondering where Black Wolf, Drew, and all the children were. Finally, she went back in the house, threw on her coat, and tramped off toward the barn in search of them.

The snow lay in deep drifts beside the barn, and Emily slipped and slithered along on the ice that had formed along the path. As she approached, she heard Josh's familiar voice ringing in the cold air. Black Wolf and Drew answered him, and from the corral she heard the sound of horses' hooves swishing over the snow. Entering the barn, Emily saw Sarah and Little Star playing in one corner with Sarah's dolls and several of Daniel's wooden animals. They didn't look up when she walked through the wide doors, and her attention was immediately drawn to the open door to her left that led into the corral.

Through the doorway, Emily caught brief glimpses of Josh and Sees Far at Night circling on ponies. They were riding bareback. Emily smiled, knowing that Joshua must be in heaven. She edged toward the door, intent on getting a fuller view of her nephew on his spotted Indian pony.

She paused just inside the door, still hidden in the shadows, when she became aware that Drew and Black Wolf were leaning against the fence to the right of the door, not five feet away from her. She could see their shadows when they moved, and she could tell that Drew had Daniel perched high on his shoulders. The men were speaking in Lakota, and as usual when she heard that language, Emily dearly wished that she understood what they were saying. A little thrill went up her spine at the sound of Drew's deep voice, and she smiled as she remembered the look in his eyes the night before. She was about to step into the corral when the men abruptly switched into English. Black Wolf's words caused her feet to freeze to the spot where she stood.

"Are you going to marry Emily now? You really ought to."

"I know," Drew answered, "but nothing's changed. I can't do it."

Chapter 20

Emily felt as though her blood had congealed, leaving her unable to move or breathe. She wanted to cry out with the wrenching pain that twisted inside her like a knife, but she couldn't. Slowly, as if in a daze, she turned back the way she had come and walked, one foot carefully placed in front of the other, until she found Sarah and Little Star.

"Dinner's ready. Will you tell everyone else, Sarah?" she asked, determined not to give in to her grief and anger.

Without waiting for an answer, she ran out the door and back to the house to give herself a few minutes alone. She'd known this moment would come, but she hadn't expected it quite so soon. Last night, she'd known, but she hadn't cared.

The children's voices alerted her that they were on their way in to dinner. She didn't turn to face them as the door burst open and the five children and two men entered with a cold blast of air. She missed the dazzling smile that Drew gave her and the look of bewilderment on his face when she didn't so much as glance at him. As they removed snowy outer clothing and boots, Emily put the food on the table and busied herself with settling the children. She didn't trust herself to look at Drew. She would have given anything if she could have simply fled the house.

The children chattered so during the meal that they didn't notice anything amiss. Drew, however, was soon scowling and trying to catch Emily's eye, though she avoided his gaze. Black Wolf noticed the tension and the stiff posture that gave away her mood even if her tone did not. She didn't eat, nor did she sit down with them. Her movements became more and more stilted, and she was having immense difficulty controlling her emotions when, suddenly, the apple cobbler she was carrying to the table somehow slipped from her hands, crashing to the floor and throwing sticky apples and pastry all over the kitchen.

The children stopped their chatter instantly, and all eyes turned solemnly to Emily. She stared for a moment at the mess. With certainty, she knew she couldn't control herself any longer, and she bolted through the dining room door.

Emily had no plan other than to get as far as possible from Drew Rutledge. She raced through the dining room and the front hall, threw back the latch on the front door, and swung it open. Before she could move through it, however, it slammed shut again, only inches from her nose. She turned her head in panic and saw that Drew was standing close behind her so that she had nowhere to go. His right arm, leaning firmly into the door, prevented her from escaping into the parlor. If she ran up the stairs to her left, he would catch her in a second. She didn't want to face the half-angry, half-confused look she saw in his eyes. She turned her accusing gaze to the floor in front of her, giving him her back.

"Emily, what the hell is wrong?" he demanded, his voice hurt and confused.

When she didn't answer, he swore under his breath. His hands went to her shoulders in an attempt to comfort her, but she shrugged away from him as if his touch were poison. He gripped her more firmly, shaking her to get her to stand still.

"Talk to me, damn it! I'm not going to try and guess what's going on inside your head, and I'm not going to leave until I know."

Still she didn't answer. She couldn't speak through the lump in her throat. With an exasperated curse, Drew jerked her around and pushed her roughly into the parlor. He closed the door behind him, turned the key and pocketed it, then faced Emily, pushing her to the sofa. She flopped into the far corner and stared at the flowered carpet. He sat next to her on the sofa, close but not touching her.

As she studied the red and pink flowers on the carpet, she was tempted to fabricate a story, but she knew that that would only serve to prolong her pain. The time had come to lay bare her soul, even if it were only to have him trample on it. She had to try. After last night, surely he must love her at least a little, she told herself.

Drew finally interrupted her thoughts.

"Are you going to tell me what's wrong?" he asked quietly, striving to keep the anger out of his voice. Her anger and hurt had been the last thing he'd expected when he'd walked into the kitchen, anxious to see her, his heart full of celebration after last night. He knew what the problem was, but he wanted her to tell him. It was time they talked as openly as he could about their future.

"Yes," she said, without looking up at him. She took a deep breath. "Our relationship cannot continue as it has been."

He wasn't surprised. "Why not?" he asked, controlling the panic that threatened to break loose inside him even though he knew exactly what stood between them.

"Because it isn't right. I want more than a lover. I need more. You were right when you said I want a husband and children. I want a family of my own, with a husband who'll be there for me and our children when we need him."

He couldn't meet her eyes.

She sighed, continuing in a defeated tone. "I don't want to feel guilty every time you touch me, Drew, thinking that there won't ever be a future for us. You know, I left Elmira because I was just as frightened of marriage without love as I am of passion without the security of marriage." She laughed wryly. "Maybe the next time I'll get it right. The third time's supposed to be the charm, isn't it?"

"What we've got doesn't happen very often, Emily. You won't find it with anyone else," Drew said.

"Perhaps not," she conceded. "But what have we got, Drew? What exactly would you call it?"

He didn't answer.

"Is it lust?"

"God, no!" he exclaimed. "Don't try and tell me you don't know it's a lot more than that. I've experienced lust plenty of times, and while I won't deny that I lust for you, I feel a damn sight more than that. You *know* that." He took her hand and squeezed it hard.

"I suppose I do," she admitted. "That's why I don't understand why you can't make a commitment to me. I was down at the barn. I heard what you told Black Wolf."

A dull flush crept upward from his collar, and his eyes uncomfortably sought the fireplace across the room. Emily looked away as well, frowning unhappily.

"Yeah," he said, exhaling. "That's the problem, isn't it?"

And he still didn't know what to do about it. His reasons for not marrying her hadn't disappeared with the coming of the snow and the cold north wind. It was looking more and more as if it would be spring before he would be able to get back to work on resolving anything, and it was only early November. He'd never felt so torn in all his life. He sighed deeply, and Emily looked at him quickly, surprised by the turmoil she saw in his eyes. He drew her into his arms and rested his chin on top of her head.

"I wish I could make you feel better," he murmured softly, the fresh scent of her hair filling his nostrils. "Do you have any idea what you do to me? These last few weeks have been heaven and hell for me. Heaven because I've seen you every day, I've shared simple joys and small pleasures with you, telling stories and playing games, washing dishes together, putting the children to bed, and so many wonderful little things. I love hearing your voice in the morning, outside my door, or late at night, soothing Daniel or Sarah. And when you touch me, I feel like I could conquer all the earth's demons but that I had enough of your caresses and your kisses. But it's been hell, because while you care, and I know that you do, Emily— you can't hide that—you hold yourself away from me. You look at me as if you know with absolute certainty that

I'll hurt you, even when you let me know how you feel. And hell because I probably will hurt you, and I can't do anything about it right now. More than anything I've ever wanted in my life, I want to be with you. I want you in my bed every night, and by my side every day. I want you desperately, Emily. Only you, and no one else.''

His words were beautiful, but his tone left her with the knowledge that there was still a profound barrier between them, that there was so much left unsaid. She only vaguely understood that it had to do with the dangerous work he was involved in, and she didn't know why he wouldn't release the burden that held them apart.

He tilted her chin up and met her lips in a searingly intense yet gentle kiss. Her heart ached with a bittersweet poignancy. He had declared his love, yet he wouldn't ask her to marry him. She even thought he wanted to marry her. Why wouldn't he? What could possibly be so important to him that he would sacrifice their happiness together?

Gradually, he ended the kiss, aware of Emily's frustration at his refusal to say more, and his own doubts about the wisdom of maintaining the wall between them.

"What are we going to do?" she asked in a small voice.

"I don't know," he admitted honestly.

He held her silently in his arms, his cheek resting against her hair, for a long time.

"I think you'd better tell me what's on your mind," Black Wolf said, following Drew around the barn as he forked hay into the horses' stalls.

"I don't want to talk about anything!" Drew panted as he tried to work out his anger and frustration.

Black Wolf understood the other man's quandary. He hadn't brought good news about Zach Steven's movements and activities, and the early snow had halted the distribution of much-needed supplies to already starving Indians. Then, of course, there was Emily. Any one of these would have been a handful in and of itself. The stress of trying to deal with all three of them together was beginning to tell on Drew.

"We can't catch Stevens yet, but he's looking more and more like our best suspect. We know he spent the early part of October on legitimate business travels that just happened to take him near several camps with visitors from the Canadian hostile groups, but he's as limited by the weather as we are. We don't have any hard evidence against him, so we can't stop him. And you know you can't change the weather. You'd be forced to wait until spring even if you weren't here at the Parkers' place. The only one of your problems that you have any control over is the one that's causing you the most anguish right now anyway. What are you going to do about her?'' Black Wolf asked seriously, concerned that Drew was expecting too much from himself.

"I said I didn't want to talk!'' Drew thundered, dumping feed sacks in a pile near the stalls.

Black Wolf trailed him, ignoring the rebuff. "They won't be back until spring, you know.''

"Who won't be back?'' Drew snapped irritably.

"Parker and his wife. A few trains are getting through, but the stages can't move, and the wagon trains are almost halted. A little more snow, and nothing will be moving at all. Have you thought about that?''

"Of course I have! I don't know what to do. I can't stay here and not sleep with her, which she won't do because of the children and because she thinks it's wrong without a marriage license. I can't very well leave after I promised Sam that I'd take care of things here. If I go ahead and marry her, what's going to happen in the spring? Do you know what it would do to me if anything happened to her, especially if it was a result of my work? Who knows what Stevens is really capable of? I can't put her in that kind of jeopardy,'' Drew finished with a defeated sigh. He sat down heavily on the feed sacks and rested his forehead on his palms.

"I suppose she wouldn't consider an Indian marriage binding?'' Black Wolf suggested. He knew enough about the white men's customs to know that Emily wouldn't be satisfied without a legal marriage. It was a ridiculous attitude to him, and it was causing an undue strain on his brother. From the Lakota perspective, the families had already had one satisfactory gift exchange, both parties were agreeable, and that was enough. Anytime Drew and Emily decided they were married, the tribe would consider them married as well. White people had to complicate things, naturally. They had to have a minister and a signed piece of paper.

"She might if it weren't for the children. As it is, she wouldn't."

"Can't you find some way to marry secretly? With this weather, folks aren't getting out much. You wouldn't have to meet people or go into town often. I doubt if Stevens will even make it out here to see her more than once or twice. He's the man you have to convince. He's caught up north now anyway. Who knows when he'll get back."

Drew looked up at his brother, turning the idea over in his mind, wondering if there would realistically be any way to keep a marriage secret. A local minister couldn't be relied upon to keep his mouth shut, and then, of course, there were the children.

Still, he didn't dismiss the idea entirely.

The next day, Drew left in the morning for Fort Meade to relay to Colonel Reynolds the information Black Wolf had brought him about the rebellion plot and Stevens's involvement. A dusting of fresh snow had fallen overnight, and the continued cold left little hope that Dakota Territory would see anything even remotely resembling Indian summer in 1880. Drew reflected that Black Wolf was right; Sam and Maggie would most likely not be back for many months.

Several hours later, he returned to the ranch, whistling, with a broad smile on his face. He rode into the barn and set about performing a task.

When he was finished, he headed for the house. He found Emily in the kitchen as he entered. The smile he gave her dazzled her, but he merely asked where Black Wolf was and then ran upstairs to find him. Emily looked after him, wondering what in the world he seemed so excited about, but when he didn't come back down immediately, she continued peeling the potatoes for their dinner. He didn't reappear until dinner, when he took a tray upstairs for Red Eagle Woman before sitting down with everyone else to eat. Emily noticed that he was in an especially fine mood, joking with the children in a constant patter, alternating between Lakota and English. Black Wolf also seemed in excellent spirits, laughing often and telling amusing anecdotes. When Emily asked why they were so merry, Drew only smiled mysteriously and wouldn't say.

When all the dishes had been cleaned up, the table wiped off, and the floor swept, Emily found herself suddenly alone with Drew. Black Wolf and the children had disappeared. Drew caught her in his arms and swung her around the room with him, laughing as though he hadn't a care in the world.

"What's going on?" she demanded laughingly, finding his mood infectious even if she didn't know the reason for it.

"I have a surprise for you," he told her, his blue eyes dancing.

"What is it?" Emily asked, her curiosity piqued. He was acting most uncharacteristically. His hands were warm on her back, sending familiar shivers along her nerves.

"I can't very well tell you. That would spoil it. All I'll tell you is that we're going out this afternoon, just you and me. How does that sound?" He grinned at her like a schoolboy.

"That sounds . . . intriguing," she said, smiling back at him. "Where are we going?"

"That's part of the surprise. Now, I want you to go put on your prettiest dress. Maybe that green one you wore to the Fort Meade dance last summer," he instructed.

"Why?" Emily was dying of curiosity.

In answer, his lips captured hers in a delightful kiss that left her breathless when he finally pulled away.

"Just do it and meet me down here in half an hour," he said as he released her and strode to the door. As it slammed shut and she listened to his footsteps crunch across the snow, she stared after him for a few seconds, wondering what in heaven's name he had planned. Then she turned and raced up the stairs to dress.

Red Eagle Woman looked on approvingly as Emily struggled into a corset for the first time in she didn't know how long and donned her pretty lace petticoats over silk stockings. The Indian woman fingered the rich green silk admiringly as she helped Emily into the dress. Then they arranged her hair in a chignon at the back of her head, leaving a few wispy golden curls to frame her face.

"You are beautiful, Emily. You will make *mišic'e* very proud," she said as they stood before the full-length mirror that hung next to the dressing table.

"Do you know where he's taking me?" Emily asked.

Red Eagle Woman smiled, but she didn't answer. Instead, she picked up the blue and white beaded necklace that Drew had given Emily at Pine Ridge. She held it up against the green silk. To Emily's surprise, it looked lovely. Red Eagle Woman tied it around her neck without a word.

When Emily was dressed, she glanced at her watch. She'd taken a little longer than half an hour. She gave Red Eagle Woman a hug, not quite sure why she felt so happy when she hadn't the faintest notion of what was going on. Then she hurried down the stairway.

Drew met her in the hall at the foot of the stairs. He looked devastatingly elegant in his black broadcloth suit and wing-collared shirt of crisp white cotton. His black tie was neatly knotted, and except for the hair that curled below his collar, one might never know that he spent most of his days dressed in Indian buckskins and beaded moccasins. He held out his arm for Emily and smiled, his even white teeth flashing white in his tanned face.

"You are a vision, Emily," he said warmly, and he thought of the many times through the years when he had seen her eyes in his dreams, wondering about the woman who lay behind them.

She blushed, but she held his gaze. There was an electricity between them that she couldn't help but respond to. What was he up to?

"Shall we go?" he asked, taking the coat that she'd

draped over her arm and helping her into it. While she adjusted her fur cap, he picked up a heavy buffalo coat and shrugged into it. He opened the door for her, and they went out.

In front of the gate, the sleigh awaited them, two of Sam's blacks harnessed to it.

"Is this the surprise?" Emily asked, her eyes excited. "A sleigh ride? But why did we get all dressed up for a sleigh ride?"

"This is part of it. You'll just have to be patient about the rest," Drew told her.

The horses blew clouds of condensed breath into the cold air as Drew handed Emily into the sleigh and tucked a warm buffalo robe around her lap. He joined her on the upholstered seat, wrapping the robes around his legs as well, the length of his hard thigh pressing solidly against her leg. He gave her an almost ridiculously silly smile, as if he were nervous, which she found difficult to believe. Then he took up the reins, and they were off.

The ride was glorious. The day was clear with a bright blue sky, though the sun held little warmth. There was no wind, and last night's snowfall still clung high up in the trees, creating the impression that they were riding through a winter fairyland. No one was about, and there were no tracks along the little road. The horses were grateful to be out of the barn and running, and Drew gave them their head for a while, allowing them to pull the little sleigh along at an exhilarating speed. He seemed to know exactly where to guide them to keep them out of ruts and snowbanks. Emily relaxed against him, enjoying the wind in her face and the sense of skimming effortlessly across the top of a serene white world.

Emily didn't keep track of how far they went or where. At one point, Drew stopped and produced a flask of whiskey, laughing heartily when Emily coughed violently upon swallowing a tiny bit. Occasionally, they passed houses with smoke curling from their chimneys, and once or twice, they saw people in the distance, but for the most part, it seemed to Emily as if they had the world to themselves.

They passed beyond the last line of hills onto the edge of the plains. Drew was guiding the horses northward along a line that might have been a road, and soon Bear Butte loomed before them. The mountain looked different to Emily with snow on it. It was more mysterious, more remote. While she watched it, she noticed that the shadows were lengthening. They must have been out for almost three hours, she decided, marveling that the time had passed so quickly. They had said almost nothing, but there was a deep feeling of communion between them that needed few words. Emily wouldn't let her worries about the future infringe on this magical time they had together.

As the sun dipped behind the hills in the west, the light failed quickly, and soon the first stars were peeping out in the cold night, bright, hard diamonds in the deepening sky. Lights appeared ahead of them in a valley as Drew turned the horses back toward the hills.

"Isn't that the fort?" Emily asked in sudden recognition. "Is that where we're going?"

A wide grin was the only answer Drew gave her.

"What's going on at the fort? Why are we going there? Is there another dance?" Emily asked excitedly. "Tell me something. Please!" she begged.

"It's a private party of sorts. A very private party," he finally revealed, still grinning.

"Who's going to be there?" she wanted to know. "What kind of a party? How did you find out about it? Have you seen Caroline and Matt?" There seemed no end to her questions.

"I'm not telling any more. You'll just have to wait," he said with finality.

It was fully dark by the time they reached the fort. To Emily's surprise, Drew left the road and steered the horses around behind the fort buildings, skirting the base of the bench hills that rose south of the encampment. Emily didn't see a soul, and she doubted that anyone was aware of their passage.

Pulling up in the shadow of a large building, Drew jumped out of the sleigh and quickly pulled the wide door open. There was no one inside. He climbed back onto the seat and drove the horses into the building. He jumped out again and slid the door closed. Then he came back and helped Emily out of the robes.

"What on earth are you about, Drew Rutledge? You're acting like you're on some sort of secret mission," Emily said.

"I am, sweetheart, and so are you. Now, we're going to run quickly over to the Reynoldses' house." He took her gloved hand in his own. "Are you ready?" His eyes glinted with excitement.

"I suppose, but . . ."

Drew didn't give her a chance to finish. He slipped the door open a foot or so, pulled her through with him, and closed it. In an instant, they were tearing across the open field that separated them from the post commander's quarters. As they raced up the steps to the front door, it opened from inside, and they slipped in. Drew peered back out through the crack before he shut it tight. His lips curved again into a smile.

"So far so good," he said, turning back to Emily's questioning eyes. "Come on." He guided her into the hall. Caroline and the colonel appeared, both of them smiling with the same ridiculous silliness that Drew was exhibiting.

"Are you both ready?" Caroline asked excitedly. "I'm so happy for—"

"We need a few minutes alone," Drew said, cutting her off.

"What's going on?" Emily asked, looking from one face to another in bewilderment.

The colonel raised an eyebrow at Drew and took his wife's elbow, ushering her into the parlor. "We'll wait in here. Take all the time you need," he said, shaking his head at Drew.

Chapter 21

Drew took Emily's coat and laid it on a chair, then removed his own. She pulled off her gloves and crossed her arms over her chest. Finally, Drew sought her hands, tugging at them to get her to release them to him. He looked nervously at her, his lips parting, then closing again in uncertainty. Emily was completely baffled by his actions.

"Did you want to say something to me? I wish you'd explain what's going on. Is this the surprise?" she asked with a mixture of doubt and chagrin. "What's going on in the parlor?"

"A wedding."

He'd never felt so uneasy in his life. He'd faced dangerous men and wild beasts alone, armed only with his wits, and had felt more confident.

"Who's getting married?" Emily's heartbeat accelerated rapidly.

The white lights in his eyes surged briefly, and a smoldering look of barely suppressed passion replaced the hesitancy that she had seen less than a second before.

"We are. If you'll have me. Will you marry me, Emily?"

The question hung in the air between them. Time ceased to flow. Emily stood silent, trapped in the blue depths of his gaze, hardly daring to believe that she had heard right. *He wanted to marry her?*

Thoughts tumbled madly through her head. Her first impulse was to throw herself into his arms and tell him that

of course she would marry him. She'd never wanted anything more in her life, and she'd thought it would never
happen. But she held back. Now that he had finally asked
her, anger was fast overriding her other reactions. He
hadn't asked until he'd put everything into place, assuming that she would agree. Damn him, didn't he ever listen
to her? This was exactly the sort of high-handed behavior
that made her feel as if she had no control over her own
life! And why had he all of a sudden changed his mind
about marrying her? Only yesterday, he had made it clear
that he wasn't willing to do so, no matter what his feelings.

More importantly, she wasn't sure he'd ever give her
the stability she wanted, married or not.

Drew watched the muscles in her jaw tighten and set.
Her lips thinned, and her eyes sparked with angry flashes.
Inwardly, he groaned, but he was prepared. She was drawing a deep breath, ready to flay him with her tongue when
he cocked his head and raised one finger and placed it
on her parted lips.

"Please, give me a minute before you say anything,"
he said. It was more an order than a request. Emily glared
at him mutinously, but she held her tongue.

"I know I shouldn't have asked you like this, but I
didn't know how else to do it. You know that I love you,
don't you?" She nodded slowly, waiting. "I've wanted to
offer you my name and my love for a long time, Emily.
The first time we made love, I wanted to take you to the
nearest church the next morning and make you mine forever. But I couldn't." His eyes pleaded with her for
understanding.

"You left instead. Without a word," she whispered accusingly, reliving the agony of that time.

"I know. And I did it again. And I told you there was
no future for us, while at the same time, I couldn't keep
my hands off you and you were constantly in my thoughts.
Emily, you have to understand that I did those things because I honestly felt that your life would be in danger if I
openly courted you. I don't want to put you in danger.
I've waited for you since I was fourteen years old. You

have no idea how much it hurt me to cause you pain and try to drive you away from me, but I didn't see any other way to protect you.'' His fingers tightened on hers as he spoke, and his eyes burned with intensity.

"What do you mean, you've waited for me since you were fourteen?" she asked, trying to keep everything he said straight.

"I saw you in a vision. At least, I saw your eyes. Do you remember that day you went to the falls?" She nodded. "In the first vision I had when I was fourteen, the eagle took me up and I flew far with him, across the whole country, and then back at last to the Hills. We landed in a tall pine above a falls, and I saw a woman walk out of the trees. I couldn't see her clearly, so we flew down to look more closely, but all I could see was her eyes. Eyes like yours, Emily, deep brown like the earth, and deep green like the pines. Your eyes.''

Emily stared at him in wonder. "How . . . ?" she asked, her voice a mere breath. She swallowed hard. Hadn't she had the feeling so often that she was called to this place, and to Drew's arms? And the eagle at the falls. The dreams. Wild images swirled before her mind's eye. "How can that be?" she repeated incredulously.

"I don't know. I can't explain it, but I can't fight it anymore either. Can you? Don't you love me, Emily?" His voice was deep with emotion.

"You know I do," she whispered, "but"—her voice grew stronger—"I don't see what's changed. Why have you decided all of a sudden that you simply can't wait another moment to marry me, when only yesterday you clearly had no intention of doing so?"

"I've had more time to think."

"Not much," she interrupted.

"But enough. You do realize that Sam and Maggie won't be able to get back before the spring, don't you? Do you really think we could stay together all that time without an awful lot of nights like we just had? Why not give ourselves what we most want?" he asked, repeating the question Black Wolf had asked him yesterday.

"So you are primarily concerned with convenience," Emily stated rather coldly.

"That's not what I meant, and you know it."

"What about all this concern for my safety? Did you catch the people who were setting you up and stealing guns?" She wasn't at all satisfied with his answers so far.

"I won't lie to you. That's still a serious problem, but it's one that nature has put on hold for the time being. I can't move in this weather, but neither can anyone else. Unfortunately, in the spring I'll have to get back to work, and that's the reason for all the secrecy tonight. No one can know that we are married—"

"*If* we get married," Emily reminded him tartly.

"—because your life will still be very much at stake if anyone finds out. Whoever's trying to set me up may try to get to me through you, or they may think you know things that could be harmful to them. And, as I've already said, I'm not willing to take that chance."

"That sounds very farfetched to me," she protested.

His eyes blazed. "Take my word for it," he warned ominously, "you'd be in far more danger than you can imagine. You'll also have to accept that until this whole mess is wrapped up, I can't tell you everything I know. That will remain as a wall between us, and if I could have it otherwise, I would. When the spring thaw comes, I'll have to leave again, and you'll have to stay behind and not know what's happening." His tone was apologetic but firm.

"I appreciate your honesty, but I'm not sure a marriage will work if that's the case. What about trust?" She regarded him warily, unsure of what to do.

"It isn't a matter of trust, Emily. It's a matter of survival. I haven't spent most of my life out here without learning a few things about what I have to do to stay alive. And right now, the most important thing to me is that you and I both live to share a long life together. I can't guarantee a safe, secure future, and I know how much that means to you, but I'll do anything and everything I can to ensure that we have a chance together. When I came out here this morning and found an itinerant preacher holed up here, it occurred to me that maybe we could make the winter pass with a great deal more joy than it otherwise might. I know I should have asked you, but it was one of those things where if I'd have waited, the opportunity would have been lost. Lots of things could happen that are out of my control, and I may not be around in the spring to marry you when I'd feel like I could do it at a church on a Sunday afternoon with the whole population of the Hills looking on. So I'm asking you now, when I know that at least we'll have the winter together. Emily, do you want to marry me tonight?''

The urgent note in his strong voice reached her heart. It was her choice. She could say no and they would walk back into the night. He hadn't decided for her. And he loved her. It wasn't a perfect situation, and there would be difficult times ahead, but he was right. At least they would have the winter. Suddenly Emily's heart swelled with love, and to her surprise, she found that she had tears in her eyes. Drew's grip on her hands was so tight she could barely feel her fingertips as she finally nodded her head.

"Yes. I want to marry you," she said clearly.

Drew crushed her to him, his breathing ragged. "Say you love me, Emily. I've never heard you say it."

"I love you, Andrew Rutledge. You are impossible." She laughed through her tears. "But I love you."

Just then, a diminutive, balding man with spectacles stuck his head out of the parlor. He wore a clerical collar and a most perturbed expression.

"Are you folks going to get married or not?" he demanded abruptly.

"We are most definitely getting married," Drew announced with pride.

The minister's face sported an immediate smile. "Glad to hear it! Shall we begin? I do love weddings," he said dreamily.

Emily and Drew looked at each other and tried not to giggle. Then they followed him into the parlor to their wedding.

The ceremony took only about ten minutes. Caroline

and Matthias Reynolds stood up as their witnesses, and the Reverend Mr. Roger Beamis of St. Louis led them through their vows. All three were sworn to secrecy, Drew having bought the reverend's silence with the provision of a guide across the prairie to Pierre, from whence the little clergyman could meet one of the last trains out of Dakota Territory. Drew presented Emily with a wide wedding band made from Black Hills gold, although she had no idea how he had gotten it on such short notice. When the ceremony was finished, Caroline showed them into the dining room where the table was laid with silver and crystal on a snowy cloth, and candles glowed on the table and from the wall sconces. They ate roasted chicken with vegetables and potatoes and drank champagne. For dessert, Caroline produced a small, white cake, decorated with white icing piped in rosettes and borders.

"Everyone should have a wedding cake," she proclaimed as she carried her creation in from the kitchen.

"Caroline, it's beautiful!" Emily exclaimed, touched that her friend had gone to so much trouble. "What would you have done if I'd said no?"

"We were a bit concerned for a while there," Caroline admitted.

"But if you'd said no, we would have still had a lovely dinner. We'd have just saved the cake for later and eaten it all ourselves," Matt Reynolds interjected, his hazel eyes twinkling.

When supper was finished, Caroline packed a basket with the leftovers and an extra bottle of champagne, which she handed to Drew as he and Emily bundled back into their coats and prepared to leave.

"Something for later," she said with a conspiratorial grin. "I'm sure you won't care to do much cooking anytime soon."

"Caroline, watch yourself," her husband warned with a smile. "You're embarrassing the bride," he pointed out, noting the deep flush on Emily's cheeks.

"Congratulations," Caroline said, reaching up to give Drew a kiss, then hugging Emily. "I wish you every happiness. Now, you'd best get going before anyone stops by and discovers you here!''

So saying, Caroline pushed them out the door, and they ran back to the shed where they had left the sleigh.

Soon they were racing over the snow-covered plains under a spangled sky, warm and happy beneath the heavy robes. Emily thought of Woḣpe and Okaga as she looked up at the bright stars, her head leaning on her husband's chest. Her husband! She laughed aloud, unable to contain the joy she felt.

"What are you thinking, *mitawin?*" he asked her lovingly.

"I was thinking of Woḣpe and Okaga. I was remembering the first night you told me their story." She sighed.

"I did that with every intention of marrying you one day, Emily. You don't know how happy I am that you said yes tonight," he said, hugging her to him.

"I think I do," she murmured. "What does *mitawin* mean? You called me that before."

"It means 'my wife, my woman,' " he told her quietly.

She looked up at him in wonder, remembering the stormy summer night when she had first heard the word. "Then why did you . . . ?"

"Because I've thought of you as my wife from the first night we made love. We belong together, and my heart knew it even though my head couldn't see how. You're mine, Emily, my woman, my wife. You always have been, and you always will be." His voice was husky with emotion.

"And you are mine, my husband, Drew Rutledge," she said, pressing her lips against his.

"Forever, Mrs. Rutledge," he promised her.

They didn't return to the Parker ranch that evening. Instead, Drew continued on to his own cabin, explaining that Black Wolf and Red Eagle Woman were only too glad to stay at the Parkers' and care for the children for the night. When the horses had been fed and sheltered, Drew pulled Emily into his arms.

"Shall we go inside?"

Emily nodded, not trusting herself to speak, and instantly found herself swept up into Drew's arms. He marched toward the cabin with her, crossed the wooden porch, and released the door latch. As he stepped into the darkened cabin, he spoke softly.

"Welcome home, *mitawin*. We'll have tonight here, but then it may be a long time before we sleep here again. I intend to make the most of our privacy."

Emily smiled as he set her down. She looked around at the shadows while she removed her hat, remembering the last time she had been carried through that door in his arms. He lit a lamp, then tossed the match into the wood already set in the fireplace.

"Everything seems ready and waiting for us," she commented, a little flustered by the hungry look in Drew's eyes as he walked toward her.

"I stopped by this morning after I was done at the fort. I wanted to be prepared," he told her, pulling her into his embrace. She shivered slightly at his touch. "Are you cold? I can think of a few ways to warm you up," he said silkily, his mouth covering hers in a possessive kiss.

Emily melted against him as his tongue demanded entrance to her mouth. The fire of their passion leapt between them, even as growing tongues of flame licked at the wood on the hearth, filling the room with a warm glow. Their tongues dueled in loving struggle, each desperate to taste the nectar of the other's kiss. At length they drew apart, breathing heavily. Drew smiled at Emily, causing butterflies to ripple through her stomach.

"I think we can at least take off our coats." He chuckled. "We have all night, and I mean to take my time with you." He slipped her coat sleeves from her shoulders. "Of course, only if you want me to," he added quickly, pulling away from her in mock deference.

"Oh, that you can be sure of. There's nothing on this earth that I want more." Her voice was sure and vibrant.

She pushed his coat away, her hands seeking the muscles of his chest under the fine shirt.

"You have too many clothes on," she complained mildly.

"My thoughts exactly," he agreed, removing his tie. "And so"—he looped the tie around her waist, pulling her closer—"do you."

Their lips met again in a dizzying kiss as their hands sought buttons and hooks, undressing each other. Emily's dress rustled to the floor, forming a deep green pool around her feet. Drew lifted her free of it, swinging her toward the bed, without removing his mouth from hers. His fingers fumbled with her corset hooks, unable to release them.

"Damn!" he muttered against her lips. "I'm going to throw this thing away if I ever get it off you!"

Emily laughed, turning in his arms so that he could see the little hooks and ties. Suddenly, her ribs were compressed as he pushed the satin material together to free it. Then he jerked the corset away from her, flinging it across the room. Instantly, his hands closed over her breasts, and he bent to taste the delicate curve of her neck. She arched against him, delighting in his hard chest, pressing into her shoulders, and his roaming hands. She wriggled her hips into him, feeling his unyielding strength supporting her, ready to carry her away to the brilliant heights of their mutual passion. Her hands reached back to stroke his thighs, while his fingers removed the final items of her clothing. In a moment, she stood naked in his arms, the fine cloth of his unbuttoned shirt brushing her breasts, the heavier material of his trousers sliding along her thighs and stomach. Easing the shirt off his shoulders, Emily rained light kisses across his chest, mesmerized by the smooth texture of his warm skin beneath the light mat of golden-brown hair. She gave herself uninhibitedly to every impulse, at the same time surrendering to Drew's bold explorations of her bare flesh.

Her fingers found his belt and tugged at it, loosening it. He tensed against the fiery assault of her touch as she undid the buttons that constrained his swollen flesh. With his hands tangled in her hair and his tongue thrusting deeply into her mouth, she slipped her hands inside his waistband, moving to the small of his back. She pushed his trousers slowly over his hips, sinking her fingers into his flanks as she did so. His hips rocked forward, and he groaned into her mouth. His hands joined hers, impatiently discarding the black pants, then clasping her to him.

Without Emily's realizing how, they moved onto the bed, their hands and mouths enticing each other, exciting them to peak after peak of ecstatic pleasure. They tumbled back and forth, Emily's long hair tangling beneath them, laughing and smiling, reveling in the lack of constraint and tension in this joyous lovemaking. Gradually they became more intent, lost in the heated demands of their bodies. Drew filled his hands with her full breasts, then dipped his fingers tantalizingly into the softness between her legs, his mouth all the while imprinting wild, impassioned kisses over every inch of her creamy skin. Emily's kisses matched his, her tongue eagerly exploring every part of him that was within reach as he lay atop her. She opened herself to him fully, delighting in the pleasure she gave him and hungrily seeking all he would give her.

Finally, Drew knelt between her legs, lifting her hips to meet him as he buried himself deep in her, as excited by her rapturous expression and the small, wild cries that rose from her throat as by the moist warmth that enfolded him. He moved inside her, slowly, erotically, in long, controlled strokes, running his hands over her, finding her small, white hands and lacing their fingers together. She opened her eyes and found his. As they moved together, matching thrust for thrust, straining forward into the eternal glory of loving release, her earthy green-brown gaze met his blue eyes, flashing with the white lights that reflected the storm of their passionate union. When they reached the pinnacle of fulfillment, they cried out as the spasms rocked their bodies. Drew fell on top of Emily, wrapping his arms around her back, crushing her to him, and she clung to him, wondering at the drop of wetness that fell from his eye onto her cheek. She had never experienced such a depth of happiness and completeness.

This night, there was nothing that could keep them apart, nothing that could diminish their love. In the morning, there would be no regrets, and no pain, but only the exquisite knowledge that they belonged to each other completely as man and wife. Emily felt almost giddy with delight, and the celebration she brought to their lovemaking lifted Drew to new heights of excitement. The complexity of sensation and emotion that engulfed them made the moments pass as eternities, whole worlds encompassed in minutes, a single touch, a look, a kiss. They savored their intimacy, spinning ever higher, the flames of their desires dancing between them, ever hotter as the night wore on. Time and time again, they took their fill of each other until, at dawn, they fell into exhausted, but blissful, slumber.

The winter passed in blessedly uneventful happiness for Drew and Emily. They told Josh and Sarah that they had gotten married and explained that they were keeping it a secret. The children had become ready accomplices, assuming the secrecy was part of some elaborate game that they didn't fully understand. They sent a telegram to Sam and Maggie, explaining that everything was under control and that they shouldn't fret over not being able to return to the Hills. The snow continued to fall at regular intervals, never melting. By the new year, no trains were moving anywhere on the plains, and life became a monotonous struggle to procure warmth and adequate food for most of the residents of Dakota, both Indian and white. They were cut off completely from the outside world, and almost as surely from even their closest neighbors. Drew's foresight and the stocks of firewood, oil, coal and canned food that he had originally gathered for his illegal distributions made life at the Parkers' easier than at most places. And for Drew and Emily, the joy of being together made all difficulties fade into insignificance.

The worst times they had that winter were the few occasions when Zach Stevens struggled over the frozen, drifted roads to call on Emily. She had wanted to tell Zach about their marriage, feeling it unfair to lead him on, but Drew had been so fiercely adamant that no one at all know, that Emily had finally accepted his will. It was risky to deceive Zach, in that it required a great deal of playacting from all of them. Drew had prayed hard that they would be able to pull off the kind of polite indifference to one another that would set Zach's mind to rest.

By the middle of March, even Emily, who had barely noticed the cold as an inconvenience, so lost was she in the joy of getting to know her husband better, began to scan the sky impatiently and test the wind, trying to determine if it hadn't warmed a degree or two. It seemed as if this terrible winter would never release its grip on the earth, and that Dakota would never again see green grass spread across the soft rises of the prairies. As March gave way to April, Drew became more and more restless. Often Emily found him standing outside, his blue eyes fixed on the implacable winter sky, a deep frown creasing his features. There was grief in his expression, and Emily knew that he was constantly aware that each day that passed without a hint of spring brought more misery, perhaps even death, to the starving bands of off-reservation Sioux.

One night in mid-April, the wind finally turned. When Emily stepped outside to shake off the tablecloth after supper, it was still frigid, driving her inside without stopping to admire the stars. Two hours later, Drew called them all to the porch. Incredibly, the air was warm and soft, carrying the scent of new leaves and wet earth. The sound of running water was already audible, and streams of melting snow cascaded off the roof. Drew explained that the warm wind was called a chinook, and that winter was finally over. He warned the children to stay far from the creek. There would be flooding as the entire winter's accumulation of snow melted in a few short days.

Emily noticed that his restless tension was more pronounced than ever and that he slept little that night, staring into the darkness with his head propped on his arms. When she awoke for the third time and he was still not asleep, she was concerned.

"Something's on your mind," she prompted, settling her head onto his shoulder. Her fingers traced idle patterns across his chest. "Can you talk about it?"

"I'm going to leave again soon." He sighed, tightening his arms around her protectively.

She'd known what he would say. Her heart pounded apprehensively.

"When?"

"As soon as the ground is firm enough to get wagons across and Sam and Maggie get back. Maybe a week. Maybe ten days. Maybe longer. It depends on the weather."

There was resignation in his voice. When he left he had no idea if he'd ever return, and if he did, what he'd return to. He had a feeling, almost a premonition, that things were going to happen fast. He sighed again, running his hands over Emily's smooth back. It was just as well. Within a month, he'd either be taking Emily to live with him at his cabin and beginning to plan their future, or he'd be dead. He had to shake off the inactivity and sense of security he'd settled into with the winter snows if he was to avoid the latter fate. He would need all his faculties to stop the rebellion plot before it could get any further and to protect himself against the bounty hunters and whoever else would be looking for his scalp. Worst of all, there would be little he could do to actively protect Emily. His absence would be her best protection, but he didn't want to let her out of his sight for fear of losing her.

Emily sensed his preoccupation. She was afraid for him and for their future, but she didn't want him to know.

"I'll be all right, you know," she said in answer to his unspoken fears. "I don't want you to go, but I understand."

He smiled at her in the dark, stroking her soft hair, and listened to the water dripping off the roof. He remembered something.

"Emily, have you had any more dreams like the one you had last summer?"

"No. I would have told you if I had. Why?" She sounded troubled.

"Just curious." He tilted her head so he could kiss her lips. The intensity of his kiss took her breath away. "I need you," he whispered into her hair, turning so that she lay half beneath him. "God, I love you so much!"

She answered by drawing his mouth back to hers. They

made love with a desperate energy, driven by their fears for the unknown future. When their passions were spent, Drew slept at last, his arms holding Emily close. Before she dropped off to sleep, she thought how lovely the winter had been for them, how unexpected. She had never thought they would resolve their differences at all. Now, she prayed that their time together would not melt with the snow, fading into memory alone. Uneasily, she felt a cold prickle of dread creep down her spine. Even the warmth of Drew's arms, surrounding her with his strength and love, could not dispel it. At length, she slipped into a restless sleep. In the morning, they would greet the spring, bidding goodbye to the winter that had given them time and kept them safe.

Chapter 22

Matt Reynolds grimly eyed the reports scattered across his desk. His jaw clenched, and he smashed a powerful fist down on top of the papers. There was a brisk knock at his door.

"Come in!" he commanded tersely.

Major Donaldson quickly entered and saluted. The colonel returned his salute perfunctorily and turned to stare out the window at the greening hills and leafing trees. Birds sang merrily in the warm spring air, but he didn't hear them.

"Have you decided what to do about Logan's report, colonel?" the man asked eagerly.

"Yes," Reynolds said between gritted teeth. He turned abruptly to his subordinate. "I want you to take Company A with you to the caves. Do not, I repeat, *do not* take Logan with you. If you find anyone there, arrest them and bring them in, but, Major Donaldson, I don't want anyone hurt, and that includes prisoners. If anyone is injured, I'll hold you personally responsible. I'll kick your butt back across the Missouri so fast you won't know what hit you. Do you understand?"

"Yes, sir," Donaldson paused. "If there are men there and they resist, colonel, what am I supposed to do?"

"I leave that up to your abilities as a creative strategist, major, but I don't want any bloodshed under any circumstances. If that means you have to get your men out of there fast, then do it. Otherwise, your orders are to seize

whatever you find. Am I making myself clear enough?''
The colonel's expression was cold and unyielding.

"Yes, sir."

"Fine. I'm taking Lieutenant Smith and Company G to
intercept the wagon train. We ride out as soon as possible."

"Yes, sir. Good luck, colonel. It will be a relief to
capture these bastards and put this rebellion plot behind
us. The men have been itching to get their hands on the
culprits behind it all winter."

"That's all, Ed. Remember your orders," Colonel Reynolds said, dismissing him.

The major marched from the room confidently. Reynolds
paused a moment before following him.

"Damn it all!" he swore, grabbing his hat and slamming the door behind him.

Emily awoke with a start, sitting up in bed, a frightened
cry dying on her lips. Gradually, her eyes focused on the
white, pink, and green quilt covering her legs, then on the
golden oak dressers and white lacy curtains. She caught
her breath. She was in her room at Sam and Maggie's.
Everything was all right.

"Emily, is something wrong?" Maggie's concerned
voice sounded just outside her door.

"Come in, Maggie. I'm fine," she replied, reaching to
turn the doorknob without getting up.

Maggie entered immediately. "You're pale as a ghost!"
she exclaimed in alarm. She placed a hand on Emily's
cheek. It was cool. "Are you ill?"

Emily shook her head. "I had another dream," she said
slowly, her eyes focused on nothing in particular while
she tried to remember. She'd been having wild, tormenting dreams since Sam and Maggie had returned two weeks
ago. And since Drew had left, as he'd said he would. But
they hadn't been the eerie, prophetic dreams of last summer. Until now. Suddenly, with blinding clarity, Emily
recaptured the terrifying picture that had awakened her.

"Maggie, it was terrible!" She turned to her sister-in-
law with wide eyes. "I saw Drew in jail, and I saw a

scaffold being built out at the fort. Soldiers were laughing, and there was the man in the smiling mask on the red horse, the one from the other dreams I told you about. They were going to hang Drew, and I was watching and I couldn't move. I couldn't help!'' Her voice rose hysterically.

Maggie grasped her arms and shook her. "Emily, it was only a dream. Get hold of yourself!''

Emily took a deep breath and controlled her rising panic, but she couldn't dispel her fear. After a minute, Maggie's hands relaxed on her arms.

"I'm all right, Maggie, but this was more than a dream.'' Emily threw the quilt and blankets away from her, swinging her feet to the floor. "It was a warning. Drew is in danger, and I have to find him. I have to try to help him.''

Emily raced around the room, throwing on a blue flannel shirt and a pair of jeans. She donned her socks, stuffed her feet into her riding boots, and grabbed a soft leather jacket.

"Where are you going? You don't have any idea where he is!'' Maggie protested. "Emily, there's nothing you can do!''

"I'm going to his cabin. Maybe there's someone there who knows where he went. I can't just stay here and wait! I couldn't bear it if anything happened to him!'' she said, flying out of her room and down the stairs.

Emily rode hard to reach Drew's cabin, pushing the mare until her coat was mottled with dark splotches of sweat. It took less than fifteen minutes to reach the meadow that led to the cabin and the limestone caves beyond. She slowed her mount and entered the edge of the pine forest, moving as quietly as she could, afraid she might already be too late to stop whatever nameless fate awaited her husband.

When she reached the cabin, she had to leave the cover of the trees. No smoke came from the chimney, and no animals were in the corral. Emily was sure Drew wasn't there, and that he hadn't been for some time from the

looks of things. Nevertheless, she went into the cabin,
hoping perhaps to find some clue that would lead her to
her husband. Realistically, she knew he might be halfway
to the Canadian border by now.

There was nothing in the cabin, and it had increased
Emily's sense of foreboding to be where she and Drew
had shared such precious times. She couldn't stand the
thought that she might never sleep in his arms again, run
her fingers through the golden-brown curls that swept his
temples, or see the joy in his eyes when she told him she
loved him. Her life would be empty without him, and
memories alone would never be enough. She wished suddenly that she were pregnant, that she hadn't allowed him
to so carefully ensure that she did not conceive. Having
his child would have eased her grief, giving her a part of
him forever. This is ridiculous! she chastised herself,
walking back to the porch. I'm thinking as if he were
dead, and for all I know, he's fine. But she couldn't quell
her fears.

Emily left the cabin and skirted the trees behind it, leading her horse toward the gully that led to the caves. A
movement inside the forest caught her eye, and she gasped
as Black Wolf stepped silently from the shelter of a mas-
sive pine trunk and beckoned to her, motioning that she
shouldn't speak. She went to him immediately. He took
the reins from her and led her high up the mountain to a
rocky underhang that overlooked the caves below. Thick
bushes hid them from view on all sides.

"What are you doing here? *Misun* told you not to come.
It's too dangerous!" Black Wolf hissed at Emily.

"I thought you went back to Pine Ridge. What are *you*
doing here?" she retorted accusingly. Black Wolf had
taken his family back to the agency as soon as it had been
possible to travel. It occurred to her that he wouldn't have
returned unless something was wrong. "Did something
happen?" she asked in sudden panic.

"No. You have to go back to your brother's, *hanka*,"
Black Wolf told her.

Emily interrupted him before he could continue. "I had

to come. I had another dream. Something terrible is going to happen, I know it. I have to try to warn Drew.''

She had his attention instantly.

"He's not here. Tell me your dream," he demanded, his black eyes flashing.

Emily told him quickly. Black Wolf shook his head and pressed his lips together.

"Where is he, Black Wolf? Can we find him before the soldiers do?'' she asked plaintively.

"I don't think Reynolds will arrest him. The colonel knows that *misun* is not the man he seeks.''

Emily relaxed slightly. She reasoned that Black Wolf was right, but she worried still. "What about the dream? It was like the ones I had before, the ones that all of you took so seriously. And you didn't answer my question. Where is he?''

Black Wolf didn't speak immediately. His keen eyes traveled out across the vista spread before them, touching on the places where the caves lay well hidden.

"He left two nights ago with a trainload of supplies, headed north. He can't be farther than fifty miles away,'' he finally conceded, knowing that Drew would be furious with him for telling Emily. He believed that her dream was a message, however. Something was wrong. Something would happen.

Emily let out a tremendous sigh of relief. "Then we can reach him by this evening if we hurry!''

"If we're not already too late,'' Black Wolf reminded her grimly. Then his whole body tensed abruptly. He turned his head slightly to the east, listening.

"Shouldn't we leave right away?'' Emily asked impatiently.

"Shhh,'' he told her. His eyes picked out a rising cloud of dust in the deep cut between the hills where the creek left the meadow, flowing toward the Parkers'. Then a hawk's cry floated across the air to them. Black Wolf signaled to Emily to get down, then he repeated the cry. She heard it twice more, echoing through the western meadow where the caves that hid supplies for the hostile Indians lay concealed.

Black Wolf dropped to the ground beside Emily and pointed to the dust cloud. She started to speak, but he shook his head.

"We're safe here, as are the other watchers, but don't move or say a word until I tell you," he said in her ear.

In silence they waited. Soon, the heavy drumming of many hoofbeats broke the sylvan quietude. In another minute, a troop of blue-coated cavalrymen rounded the base of the hill and entered the valley, riding two abreast, the standardbearer carrying the red and blue swallow-tailed guidon of the Seventh Cavalry as if they were riding into battle. Emily's breath hissed through her teeth at the sight. Only the knowledge that Drew was miles away kept her from crying out in dismay.

Upon reaching the cabin, the troops split up, a small party of them dismounting to search the area near the small house. The larger group headed unerringly into the gully and within minutes was fanning out through the valley where the caves were.

The soldiers who searched the cabin and corral soon joined the rest of the company near the mouth of the gully. A call rang out, and the men searching the forest rejoined the main body of soldiers. The major leading them began issuing orders, pointing to the valley walls and sending groups of four and five soldiers to various points along the meadow. He kept glancing down at a large piece of white paper in his hands.

Emily sensed Black Wolf tense beside her. The bluecoats in the valley pulled at bushes and rocks, uncovering the openings to the caves that Emily had seen only once before. She exchanged an apprehensive look with Black Wolf but made no comment. She hoped that Drew had taken most of what had been stored in the caves and that the soldiers wouldn't find anything. She knew that simply finding the goods could not possibly be enough evidence to support criminal charges against Drew. At any rate, he would have taken precautions so that nothing incriminating could be found either at the cabin or in the caves.

Emily and Black Wolf watched the soldiers drag all manner of empty crates and boxes out of the dark holes in the mountain sides. Some of the boxes held blankets and bolts of cloth that spilled into the dirt when they broke open, only to be carelessly thrown into disordered piles at the mouth of each cave. Most of the boxes were empty, however, and the soldiers began to lose interest in their task.

A sudden shout drew all of the soldiers' attention. Several of them wandered over to a group that was pulling numerous long, narrow crates into the bright morning sunlight. There were several whoops and loud calls as the boxes were opened. Major Donaldson signaled for a wagon that had just arrived to be moved into position, and the boxes were loaded into it.

Emily couldn't see what was in the boxes. When she glanced at Black Wolf, she was almost frightened by the startled fury she saw in his face. Her eyes returned to the scene in the meadow below just in time to see one of the crates fall off the wagon tailgate. Her mouth dropped open in shock. A dozen brand-new rifles tumbled to the ground like so many matchsticks.

Emily's mind whirled. Drew would be arrested if they found him. She had to warn him. Then she remembered his words, so calm, so sincere, assuring her that he had nothing to do with the stolen guns and the murders committed during their theft. Could he have lied? Could he have been behind the rebellion plot all along and cleverly put her off guard by directly confronting her worst fears and brazenly lying to her? Emily lifted herself to her knees, a cry already forming in her throat.

Black Wolf clapped his hand to her mouth and pushed her back down. He spoke right in her ear again.

"Say nothing. It's not what you think. He had nothing to do with stealing anything. The guns were not there two days ago. I saw for myself. You will be quiet?"

Emily nodded, and Black Wolf eased the pressure of his fingers. She took a deep breath, wondering what the truth was. Her heart told her that Drew hadn't lied to her, that he was exactly as he had said he was. She knew he hadn't pretended his feelings for her, but he had always been so secretive about where he went and what he did. He'd flatly refused to speak about his work, always insisting that the less she knew, the safer she was. Had he really been protecting his own secrets as she had originally suspected, so long ago, and nothing more? A dull pain throbbed in her chest.

Most of the soldiers left when the wagon pulled out of the valley, but a guard was posted near the caves and another near the cabin. Emily and Black Wolf crept cautiously along the hill until they were well away from view from either of the valleys.

"What are we going to do?" she asked desperately. "We have to warn him, Black Wolf!"

"We'll have to go out over the hills. It'll take more time, but we can't risk meeting any soldiers."

"How long will it take?"

"Maybe an hour."

"Then how long to find Drew?"

"It's hard to say. Maybe by dusk."

"Will we be too late, Black Wolf?"

"I fear so, *hanka*. There's a bad feel to this day."

"He is innocent, isn't he?" Her voice was small.

"The guns were intended to frame him, but he has aided the hostiles. If the army catches him with the supply train, it won't be good."

"It would be treason, wouldn't it?"

"Yes, *hanka*." Black Wolf sighed.

"Will they hang him?" Tears threatened to spill from her eyes.

"We won't let them," Black Wolf assured her with a conviction he didn't feel. "Now, come. We have to hurry."

Emily followed him through the trees, willing herself to be strong and have hope. Everything had to work out. They'd come too far, against too many obstacles, for it to be any other way. Wakantanka had brought them together. They would make it in time to warn Drew.

Late that afternoon, Black Wolf and Emily were met by Yellow Thunder and his nephew, riding Drew's buckskin, at the crest of a hill overlooking the Belle Fourche River.

One look at Black Wolf's face told Emily all she needed to know.

"The army found him?" she asked, fighting to keep the images from her dream out of her mind.

"Yes." Black Wolf sighed. He spoke rapidly in his own language with Yellow Thunder. Finally, Emily could stand waiting no longer.

"Tell me what happened," she begged.

"He almost got away, but there was an accident with the boy's horse. Drew reached to pull him onto his own horse when one of the soldiers fired his rifle. He took a bullet in the shoulder and fell. He insisted that the boy take his horse, and he was left behind. The soldiers took him. Colonel Reynolds was with them," Black Wolf related solemnly. "Drew was very courageous and generous, *hanka*. He saved the boy. The soldiers would have killed the Oglalas if they'd caught them, and some of them would have died in the fight. Drew kept many people from death this day, and many more that would have died in reprisals."

"Yes," Emily said through a fog of pain that engulfed her heart, acknowledging her pride in his courage and concern for others. "How badly was he hurt?"

"The boy isn't sure. He thinks the bullet hit high in the shoulder. It wouldn't be fatal."

Emily closed her eyes, blinking back hot tears. A picture was etched in her mind: an eagle with piercing blue eyes, falling to the earth with an arrow in its breast.

Matt Reynolds was staring out his office window, watching the billowy spring clouds race across the darkening sky, blown along by a brisk west wind, when he heard the sharp rap of bootheels on the wooden steps, then the porch. The footsteps didn't stop at his aide's desk but continued without hesitation to his door. The colonel heard his aide's chair scrape across the floorboards, then his voice.

"Wait a minute, ma'am, you can't just . . ."

The door flew open, banging back on its hinges.

"I want to see my husband!" Emily demanded, whipping a long strand of blond hair away from her sunburned cheeks.

Colonel Reynolds faced her with a grim countenance. He noted her wrinkled shirt and dust-streaked face. Her hair hung in tangled disarray.

"Sit down, Emily," he said calmly, nodding to the young officer standing in the open doorway. The man backed out and closed the door.

"I am not going to sit down until I know exactly why you arrested Drew and when you're going to release him!"

The colonel walked around from behind his desk. "I arrested Andrew Rutledge on the charges of theft of U.S. Army weapons and ammunition, murder of the teamsters transporting said weapons, high treason for plotting to overthrow the representatives of the U.S. Government in this territory, and aiding and abetting the enemy by supplying them with goods and provisions, also a treasonous act. He will not be released."

Emily paled and crossed her arms over her chest involuntarily. She swallowed hard.

"You know he didn't do those things, Matt," she whispered, her eyes pleading with him. "What are you doing to him? Why?"

"We caught him with a wagon train full of supplies, headed north," Colonel Reynolds told her, picking up the pile of folders from his desk.

"That doesn't prove anything. And you know that he didn't do the other things! You know!" Emily cried.

"Major Donaldson found the stolen guns in the caves on Rutledge's land this morning. What am I supposed to do, Emily?" His eyes held hers. "Pretend it didn't happen?"

"But you know he's being framed!" she shouted. "How can you do this? He could hang! Matt, please tell me what's going on!"

"I know what he did and didn't do, Emily, and he has been supplying the hostiles illegally. As I said, that's an act of treason, regardless of the other charges. My hands are tied. The intelligence reports went to Donaldson first, and there was nothing I could do except try to protect

Drew's life. I'm sorry, Emily." He flung the reports back down on the desktop.

"Protect his life?" she wailed disbelievingly. "Is that why you let your men shoot him? I thought you were his friend! You have to get him out!"

"I can't do that."

"Why not? You must! Do you want his death on your hands?"

"I'll do my best to avoid that; you have my word."

"Oh, God!" Emily gasped, sinking at last into the chair behind her, her head in one hand. "Matt, you can't let anything happen to him. I love him so much. I don't want to live without him. You have to help me."

Colonel Reynolds closed his eyes briefly against her despair.

"Do you want to see him?" he asked gently. "I'll take you in. He lost quite a bit of blood from the bullet wound, but the surgeon got the slug out. He's probably asleep now."

"Is that all you're going to say?" she asked accusingly, lifting her head.

He didn't answer but met her gaze steadily.

"Yes. I want to see him," Emily finally said desperately.

Drew lay on a narrow cot, covered only with a single worn blanket in a small dark cell. There was a tiny barred window high up on one wall, and the door was made of heavy iron bars. The guard handed the keys over to the colonel, and as soon as he unlocked the door, Emily raced to Drew, falling on her knees beside the cot. The colonel followed, carrying a lantern. In the dim light, Drew's face looked gray. There was a large bandage wrapped around his left shoulder, and his face was streaked with dirt and sweat.

"It's freezing in here, and he's a mess. He needs more blankets, and I want hot water, soap, and towels," Emily announced. Her defiant manner dared the colonel to refuse her.

"Get the things the lady wants." He nodded to the guard, who immediately disappeared down the hall.

The voices roused Drew, and his eyes opened slowly. He started to sit up, but the pain in his shoulder caused him to wince. Emily pushed him back down gently.

"Don't try to sit up yet," she cautioned, managing a feeble smile. "You've lost a lot of blood, but I'm sure you'll be back to normal in a few days."

"If that damn surgeon didn't use filthy instruments, I will be," he growled. His eyes moved past Emily and settled on Matt Reynolds. Emily missed the look of understanding that passed between them as she pulled the thin blanket up higher over Drew's bare chest.

"We were coming to warn you, Black Wolf and I," she told him, catching his blue gaze. "I had another dream last night. I saw you in jail, and I saw—I tried to find you, but we were too late. I'm so sorry, Drew." She stopped for fear she would cry.

Drew rubbed his fingers across her cheek, wiping at the single tear that spilled from her eye. "Emily, don't cry. There was nothing you could do, so you mustn't feel bad. I'm going to need you to be very strong right now, so we can get through this. Can you do that?"

"I don't know," she answered honestly. "What's going to happen to you?"

"I'm not sure exactly, but it looks like I'm going to be here a while," he said. He took a deep breath. "Emily, I don't want you to say anything about our marriage or to come see me. It's too dangerous. You could get hurt." He spoke very softly.

The look of pain that shot across Emily's face cut Drew to the core. She stared at him, uncomprehending for a moment.

"You don't want to see me?" she whispered.

"You know I want to see you. That isn't the point."

"How can I still be in any danger? The worst has happened! You're in jail facing charges that could see you hanged! And you don't want to see me? I don't understand."

The guard arrived then with the water and blankets. Emily took the basin and cloths from him and set them on the floor beside the cot. Glaring at Drew all the while, she bathed his face and chest, then dried him off. His jaw clenched when she jarred his injured shoulder. When she finished, she grabbed the blankets and settled them around him. She could tell he needed sleep and that there was no sense in arguing with him until he was more rested, but she was hurt and confused that he didn't want her to visit him.

When she had finished, she leaned forward to kiss his mouth gently. His eyes closed, and his right arm stole around her waist, holding her tightly.

"How does your shoulder feel?" she asked anxiously, aware that there was so much she wanted to say, little time, and no privacy.

"It will be fine in a day or two," he said. Then his voice became more urgent. "Emily, I'm so sorry to do this to you. I knew how easily I could be arrested. That's why I tried to fight our love for so long. I didn't want you to have to suffer the consequences of what I've done."

"But you haven't done anything wrong!" she insisted.

"Maybe not morally, but in the eyes of the law I have, and more than enough to send me to the gallows."

"Don't talk like that! I will not see you hang! I'll find a way to get you out of here," she said lowering her voice. "I will not lose you, Drew Rutledge. I love you, and I plan to spend the rest of my life with you. That's a promise."

Drew pulled her hands up to rest on his chest. "I love you," he whispered huskily, "but I won't allow you to put your life on the line by doing anything foolish. There's nothing you can do to get me out of this, Emily, and I would gladly die a thousand times over before I'd see you hurt. Maybe things won't go so badly for me, after all. We just have to wait and see."

"I'll be back tomorrow, and we'll talk then. Go to sleep now and build your strength. I won't let anything happen to you," she promised against his ear.

"Emily . . ."

"Shhh," she said, kissing him again lightly. "I love you, Drew Rutledge."

"I love you so much, *mitawin.*"

"Go to sleep, my love," she murmured, and within a

few minutes, his breathing was deep and regular, and the drawn lines in his face relaxed.

"I think we should leave now." Colonel Reynolds spoke quietly so as not to disturb Drew.

Emily rose reluctantly and followed him out of her husband's cell. When they reached his office again, Matt led her to one of the deep armchairs and poured her a brandy.

"Drink this. It'll help settle your nerves."

Emily drained the glass obediently. She sat dejectedly staring at her reflection in the windows and the black night beyond.

"I'll have one of the officers ride with you to make sure you get home all right," the colonel offered. "Unless, of course, you'd rather stay here tonight. You're more than welcome to stay with Caroline and me."

"No thank you," Emily replied coldly. "All I want from you is for you to release my husband. I don't see how you can hold him on these ridiculous charges. If that wound becomes infected, I'll scream all the way to Washington about your incompetent doctor and your callous treatment of an injured man."

"Emily, I'll personally see to it that he gets the best care the U.S. Army has available, for your sake," he reassured her.

She rose and walked to the door. "I would appreciate it," she told him, more graciously. "I'd better go."

"One last thing, Emily. Drew was right, it would be wise not to let people know that you two are married. Angry citizens might decide to vent their aggressions on you or your brother's family if they know."

She paled. It hadn't occurred to her that this was a possibility.

"What about your aide and the guard? I didn't think about that when I came in."

"I'll talk to them. They're trustworthy men who are loyal to me and who wouldn't want to see an innocent woman hurt."

"What about an innocent man, Matt?"

She opened the door and walked out.

Chapter 23

~~~ ◦✦◦ ~~~

The gray light of dawn had barely streaked the eastern sky when Matt Reynolds slipped into the camp stockade. He relieved the young man guarding the prisoner.

"I thought I'd see if I can't find out anything while he's still a bit out of sorts. Maybe his guard will be down," the colonel told the young soldier.

"I hope so, sir. I heard he's a tough one, though. Grew up with them damn Sioux."

"He did at that. Come back in half an hour, corporal."

"Yes, sir." The guard saluted smartly, glad for the break from the dull duty of watching over a sleeping, injured prisoner.

Drew was sitting up when the colonel entered his cell. He nodded in greeting, yawned, and swept the room in a grand gesture with his good arm.

"I'd offer you a seat, but the management neglected to provide me the resources for entertaining," he quipped.

"How are you feeling, Rutledge?"

"About as well as can be expected."

"I gave orders that no one was to fire a shot. The man who winged you is cooling his heels for a few days in cell number four."

"Did your men find any of the Indians?"

"No. Much to their regret, I wouldn't allow them to go after them."

"Thanks." He paused. "What happened?"

"Logan gave reports of your activities and of hearing word of the stolen weapons in your caves to Donaldson

350

while I was out with a patrol. By the time I got back, the officers were in an uproar. I sat on it as long as I could, ostensibly completing my own investigations, but I couldn't ignore it indefinitely.''

Drew nodded grimly. "I thought it was something like that. What's Stevens been doing during all this?"

"Not a damn thing except selling his lumber, to all appearances. We just can't catch him."

Both men were silent for a moment.

"I know it's him, Matt. I can feel it in my gut. Maybe he'll be less careful now that I'm in jail," Drew speculated. "Do you think we could force his hand somehow? He wouldn't have put *all* the guns into my caves where the army would take them. He must have the rest of them stashed somewhere close by."

"I'd like nothing better than for him to make a mistake."

"Yeah," Drew agreed. "Black Wolf will be keeping an eye on him, too."

"We have another very pressing problem."

Drew moved slightly, testing his shoulder. The pain wasn't as sharp as it had been. "Which one?" he asked without enthusiasm.

"Saving your neck from the noose. I sent a wire to your uncle in Washington and one to the Office of Indian Affairs before I left yesterday, so more than likely you'll be spared an official trial, but I can't say I'm as optimistic about the locals. They might not buy that you've been working for the commissioner of Indian Affairs, and there is the matter of your extracurricular activities. I'm sure your uncle can secure a pardon for you, but that isn't likely to make any difference to a vigilante squad. I don't dare let you out of this place for your own safety."

Drew waved his good hand impatiently. "I can take care of myself. I always have."

"You have an amazing faith in yourself," Matt observed dryly.

"My faith isn't in myself, but in God. My work isn't finished yet, so Wakantanka will protect me."

"I'm afraid I don't know too much about your Indian

religion, but I wouldn't discount the danger of an angry mob, Rutledge, God or no God, Wakantanka or Jehovah or whoever. I won't let you out of here until we've got another suspect in custody and your uncle, the good senator from Massachusetts, has a pardon for you signed by the President.''

"I can't just sit here doing nothing, Reynolds!" Drew exclaimed angrily.

"That's exactly what you're going to do until Zachary Stevens makes a mistake and we can arrest him for engineering a plot to organize an armed rebellion among the Sioux. Believe me, if I felt there was any other choice, I'd arrange a quiet escape for you. It gives me absolutely no pleasure to lock up a friend. I've never felt like as great a cad as I did yesterday evening when Emily stormed into my office, nearly in tears with worry about you, and all I could do was tell her that I'd arrested you for crimes I know you didn't commit. But I did promise her that I'd do everything I can to see that you don't come to further harm, and I mean to keep that promise." His tone was firm.

"So I'm stuck here." He sighed heavily. "What about Emily? Can you keep her away? If Stevens finds out we're married, I don't even like to think about what he might do."

"How much does she know about all this?"

"Nothing about Stevens. Just that someone's been trying to set me up and rile the Indians. She doesn't know that I work for the commissioner of Indian Affairs. She must be worried sick, but I don't want her to know anything more until you get Stevens."

"She's coming back to see you this morning. Can you convince her to stay away from you?"

"It'd be easier on me if you'd forbid me visitors. Her, too, I think."

"I was afraid you'd say that," Matt said, shaking his head. "All right, I'll do it, but only to make up for your catching that bullet. By the way, I thought you told me once that you were bulletproof, like Crazy Horse. What the hell happened?"

Drew chuckled grimly, wincing as the movement hurt his shoulder. "What the hell happened to Crazy Horse? At least I didn't get killed. No, my power is still strong. We're going to get Stevens, Matt, you'll see."

Footsteps, resounded along the wooden planks of the hallway, signaling the young guard's return. Colonel Reynolds let himself out the door and locked it behind him.

"I hope you're right, Rutledge. I surely do."

The next days were hell for Emily. Colonel Reynolds refused to allow her to visit Drew, and he would tell her nothing about when formal charges would be brought up or when he expected Drew to come to trial. When she had protested violently, he'd threatened to bar her from the post, if he had to, to keep her away from Drew. Unexpectedly, Sam hadn't supported her. He'd doggedly maintained that the colonel was a capable man, and if he thought it best that Drew not have any visitors, then Sam accepted the decision. Sam made it clear that he understood his sister's frustration and fears, but that he would not, under any circumstances, become involved in trying to thwart Matt's orders. Emily's hopes that Sam might help arrange for Drew to escape were dashed.

Each day that passed made Emily more certain that Drew would end up on the gallows she had seen in her dream. She accompanied Maggie into town on a shopping trip one day, and everywhere they went, she heard Drew's name on people's lips. Several well-meaning citizens ventured that the Parkers' must be very relieved that such a vile criminal had been caught. After all, they were his nearest neighbors, and he had even lived at their house that winter. To think that they had trusted him with their children! Emily heard at least six men proclaim loudly that they had always known that Rutledge fellow was a bad one, throwing aside his upbringing to live like a savage Indian. Every unsolved crime in the territory was laid at his feet, from harassing settlers and stealing chickens to scalpings and coldblooded murders. It was all Emily could do to hold her tongue in the face of such outrageous claims. The strain of trying to be civil became too much for her, and she finally left Maggie and returned to the livery where they had left the wagon to wait.

With a start, she recognized her name being called. She raised her head and looked around.

"Zach!" she exclaimed in surprise. "I didn't hear you, I'm sorry. How have you been?"

"Never better," he said with an easy smile. "What are you doing hiding out here in the livery?"

"Oh, nothing. Maggie and I were shopping and I got tired, so I decided to wait for her here. It's quiet, and I don't have to keep up a polite chatter with the horses."

"Can I talk you into having a late lunch with me?" A wide grin accompanied his invitation.

"I wish I'd run into you sooner," Emily said sincerely, "but Maggie and I ate earlier. Besides, I don't think she'll be very much longer. She only had a few more items on her list when I left. Thank you for asking."

Zach's eyes narrowed fractionally. "Are you avoiding me, Emily?"

She looked up a little too quickly, her eyes wide. "Why would I avoid you?"

"That's what I'd like to know. Why would you?" There was a trace of bitterness in his tone that made Emily feel horribly guilty. She looked back at the horse's withers.

"I'm not avoiding you."

"I don't believe you, but I won't press you. You know how I feel about you, Emily. I don't want to frighten you, but I don't want to wait forever, either. It's hard to care for someone who keeps you at arm's length." He reached out and tipped her chin up. "Are you afraid of me, Emily, or my affections?"

She was afraid. Afraid that she had been unfair to Zach and that he would hate her when he found out about her deception. For now, however, there was nothing she could do except continue to evade the truth. "I'm not afraid of you, Zach, but your feelings for me make me a little uneasy. You know that, and you know that it doesn't mean that I don't care very much for you and consider you one of my closest friends."

He released her chin. "That isn't enough for me. I want

much more from you. You could learn to love me, you know. I'd do anything to make you happy.''

"Please, Zach," she pleaded softly. She couldn't meet his gaze. "I'm sorry. Why don't we have lunch another day.''

"Another day," Zach finally agreed. "By the way, I was sorry to hear about Rutledge. You must have been upset when he was arrested. I mean, you must have gotten to know him pretty well this winter with him staying with you folks. Probably came as quite a shock.'' There was no censure in his expression, only concern.

"Yes, it did," Emily conceded, grateful for Zach's restraint from judgment. When she said nothing further, he continued.

"Well, just remember, if you ever need anything, you can rely on me, Emily. I'll do anything I can.'' He held her gaze intently for a long moment. "Anything," he added before he walked away.

It wasn't difficult for Emily to decide on a plan to rescue Drew, as she'd given the matter considerable thought over the past week. She would go in the early hours before dawn, when there was the least activity at the fort. She felt certain that she could distract the guard at the cell door and get his keys to Drew if she could only take care of the officer on duty in the room that served as the stockade's office. And then she would need a diversion outside so she and Drew could ride away unnoticed. One other person was all that was really needed, but she didn't know who would help her. All of her friends were either inaccessible or actively working against her.

Then she remembered Zach's words. If she ever needed anything, he had told her, she had to but ask. Would he help her break Drew out of the Fort Meade prison? Would that be asking too much of him? She had hope in Zach because he had proved such a loyal friend. His quiet support had often seen her through trying times with Drew, and he'd never pressed for more than she had been willing to give. Emily sat down on her bed again and thought about the idea.

She decided that in all fairness to Zach, if she were to ask for his help she'd have to tell him that she and Drew were married. Then, if he had no wish to become involved, she could hardly blame him. It would put him in an awkward position, but at length, when she could think of no one else to go to, she decided that Drew's life was more than worth the risk. If there were anyone else, she wouldn't ask Zach, but in such desperate circumstances, she had to act quickly.

Her decision made, Emily dressed quickly in her riding habit. She braided her hair and wound it into a knot at the back of her head. On her way out, she picked up a leather bag and stuffed her jeans and an old shirt into it. She pulled open the top drawer of her dresser and picked up the pistol that Drew had given her when he left. It was cold and heavy in her palm. When he had handed it to her, Drew had said he hoped she never needed it. Shaking her head, Emily picked up a handful of shells and placed the gun and ammunition in her saddlebag before leaving the room.

Not wishing to run into Maggie or the children, she slipped out of the house and ran to the barn where she quickly saddled her horse and put a bridle on the pony Long Feather had sent last fall as a wedding present. Drew would need a mount.

Luck was with her, and she made it out of the corral without seeing anyone. It was about four in the afternoon, and she thought she should be able to make it to Zach's sawmill well before dark, even considering that she didn't know exactly where it was. She had a good idea, and she knew which cutoff from the main trail through Boulder Park to take.

Emily saw several other riders, but no one she recognized on her way through Boulder Canyon. It was with relief that she turned up the steep trail that would lead her to Zach's mill.

After ten minutes, the sounds of machinery and men's voices reached Emily through the trees. She immediately veered off the trail into the woods where she would not meet anyone. The fewer people who saw her, the better.

In another minute, she could see a clearing beside the creek and the large mill building. Emily dismounted and sat down on a rock behind a screen of bushes to wait until the other men had left.

She didn't have to wait long.

The lowering sun cast weird shadows among the high log piles. The hills of sawdust threw huge, dark shadows like mountains across the clearing, and the hiss from the boiler still punctuated the cool air. Emily stopped at the mill entrance and peered in, squinting in the gloom.

"Zach?" she called tentatively. "Zach? Are you in here?" She took a step into the mill.

A man's form emerged from the shadows at the other end of the spacious mill.

"Emily? Is that you?" Zach's voice called out. He walked quickly toward her. When the light caught his face, Emily saw that he was smiling. "What a nice surprise to see you here."

"Good evening, Zach," she began, suddenly unsure of how to broach the reason for her visit. "This is quite an impressive operation," she observed, glancing around her.

"I'm glad you approve," he said evenly.

He was in his shirtsleeves, and a light dusting of pine shavings covered his dark hair. He ran a hand quickly through his hair, shaking it clean. His brown eyes held the same excited light that they had the other day in town. Emily hesitated long enough for Zach to pick up the conversation.

"What are you doing out here? Not that I'm not happy to see you, Emily, but I somehow doubt that you came all this way, and with two horses, just to inspect my business," he added, flashing a smile.

Emily looked at the ground guiltily before answering.

"You're right, I do have a particular reason for coming here. I . . . I don't know how to begin really, but do you remember a few days ago when you told me that if I ever needed help with anything, I could feel free to ask you?" She looked at him now, her eyes pleading for understanding.

Zach nodded. "I meant that, Emily. Do you need my help? Is that why you're here?" he asked.

"Yes, it is. You're the only person I could think of who can help me, Zach. You've been such a kind friend since I came to the hills. What I'm going to ask, though, may be too much, even for you, and if it is, I'll understand." She paused, seeking reassurance in his warm eyes.

"Go on," he coaxed. "Tell me what I can do to help you."

"I want to help Drew escape from the Fort Meade stockade, and I can't do it by myself." She noticed Zach draw his shoulders back, but she didn't look at his face. "Before you answer, though, I feel that I have to be honest with you about my relationship with Drew. This winter, I'm ashamed to admit that we lied to you when we pretended that there was nothing between us."

Zach became very still. Emily forced herself to continue, her eyes glued to her hands.

"We're very much in love, Zach. In fact, we were married in a secret ceremony last November when it became apparent that Sam and Maggie couldn't get back and Drew would be spending the winter with us. So you see why I can't stand by and see him hanged for crimes he didn't commit. He's my husband. Someone is trying to frame him, and there's nothing I can do except help him escape." She stopped before she lost control of her emotions. "Will you help me, Zach?" she whispered.

When Zach didn't reply, Emily looked up at him. What she saw, however, chased all thoughts from her mind. Zach's expression bore no resemblance to the smiling friend she had faced but moments ago. His face was contorted by rage, and his eyes flashed with vengeance and fury. Emily gasped and took a step backward.

Zach reached for her arm with lightning speed and pulled her toward him.

"You married him?" he asked coldly.

Emily nodded.

"And now you want me to help you break him out of the fort prison?"

Emily could see that she'd made a terrible mistake to

ask Zach. "I'm sorry, Zach, I shouldn't have asked. I see that now. If you'll let go of me, I'll leave."

"No, you won't," he said sharply. "How could you come here, knowing how I feel about you, Emily, knowing that I've been in love with you from the first minute I saw you, and that I've patiently waited for you to accept my love and hoped that maybe, maybe someday, if I were truly lucky, you might learn to care for me in return? How could you come here, telling me that you're married to Drew Rutledge, and ask me sweetly to help you rescue him so the two of you can live happily ever after?" Zach asked smoothly, his voice curiously not reflecting the wrath in his expression.

Emily was suddenly very frightened. As she looked into Zach's face, she remembered many little things she had noticed over the months: the fleeting possessiveness in his eyes, always quickly shielded, his evident dislike of Drew, a certain elusive intensity that disappeared whenever she began to attend to it. Then, in a rush, she remembered the day last September when Zach had found her at Pine Ridge. She remembered him riding toward her on his sorrel stallion, and she recalled her inexplicable fear before recognizing Zach. Looking into his face now, with the smiling mask replaced by twisting hatred, Emily knew him for who he was.

"You!" she breathed incredulously. "You're the man who's been organizing Canadian hostiles to attack the army!"

Chapter 24

Zach looked surprised for an instant. Then he laughed softly, and his eyebrows raised in appreciation. "Very clever, Emily. Since you bring it up, I won't deny it. But you do understand why I can't help you."

She was startled by his ready admission. "Then it was you who put the stolen army guns in Drew's caves and arranged things so that Colonel Reynolds had to arrest him!" Revulsion swept through her with this realization, and she tried to pull away from him. His fingers bit into her wrist, holding her firmly. "Why did you do it? What did he ever do to hurt you?"

"Oh, he's done plenty, my dear. But for Drew Rutledge I'd have had those Indian renegades on the warpath last summer. By now, they and all their peaceful red cousins on the agencies would have been wiped from the face of the earth by the U.S. Army, and I'd have been a rich man profiting off the increased white immigration into the territory. And then, of course there is you, Emily. That bastard Rutledge turned your head so fast I never had a chance, but I always knew I'd have you in the end. And here you are." He smirked.

"You did all this for money? Just for money, you were going to exterminate an entire people?" Emily gasped, horrified.

"And for you, Emily," he replied with sickening sweetness. "I could give you the best of everything. I may have suffered a few delays, but there's really nothing to stop me."

"I'll stop you, by God, or I'll die trying!" she exclaimed, wrenching violently to escape him. Zach pinned her arms easily against her back and pushed her against the mill wall, leaning his weight into her so that she couldn't kick. He chuckled.

"I doubt that very much. It would be a shame to force me to kill you, Emily, but believe me, if you leave me no other choice, I'll do it. On the other hand, I can think of many more pleasurable ways to spend our time together." He ran a finger along her jaw, then rested his thumb against her lower lip. "Ways that you might find as enjoyable as I will, once you accept that your beloved husband is not long for this world."

"Don't touch me!" she ground out between clenched teeth.

"I'm the one who's giving the orders here, in case you hadn't noticed, Emily. I suggest you speak civilly to me, or I just might forget how much I want you in a moment of anger."

Emily was terrified. Why hadn't she realized who he was? The truth had been right in front of her nose, and she had walked directly into a trap. She had to get away, or she'd never be able to help Drew. If she could only tell Colonel Reynolds or Sam what she knew, they would have to release Drew. She realized suddenly that Drew must have suspected Zach for some time, probably since they had met him on the reservation. How she wished he had told her! For the moment, though, her immediate concern was with finding a way to escape Zach.

"In fact, Emily," Zach was continuing, the false smile spreading across his features, "I think we should take this opportunity to get to know each other a little better. As you're an experienced woman now, I see no reason to wait any longer. After all, I've already been waiting for months, and you feel so soft and inviting. Finally—"

"Well, well, what have we got here, Stevens? Takin' a little time off work, are ya?" A man wearing a Seventh Cavalry officer's uniform walked toward them. Emily recalled that his name was Logan. She'd seen him several times at Fort Meade.

"What are you doing here?" Zach snapped brusquely, not shifting his pose. Emily was uncomfortably aware of Lieutenant Logan's pale blue eyes resting on her.

"One of our contacts is camped out on Alkali Creek waitin' for our first delivery, and I heard a little gossip that I thought might interest ya, Stevens." Logan answered. "Seems your favorite Indian friend had his uncle, the United States senator, organize a pardon, signed by President Garfield himself. It arrived by special messenger today, so the colonel would appear to be buildin' the case to release him. Of a bit more interest, though, word at the telegraph office is that the commissioner of Indian Affairs himself is on a train west right now. It could prove inconvenient, if ya know what I mean, but if we move fast enough, we can be finished wi' Rutledge before the commissioner gets here. And get our deliveries completed if we're lucky."

"Damn!" Zach swore.

"Aye," Logan agreed. "Looks like we didn't figure on a dog who lives with the Sioux havin' so many high-placed connections. Sneaky, that Rutledge is, damn sneaky. I thought for sure he was a free-lancer."

"What are you talking about?" Emily demanded, her attention riveted on the bandy officer. "What do you mean that Drew is a free-lancer? What is this all about? Tell me!"

Logan laughed at her. "Looks like Rutledge has a close mouth even in his bed," he commented to Zach.

Zach was so close to her that she could feel his breath on her face when he spoke. "I find it hard to believe that you know nothing about your husband's work, Emily. That hardly indicates a trusting relationship, does it?"

"He didn't tell me anything in order to protect me! He kept saying it was too dangerous for me to know what he was doing," she said, struggling to no avail to place a little distance between herself and Zach.

"Relax, my dear, I'm not letting you go, and I won't tell you what you want to know until you stand still."

Emily ceased squirming at once.

"That's better. Well, as I'm sure you gathered from the

lieutenant, you married into a prominent Boston family, one member of whom is a U.S. senator, no less. We fully expected the pardon for Rutledge on the charges that he aided the hostile Indian camps, but we did think that Reynolds would have a harder time ignoring the guns found in the caves. Even a senator's nephew wouldn't be likely to be pardoned for organizing a full-scale Indian war, and without another suspect in custody, Rutledge is as good as dead. Unfortunately, we didn't have confirmation until now that your dear husband works directly for the commissioner of Indian Affairs. He managed to keep that under his hat most effectively. And that complicates the picture somewhat, although government agents are far from immune to corruption, because if it becomes broadly known that he was working for the commissioner, some influential people may begin to doubt Rutledge's guilt. There will be other plausible explanations for his actions besides criminal intent, and he will have powerful advocates.''

"What do you mean, he works for the commissioner?" Emily asked, puzzled.

"I mean he's an in-house spy. He keeps tabs on the agents and other government officials involved with the Indians. We miscalculated slightly, assuming that he worked alone on behalf of the Sioux, using whatever resources he could muster. But rest assured this is only a minor error. All we have to do is set our mob in action before the commissioner gets here, and Rutledge will be out of the way for good. We're ready to begin delivering weapons and ammunition to the Sioux who've thrown in their lot with us, so within a few weeks, all hell will break loose in the territory, commissioner or no commissioner. Then all we do is sit back and watch the army slaughter the Sioux. Rather simple, isn't it?''

Emily didn't respond. It was staggering to contemplate that she had trusted this man as her friend. Miserably, she realized too late that Colonel Reynolds was holding Drew for his own safety, after having been manipulated into arresting him, to keep him out of the hands of angry men who would kill him without asking if he were guilty or not. Using bureaucratic procedures as an excuse to gain time, Reynolds had set about gathering the evidence necessary to clear Drew. If only she had known! Instead, she had needlessly put herself in the worst possible danger and increased the threat to Drew's life in the process.

"She doesn't look too happy, Stevens. Maybe ya have plans to cheer her up a mite?" Logan snickered.

"That will have to wait, I'm afraid. I need to get out to Alkali Creek."

"What will you do with the girl?"

"Get some rope from downstairs. We can leave her tied up in the storeroom here. I don't want to take any chances."

Logan left the office quickly. Zach turned back to face Emily.

"I hope you won't be too terribly uncomfortable, Emily, but I'll be back in the morning when we can resume, ah, business?" he said. "That will give you something to look forward to through the night," he added with a nasty chuckle.

"You are the most repulsive, vile man I have ever met, Zach Stevens. Hasn't it been a strain keeping up the pretense of being a law-abiding member of the community?"

"Not everything is an act, Emily. Some of us simply don't have the simpleminded straightforwardness that is so prized by our society. We could be happy together, you and I." Logan reentered the room carrying a coil of rope. "Think about your other options," he advised confidently while Lieutenant Logan bound her feet.

Sam banged unceremoniously on the front door of the Reynoldses' quarters. The housekeeper opened the door with a disapproving frown, then smiled when she saw Sam.

"Is the colonel in? I need to talk to him right away," Sam said, brushing past her into the hall. Matt came out of the parlor at that moment.

"It's all right, Mrs. Willy," he said, excusing the housekeeper. "What is it, Sam?"

"Emily disappeared late this afternoon, I'm not sure exactly when, with two horses, one of them our Indian pony. It looks like she's planning to get Drew out of the stockade, and I wanted to let you know. I don't want her to get hurt," Sam told him quietly.

Matt Reynolds frowned. "This whole business has to have been hell for her," he said, shaking his head. "I'll see that she isn't hurt if I have to sit down there all night myself," he promised.

"You going to tell Rutledge?" Sam asked.

"Yeah, I suppose I will. He's not going to be pleased."

Sam managed a weak smile. "Better you than me telling him. I'm supposed to be looking after her for him. If anything happens to Emily I hate to think what he'd do."

"Thanks for letting me know, Sam," the colonel said.

"I'm going to see if I can't find Black Wolf and put him on her trail. If he can find her, maybe he can talk her out of anything rash," Sam said, his hand on the door.

"Good idea," Matt agreed.

Drew tossed and turned on his narrow bed. A sense of foreboding had settled over him when Colonel Reynolds relayed the news that Emily was missing and that her brother feared she would foolishly try to help him escape from jail. He wished fervently that he'd told her that no formal charges would be brought against him. He wondered why she'd left that afternoon, when Sam and Maggie were sure to note her absence. Where was she now? What was she planning? Surely she didn't think she could pull off a jailbreak alone, but who would she get to help her? Drew stared at the dark walls of his cell, trying to pinpoint the exact source of his unease. Absently, he flexed his injured shoulder, testing the muscles, noting that it was still a bit stiff. He glanced out the tiny window at the stars wheeling by in their nightly procession. It was past midnight. He resigned himself to no sleep until Emily came. If she came.

He lay on the ground, blood streaming from his chest, yet, curiously, he felt strong. He looked up. Large, dark eyes locked with his. In the firelight, they glowed with the colors of the earth, forest greens and browns. He recog-

nized the eyes. He had seen them many times before, the first time by the waterfall, so long ago. Never, though, had he seen such pain in them. Tears streamed down her face.

He looked around him. He saw the huge red stallion, and he remembered. He looked down at his chest and saw the arrow shaft protruding from his breast. The masked rider was not looking at him now, but at the girl. Reaching down with his beak, the eagle plucked the arrow from his own breast, and before his eyes, he watched the wound close and the blood cease to flow. He looked around again. Where were the people? Had they all left? No! There they were, just beyond the shadows. They were watching the rider.

The Mask Wearer, laughed triumphantly as he rode toward the woman. She didn't move but stared at him in horror. Then the mask began to slip. The eagle saw it fall to the ground, but the rider's back was to him. The woman gasped. He felt a warm breath on him and looked up at the buffalo. With its breath, his power returned, and he spread his wings and rose again into the air with a great rushing sound. The woman's gaze left the rider when she saw him, and wonder filled her eyes. The rider turned. His unmasked face was terrifying. It was a jumbled puzzle of open sores, horns, and misshapen features. Some parts were well formed and would have been fair had they stood alone, but the combination was horrible. The rider drew his bow and faced the eagle once again. Determination and hatred lit his eyes, and his cruel laughter echoed in the night.

The eagle flew in the rider's face, but he was beaten back with the bow. The rider's arrows spilled on the ground, but he pulled a knife from his belt to slash at the beating wings in his face. They struggled fiercely, neither able to stop the other, each growing more determined to end their combat victoriously. The intensity of their blows increased, but the rider did not weaken. His hatred burned furiously, and he fought with the strength of many. The eagle felt his wound begin to pain him. He threw himself ever more vigorously into his attack, but he knew he had

*not the strength to win alone. Yet he must endure, he must
protect the people from the rider. He must!*

"Rutledge! Wake up!" the guard hollered. "Keep it
down in there! What the hell is going on?"

Drew jumped to his feet, disoriented. It was still dark.
He was in his cell. A quick glance at the window told him
that it was less than two hours before dawn. The guard
was standing at his door. Then the images from the dream
hit him again.

He clutched his shoulder, gasped, and collapsed onto
the floor, moaning and breathing with great difficulty.

"What the—?" the young guard exclaimed in alarm.
"Hang on, I'm coming in."

He fumbled for his keys and unlocked the door. He had
come to like Rutledge and respect him as an honest man,
no matter what the charges were against him. Pushing into
the cell, he left the door ajar in his haste to see what was
wrong. He knelt on the floor beside the gasping prisoner
and put out a hand to pull back his shoulder for a better
view. Drew appeared to flinch, but in the next instant, he
delivered a numbing blow to the young man's head. The
guard sagged against him, whereupon Drew quickly lifted
him onto the cot, gagged him, and secured his handcuffs
to the bed frame. He relieved the guard of his revolvers
and keys, automatically checking to see that the guns were
loaded. Then he stepped silently through the door, locking
it behind him.

Drew crept down the corridor toward the small office.
The man on duty there was sitting behind the desk sleeping with his feet propped on a trash basket. Drew slipped
the sleeping man's gun out of his holster and tucked it into
the back of his pants. Then he pressed the muzzle of one
of the other pistols against the guard's forehead and
thumbed back the trigger. The guard's eyes popped open,
and he began to protest. Pulling the man's arm up behind
him in a sudden motion, Drew whispered into his ear.

"I don't want to hurt you, but I will if you don't co-
operate. I have to get out of here fast, and I know the

colonel is outside somewhere. Do you have a signal to get his attention?''

The frightened guard nodded.

"What is it?''

"I wave my cap in the window by the door. Twice.''

"Don't worry. I won't tell the colonel I caught you sleeping on duty.'' Drew chuckled softly.

"Are you going to kill him? And me?'' the guard asked in a strangled whisper.

"Not if you shut up and don't waste any more of my time talking,'' Drew growled. Then he whipped the revolver around and brought the butt down against the man's skull. Linking his arms around the man's chest, he hauled him back toward the nearest cell and locked him inside. Drew took the guard's cap with him and returned to the outer room. Stooping low, he crossed to the window and waved the cap, hoping the guard hadn't lied. Then he positioned himself behind the door to wait.

When Matt Reynolds cautiously stepped through the door a few minutes later, Drew pushed one of his guns into his ribs and whirled him against the wall, deftly disarming him before the colonel realized what was happening. Drew slipped the second guard's handcuffs onto Matt's wrists behind his back.

"I'm sorry about this, Reynolds, and I wouldn't do it if I thought for a minute that you'd let me out of here any other way,'' Drew said quietly, pushing his friend into a chair. He pulled a handkerchief from the colonel's pocket and tied it across his mouth. "Emily isn't coming for me tonight, but I'm afraid she's in trouble. I had one of those dreams you don't place too much stock in.'' Matt rolled his eyes and grunted. "I think Stevens may have Emily, so I'm going to the mill. If you're not too put out with me for being such an ungrateful guest, you might think about sending a patrol up that way once you're loose again. I only hope I'm not too late.''

A few more rapid movements, and the colonel was securely bound to the chair. Matt regarded him doubtfully.

"Now I know how you felt when you arrested me, Matt. Sometimes circumstances force our hand. I'm afraid I'm going to be forced to borrow a horse, too. See you later, I hope," Drew said as he slipped out the door into the night.

Again she watched the eagle drop to the earth, pierced through the breast. The rider advanced confidently, blocking the fallen eagle from her view. His mask, so at odds with his tormenting laughter, began to slip. Slowly, it slid from his face to the ground, revealing his true features below. She gasped, her eyes widening at the ghastly spectacle of twisted flesh before her. What kind of malice had created such a visage? It was terrible to behold.

Then, to her amazement, a dark shape rose behind the rider, and the thunder of beating wings drowned out the wild laughter. The eagle! He wasn't dead. He looked strong and powerful, and the rider turned toward him, his face gruesomely twisted with rage. He reached for the bow, then for his arrows, but the bird dashed them to the ground as he flew into the rider's face. The rider swung the bow, and it landed heavily across the eagle's right wing, but it didn't stop him. On and on they fought, the great bird rising high in the air to swoop low, razor-sharp talons first, the rider rearing back, encouraging his horse to kick with powerful hooves, swinging the bow like a club and using it as a shield. She watched in horror as the eagle began to weaken. His wound had left him weak, and he would not last against the rider's furious strength.

Then the rider reached to his belt and drew a knife, the blade glinting bright and cold in the red firelight. When the knife slipped free, something else fell to the ground, something gray and heavy. She darted to pick it up. It was a gun. She knew how to shoot. She picked it up and trained it on the rider. If only he would stay in one place long enough, she would kill him. She would help the eagle. But the rider kept moving, and she grew more and more tense, afraid to pull the trigger lest she wound the bird a second time.

Suddenly, the gun exploded in her hands. She watched in surprise as the rider fell from his saddle, blood pouring from his heart. His face changed as he landed in the dirt

*at her feet, and all the warped features coalesced into the
once handsome face of a man she had known as a friend.*

Emily awoke screaming, her heart pounding furiously.
She couldn't move, and she began to panic. Something
was confining her arms and legs, and she kept bumping
into things. The sharp pain in her arms finally forced her
to sit still, and she remembered where she was. With dismay, Emily realized that she had slept through the night
and that it was dawn. Zach would return at any time, and
she hadn't freed herself. And she had dreamed again. Oh,
God, such a horrible dream! She choked back a sob. What
had Long Feather said? That she would have the strength
to do what she must, but she had never thought she could
kill a man. Would she be able to do it? Even to save
Drew? Uncertainty and a wasting sense of inadequacy
flooded her.

She heard voices coming from outside, and her heart
went chill. It was Zach and Lieutenant Logan. She could
dimly hear the sounds of horses, doors being opened and
shut, and then the clanking of pipes and machinery. Long
minutes passed before she heard footsteps on the stairway,
then along the open platform that led to the storage room
where she sat. Her blood froze in her veins.

There was a soft click as the key turned in the lock.
Zach pushed open the door and squeezed into the cramped
room. He smiled broadly when his eyes met Emily's.

"Good morning, my dear. I trust you slept better last
night than I did," he said cheerfully. He crossed the short
distance between them and lifted Emily by her shoulders.
Her feet were so numb from lack of movement that she
stumbled against him. His arms slipped instantly around
her waist to support her.

"If you untie my feet, I can walk by myself," she
pointed out acidly.

"I can see that sleep hasn't improved your temper any.
No matter," he replied, stooping to cut the cords at her
feet with his knife. "One of the things I like about you is
your spirit."

"Aren't you going to untie my hands?" she snapped,

stepping from one foot to the other to start the blood flowing to her feet again.

Zach looked at her hard, then shrugged.

"I guess it won't hurt. There's no one here, and nowhere for you to go. By the time the Sunday crew gets here, we'll be long gone." He stepped behind her to free her hands. "If you try to run from me or make a move for one of my weapons, you will be very, very sorry, I promise you," he whispered in her ear.

"Where are we going?" she asked, ignoring his threat.

"I imagine that you would prefer that I make love to you in a bed rather than here in the mill, and I find that this morning, I'm of a similar mind myself." Emily cringed at his words. "So we are going to my bed, Emily darling."

She didn't reply, but she felt the blood drain from her face.

Emily tripped and stumbled along behind Zach on the platform that overlooked the mill works. The great doors were still shut, and somewhere in the darkness she could hear Logan moving about. He met them at the bottom of the stairs, using a dirty rag to wipe hands smeared with coal dust.

"Boiler's fired up and ready to go, Zach. Mind if I take some of that yellow pine back to the fort?" Logan asked with a meaningful glance at Emily. "Good wood for a coffin," he added with a snicker.

Zach laughed with him. "Take all you need for such a worthy cause," he offered magnanimously.

Emily could hardly control her rage. Zach callously joked about killing Drew, her husband, one second, then expected her to fall into his arms the next. It was worse than any of her nightmares. She looked frantically about, desperate to escape. Through a dirty window, she saw Zach's sorrel, just outside the door. Casting her fears to the winds, Emily decided to make a run for the horse.

A soft voice stopped her.

Chapter 25

❝ **S** ounds like you folks are set on going to a funeral,'' Drew said conversationally. ''Wouldn't
happen to be anyone I know, now, would it?''

Zach laughed delightedly, but he pulled Emily close in
front of him and slid his gun from its holster.

''Drew! Thank God!'' she cried in relief. She searched
the gloomy mill for him but couldn't see him.

''What the hell? How'd he get here?'' Logan exclaimed
in surprise, drawing his pistol and spinning around.

''That doesn't really matter,'' Zach observed with cold
amusement. ''The real question is, how will he leave?
Perhaps in the same wagon with the boards to build his
coffin. How fitting, though not quite the spectacular end I
had envisioned for the great white warrior of the Lakota.
Which would you prefer Rutledge? A public, albeit not
very official, hanging for treason, or the unfortunate death
of an escaped criminal in the course of recapture?''

''The latter makes you more of a hero, Stevens,'' Drew
taunted, his voice coming from a different part of the shadows. ''It'd get you lots of press, probably some nice civic
award from the sheriff.''

Logan fired a shot in the direction of Drew's voice. The
bullet passed harmlessly through the outer mill wall, leaving a gap where sunlight streamed into the dim interior.
Blue gunsmoke spiraled upward, mixing with the dust
motes sparkling in the bright rays that streaked above their
heads.

Drew spoke again, from yet another position.

"Then again, it's messier to kill me yourself. Sort of goes contrary to your usual style of having other folks do your dirty work for you. Might make folks think you aren't as refined and gentlemanly as you want them to."

Emily felt Zach stiffen. Another shot exploded, this time the bullet crashing into one of the wall studs, splintering it. Logan narrowed his eyes, sweeping the large room in a vain attempt to locate his target. Emily's eyes followed his gaze, praying that Drew would keep out of sight. The night before she hadn't really looked at the room, but now she saw that it was a big rectangle with wide doors, still shut, at either end. In the center, there was a saw pit and a bank of control switches that operated the steam-driven saws, planes, sanders, and belts that moved the lumber from one machine to the other. The raised platform that supported the office and storeroom was at her back, and there were worktables and stacks of lumber in varying stages of completion piled neatly throughout the building. At the far end of the room, a huge metal boiler hissed and clanged as it heated up for the day. The ceiling was high, and the morning sun was just beginning to throw blinding rays through a couple of east windows, high up on the unfinished walls. Drew could be concealed behind any number of objects, for the mill was full of wood and machinery, all casting eerie, odd-shaped shadows in the half light.

"You're just wasting your bullets," Zach told Logan with some impatience. "He's not going to let you touch him until he comes into the open. *If* he's got the guts to come out into the open. He's just like his damn, sneaking redskin friends, skulking about in the shadows," he added derisively.

Logan looked at Zach apprehensively. "I've fought with Indians before, Stevens. They may sneak around, but it ain't out of cowardice."

"Logan, you're the stinking coward," Zach said coldly. "Get the hell out of here if you're so scared of one foolhardy bastard who likes to pretend he's an Indian when he's really a goddamn Eastern lawyer just like all those asinine politicians in Washington who want to tell us how to run our territory. Go on! Leave!'' he yelled. ''I'll handle this myself, but I'll also handle you when I'm through.''

Emily watched the sweat pour off Logan, despite the chill in the air. He was clearly torn between his fear of the two men, both of whom were far stronger and more driven than he.

A shot resounded in the empty mill. Logan fell to the ground, gripping his right arm and screaming in pain. More shots followed rapidly. Zach raced to a table, flipped it on its side, and dropped behind it, taking Emily with him. He pressed the cold barrel of his gun into her ribs.

''Knock it off, or I'll shoot Emily, Rutledge,'' Zach shouted.

Logan writhed on the dusty floor, his entire right arm dark with blood.

''Get on out of here, Logan,'' Drew called. ''If I ever see you again and you're not on the gallows already, I'll slit your gut open and let you watch your innards spill into the dirt, your life slipping away with them, just as you would have watched the Lakota slip away into oblivion.''

Logan scrambled for the door without a second thought. Within seconds, hoofbeats broke the silent morning, then faded rapidly.

''All right, Rutledge, you've got yourself a fair fight now. But to reach me, you're going to have to go around your pretty little wife, or should I say your soon-to-be widow?'' Zach sneered.

''Let her go, Stevens. This is between you and me. You know you don't want Emily hurt anymore than I do,'' Drew answered. Every time he spoke, his voice seemed to come from a different corner of the room.

''No, you're right. I don't want her hurt, but I do want her to see me defeat you.''

Drew said nothing. Emily wondered what he was doing and where he was. If he had a plan, she must be alert and ready to act on a split second's notice.

Zach hauled Emily to her feet and ran across a short open area to the shelter of a stack of newly cut siding. The double doors that led into the lumberyard were at their backs. Drew made no sound or movement. Zach spoke again, his voice full of bitterness, cold and disdainful.

"You've probably always had everything go your way, Rutledge, but your luck has run out. There's no rich family here to bail you out and smooth the way for you, no powerful relatives to save your neck, no filthy Indians to scare everyone for you, nobody but you. Alone. Have you ever done anything alone in your whole goddamn life, Rutledge? You like to pretend that you're a loner, but you're always surrounded by people who look out for you. You've never built anything yourself, done anything on your own. You didn't even court Emily by yourself! You had her family and those thieving red vermin you call your relatives all acting on your behalf. Even that old windbag Red Cloud, for God's sake!

"But now it's time, Rutledge. Now you're facing me alone, and you haven't beat me yet. You *can't* beat me. I'm strong, stronger than you are because I've done everything alone."

Suddenly, the doors behind them flew open with a noisy crash. Zach whirled to face them, Emily still clamped to his side. Zach fired four shots in quick succession through the doors. There was no one there. Light spilled into the mill from the empty yard beyond. Emily heard a meadowlark call, its jubilant song hopelessly out of step with the scene inside the mill.

A shot rang out, the bullet whizzing just over Zach's head. They spun again, this time facing the banks of machinery and lumber. Zach pulled Emily directly in front of him.

"Nice shot, Rutledge. But today bullets won't hit me. One of the few Indian tricks I thought worth learning. Try again if you like." Emily could hear the confident grin in his voice.

Zach stepped out into the small clear area in front of the saw pit, chuckling with perverted amusement.

"I think I've had about enough of these hide and seek games. Show yourself, Rutledge. It's time we face each other squarely. Face me like a man," he challenged.

"No!" Emily screamed. "Don't! He'll—"

In that instant, Drew hurled himself at them from the railing of the office platform. He crashed into them, throwing them to the floor. Emily jerked free of Zach's hold, and his gun thudded to the ground. Before she could grab it, his fingers closed over the butt. Drew reached to stay Zach's hand.

"Emily, get back!" he shouted. "Run!"

She obeyed immediately, scrambling to her feet and backing toward the shelter of the overturned table. She hesitated when Zach brought his knee up hard into Drew's stomach. Drew slammed his fist under Zach's chin, driving his head back into the dirt. The gun in his hand, Zach tried to turn the barrel toward Drew, who delivered a bone-crushing blow to Zach's forearm. The gun went off with a roar, and Emily screamed, fearful that Drew had been hit. Instead, he knocked the gun from Zach's grasp, and it scuttled across the floor. Emily raced to where it lay and picked it up, raising the barrel under her left hand, ready to shoot.

"Stop it!" she shouted. "I have the gun."

The images from her dream wove in and out with reality before her eyes. Drew and Zach seemed unaware of her, rolling over each other, pummeling one another viciously. She was afraid that if she fired, she would hit Drew. The two men were evenly matched in build and strength. Then Zach thrust his elbow solidly into Drew's left shoulder. Drew gasped for breath, and his face went white for an instant as the pain shot through the still stiff muscles near the healed bullet wound. His grip slackened, and Zach leaped to his feet, grabbing a long two-by-four that was propped against a post. He laughed wickedly and raised the beam above his head. He stood directly over Drew.

"Drew!" Emily shouted, frozen by fear, forgetting the gun in her hands in the split second it took Drew to jump to his feet.

Drew reached out and found a club of his own. Zach moved back and forth like a tiger stalking its prey, keeping Drew between himself and the wavering gun in Emily's grasp. He feinted at Drew with the staff, laughing cruelly. Finally he brought a heavy blow down on Drew's injured shoulder, following it with a rapid thrust that pushed him backward toward the saw pit.

Drew stumbled against the machinery panel that hung from the central building supports. All at once noise filled the air, the whirring, whining, inhuman sounds of rapidly spinning metal blades and the loud hiss of steam. In an instant, Zach was upon him again, raining hard blows on his upper body, targeting his head. He managed to deflect the worst of the onslaught with his own stick, but his shoulder wasn't strong enough to give him the power he needed to strike with enough force to drive Zach back.

Emily watched in horror as Zach pushed Drew ever closer to the screaming machinery. She hovered just beyond the men, trying desperately now to get a clear shot at Zach. It was apparent that he intended to push Drew into the saw pit. If he went down, one blow to his head could spell his death. It was like her dream. She would have to shoot Zach. Fear for Drew's life pushed her to be resolute, though the bile rose in her throat.

Drew's club split suddenly with a crack that echoed above the whine of the saws. Pieces flew backward into the tangle of steel and rotating blades, shattering into splinters when they hit the deadly saw teeth. Small fragments of wood were thrown in a wide arc around the mill. Almost before Zach realized that Drew was without his weapon, Drew threw himself inside Zach's swing, caught him around the waist, and drove him into the post that supported the control panel. As Zach's head snapped back up against the uneven surface, covered with dials, knobs, and gauges, Drew saw one large gauge with the needle pressing into a red warning zone. Below it in neat block letters were the words BOILER PRESSURE.

"Emily! Get out of here! The boiler may explode," Drew shouted at her.

Drew was weakening, and he had no weapon. He threw one of the empty revolvers at Zach, clipping him in the jaw and opening a long red welt. Zach swung back hard with the beam.

Drew caught it just in time to stop it hitting under his chin. Ignoring the gut-wrenching pain in his left shoulder, he jerked the piece of wood out of Zach's grip and swung it so that he held it across his body. In one rapid, powerful motion, he thrust forward with all his strength, feeling the muscles tear in his shoulder, catching Zach across the chest with the blow and driving him backward once again. Drew put all his weight into the beam, and Zach fell back several feet, landing heavily on his back in the dust. Drew himself stumbled to one knee, carried by his own momentum.

"Zach!" Emily screamed over the din. "Zach, stop! I'll shoot!"

She should shoot now, she knew, but something held her back.

"Go ahead, Emily. Shoot, if you can," he laughed. He rose, panting. "Shoot me!" he bellowed over the roar and hiss, his dark eyes glittering triumphantly.

She leveled the gun at Zach's chest with a cold and sudden certainty and squeezed the trigger.

Zach fell to his knees, a startled look on his face, as if he hadn't thought she would ever do it. His hands clutched his chest, and a bright red stain seeped through his shirt. He looked up at her in amazement, his mouth open, his eyes wide with disbelief.

Emily stared in confusion. There had been no explosion, no recoil when she pulled the trigger. There was no smoke coming from the barrel of the pistol. There had only been a tiny click, lost in the noise around her. There were no bullets left in the chamber.

A trickle of blood appeared at the corner of Zach's mouth, and he jerked convulsively. The look of baffled incredulity faded as his eyes glazed and his face settled into its final mask. His body toppled forward. Emily stared at him, uncomprehending.

Zachary Stevens's back was pierced full of feathered arrows from his shoulders to his waist.

Emily tore her eyes from the gruesome sight, seeking Drew. He, too, was staring in disbelief. Then a high-pitched wail began to build to a screaming pitch. Drew's eyes flew to the steam gauge. It was past the red area, past extreme danger.

He leaped to Emily's side and pushed her toward the

open doors. They ran hard, into the yard, the screaming hiss of steam all around them. Drew pointed to a large pile of huge ponderosa pine logs, and they scurried behind it. Drew pushed Emily onto the ground and threw himself on top of her.

There was a tremendous roar and crash and a bright flash of flame, followed by a billowing cloud of scalding steam. The ground shook, and the logs beside them bounced slightly. Some of the smaller log piles clattered to the ground, and bits of burning wood and hot metal rained down all over the yard. Gradually, it subsided, leaving only the dull roar of flames and the acrid smell of smoke hanging in the clearing.

"Are you all right?" Drew asked anxiously, lifting his head and raising himself on his elbows above Emily.

"I think so," she answered, her voice weak. "What about you?"

Drew's face was swollen, and blood oozed from cuts on his face and arms. His shirt was torn, and he was covered with dust and soot. He stretched a little and prodded gingerly at his left shoulder.

"No permanent damage," he said, though he winced.

"You look terrible," she told him, wiping at the blood on his face with her sleeve.

"Thanks."

"But, God, am I glad to see you!" she said, throwing her arms around him in a tight hug.

"Easy!" He flinched when she touched his shoulder. "I'm pretty glad to see you, too. I don't think I would have gotten out of there without you."

"I didn't do anything, and it was my fault you were there in the first place. How did you know where to find me?"

His blue eyes met hers solemnly.

"I had a dream," he said simply.

"Last night?"

He nodded.

"So did I."

A shadow passed over them, and from just above the

treetops came a shrill cry, high and piercing. An eagle's cry.

Emily shuddered and found tears springing into her eyes. Tears of relief and thankfulness. Drew buried his face in her neck and held her close until she stopped shaking. His own lashes were wet when he finally lifted his head.

"Do you think you can ride back to the fort?" he asked quietly. "I told Reynolds when I left him tied up at the stockade last night that I'd come back."

"You didn't tie him up!" Emily exclaimed in horror. "Oh, God, now they really will be able to press charges against you!"

"I don't think so. Not after everything that's happened. Reynolds wouldn't put you through it. Besides, we're even now," he added lightly. "He had to arrest me, I had to escape."

Hoofbeats sounded on the trail through the woods. Emily looked up in alarm.

"Who's that?" she asked, thinking it might be Zach's employees.

"It's okay. It's probably the patrol I asked Reynolds to send after me."

The first rider entered the yard. It was Colonel Reynolds himself. He reined in his horse and stared at the burning mill.

A thought occurred to Emily.

"Where is Black Wolf? If the soldiers see them . . ."

"He and the others are long gone. They've probably got Logan with them, but they'll turn him over to the colonel."

"How did they know to come?"

"I don't know. Maybe your brother told Black Wolf that you were missing and they tracked you. Maybe they followed me. However they got here, I'm sure as hell glad they did," he said emphatically. "We'd better let Reynolds know we're here."

Before he stood, Drew pressed a kiss to his wife's lips, a slow, sweet caress that spoke of abiding love and hopes for a bright future. For the first time since he had met her, there was nothing that could keep them apart. Despite the grief, ugliness, and fear of the morning, they had triumphed. Together, with the help of Wakantanka and the people.

A tremor shook Drew from head to feet. He rested his forehead against Emily's for a second, then rose, offering her his good arm and pulling her up beside him. They turned their backs on the smoking mill and faced the approaching cavalry and the bright morning sun.

Emily dropped the last of the weeds she had pulled from around the struggling pansies into her basket and rose, her attention drawn away from the garden by the sound of hoofbeats carrying up from the road. She wiped her hands on her apron and called to her sister-in-law in the kitchen.

"Maggie! They're back!"

As Maggie met her on the porch, Drew and Sam appeared at the gate, their faces somber.

Emily hesitated for a moment, unsure. Then Drew smiled and opened his arms to her. She ran to him, flinging herself against him. Their lips met in a quick, burning kiss.

"Well?" Maggie asked, walking to Sam's side. "What happened?"

"It's all over," Drew said, pulling Emily to his side, his arm still tight around her. "I have officially been pardoned and am free to resume a normal life. The hearing was quick, my uncle delivered the pardon in person, and that was that."

"Except for the warning," Sam interjected.

"What warning?" Emily's brow furrowed.

"My good friend the colonel told me in no uncertain terms that I'd better watch myself and forgo any and all illegal activities in the future if I want to see my children grow into long pants. He declared that I would get no more preferential treatment at his hands, that I was too much of a nuisance, and he'd see me dead before going through the indignity of being tied up in his own stockade again," Drew informed them casually. Too casually.

"Drew," Emily began in a stern voice.

"What children?" Sam inquired, interrupting her. "You got some news for us?"

"The ones we're going to get started on tonight." Drew

chuckled wickedly, looking into his wife's dark eyes. He was rewarded by a bright flush of color that swiftly mounted her cheeks.

"Drew!" she exclaimed. Sam and Maggie laughed. "What took you so long? I was so worried when you didn't come back this morning," she said to change the subject. "I kept seeing the gallows from those dreams. I've been so afraid that something else was going to happen."

The men's faces grew serious once again. "We stayed to hear the results of Logan's court martial and see if they were able to get him to name the others that helped them. He wouldn't give an inch, though. Showed a lot more fortitude than anyone figured he had. With the guns found at the mill after the explosion and the ledger in the safe, though, and his own admission to arranging for some of the guns to be placed in Drew's caves, a guilty verdict on all the charges was a foregone conclusion. We were curious about the sentence though. Unfortunately, Emily, it seems you were right about a hanging, but it isn't going to be your husband's neck in the noose."

"Oh, dear. How soon will it be?" Maggie asked, her mouth pursed.

"Tuesday at dawn," Drew added quietly, his arm tightening around Emily's waist.

They were silent for a moment. As much as Emily hated what Zach and Logan had done, she hated to see yet another death come of it. And she would never forget how easily it could have been Drew.

"You will listen to Matt and stop anything illegal, won't you?" Emily pleaded softly. "Even if it means that the Lakota . . ." She couldn't finish.

"There isn't going to be much more need for my little operation. While we were waiting, a courier from Fort Peck rode in, a man I've worked with some in the past. He told me that the Canadian refugees are coming in by the droves. The winter was too much for even the strongest of them, and Sitting Bull can't hold them with him. Word is that the old man himself is planning on surrendering to the army within a couple of months, and after that, nearly all the Lakota will be settled on one or another of the reservations.'' There was sorrow in his voice. Then he continued with renewed conviction. ''But there are things I can do, even so.''

Emily raised her eyebrows dubiously.

''Legal things,'' he assured her. ''You see, I had the most interesting conversation with my uncle and the commissioner.'' He grinned maddeningly and closed his mouth.

''I'm sure you did, and I'm also sure that you're not going to be fathering any children to nurture to adulthood if you don't tell me every word of it. I've had it with your secrets, Drew Rutledge,'' Emily said firmly but with a rueful smile.

He looked at her appraisingly for a minute, a smile playing at the corners of his mouth. ''Are you trying to blackmail me, woman?'' he queried with mock disbelief.

''No,'' she retorted briskly. ''I'm threatening you. And I'm making decisions for you. But all to protect you, you must understand. I wouldn't want to see you make a complete success of hanging yourself the next time.''

''Who asked you to butt into my life, anyhow?''

''You did. Don't you remember? You took my hand, looked at me like a sick cow, and asked me to marry you, and— Hey! What do you think you're doing? Put me down!''

Drew hoisted Emily over his shoulder and turned to Sam and Maggie. ''Excuse us, please. My recalcitrant wife is making threats that I can't allow to go unanswered. Keep the kids out of the barn, will you, Sam?''

''Oh, you are the most impossible man I have ever met!'' Emily exclaimed with a combination of amusement, embarrassment, and love as he pushed through the gate.

''And you wouldn't want me any other way,'' he responded blithely.

Sam looked on with a satisfied smile. ''What did I tell you, Mags? A well-matched pair if ever there was one!'' He slung one arm around Maggie's shoulder and led her toward the house, grinning all the way, the sounds of Drew's and Emily's arguing voices fading behind them across the yard.

Epilogue

~~~~~~~~~~~~~~~~~

“**T**his is ridiculous, you know,” Emily fussed while Maggie and Caroline arranged the white silk tulle veil over her golden hair, securing it with pearl combs. “I had one perfectly good wedding. It's silly to have another one.”

Maggie laughed happily. “You're enjoying this as much as Drew is; you can't fool us. I think it's the best idea he ever had. We all needed something to look forward to to take our minds off . . .” She thought of the recent hanging. “I'm not even going to mention it on this wonderful day. So stop frowning at your hair and smile. You look lovely.”

“Drew is the envy of every bachelor in the Hills, Emily, and most of the married men,” Caroline teased. “It's only natural he'd want to show you off, and another wedding is the best way to do it. And certainly the most fun.”

The door burst open, and Sarah ran in, trailing pink ribbons and a basket filled with delicately colored flower petals.

“Papa says the minister is ready to start,” she announced. “Grandma's already gone in to sit down. Are you ready, Aunt Emily?” Her blue eyes were dancing with anticipation.

Emily took one last look in the full-length mirror. The white silk gown hung in elegant folds from a tight waist and high bodice decorated with white embroidery and trimmed with tiny pearls and white satin ribbons. It was white at Drew's insistence and over her protests, but Emily had to admit that the color suited her. Her complexion glowed ivory and pink, her full lips flushed deeper red, her dark eyes mysterious under the wispy veil. She was happy, and it showed.

Sam stuck his head around the door. He whistled when he caught sight of his sister.

"Lord, Emmy, now I see why Drew insisted on going through with this shindig," he said appreciatively. "With the obvious exception of my own beautiful bride, I have never seen another lovelier, even if you are a matron." He chuckled as he offered her his arm.

When Maggie and Caroline had been escorted to their seats, the rich notes from the organ swelled out over the assembled crowd. There were more dignitaries present than Deadwood had ever before seen together in one place. All the local people of consequence had wrangled invitations or simply shown up, unwilling to miss the affair. In addition, the commissioner of Indian Affairs was there, along with most of the agents from the reservations. All of the officers from Fort Meade had come, and a few visiting dignitaries from the capital in Yankton. Most impressive were the groom's father, a prominent Eastern business-man, and his Uncle Edward, the senator from Massachu-setts. Emily's mother had been bowled over by the older Rutledge brothers, both of whom looked like mature ver-sions of Drew. Mrs. Parker had been rather unnerved by Drew, finding him a trifle irregular, but his patient manner had soon dissolved most of her misgivings about her son-in-law. After all, Emily did seem terribly happy with him.

Emily saw no one but her husband as she walked down the aisle to stand by his side for the public recitation of their vows. She felt Sam's arm beneath hers, but she didn't notice where he went after he placed her hand in Drew's.

Her groom was resplendent in a fine new suit that, if anything, made his broad shoulders look wider and his trim waist narrower. His smile dazzled her, and she basked in his loving gaze. Her voice caught with emotion when she repeated her vows after the minister, and many in the congregation dabbed joyfully at their eyes. It was a beautiful ceremony.

And the party that followed! It provided the grist for many provocative conversations and fond memories throughout that summer. For more than a year, all weddings in the northern hills were judged to its standard. There was wine, music, dancing, and feasting late into the night.

The second-time-around bride and groom were not a part of the festivities, however. As soon as they were able, they changed into riding gear and slipped away into the hills. They rode through winding canyons and narrow gulches, among the towering pines and through fields bright with June wildflowers. At last they came to a meadow where a short falls spilled into a deep pool.

"Look!" Emily exclaimed, pointing. "A tipi! Where did it come from?"

The hide-covered lodge stood near the pool, between the trees and the bank out of which grew the mighty ponderosa pine where the eagle had perched before. Smoke curled up from the opening at the top. On the sides, bright figures had been painted: an eagle soaring in flight above a buffalo cow, and two faces, one with deep blue eyes, the other with forest green and brown ones.

"It's a gift from my other father, Long Feather, and his family. Can't you tell?" Drew asked, sliding from his saddle. He placed his hands on Emily's waist and lifted her from her horse.

"Is someone here?" she asked doubtfully, eyeing the wisps of smoke.

"Nope. Not a soul besides you and me, sweetheart."

"Who set up the lodge, then?" she persisted.

"So many questions! I have other things on my mind, *mitawin,*" he said, bending to kiss her neck just below her ear.

Emily felt a familiar flutter deep inside at his touch. Her hands stole up to cradle his head. Her eyes, however, were still focused on the painted tipi.

"Did Black Wolf put up the lodge?"

"Yeah, he did," Drew whispered against her throat, his lips gliding along the smooth skin.

"Did you ever notice that your eyes are like the sky and

mine are like the earth?'' she asked in sudden wonder, looking at the faces on the lodge.

Drew raised his head now and gazed deeply into her eyes, his face serious.

''Iśte Śkan Niyapi and Iśte Maka Niyapi, eyes that are alive with the sky, and eyes that are alive with the earth. Together we are one creation, one being, complete in each other,'' he said softly.

Emily's heart raced, and the sense of wonder that she had never felt before coming to the Hills, along with the sense of completion that she felt only when she was with Drew, overcame her. High, high above them, the faint cry of an eagle mingled with the winds.

''Complete in our love,'' she whispered.

''Forever,'' Drew said, as his lips met hers in confirmation.

Author's Note

Many of the events in this book are based on happenings in and around the Black Hills in 1880–81. Red Cloud did bring a group of his warriors to Deadwood to testify at a trial and they did, in fact, dance there on a hot August afternoon. Indian Agent Major V. T. McGillycuddy and Red Cloud did have a stormy relationship, one point of contention being the introduction of schools at the agency. My own great-grandfather and his brothers operated a sawmill near Boulder Park and the winter of 1880–81 was every bit as severe as I have depicted it. An autumn blizzard struck the plains on October 15, 1880, and the last snowfall came on April 10, 1881. It was a disheartening season for which few in Dakota Territory were prepared. Virtually all travel on the plains was halted early that winter, and by the beginning of January, even the trains along the Union Pacific line in Nebraska had ceased running.

This harsh winter effectively ended the resistance of the Sioux who had fled to Canada with Sitting Bull and Gall after the United States forced the Lakota onto reservations following the Battle of the Little Bighorn in 1876. Sitting Bull returned to Dakota Territory with the last of his followers in July 1881.

With respect to Lakota courting ritual, I have created a fictional interpretation of Drew and Emily's mock engagement based on historical and contemporary research. I make no pretense to claiming that Lakota betrothals ever followed the exact course presented herein, but I couldn't pass up including Okaga and Wohpe's tale. It's a Dakota romance original.

As you may have guessed, I have a special place in my heart for the Black Hills and the surrounding country. I was born in Deadwood, and my grandparents had a ranch a few miles east of Bear Butte. It's a beautiful land, open and mysterious, resonant with voices just beyond hearing and ripe with images just beyond sight. It is a land full of romance and dreams.

The Sizzling Night Trilogy by
New York Times Bestselling Author

NIGHT STORM
75623-4/$4.95 US/$5.95 Can

Fiery, free-spirited Eugenia Paxton put her heart to the sea in the hands of a captain she dared not trust. But once on the tempestuous waters, the aristocratic rogue Alec Carrick inflamed her with desires she'd never known before.

NIGHT SHADOW
75621-8/$4.50 US/$5.50 Can

The brutal murder of her benefactor left Lily Tremaine penniless and responsible for the care of his three children. In desperation, she appealed to his cousin, Knight Winthrop—and found herself irresistibly drawn to the witty, impossibly handsome confirmed bachelor.

NIGHT FIRE
75620-X/$4.95 US/$5.95 Can

Trapped in a loveless marriage, Arielle Leslie knew a life of shame and degradation. Even after the death of her brutal husband, she was unable to free herself from the shackles of humiliation. Only Burke Drummond's blazing love could save her . . . if she let it.

*If you enjoyed this book, take advantage
of this special offer. Subscribe now and . . .*

GET A *FREE*
HISTORICAL ROMANCE
—— NO OBLIGATION(a $3.95 value) ——

Each month the editors of True Value will select the four best historical romance novels from America's leading publishers. Preview them in your home Free for 10 days. And we'll send you a FREE book as our introductory gift. No obligation. If for any reason you decide not to keep them, just return them and owe nothing. But if you like them you'll pay *just* $3.50 each and save at least $.45 each off the cover price. (Your savings are a minimum of $1.80 a month.) There is no shipping and handling or other hidden charges. There are no minimum number of books to buy and you may cancel at any time.

send in the coupon below